ON THE BLOODY STREETS OF L.A.

"Now, partner," I whispered, as we flattened ourselves up against the corner building when two gunmen came running out with guns drawn. They saw us and aimed their .45's just as Wacky and I opened fire. I squeezed off three shots, and the first gunman spun to the pavement. Wacky sent off two wild shots at the other man, who spun and fired at me.

I returned his fire, hitting him and knocking him into the gutter. Wacky fired twice more at the man on the pavement when I saw the gunman in the gutter take aim. I was moving toward him when I heard another shot. Wacky was staggering backward, stunned, grasping at his chest. He dropped his gun and screamed, "Freddy!" and then fell.

Avon Books are available at special quantity discounts for bulk purchases for sales promotions, premiums, fund raising or educational use. Special books, or book excerpts, can also be created to fit specific needs

For details write or telephone the office of the Director of Special Markets, Avon Books, Dept. FP, 1350 Avenue of the Americas, New York, New York 10019, 1-800-238-0658.

CLANDESTINE

James Ellroy

AVON BOOKS ◆ NEW YORK

CLANDESTINE is an original publication of Avon Books. This work has never before appeared in book form.

AVON BOOKS
A division of
The Hearst Corporation
1350 Avenue of the Americas
New York, New York 10019

Copyright © 1982 by James Ellroy
Published by arrangement with the author
Library of Congress Catalog Card Number: 82-90488
ISBN: 0-380-81141-3

First Avon Books Printing: December 1982

AVON TRADEMARK REG. U.S. PAT. OFF. AND IN OTHER COUNTRIES, MARCA REGISTRADA, HECHO EN CANADA

Printed in Canada

UNV 10 9 8 7

TO
Penny Nagler

PROLOGUE

During the dark, cold winter of 1951 I worked Wilshire Patrol, played a lot of golf, and sought out the company of lonely women for one-night stands.

Nostalgia victimizes the unknowing by instilling in them a desire for a simplicity and innocence they can never achieve. The fifties weren't a more innocent time. The dark salients that govern life today were there then, only they were harder to find. That was why I was a cop, and why I chased women. Golf was no more than an island of purity, something I did exceedingly well. I could drive a golf ball three hundred yards. Golf was breathtaking cleanliness and simplicity.

My patrol partner was Wacky Walker. He was five years my senior, with the same amount of time in the department. We first bumped into each other in the muster room of Wilshire Station, each of us lugging a golf bag. We both broke into huge grins and knew each other instantly—and completely.

With Wacky it was poetry, wonder, and golf; with me it was women, wonder, and golf. "Wonder" meant the same thing to both of us: the job, the streets, the people, and the mutable ethos of we who had to deal daily with drunks, hopheads, gunsels, wienie-waggers, hookers, reefer smokers, burglars, and the unnamed lonely detritus of the human race. We became the closest of friends, and later partners on day watch.

The day watch commander, Lieutenant William Beckworth, was a golf fanatic and hopeless ball beater. When he heard I shot scratch he had me put on day watch in exchange for lessons. It was a fair trade, but Beckworth was

unteachable. I could wrap the lieutenant around my little
finger—I even had him caddying for me on Saturday mornings, when I hustled games at country clubs and municipal
courses—so it was easy to get Wacky bumped off night
watch and assigned to days with the two of us as partners.
Which took us deeper.

Herbert Lawton Walker was thirty-two years old, death-
obsessed, and an alcoholic. He was a genuine hero—a
World War II recipient of the Congressional Medal of
Honor, which he was awarded for wiping out two machine
gun nests full of Japs on Saipan. He could have gotten any
job he wanted. Insurance companies were deluging him
with offers when he went touring for war bonds, but he
opted for the Los Angeles Police Department, a blue suit, a
gun, and the wonder.

Of course, as a juicehead his perception of the wonder
was somewhat predicated on the amount of booze he consumed. I was his watchdog, denying the sauce to him in
the mornings and regulating his intake until our tour
ended and we returned to the station.

In the early evenings, before I went out looking for
women, Wacky and I would belt a few at his apartment
and discuss the wonder or talk about the war I had avoided
and he made his name in. Wacky was convinced that killing the fifteen Japs on Saipan had made him a wonder addict, and that the key to wonder was in death. I disagreed.
We argued. I told him life was good. We agreed. "We are
the sworn protectors of life," I said. "But the key is in
death, Freddy," he said. "Can't you see that? If you ever
have to kill you'll know." We always came to that stale-
mate. When that happened Wacky would lead me to the
door, shake my hand warmly, and retire back to his living
room to drink and write poetry. Leaving me, Frederick Upton Underhill, twenty-six-year-old outsized crew-cut cop,
on his doorstep contemplating nightfall and neon and
what I could do about it in what I would later know to be
the last season of my youth.

That season was to become a rite of passage composed of
many false starts and erroneous conclusions. I was to blun-
der love and call it many different things; I was to savor
the amenities of life on the make and feel last surges of cal-
low power. I was finally to kill—and conclusively disprove

Wacky's thesis, for even with hero's blood on my hands and laurels at my feet, the wonder in its ultimate state eluded me like a beacon whose light remained fixed while the turbulent waters around it constantly shifted in death and self-renewal.

It was those waters that grabbed me and gave me, many years later, my salvation. If you trace every link in the Eddie Engels case backward and forward in time you will find no beginning and no end. When my rapacious ambition thrust me into a brutal labyrinth of death and shame and betrayal in 1951, it was only *my* beginning. At the final unraveling in 1955 I knew that my willingness to move with and be part of a score of hellishly driven lives in clandestine transit was the wonder—as well as my ultimate redemption.

I

LAST SEASON

1

Wacky and I had been partners for three months when Night Train entered our lives. The roll call sergeant told us about him as we were getting into our '48 Ford black-and-white in the parking lot at Wilshire Station.

"Walker. Underhill. Come here a second," he called at us. We walked over. His name was Gately; he needed a shave and he was smiling. "The loot's got a good one for you guys. You golfers get all the breaks. You like dogs? I hate dogs. We got a dog who's terrorizing little kiddies. Stealing their lunches over at the elementary school off Orange and Olympic. Mean old trash can dog, used to belong to a wino. The janitor at the school's got him. Says he's going to kill him, or cut his balls off. The Animal Regulation guys don't want the squeal, 'cause they think the janitor's crazy. You guys go take the mean old dog to the pound. Don't shoot it, 'cause there's all kinds of little kiddies might get upset. You golf guys get all the breaks."

Wacky pulled the black-and-white out onto Pico, laughing and talking in verse, which he sometimes did when coffee reactivated the previous night's booze still in his system.

"Whither thou, o noble beast, the most we do is ne'er our least, o noble hound, soon to be found, awaits the pound thence gas and ground."

I laughed on while Wacky continued, driving his poetry into the pavement.

The janitor at Wilshire Crest School was a fat Japanese guy of about fifty. Wacky waggled his eyebrows at him, which broke the ice and got a laugh. He led us to the dog, who was locked up inside a portable construction toilet. As

7

we approached I could hear a keening wail arise from the
flimsy structure.

At the prearranged signal from Wacky, I kicked a hole
in the side of the outhouse and shoved in our combined
lunches—two ham-and-cheese sandwiches, a sardine sandwich, one roast beef on rye, and two apples. There was the
sound of furious masticating. I threw open the door,
glimpsed a dark furry shape with glittering sharp teeth,
and slugged it full force, right in the chops. It collapsed,
spitting out some ham sandwich in the process. Wacky
dragged the dog out.

He was a nice-looking black Labrador—but very fat. He
had a gigantic whanger that must have dragged the
ground when he walked. Wacky was in love. "Aww,
Freddy, look at my poor baby. Awww." He picked the unconscious dog up and cradled him in his arms. "Awww.
Uncle Wacky and Uncle Freddy will take you back to the
station and find a nice home for you. Awww."

The janitor was eyeing us suspiciously. "You killee
dog?" he asked, drawing a finger across his throat and
looking at Wacky, who was already carrying his new-
found friend lovingly back to the patrol car.

I got in the driver's side. "We can't take this mutt back
to the station," I said.

"The hell you say. We'll stash him in the locker room.
When we get off duty I'm taking him home. This dog is
gonna be my caddy. I'm gonna fix him up with a harness so
he can pack my bag."

"Beckworth will have your ass."

"Beckworth can *kiss* my ass. You take care of Beckworth."

The dog came awake as we pulled into the parking lot of
the station. He started barking furiously. I turned around
in my seat to slug him again, but Wacky deflected my arm.
"Awww," he said to the beast, "Awww, Awww!" And the
dog shut up.

I led the dog around to the locker room from the back entrance. Wacky made the run to the hot dog stand next to
Sears, and came back with six cheeseburgers. I was pet-
ting the hound in front of my locker when Wacky came
back and dumped the greasy mess on the floor in front of
me. The dog tore into it, and Wacky and I shot out the door

and resumed patrol. So began the odyssey of Night Train, as the dog came to be known.

When we returned from our tour of duty that night we heard Reuben Ramos's saxophone honking from the locker room. Reuben is a motorcycle officer who picked up a love of jazz from working Seventy-seventh Street Vice, where he raided the bop joints of Central Avenue regularly, looking for hookers, bookies, and hopheads. He had taught himself to play the sax by ear—mostly honks and flub notes, but sometimes he gets going on some simple tune like "Green Dolphin Street." Tonight he was really cooking—the main theme from "Night Train" over and over.

When Wacky and I entered the locker room we couldn't believe our eyes. Reuben, in his Jockey shorts, was twisting all around, blasting out the wild first notes of "Night Train" while the fat black Lab writhed on his back on the concrete floor, yipping, yowling, and shooting a tremendous stream of urine straight up into the air. Groups of off-duty patrolmen walked in and walked out, disgusted. Reuben got tired of the action and went home to his wife and kids, leaving Wacky to yell and scream of the dog's "genius potential."

Wacky named the dog "Night Train" and took him home with him. He serenaded the dog for weeks with saxophone music on his phonograph and fed him steak, all in the fruitless hope of turning him into a caddy. Finally Wacky gave up, decided that Night Train was a free spirit, and cut him loose. We thought we had seen the last of the beast—but we hadn't. He was to go on to assume legendary status in the history of the Los Angeles Police Department.

Two days after his release, Night Train showed up at Wilshire Station with a dead cat in his jaws. He was chased out by the desk sergeant, who threw the cat in a trash can. Night Train showed up the following day with another dead cat. This time he was chased out with the cat still in his mouth. He came back later that day with the same cat, somewhat the worse for wear. He came back at the right time, for Wacky and I were just getting off duty. When Night Train saw Wacky he swooned with joy, dropped the battered feline gift of love, ran to Wacky's outstretched arms, and urinated all over his uniform. Wacky

carried Night Train to my car and locked him in. But
Wacky was pissed at Lieutenant Beckworth. Beckworth
was supposed to have come across with two cases of Cutty
Sark at 75 percent off from a fence he knew, but he had
reneged.

Wacky wanted revenge, so he retrieved the mangled
dead cat and attached a note with a straight pin to the cat's
hide. The note read: "This is all the pussy you're ever going to get, you cheap cocksucker." He then placed the cat
on the lieutenant's desk.

Beckworth found it the next morning and went insane.
He ordered an all-points bulletin for the dog. He didn't
have to look far. Night Train was discovered where he had
been placed the previous night—in the back seat of my car.
Beckworth couldn't mess with me because he knew I could
stop his golf lessons, but he could fuck over Night Train for
dead sure. He had the dog arrested and placed in the drunk
tank. It was the wrong thing to do. Night Train attacked
and almost killed three winos. When the jailer was
aroused by their screams and rushed to open the tank door,
Night Train ran straight past him, out the door of Wilshire
Station, across Pico Boulevard and all the way home to
Wacky's apartment, where the two of them lived happily—listening to saxophone music—until the end of the last
season of my youth.

A week after the dead cat episode, Beckworth was still
pissed.

We were at the driving range at Rancho Park, where I
was trying, unsuccessfully, to correct his chronic slice. It
was hopeless. The price of working day watch was high.

"Fuck. Shit, fuck. Oh, God," Beckworth was muttering.
"Show me again, Freddy."

I grabbed his 3 iron and sailed off a smooth one. Two-
twenty. Straight. "Shoulders back, Loot. Feet closer
together. Don't reach for the ball, meet it."

He had it perfect until he swung his club. Then he did
everything I had told him not to and shank-dribbled the
ball about ten yards.

"Easy, Loot. Try it again."

"Goddamnit, Freddy, I can't think today. Golf is ninety

percent concentration. I've got the coordination of a superb athlete, but I can't keep my mind on the game."

I played into it. "What's on your mind, Loot?"

"Little things. Minor things. That shithead partner of yours—I've got a feeling about him. Medal of Honor winner, okay. High scores at the academy, okay. But he doesn't look, or act, like a cop. He spouts poetry at roll call. I think he's a homo."

"Not Wacky, Loot. He loves dames."

"I don't believe it."

I played into the lieutenant's sub rosa but well-known love of Negro tail. All the Seventy-seventh Street harness bulls knew him to be a frequent visitor at Minnie Roberts's Casbah—the swankiest colored whorehouse on the South Side.

"Well, Loot," I said, keeping my voice at a whisper, "he loves dames, but he's gotta have a certain kind of dame, if you follow my drift."

Beckworth was getting titillated. He smiled, something he rarely did, and exposed the two snaggle teeth at the corners of his mouth. "Drift it my way, Freddy boy."

I looked in all directions, broadly searching out eavesdroppers. "Korean women, Loot. He can't get enough of them. Only he doesn't like to talk about it, because we're at war over there. Wacky goes goo-goo for gooks. There's a cathouse on Slauson and Hoover that specializes in them. It's right next to that dump with all the colored girls—what's the name of the place?—Minnie's Casbah. Wacky goes to this chink place. Sometimes he sits in his car and has a few belts before he goes in. He told me he's seen a shitload of department brass go into the Casbah looking for poontang, but he won't tell me who. Wacky's a stand-up guy. He doesn't hate the brass hats the way a lot of street cops do."

Beckworth had gone pale, but came out of it fast. "Well, he may not be a queer, but he's still a shithead. The bastard. I had to get my office fumigated. I'm a sensitive man, Freddy, and I had *nightmares* about that dead cat. And don't tell me Walker didn't do it—because I know."

"I don't deny it, Lieutenant. He did it. But you got to look at his motives."

"What motives? He hates me. That's his motive."

"You're wrong, Loot. Wacky respects you. He even envies you."

"Respect! Envy! What the hell are you talking about?"

"It's a fact. Wacky envies your golfing potential. He told me so."

"Are you crazy? I'm a hacker. He's a low handicapper."

"You wanna know what he said, Loot? He said, 'Beckworth has all the moves. It's just his concentration that's fucking up his game and keeping him from putting it all together. He's got a lot on his mind. He's a good cop. I'm glad I'm just a dumb harness bull on the street. At least I can break eighty. The lieutenant is too conscientious and it fucks up his game. If he weren't such a good cop, he'd be a scratch player.' That's what he said."

I gave it a minute to sink in. Beckworth was aglow. He put down the 4 iron he was mauling and smiled at me beatifically. "You tell Walker to come and see me, Freddy. Tell him I've got some good Scotch for him. Korean pussy, Jesus! You don't think he's a red, do you, Freddy?"

"Wacky Walker? Staff sergeant, U.S. Marines? Bite your tongue, Lieutenant!"

"You're right, Freddy. That was unworthy of me. Let's go. I've had enough for today."

I drove Beckworth back to his car, then went home to my apartment in Santa Monica. I showered and changed. Then I put my off-duty .38 snub-nose into a small hip holster and attached it to my belt next to my spine in case I went dancing and got romantic. Then I got into my car and went looking for women.

I decided to follow the red trolley car. It ran from Long Beach all the way up into Hollywood. It was Friday night, and on weekend nights the red car carried groups of girls looking for an evening's fun on the Strip that they probably couldn't afford. The red car ran slightly elevated on a track in the middle of the street, so you could hardly see the passengers. Your best bet was to drive abreast of it and watch the girls as they boarded.

I liked L.A. girls the best, they were lonelier and more individual than girls from the "suburbs," so I caught the red car at Jefferson and La Brea. I wanted to give myself five minutes or so of suspense before the Wilshire Boulevard bonanza: clusters of salesgirls from Ohrbach's and the May Company, and secretaries from the insurance companies that lined L.A.'s busiest street. I kept my '47 Buick ragtop with the gunsight hood ornament dead even with the red car and watched keenly as passengers boarded.

The parade up to Wilshire was predictable—old-timers, high school kids, some young couples. At Wilshire, a whole knot of high-voiced gigglers jumped on board, pushing and shoving good-naturedly. It was cold out; overcoats obscured their bodies. It didn't matter; spirit is more important than flesh. They boarded fast, so I couldn't discern faces. That put me at a disadvantage. If they got out at Fountain or Sunset en masse, I would have to park quick and chase them with no time to work on a line suited to one particular woman.

But it didn't matter, not tonight, because on La Brea just short of Melrose I saw her, running out of a Chinese restaurant, handbag flying by its straps, framed for a few brief seconds in the neon glow of the Gordon Theater: an unusual-looking girl, identifiable not by type, but by an intensity of feeling. She seemed to have a harried, frightened nervousness that blasted open the L.A. night. She was dressed with style, but without regard for fashion: men's baggy-cuffed slacks, sandals, and an Eisenhower jacket. Men's garb, but her features were soft and feminine and her hair was long.

She barely made the red car, hopping aboard with a little antelope bound. Her destination eluded me—she had too much stuff to be running for the Strip. Maybe she was headed for a bookstore on Hollywood Boulevard, or a lover's rendezvous that would ace me out. I was wrong; she got off at Fountain and started walking north.

I parked in a hurry, placed an "Official Police Vehicle" sign under my windshield wiper and followed her on foot. She turned east on De Longpre, a quiet residential street on the edge of the Hollywood business district. If she was going home I was out of luck for tonight—my methods required a crowded street or public place, and the best I could hope for was an address for future reference. But I could see that half a block up two black-and-whites were double-parked with their cherry lights on: a possible crime scene.

The girl noticed this, hesitated, and walked back in my direction. She was afraid of cops, and this compounded my interest. I decided to risk all on that fear, and intercepted her as she passed me. "Excuse me, miss," I said, showing her my badge. "I'm a police officer, and this is an official crime scene. Please allow me to escort you to a safe place."

The woman nodded, frightened, her face going pale and blank for a brief moment. She was very lovely, with that strength-vulnerability combo that is the essence of my love and respect for women. "All right," she said, adding "Officer" with the thinnest edge of contempt. We walked back towards La Brea, not looking at each other.

"What's your name?" I asked.

"Sarah Kefalvian."

"Where do you live, Miss Kefalvian?"

"Not far from here. But I wasn't going home. I was going up to the boulevard."

"Whereabouts?"

"To an art exhibit. Near Las Palmas."

"Let me take you there."

"No. I don't think so."

She was averting her eyes, but as we got to the corner of La Brea she gave me a spirited, defiant look that sent me. "You don't like cops, do you, Miss Kefalvian?" I said.

"No. They hurt people."

"We help more people than we hurt."

"I don't believe it. Thank you for escorting me. Good night."

Sarah Kefalvian turned her back to me and started striding off briskly in the direction of the boulevard. I couldn't let her go. I caught up with her and grabbed her arm. She yanked it away. "Look," I said, "I'm not your average cop. I'm a draft dodger. I know that there's a Picasso exhibit at that bookstore on Las Palmas. I'm hot to learn culture and I need someone to show me around." I gave Sarah Kefalvian the crinkly smile that made me look a bashful seventeen. She started to relent, very slightly. She smiled. I moved in. "Please?"

"Are you really a draft dodger?"

"Kind of."

"I'll go with you to the exhibit if you don't touch me or tell anyone that you're a policeman."

"It's a deal."

We walked back to my illegally parked car, me elated, and Sarah Kefalvian interested, against her will.

The exhibit was at Stanley Rose's Bookshop, a longtime hot spot for the L.A. intelligentsia. Sarah Kefalvian walked slightly ahead of me, offering awed comments. The pictures were prints, not actual paintings, but this didn't faze her. It was obvious she was warming to the idea of having a date. I told her my name was Joe Thornhill. We stopped in front of "Guernica," the one picture I felt confident enough to comment on.

"That's a terrific picture," I said. "I saw a bunch of photographs on that city when I was a kid. This brings it all back. Especially that cow with the spear sticking out of him. War must be tough."

"It's the cruelest, most terrible thing on earth, Joe," Sarah Kefalvian said. "I'm devoting my life to ending it."

"How?"

"By spreading the words of great men who have seen war and what it does."

"Are you against the war in Korea?"

"Yes. All wars."

"Don't you want to stop the Communists?"

"Tyranny can only be stopped through love, not war."

That interested me. Sarah's eyes were getting moist. "Let's go talk," I said, "I'll buy you dinner. We'll swap life stories. What do you say?" I waggled my eyebrows a la Wacky Walker.

Sarah Kefalvian smiled and laughed, and it transformed her. "I've already eaten, but I'll go with you if you'll tell me why you dodged the draft."

"It's a deal." As we walked out of the bookstore I took her arm and steered her. She buckled, but didn't resist.

We drove to a dago joint on Sunset and Normandie. En route I learned that Sarah was twenty-four, a graduate student in History at U.C.L.A. and a first-generation Armenian-American. Her grandparents had been wiped out by the Turks, and the horror stories her parents had told her about life in Armenia had shaped her life: she wanted to end war, outlaw the atom bomb, end racial discrimination, and redistribute the wealth. She deferred to me slightly, saying that she thought cops were necessary, but should carry liberal arts educations and high ideals instead of guns. She was starting to like me, so I couldn't bring myself to tell her she was nuts. I was starting to like her, too, and my blood was roiling at the thought of the lovemaking that we would share in a few hours' time.

I appreciated her honesty and decided that candor would be the only decent kind of barter. I decided not to bullshit her: maybe our encounter would leave her more of a realist.

The restaurant was a one-armed Italian place, strictly family, with faded travel posters of Rome, Naples, Parma, and Capri interspersed with empty Chianti bottles hanging from a phony grape arbor. I decided to forgo chow, and ordered a big jug of dago red. We raised our glasses in a toast.

"To the end of war," I said.

"Do you really believe that?"

"Sure. Just because I don't carry placards or make a big deal out of it doesn't mean I don't hate it."

"Tell me why you dodged the draft," Sarah said softly.

I drained my glass and poured another. Sarah was sipping hers slowly.

"I'm an orphan. I grew up in an orphanage in Hollywood. It was lousy. It was Catholic, and run by a bunch of sadistic nuns. The food stank. During the Depression we ate nothing but potatoes, watery vegetable stews, and powdered milk, with meat maybe once a week. All the kids were skinny and anemic, with bad complexions. It wasn't good enough for me. I couldn't eat it. It made me so angry my skin stung. We got sent out to a Catholic school over on Western Avenue. They fed us the same slop for lunch. When I was about eight, I *knew* that if I continued to eat that garbage I would forfeit my claim to manhood. So I started to steal. I hit every market in Hollywood. I stole canned sardines, cheeses, fruit, cookies, pies, milk—you name it. On weekends the older kids used to get farmed out to wealthy Catholic families, to show us a bit of the good life. I got sent regularly to this family in Beverly Hills. They were loaded. They had a son about my age. He was a wild kid, and an accomplished shoplifter. His specialty was steaks. I joined him and we hit every butcher shop on the West Side. He was as fat as a pig. He couldn't stop eating. A regular Goodyear blimp.

"During the depression there was a kind of floating hobo jungle in Griffith Park. The cops rousted the bums out of there regularly, but they would recongregate in another place. A priest from Immaculate Heart College told me about it. I went looking for them. I was a curious, lonely kind of kid, and thought bums were romantic. I brought a big load of steaks with me, which made me a big hit. I was big enough so that no one messed with me. I listened to the stories the old bums would tell—cops and robbers, railroads and Pinkerton men, darkness. Strange things that most people had no inkling of. Perversions. Unspeakable things. I wanted to know those things—but remain safe from them.

"One night we were roasting steaks and drinking some whiskey I had stolen when the cops raided the jungle. I scampered off and got away. I could hear the cops rousting out the bums. They were firm, but humorous about the whole thing; and I knew that if I became a cop I could have the darkness along with some kind of precarious impunity. I would *know,* yet be safe.

"Then the war came along. I was seventeen when Pearl Harbor was bombed. And I *knew* again, though this time in a different way. I knew that if I fought in that war I would die. I also knew that I needed an *honorable* out to insure getting on the police department.

"I never knew my parents. My first adopted parents gave me my name before they turned me over to the orphanage. I devised a plan. I read the draft laws, and learned that the sole surviving son of a man killed in a foreign war is draft exempt. I also knew I had a punctured eardrum that was a possible out, but I wanted to cover my bets. So I tried to enlist in '42, right after I graduated from high school. The eardrum came through and they turned me down.

"Then I found an old wino woman, a down-and-out actress. She came with me when I made my appeal to the draft board. She yelled and screamed that she needed me to work and give her money. She said her husband, my dad, was killed in the Chinese campaign of '26, which was why I was sent to the orphanage. It was a stellar performance. I gave her fifty bucks. The draft board believed her and told me never to try to enlist again. I pleaded, periodically, but they were firm. They admired my patriotism—but a law was a law, and ironically the punctured eardrum never kept me from becoming a cop."

Sarah loved it, and sighed when I finished. I loved it, too; I was saving the story for a special woman, one who could appreciate it. Aside from Wacky, she was the only person to know of that part of my life.

She put her hand on mine. I raised it to my lips and kissed it. She looked wistful and sad. "Have you found what you're looking for?" she asked.

"Yes," I said.

"Will you take me by that hobo jungle? Tonight?"

"Let's go now. They close the park road at ten o'clock."

It was a cold night and very clear. January is the coldest, most beautiful month in L.A. The colors of the city, permeated by chill air, seem to come into their own and reflect a tradition of warmth and insularity.

We drove up Vermont and parked in the observatory parking lot. We walked north, uphill, holding hands. We talked easily, and I laid on the more gentle, picaresque side of police work: the friendly drunks, the colorful jazz musicians in their zoot suits, the lost puppies Wacky and I repatriated to their youthful owners. I didn't tell her about the rape-o's, the abused kids, the stiffs at accident scenes or the felony suspects who got worked over regularly in the back rooms at Wilshire Station. She didn't need to hear it. Idealists like Sarah, despite their naiveté, thought that the world was basically a shit place. I needed to temper her sense of reality with some of the joy and mystery. There was no way she could accept that the darkness was part of the joy. I had to do my tempering Hollywood-style.

I showed her the site of the old jungle. I hadn't been here since 1938, thirteen years, and now it was just a clearing overgrown with weeds and littered with empty wine bottles.

"It all started here for you?" Sarah asked.

"Yes."

"Time and place awes me."

"Me, too. This is January 30, 1951. It's now and it won't ever be again."

"That scares me."

"Don't be scared. It's just the wonder. It's very dark here. Are you afraid of the dark?"

Sarah Kefalvian raised her beautiful head and laughed in the moonlight. Big, hearty laughter worthy of her Armenian ancestors. "I'm sorry, Joe. It's just that we're speaking so somberly, so symbolically that it's kind of funny."

"Then let's get literal. I've confided in you. You confide in me. Tell me something about yourself. Something dark and secretive that you've never told anyone."

She considered this and said, "It'll shock you. I like you and I don't want to offend you."

"You can't shock me. I'm immune to shock. Tell me."

"All right. When I was an undergrad in San Francisco I had an affair—with a married man. It ended. I was hurt and I started hating men. I was going to Cal Berkeley. I had a teacher, a woman. She was very beautiful. She took an interest in me. We became lovers and did things—sexual things that most people don't even guess about. This woman also liked young boys. *Young* boys. She seduced her twelve-year-old nephew. We shared him."

Sarah backed away from where we stood together, almost as if fearing a blow.

"Is that it?" I asked.

"Yes," she replied.

"All of it?"

"Yes! I won't get graphic with you. I loved that woman. She helped through a difficult time. Isn't that dark enough for you?"

Her anger and indignation had peaked and brought forth in me a warm rush of pure stuff. "It's enough. Come here, Sarah." She did and we held each other, her head pressed hard into my shoulder. When we disengaged, she looked up at me. She was smiling, and her cheeks were wet with tears. I wiped them away with my thumbs. "Let me take you home," I said.

We undressed wordlessly, in the dark front room of Sarah Kefalvian's garage apartment on Sycamore Street.

Sarah was trembling and breathing shallowly in the cold
room, and when we were naked I smothered her with my
body to stanch her tremors, then lifted her and carried her
in the direction of where the bedroom had to be.

There was no bed; just a mattress on a pallet covered
with quilts. I laid her down and sat on the edge of the mattress, my long legs jammed up awkwardly. A shaft of light
from a streetlamp cast a diffuse glow over the room and let
me pick out shelves overflowing with books and walls
adorned with Picasso prints and labor activist posters from
the Depression.

Sarah looked up at me, her hand resting on my knee. I
stroked her hair, then bent over and placed short dry
kisses on her neck and shoulders. She sighed. I told her she
was very beautiful, and she giggled. I looked for imperfec-
tions, the little body flaws that speak volumes. I found
them: a small growth of dark hairs above her nipples, an
acne cluster on her right shoulder blade. I kissed these
places until Sarah grabbed my head and pulled my mouth
to hers.

We kissed hard and long, then Sarah opened up yawn-
ingly and arched to receive me. We joined and coupled violently, strongly, muscles straining in our efforts to stay in-
terlocked as we changed positions and thrashed the quilts
off the mattress. We peaked together, Sarah sobbing as I
mashed my face into her neck, rubbing my mouth and nose
in the little rivulets of our combined sweat.

We lay still for a long time, gently stroking odd parts of
each other. To talk would have been to betray the moment;
I knew this from experience, and Sarah from instinct. After a while she pretended to sleep, a silent, loving way to
ease the awkwardness of my departure.

I dressed in the dark, then reached over and brushed
back her long dark hair and kissed the nape of her neck,
thinking as I left that maybe this time I had given as much
as I had taken.

I drove home and got out my diary. I wrote of the circumstances of my meeting Sarah, what we had talked about,
and what I learned. I described her body and our lovemaking. Then I went to bed and slept long into the afternoon.

2

"Getting laid, Freddy?"

Wacky and I were pulling into the parking lot at Rancho Park Municipal Golf Course very early the following Saturday morning. I was hungry for golf, not masculine banter, and Wacky's question felt like a knife in the side. I ignored it until Wacky cleared his throat and started to speak in verse:

"Whither thou, O pussy-hound, O tireless fiend for Venus Mounds, O noble cop, you'll never stop . . ."

I set the hand brake and stared at Wacky.

"You haven't answered my question," he said.

I sighed: "The answer is yes."

"Great. What's it costing you?"

"Very little. I go to bars only as a last resort." I hauled my clubs out of the back seat and motioned Wacky to follow me. As I slung my golf bag over my shoulder and locked the car, Wacky gave me one of his rare cold sober looks.

"That wasn't what I meant, Fred."

"What *did* you mean, Wacky? I came here to hit golf balls, not write my sexual memoirs."

Wacky clapped me on the back and waggled his eyebrows. "Are you still planning on being chief of police someday?" he asked.

"Of course."

"Then I hope you realize that the commission will never appoint a bachelor pussy-fiend as chief. You know that they're going to get to you, don't you?"

I sighed again, this time angrily. "Exactly what are you talking about?"

"Price, Freddy. The dames are going to start to get to

21

you. You're going to get tired of one-nighters and go loony
romantic and start searching for some tomato you screwed
back in '48. *The* woman, who'll never be able to compete
with the thrill of one-nighters. You'll be screwed both
ways. You make me damn glad I'm not big and handsome
and charming. You make me damn glad I'm just a poet and
a cop."

"And a drunk." I regretted saying it immediately and
fished around for something to make it right.

Wacky preempted me: "Yeah, and a drunk."

"Then you watch the price, Wack. When I'm chief of police and you're my chief of detectives I don't want you
croaking of cirrhosis of the liver."

"I'll never make it, Fred."

"You'll make it."

"Shit. Haven't you heard the rumors? Captain Larson is
retiring in June. Beckworth is going to be the new top dog
at Wilshire, and I'm going to Seventy-seventh Street—
Niggerland, U.S.A. And you, Beckworth's golf avatar and
fair-haired boy, are going to Vice, a nice assignment
for a cunt-hound. I have this on very good authority,
Freddy."

I couldn't meet Wacky's eyes. I had heard the rumors,
and credited them. I started thinking of stratagems I could
use to keep Beckworth from transferring Wacky, then suddenly realized I was supposed to meet Beckworth at seven
o'clock that morning at Fox Hills for a lesson. I dropped my
bag to the ground in disgust. "Wacky?" I said.

"Yes, Fred?"

"Sometimes you make me wish that *I* were the drunk
and the fuck-up in this partnership."

"Will you elaborate on that?"

"No."

The driving range was deserted. Wacky and I dug our
stash of shag balls out of their hiding place in a hollowed-
out tree trunk and settled in to practice. Wacky warmed
up by chugalugging a half pint of bourbon, while I did deep
knee bends and jumping jacks. I started out hitting 7
irons—one seventy with a slight fade. Not good. I shifted
my stance, corrected the fade and gained an additional ten

yards in the process. I was working toward my optimum when Wacky grabbed my elbow and hissed at me: "Freddy, psst, Freddy!"

I slammed the head of my club into the dirt at my feet and pulled loose from Wacky. "What the fuck is wrong now?"

Wacky pointed to a man and woman arguing nearby on the putting green. The man was tall and fat, with a stomach like an avocado. He had wild reddish-brown hair and a nose as long as my arm. There was an appealing ethnic roguishness to him, broad laughter lines around his mouth, his whole face spelling out fifty-five years of good-natured conniving. The woman was about thirty, and obese—probably close to two-seventy-five. She bore the man's long nose and reddish hair, then did him one better by sporting a distinct downy mustache. I groaned. Wacky was only nominally interested in women, and fat ones were the only kind that aroused him. He pulled a fresh half pint from his back pocket and took a long pull, then pointed to the couple and said, "Do you know who that *is*, Freddy?"

"Yeah. It's a fat woman."

"Not the tomato, Freddy. The old guy. It's Big Sid Weinberg. He's the guy who produced *Bride of the Sea Monster,* remember? We saw it at the Westlake. You went bananas for that blond with the big tits?"

"Yeah. And?"

"And I'm gonna get his autograph, then I'm gonna sell him 'Constituency of the Dead' for his next picture."

I groaned again. Wacky was a horror-movie fanatic, and "Constituency of the Dead" was his attempt to capture Hollywood's monster madness in prose. In his poem, there was a world of the dead, existing concurrent with the real world, but invisible to us. The inhabitants of this world were all wonder addicts, because they had all been murdered. I considered it one of his poorer efforts.

Wacky waggled his eyebrows at me. "One thing, partner," he said, "one thing I promise."

"What's that?"

"When I'm a big-time Hollywood screenwriter I'll never high-hat you."

I laughed: "Watch out, Wack. Hollywood producers are

notorious shit-heels. Go for the daughter instead. Maybe you can marry into the family." Wacky laughed, and trotted away, while I returned to the blessed solitude of golf.

I was at it for over an hour, savoring the mystical union that takes place when you know that you're a gifted practitioner of something much greater than yourself. I was crunching three-hundred-yard drives with fluid regularity when I gradually became aware of eyes boring into my back. I stopped in mid-swing and turned around to face my intruder. It was Big Sid Weinberg. He was lumbering toward me almost feverishly, right hand extended. Taken aback, I extended mine reflexively, and we exchanged names in a mutual bone-crusher. "Sid Weinberg," he said.

"Fred Underhill," I said.

Still grasping my hand, Weinberg eyed me up and down like a choice piece of meat. "You're a six, but you can't putt, right?"

"Wrong."

"Okay, you're a four, and you can hit the shit out of the ball, but your short game stinks. Right?"

"Wrong."

Weinberg dropped my hand. "So you're—"

I interrupted: "I'm a hard scratch, I can drive three hundred yards, I've got a demon short game, I can putt better than Ben Hogan and I'm handsome, charming, and intelligent. What do you want, Mr. Weinberg?"

Weinberg looked surprised when I mentioned his name. "So that lunatic was right," he said.

"You mean my partner?"

"Yeah. He told me you two guys were cops together, then he tells me some lunatic story about a city of stiffs. How the hell did he ever make the force?"

"We've got lots of crazy guys, only most of them hold it better."

"Jesus. He's reading his stuff to my daughter now. They're soul mates; she's as crazy as he is."

"What do you *want*, Mr. Weinberg?"

"How much do you make with the cops?"

"Two hundred ninety-two a month."

Weinberg snorted. "Spinach. Peanuts. Worse than that, popcorn. The ducks in the lake at Echo Park make more moolah than that."

"I'm not in it for the money."

"No? But you like money?"

"Yeah, I like it."

"Good, it ain't a crime. You wanna walk across the street to Hillcrest and play a class-A kosher course? Scramble? The two of us versus these two ganefs I know? We'll slaughter 'em. C-note Nassau? What do you say?"

"I say you put up the money, and my partner comes with us to read our greens. He gets twenty percent of our action. What do *you* say, Mr. Weinberg?"

"I say you musta been Jewish in a previous life."

"Maybe in this one."

"Whaddaya mean?"

"I never knew my parents."

Big Sid raised his head and roared: "Ha-ha-ha! That's par for the course, kid. I got two daughters and I don't know them from a hill of beans. You got yourself a deal."

We shook hands on it, sealing the last carefree alliance of my youth.

Hillcrest was only a block away geographically, but it was light-years away from Rancho in every other respect: lush, manicured fairways, well-tended, strategically placed bunkers and sloping greens that ran like lightning. There were eight of us in the group: Big Sid and I, our opponents, two caddies, and our giggling, moonstruck gallery—Wacky and Big Sid's gargantuan daughter, Siddell. Those two seemed to be rapidly falling into lust, swaying into each other as they trudged fairway and rough, holding hands surreptitiously when Big Sid had his back to them.

And Sid was right; it was a slaughter. Our opponents—a Hollywood agent and a young doctor—were pitifully mismatched; shanking, hooking, slicing into the trees and blowing their only decent approach shots. Big Sid and I played steadily, conservatively, and sunk putts. We were well-aided by Wacky's superb green reads and the club selections and yardage calls of our short-dog–sucking wino caddy, "Dirt Road" Dave.

"Hey, hey, shit, shit," Dave would say. "Play a soft seven and knock it down short of the green. It breaks left to right off the mound. Hey, hey, shit, shit."

Dave fascinated me: he was both sullen and colloquial, dirty and proud, with an air of supreme nonchalance undercut by terrified blue eyes. Somehow, I wanted his knowledge.

The match ended on the fourteenth hole, Big Sid and I closing our opponents out 5–4. Nine hundred dollars changed hands, four hundred and fifty for Big Sid, four hundred and fifty for me. I felt rich and effusive.

Big Sid clapped me on the back. "It's just the beginning, doll! You stick with Big Sid and the sky's the limit! Va-va-va-voom!"

"Thanks, Sid. I appreciate it."

"Va-va-va-voom, kiddo!"

I looked around. Wacky and Siddell had disappeared into the woods. Our opponents were heading back to the clubhouse dejected, their heads down. I told Big Sid I would meet him at the clubhouse, then went looking for Dirt Road Dave. I found him walking across the rough toward the eighteenth hole with Big Sid's bag as well as mine slung across his bony right shoulder. I tapped him on that shoulder and when he turned around stuck a fifty-dollar bill into his callused, outstretched palm. "Thanks, Dave," I said. Dirt Road Dave unhitched the bags, put the money into his pocket and stared at me. "Talk to me," I said.

"About what, sonny boy?"

"About what you've seen. About what you know."

Dirt Road Dave let my bag fall to the grass at my feet, then he spat. "I know you're a smart-mouth young cop. I know that's a roscoe and handcuffs under your sweater. I know the kind of things you guys do that you think people don't know about. I know guys like you die hungry." His finality was awesome. I picked up my bag and walked to the clubhouse—only to be ambushed by another madman en route.

It was Wacky, materializing out of a grove of trees, scaring the shit out of me. "Jesus!" I exclaimed.

"Sorry, partner," Wacky whispered, "but I had to catch you out of earshot of Big Sid. I need a favor, a big-o-rooney."

I sighed: "Name it."

"The car—for an hour or so. I've got a hot date that won't wait, passion pie in the great by-and-by. I'm eating kosher, partner. You can't deny me."

I decided to do it, but with a stipulation: "Not in the car, Wack. Rent a room. You got that?"

"Of course, I'm a cop. Would I break the law?"

"Yes."

"Ha-ha-ha! One hour, Fred."

"Yeah."

Wacky disappeared into the trees, where his high-pitched laughter was joined by Siddell Weinberg's baritone sighs. I walked to the clubhouse feeling sad, and weighted down by strangers.

3

I figured that Wacky would be at least two hours late returning my car, and moreover that good taste dictated I remain to drink and shoot the shit with Big Sid. I wanted to take a run to Santa Barbara and look for women, but I needed my car for that.

I showered in the men's locker room. It was a far cry from the dungeonlike locker room at Wilshire Station. This facility had wall-to-wall deep-pile carpets and oak walls hung with portraits of Hillcrest notables. The locker room talk was about movie deals and business mergers with golf a distant third. Somehow it made me uneasy, so I showered fast, changed clothes, and went looking for Big Sid.

I found him in the dining room, sitting at a table near the large picture window overlooking the eighteenth hole. He was talking with a woman; she had her back to me as I approached the table. Somehow I sensed she was class, so I smoothed my hair and adjusted my pocket handkerchief as I walked toward them.

Big Sid saw me coming. "Freddy, baby!" he boomed. He tapped the woman softly on the shoulder. "Honey, this is my new golf partner, Freddy Underhill. Freddy, this is my daughter Lorna."

The woman swiveled in her chair to face me. She smiled distractedly. "Mr. Underhill," she said.

"Miss Weinberg," I replied.

I sat down. I was right: the woman was class. Where Siddell Weinberg had inherited the broadness of her father's features, Lorna exhibited a refined version: her hair was more light brown than red, her brown eyes more pale and crystalline than opaque. She had Big Sid's pointed chin and sensual mouth, but on a softer, muted scale. Her nose was large but beautiful: it informed her face with intelligence and a certain boldness. She wore no makeup. She had on a tweed suit over a white silk blouse. I could tell that she was tall and slender, and that her breasts were very large for her frame.

I immediately wanted to know her, and quashed a corny impulse to take and kiss her hand, realizing that she wouldn't be charmed by such a gesture. Instead, I took a seat directly across from her where I could maintain eye contact.

Big Sid slammed me so hard on the back that my head almost hit the linen tablecloth. "Freddy, baby, we killed them! Four hundred and fifty simoleons!" Big Sid leaned over and explained to his daughter: "Freddy's my new gravy train. And vice versa. What a swing!"

Lorna Weinberg smiled. I smiled back. She patted her father's hand and looked at him with exasperated fondness. "Dad's a fanatic, and a hyperbolic personality. He loves to classify people with colloquialisms. You must forgive him." She said it lovingly, but with the slightest air of condescension to her father—and of challenge to me.

Big Sid laughed, but I took the challenge. "That's an interesting perception, Miss Weinberg. Are you a psychologist?"

"No, I'm an attorney. And you?"

"I'm a police officer."

"In L.A.?"

"Yes."

Lorna smiled guardedly. "Are you as good at police work as you are at golf?"

"I'm better."

"Then you're a double threat."

"That's a colloquialism you'd better elaborate on."

"Touché." Lorna Weinberg's eyes bored in on me. They were dancing with a bitter mirth. "I'm a deputy district attorney, for the city of Los Angeles. We have the same employer. I would rather be a deputy public defender, but that's the rub of the green, as Dad would say. I deal with policemen every day—and I don't like them. They see too little and arrest too often. What they can't understand or won't accept, they arrest or beat up. The jails in Los Angeles are full of people who don't belong there. My job is to prepare cases for the grand jury. I wade through tons of reports from overzealous detectives. Frankly, I see myself as watchdog on arrest-crazy police agencies. This gets me a lot of flak from my colleagues, but they accept me, because I'm damn good at what I do, and because I save them a lot of work."

I breathed it all in, and gave what I hoped would pass for an ironic grin: "So you don't like cops," I said. "Big deal. Most people don't. Would you rather have anarchy? There's only one answer, Miss Weinberg. This is not the best of all possible worlds. We have to accept that, and get on with the administration of justice."

Big Sid noted the fire in his daughter's eyes, and hurried off in the direction of the bar, embarrassed by the intensity of our conversation.

Lorna did not relent. "I can't accept that, and I won't. You can't change human nature, but you can change the law. And you can weed out some of the sociopaths who carry badges and guns.

"For example, my father told me you were curious about that man who caddied for you today. I know about him. He's one of your victims. An attorney who's a member of this club once represented Dirt Road Dave in his suit against the Los Angeles Police Department. During the Depression he had stolen some food from a grocery. Two policemen saw him do it and chased him, and when they finally caught him they were angry. They beat him unconscious with their billy clubs. Dave suffered internal hemorrhaging and almost died. He sustained irreparable brain damage. The A.C.L.U. sued your police department, and lost. Cops are above the law and can do what they please. Abe Dolwitz, the attorney, looks after Dave somewhat, but Dave's only lucid half the time. I imagine the other half of the time is a nightmare for him. Do you understand what I'm saying?"

"I understand that you're moving into areas way beyond your bailiwick, counselor. I understand that your opinion of cops is academic and one-sided and removed from the daily context we work in. I understand your compassion, and I understand that the problems you've described are insoluble."

"How can you be so jaded?"

"I'm not. I'm just realistic. You said that cops see too little and arrest too much. It's the opposite with me. I'm in the job for what I see, not the crummy salary I make."

Lorna Weinberg dropped her voice condescendingly: "I find that very hard to believe."

I dropped mine to match hers. "I don't really care, counselor. But one question. You called me a '*double* threat.' What in the world is threatening about golf?"

Lorna sighed. "It keeps people from thinking about the important things in life."

"It also keeps them from thinking about the unimportant things," I countered. She shrugged. We were even. I got up to go, chancing a parting shot: "If you hate golf so much, why do you come to this club?"

"Because they have the best food in L.A."

I laughed, and took Lorna Weinberg's hand casually "Good day, Miss Weinberg."

"Good day, officer," Lorna said, her voice now richly ironic.

I found Big Sid, thanked him for the pleasure of his golfing company, and promised to call him soon for another game. Big Sid's offer of friendship was touching, but my encounter with Lorna Weinberg left me feeling aggressive and enervated.

I picked up my clubs and walked out to the parking lot to look for my car. It wasn't in the main lot for members, or the one for club employees. I walked out the gate onto Pico. Wacky was getting to be too unreliable to trust.

I crossed the street, deciding to kill time by taking a walk around the outskirts of the 20th Century-Fox studio. I walked north, past a large expanse of vacant lots.

The sky was darkening, black clouds competing for primacy with a brilliant blue sky. I hoped for rain. Rain was a good catalyst. It was good to look for women on rainy nights—they seemed more vulnerable and open when foul weather raged.

I was almost up to Olympic when I spotted my red and white '47 Buick in an alley behind the studio's prop department. It was rocking and there were moans coming from inside. I walked up and peered in the driver's side window. It was fogged from heavy breathing, but I could still plainly see Wacky and Siddell Weinberg writhing in a hot nude embrace.

I felt the perfect calm that settles on me when I get very angry. I took a 5 iron out of my bag and opened the door of the car. "Police officer!" I called as Wacky and Siddell started to shriek and attempted to cover themselves. I didn't let them. I poked my 5 iron roughly between them, probing, kneading, and pushing at where they were joined. "Get the fuck out of my car, you stupid shitheads!" I screamed. "Now! Get out! Get the fuck *out!*"

Somehow they disengaged themselves and tumbled out the door. Siddell was sobbing and trying to cover her breasts with her arms. I threw their clothes out after them, and hurled Wacky's holstered .38 and handcuffs over the fence into the prop department. As he tried to pull on his pants I kicked him hard in the ass.

"Don't fuck with me, you asshole! Don't fuck with my career, you fucking disgrace of a cop! Take your fucking fat pig and get the fuck out of my life!"

They stumbled off down the alley, pulling on clothes as they went. I looked into my car. There was a half empty fifth of bourbon on the floor. I took a long drink and threw it after them. The dark clouds had almost completely eclipsed the blue sky.

I retrieved the bourbon bottle and drank while awaiting the rain. I thought of Lorna Weinberg. When the first raindrops fell I discarded the bottle and started the car, with no particular destination in mind.

Aimless driving consumed three hours. Lorna Weinberg, Wacky, and Dirt Road Dave consumed most of my thoughts. They were depressing thoughts, and my random driving reinforced my grim state of mind.

The rain was coming down in sheets, driven by a fierce north wind. It turned dark early, and for no logical reason I was drawn to the winding, treacherous Pasadena Freeway. Maneuvering its abrupt turns on rain-slicked pavement at top speed got me feeling better. I started thinking about my opportunities for advancement and the wonder-seeking that working Vice would afford me.

That provided me with a destination. As soon as I hit
Pasadena I turned around and drove back to L.A., to Wilshire Division, to some vice hot spots old-timers had told
me about. I drove by the hooker stands on West Adams
where knots of Negro prostitutes, probably hopheads,
waited under umbrellas on the off chance that a customer
would brave the rain and supply them with money for
dope. I cruised by the known bookie joints on Western,
then parked and watched bettors come and go. They
seemed as desperate as the hopheads.

I got the feeling that Vice wonder would be sad wonder,
pathetic and hopeless. The neon signs on the bars and
nightclubs I passed looked like cheap advertisements for
loneliness eradicator.

It was almost nine o'clock. I stopped at the Original Bar-
becue on Vermont and took my time with a sparerib dinner, wondering where to go look for women. It was too late
and too wet to chance anything but bars, and women who
were looking for the same thing I was. That made me sad,
but I decided that while I cruised I could peruse the bar
scene from the standpoint of a rookie Vice cop and maybe
learn a few things.

The joint on Normandie and Melrose was dead. Its main
draw was the television above the bar. Slaphappy locals
were laughing at the "Sid Caesar Show." I left. In the next
place, near L.A. City College, there were nothing but ani-
mated college kids, all coupled off, most of them shouting
about Truman and MacArthur and the war.

I made my way southwest. I found a bar on Western that
I had never noticed before—the Silver Star, two blocks
north of Beverly. It looked warm and well kept up. It had a
tri-colored neon sign: three stars, yellow, blue, and red, arranged around a martini glass. "Silver Star" flashed on
and off in bright orange.

I parked across the street at Ralph's market, then
dodged cars as I ran toward the neon haven. The Silver
Star was crowded, and as my eyes became accustomed to
the indoor fluorescent lighting I could tell that the place
served more as a pickup joint than a local watering hole.
Men were making advances to women seated beside them.
The gestures were awkward, and the women feigned interest in the spirit of booze-induced camaraderie. I ordered a

double Scotch and soda and carried it over to a dark row of booths against the back wall, choosing the only empty one. My legs were too long to keep from jamming into the table, so I stretched them out and sipped my drink, trying to look casual while remaining alert, with my eyes on the bar and front door.

After an hour and two more drinks, I noticed a comely woman enter the bar. She was a honey blond in her middle thirties. She walked in hesitantly, as though the place were unfamiliar and potentially hostile.

I watched as she took a seat at the bar. The bartender was busy elsewhere so the woman waited to be served, fiddling with the contents of her purse. There was an empty stool next to her, and I made for it. I sat down and the woman swiveled to face me.

"Hi," I said, "it's kind of busy tonight. The barman should be with you by Tuesday afternoon, though." The woman laughed, her face slightly averted. I could tell why; her teeth were bad, and she wanted to be fetching without exposing them. It was the first endearment in what I hoped would be a long night of them.

"This is kind of a nice place, don't you think?" she asked. Her voice was nasal and slightly midwestern.

"Yes, I do. Especially on a night like this."

"Brrr," the woman said. "I know what you mean. I've never been here before, but I was driving by in a cab and it looked so warm and inviting that I just had to stop in. Have you been here before?"

"No, this is my first time, too. But please excuse my bad manners. My name is Bill Thornhill."

"I'm Maggie. Maggie Cadwallader."

I laughed. "Oh, God, our names are so solid, like a trip to Great Britain."

Maggie laughed. "I'm just a Wisconsin farm girl."

"I'm just a big-city hick."

We laughed some more. It was good laughter; we were playing our roles with both naturalness and refinement. The bartender came and I ordered a beer for myself and a stinger for Maggie. I paid. "How long have you lived in L.A., Maggie?" I asked.

"Oh, for years. What about you, Bill?" From that added

intimacy I *knew* it was going to be. Relief and ardor flooded through me.

"Too long, I think. Actually, I'm a native."

"One of the few! Isn't it some place, though? Sometimes I think I live here because anything can happen, do you know what I mean? You can be walking down the street and something crazy and wonderful might happen, just like that." The wonder in a nutshell. I started to like her.

"I know exactly what you mean," I said, and meant it. "Sometimes I think that's what keeps me from moving away. Most people come here for the glamour and the movies. I was born here, so I know that's a lot of baloney. I stay here for the mystery."

"You put that so well! Mystery!" Maggie squeezed my hand. "Wait a second," she said as she finished her drink. "Let me see if I can guess what you do. Are you an athlete? You look like one."

"No, guess again."

"Hmmm. You're so big. Is it an outside job?"

"No hints. Guess again."

"Are you a writer?"

"No."

"A businessman?"

"No."

"A lawyer?"

"No."

"A movie star!"

"Hah! No."

"A fireman?"

"No."

"I give up. Tell me what you do, and I'll tell you what I do."

"Okay, but prepare yourself for a letdown. I sell insurance." I said it with boyish mock humility and resignation. Maggie loved it.

"What's so bad about that? I'm just a bookkeeper! What we *do* isn't what we *are,* is it?"

"No," I lied.

"So there!" Maggie squeezed my hand again.

I signaled the bartender, who brought us refills. We raised our glasses in a toast. "To mystery," I said.

"To mystery," she repeated.

Maggie finished her drink quickly. I sipped my beer. It felt like time to make a move. "Maggie, if this weather weren't so damn rotten, we could take a drive. I know L.A. like the back of my hand, and there's lots of beautiful places we could go."

Maggie smiled warmly, this time not worrying about showing her teeth. "I feel like getting out of here, too. But you're right, the weather is rotten. We could go to my apartment for a nightcap."

"That sounds nice," I said, my voice tightening.

"Did you drive? I came in a cab."

"Yeah, I drove. We can take my car. Where do you live?"

"In Hollywood. On Harold Way. That's a little street off of Sunset. Do you know where it is?"

"Sure."

"That's right, you know L.A. like the back of your hand!"

We both laughed as we left the bar and hurried across rainy Western Avenue to my car.

Driving north on Wilton Place, the rain started to abate. Maggie and I avoided flirting, and talked instead about things like the weather and her cat. I didn't particularly like cats, but faked great interest in meeting hers. I kept wondering about her body. In the bar she had never taken off her coat. Her legs were well formed, but I wanted to know the size of her breasts and breadth of her hips before we were nude together.

Harold Way was a small, dimly lighted side street. Maggie showed me where to park. Her apartment building was postwar ugly with a Hawaiian motif. It was a giant boxlike structure of eight or ten units, stucco, with phony bamboo trim along the doors and windows. The entrances were along the side of the building.

Maggie and I chatted nervously as we walked down the long entranceway to her apartment. When she opened the door and flipped on the lights a fat gray cat jumped out of the darkness to greet us. Maggie put down her umbrella and picked him up. "Mmmm, my baby!" she cooed, hugging the captive feline. "Lion, this is Bill. Bill, this is my protector, Lion."

I patted the cat's head. "Hello, Lion," I said naturally, not changing my voice. "How are you this fine winter's evening? Caught any rodents lately? Are you earning your keep in this wonderful abode your lovely mistress has given you?"

My deadpan expression and voice sent Maggie into gales of laughter. "Oh, Bill, that's so funny!" she gasped. She was slightly drunk.

I took the cat as Maggie locked the door behind us. Lion was very fat, probably not a ball bearing mouse trap. I looked around the living room. It was tidy, and a virtual ode to faraway places: Greece, Rome, France, and Spain were represented on the four walls, courtesy of Pan American Airways. I dropped the cat to the floor, where he started to sniff my trouser legs.

"It's a nice apartment, Maggie. You've obviously taken a lot of care with it."

Maggie beamed, then took my hand and led me to a plush overstuffed sofa. "Sit, Bill, and tell me what you'd like to drink."

"Cognac, neat," I said.

"One minute."

While Maggie was in the kitchen I transferred my gun and cuffs from my belt to my coat pocket. She returned a moment later with two snifter glasses each containing a solid three ounces. She sat next to me on the sofa. We toasted silently. As the brandy hit my system I realized that I had little to say. There was nothing I could impart to this woman—who was probably ten years my senior—that she didn't already know.

Maggie took the matter out of my hands. She finished her brandy and placed her glass on the coffee table. The cat scampered up to us and I playfully lunged at his tail. Maggie reached down to pet him and our shoulders brushed together. We looked at each other for a split second, then I grabbed her and we fell to the floor. She giggled, and I took my cue. I barked like some breed of gentle dog and covered her shoulders with gentle dog bites, barely pinching her skin beneath the fabric.

Maggie laughed and laughed. She tightened her arms around me. "Oh, Bill. Oh, Bill. Oh, Bill," she squeaked between laughing fits.

I dog-nipped my way down her back, turning and looking every few seconds at her tear-stained face. I lifted the
hem of her skirt and bit my way down her legs to her ankles, trying not to snag her nylons. Her hand was stroking
and mussing my hair. I pulled off her shoes and bit her
toes, one at a time, barking "Woof! Woof!" between each
bite. Maggie was shrieking now, her whole body wracked
with uncontrollable laughter.

Now that I knew what I had come to give, I rolled her
over onto her side and elbowed myself up until we were
face to face. We had a long interim where Maggie held me
tightly and I stroked her hair. Just as her laughter would
subside, I would "woof, woof" tenderly into her ear and
kiss her neck until she cracked up again.

Finally Maggie took her head from my chest and looked
at me. "Woof, Bill Thornhill," she said.

"Woof, fair Maggie Cadwallader," I said.

Maggie's lipstick was gone, mashed into my lapels and
shirtfront. Her mouth was completely guileless as I bent in
slow motion to kiss it. Maggie's lips parted and her eyes
closed as she sensed my intention. Our lips and tongues
met and played in perfect, experienced unison. We rolled
together as we kissed, kicking over the coffee table, sending magazines and artificial flowers to the floor. We broke
our long kiss, and Maggie made small noises as my hands
fumbled at the clasp at the back of her dress.

"The bathroom first, Bill, please." As I released her, she
leaped out of my embrace and stumbled to her feet, making more small noises as she moved to the bathroom.

I got to my feet and took off my clothes, laying them
neatly on the sofa. Wearing only undershorts, I walked
softly to the bathroom. The door was slightly ajar and the
light was on. I could hear Maggie rummaging in the medicine cabinet. There was a ritual going on that I had long
wanted to observe.

I pushed open the door. Maggie was starting to insert
her diaphragm when she saw me. She jumped, startled and
angry, into the bathtub, where she covered herself with
the shower curtain.

"Bill," she said, flushed. "Please, goddamnit, I'll just be
a minute. Wait in the bedroom, honey. Please. I'll be right
there."

"I just wanted to watch you, sweetheart," I said. "I wanted to help you with it."

Maggie said nervously, "It's a private thing, Bill. A woman's thing. If you don't see me do it, then you don't really know it's there. It's better for you. Believe me, honey."

"I believe you, but I want to see. Show me, please."

"No."

"Please?"

I lowered my head and nudged Maggie back against the shower wall. She started to giggle. I pulled her away from the bathtub, hoisted her into the air, spun her around and set her down in the same posture she had been in when I had pushed open the bathroom door.

"Do you ever lose at anything, Bill?"

"No."

"How old are you?"

"I'll be twenty-seven next week."

"I'm thirty-six."

"You're beautiful. I want to love you so much."

"You're very handsome. You've never seen a woman put in her diaphragm?"

"No."

"Then I'll show you."

She did. "You're a strange, curious young man, Bill."

"Intimate things like that mean a lot to me."

"I believe you. Now make love to me."

Maggie led me to her bedroom. She left the light off. She unbuttoned her blouse, unhooked her bra and let the garments fall to the floor. I stepped out of my undershorts. We lay on the bed and held each other for a long time. I stroked Maggie's hair. She cooed into my chest. I grew tired of it, and tried to bring her chin up so I could kiss her, but she resisted, pushing her head harder against me. After a while her grip loosened and I was able to cover her neck with kisses. Maggie sighed, and I began to suck her breasts. I felt her hand between my legs, urging me toward her. She positioned herself beneath me and guided me in. I began to move. Maggie didn't respond. I tried slow, exploratory thrusts, then hard insistent ones. Maggie just lay there, motionless. I propped myself up on my hands, the better to look at her face. Maggie looked up at me, smiling.

She reached up and framed my face with her hands, her smile more beatific as my thrusts multiplied in their urgency. I came very hard. I groaned, shuddered and collapsed on top of her. She never said a word. When I finally managed to look at her she was still smiling; and I realized I had been thinking of Lorna Weinberg.

Maggie had seemed to change during our lovemaking. She had gotten what she wanted, and it wasn't love, or sex. Her smile and post-lovemaking ritual of bringing in brandy and snifters on a tray seemed to be saying, "Now that we have gotten that over with, we can get down to the real business of our meeting."

We sat in bed and sipped brandy, both of us nude. I liked Maggie's body: pale, freckled skin, gently rounded shoulders, soft stomach, and small soft breasts with large dark red nipples. I liked her openness in showing it to me even more, and had no desire to leave. The brandy was good, but I watched my intake. Maggie was sipping steadily, and would soon be pie-eyed. Maggie beamed at me as I shifted postures. I waggled my eyebrows a la Wacky Walker. Maggie beamed some more. I told her some lies about the insurance racket. She still beamed.

Finally she said, "Bill, let's go into the living room, okay?" She dug two terry cloth robes out of her bedroom closet, then led me into the living room, gave me a big kiss on the cheek, and sat me down on the couch like a loving mother or schoolteacher. She went back into the bedroom and returned with a large leather-bound scrapbook.

She sat down between me and my piled-up clothes and poured herself more brandy. My robe was well worn and smelled fresh. As Maggie arranged the scrapbook on the coffee table I adjusted her robe to show off a fair amount of cleavage. She reacted with a prim kiss on my cheek. I disliked her for it. The ten-year gap in our ages was beginning to show.

"Memory lane, Bill," Maggie said. "Would you like to take a little trip down memory lane with old Maggie?"

"You're not old."

"In some ways I am."

"You're in your prime."

"Flatterer."

She opened the scrapbook. On the first page were photographs of a tall, light-haired man in a World War I doughboy's uniform. He stood alone in most of the sepia-tinted photos, and in a preeminent spot in the group shots.

"That's my daddy," Maggie said. "Mama used to get exasperated with him sometimes, and say bad things about him. When I was a little girl I asked her once, 'If Daddy was so mean, why did you marry him?' and she said, 'Because he was the handsomest man I'd ever seen.'"

She turned the page. Wedding pictures and baby pictures.

"That's Mama and Daddy's wedding—1910. And that's me as a little baby, just before Daddy went into the army."

"Are you an only child, Maggie?"

"Yes. Are you?"

"Yes."

She flipped the pages more rapidly. I watched time pass, seeing in minutes Maggie's parents go from young to old and seeing Maggie go from infancy to lindy-hopping adolescent. Her face, as she danced at some long-gone high school sock-hop, was a heartbreakingly hopeful version of her current one.

She drank brandy, talking on in a wistful monotone, barely heeding my presence. She seemed to be leading up to something, working slowly toward some goal that would explain why she wanted me here.

"End of volume one, Bill," Maggie said. She got up unsteadily from the sofa and knocked over my folded sportcoat. When she picked it up, she noted its heaviness and started to fumble in the pocket where I had put my gun and handcuffs. Before I had a chance to stop her, she withdrew the .38, screamed, and backed away from me, holding the gun shakily, pointed to the floor.

"No, no, no, no!" she gasped. "Please, no! I won't let you hurt me! No!"

I got up and walked toward her, trying to remember if both safety locks were on. "I'm a policeman, Maggie," I said softly, placatingly. "I don't want to hurt you. Give me the gun, sweetheart."

"No! I know who sent you! I knew he would! No! No!"

I picked up my trousers and pulled out my badge in its

leather holder. I held it up. "See, Maggie? I'm a police officer. I didn't want to tell you. A lot of people don't like policemen. See? It's a real badge, sweetheart."

Maggie dropped the gun, sobbing.

I went over and held her tightly. "It's all right. I'm sorry you were scared. I should have told you the truth. I'm sorry."

Maggie shook her head against me. "I'm sorry, too. I was a ninny. You're just a man. You wanted to get laid, and you lied. I was a ninny. I'm the one who should be sorry."

"Don't say that. I care about you."

"Sure you do."

"I do." I kissed the part in her hair and pushed her gently away. "You were going to show me volume two, remember?"

Maggie smiled. "All right. You sit down and pour me a brandy. I feel funny."

While Maggie got her other scrapbook I put my gun back in my coat pocket. She came back hugging a slender black leather album. She beamed as if the gun episode had never happened.

We took up where we left off. She opened the album. It contained a dozen snapshots of a little baby, probably only a few weeks old, still bald, peering curiously up toward some fascinating object. Maggie touched her fingers to her lips and pressed them to the photos.

"Your baby?" I asked.

"Mine. My baby. My love."

"Where is he?"

"His father took him."

"Are you divorced?"

"He wasn't my husband, Bill. He was my lover. My true love. He's dead now. He died of his love for me."

"How, Maggie?"

"I can't tell you."

"What happened to the baby?"

"He's in an orphanage, back east."

"Why, Maggie? Orphanages are terrible places. Why don't you keep him? Children need parents, not institutions."

"Don't say that! I can't! I can't keep him! I'm sorry I showed you, I thought you'd understand!"

I took her hand. "I do, sweetheart, more than you know. Let's go back to bed, all right?"

"All right. But I want to show you one more thing. You're a policeman. You know a lot about crime, right?"

"Right."

"Then come here. I'll show you where I keep my buried treasure."

We went back into the bedroom. As I sat on the bed, Maggie unscrewed the left front bedpost. She pulled off the top part and reached down into the hollowed-out bottom piece. She extracted a red velvet bag, its end held together by a drawstring.

"Would a burglar look in a place like that, Bill?" she asked.

"I doubt it," I said.

Maggie opened the velvet bag and drew out an antique diamond brooch. I almost gasped: the rocks looked real, perfectly cut, and there were at least a dozen of them, interspersed with larger blue stones, all mounted on heavy strands of real gold. The thing must have been worth a small fortune.

"It's beautiful, Maggie."

"Thank you. I don't show it to many people. Only the nice ones."

"Where did you get it?"

"It's a love gift."

"From your true love?"

"Yes."

"You want some advice? Put it in a safe-deposit box. And don't tell people about it. You never know the kind of person you might meet."

"I know who I can trust and who I can't."

"All right. Put it away, will you?"

"Why? I thought you liked it."

"I do, but it makes me sad."

Maggie replaced the brooch in its hiding place. I lifted her and set her down on the bed.

"I don't want to," she said. "I want to talk and drink some more brandy."

"Later, sweetheart."

Maggie slipped off her robe reluctantly. I tried to be passionate, but my kisses were perfunctory, and I was filled with a sense of loss that not even lovemaking could surmount.

When it was over Maggie smiled and kissed my cheek absently, then threw on her robe and went to the kitchen. I could hear her digging around for bottles and glasses. It was my cue. I padded softly into the living room and dressed in the semidarkness.

Maggie came out of the kitchen carrying a tray with a liqueur bottle and shot glasses on it. Her face crashed for an instant when she saw I was leaving, but she recovered quickly, like the veteran she was.

"I have to go, Maggie," I said. She did not put down the tray, so I leaned over it, bumping it slightly, and brushed my lips against her cheek. "Goodbye, Maggie." She didn't answer, just stood there holding the tray.

I walked to my car. The cold air felt good, and dawn was just starting to break.

I knew that this Saturday, February 6, 1951, had been a red-letter day for me. When I got home I wrote in my diary only what I knew: Maggie Cadwallader and Lorna Weinberg. I would not realize until later that this had been the pivotal date of my life.

4

Beckworth called me into his office on Monday morning. I had expected him to be angry with me for standing him up, but he was surprisingly magnanimous. He told me flat out what I had already heard from several other less reliable sources: come June he would be the new commander of Wilshire Station, and would initiate a purging of "shit-head deadwood" sending a half dozen "fuck-up bluesuits" to Seventy-seventh Street Division, "Niggerland, U.S.A.," where they could learn "the real meaning of police work." He never mentioned names—he didn't have to. Wacky Walker would obviously be on the first stage to Watts, and I gravely accepted the fact that there was nothing I could do about it.

Wacky and I had resolved our differences that weekend through booze and poetry. I had gone over to his apartment Sunday bearing gifts—a crisp C-note as payment for his green-reading duties, handcuffs and gun, a bottle of Old Grand Dad and a limited edition volume of the early poetry of W. H. Auden. Wacky was delighted and almost wept in his gratitude, causing me to feel the strangest detachment; love mixed with pity and bitter resentment at his dependence on me. It was a feeling I would carry with me until the end of the last season of my youth.

I walked into the muster room for the immortal police ritual of Monday morning roll call. The room was noisy, and filled with cigarette smoke. Gately, the muster sergeant, needed a shave as usual.

I found a seat next to Wacky. He was staring into his lap, pretending to read traffic reports. As I sat down, I glanced

45

at his real reading material: enclosed in the traffic holder
was a copy of the *Four Quartets* by T. S. Eliot.

Gately made it brief. No drunk arrests—the Lincoln
Heights drunk tank had flooded during the recent heavy
rains—and lots of traffic summonses; the city attorney
wanted shitloads of them—the heavy implication being
that the city needed moola. We were told to lay off the
streetwalkers on West Adams, and to look out for a stickup
team: two Mexican gunsels had hit a liquor store and a
couple of markets on the Southern border of the division,
near the Coliseum. The dicks had learned from eyewitnesses that they drove a souped-up white Ford pickup.
They were packing .45 automatics. When Gately mentioned this there was an immediate reaction in the
room—this is why we are all here, every cop in the room
seemed to be thinking. Even Wacky stirred and looked up
from his Eliot. He pointed his right index finger at me and
cocked his thumb. I nodded; it was why I was there, too.

We got our black-and-white from the lot and cruised east
on Pico to Hoover, then south toward the Coliseum. Wacky
wanted to spend some time warning local merchants about
the Mexican heisters. He was in an effusive mood and
wanted to gab with his "constituents."

We parked, and Wacky insisted that I accompany him to
talk to Jack Chew. Jack Chew was a Chinaman with a
Texas drawl. He owned a little market-butcher shop at
Twenty-eighth and Hoover and said things like, "Ah, sooo,
pardner." Wacky loved him, but he hated Wacky because
he helped himself to the canned litchi nuts that Jack kept
behind the counter for the cops on the beat. Jack was very
courtly and Old World: he liked to offer or be asked, and he
thought that Wacky was a pig for grabbing.

He was behind the meat counter when we walked into
his open-air store, wrapping up some kind of candied duck
for an old Chinese lady.

"Hey there, Jack," Wacky called, "where'd you get that
quacker? I thought the guys at Rampart told you to quit
raiding Westlake Park. Don't you know all those used rubbers they got floating round in the lake spoil the flavor?
The guys at Rampart told me the ducks wear the rubbers
at night to keep their beaks warm. Whither thou, O
quacker beak; Peter juice and soon you'll peak; O noble

duck, Such bad, bad luck; To end at Jack's you're really fucked."

Jack groaned and the old woman giggled as Wacky did his Frankenstein imitation, walking toward her slowly, arms extended, groaning deeply.

"Fuck you, Walker," Jack said. To me he said, "Ah, sooo, Officer Freddy," then handed me an open can of litchi nuts. Jack spoke a few words to the woman in Chinese. She left, giggling and waving at Wacky.

"They all love me, Jack. What is it about me?" Wacky said. "But this isn't a social call."

"Good," Jack said.

Wacky laughed and went on, "Jack, we got some bad hombres operating on this side of the range, carrying hardware. They like little markets like yours, and being greasers they probably don't know that Chinamen are tough giver-uppers. They're in their mid twen—"

Wacky didn't get to finish. A young woman ran into the market. She was opening her mouth to scream, but no sound was coming out. She grabbed at Wacky's arm.

"Ow, ow, ow, ow, ow," she choked.

Wacky held both her hands to her sides. He spoke calmly. "Yes, dear. 'Officer.' Now what's wrong?"

"Off . . . ic . . . er," she got out, "Ma, ma—my neighbor . . . dead!"

"Where?" I said.

The woman pointed to Twenty-eighth Street. She started to run in that direction. I ran after her. Wacky followed me. She led us halfway down the block and up to an old, white wood-framed four-flat. She pointed up the stairs leading to the second story. The door was wide open.

"Uh, uh, uh," she stammered, then pointed again and backed up against a row of mailboxes, biting at her knuckles.

Wacky and I looked at each other. We both nodded and Wacky gave me the beginning of a smile. We drew our guns and raced up the stairs. I entered first, into what had once been a modest living room. Now it was in a shambles: chairs, bookshelves, and cabinets were overturned and the floor was covered with broken glass. I held my breath, and advanced slowly, my gun held in front of me. Behind me, I could hear Wacky breathing hoarsely.

There was a small kitchen straight ahead. I tiptoed up to
it. The white linoleum was broadly spattered with con-
gealed blood. Wacky saw it and immediately tore back into
the rear rooms of the apartment, completing forgetting
caution. I ran after him, almost knocking him over in the
bedroom doorway just as I heard his first exclamations of
horror: "Oh, God, Freddy!"

I pushed him aside, and looked into the bedroom. Lying
on the floor on her back was a nude woman. Her neck was
black and purple and twisted to the side. Her tongue was
hugely swollen and stuck out obscenely. Her eyes bulged
in their sockets. There were puncture wounds on her
breasts and abdomen and deep gashes on the insides of her
thighs. She was covered with dried blood.

I checked my watch—9:06 A.M. Wacky stared at the dead
woman and then at me as if he couldn't believe what he
was seeing. His eyes moved back and forth frantically
while he remained motionless.

I ran downstairs. The woman who had summoned us
was still next to her open apartment door, still gnawing at
her knuckles. "The phone!" I yelled at her. I found it in her
crowded front room and called the station, requested a
team of detectives and a meat wagon, then ran back upstairs.

Wacky was still staring at the dead woman. He seemed
to be committing to memory the details of her desecration.
I walked through the apartment, writing down descrip-
tions: the overturned furniture, the broken glass, and the
configuration of the dried blood in the kitchen. I knelt
down to check the carpet: it was a dark-orange phony Persian, but light enough so that the trail of blood was still
visible. I followed it into the bedroom where the dead
woman lay. Wacky suddenly spoke out behind me, causing
me to almost leap through the ceiling: "Jesus fucking
Christ, Freddy. What a mess."

"Yeah. The dicks and the coroner are on their way. I'm
gonna keep looking around here. You go downstairs and
get a statement from the woman."

"Right."

Wacky took off and I returned to my note-taking. It was
just a homey middle-class apartment, clean and comfortable looking, not the kind of place that even a desperate

hophead would burglarize, but that was what this looked like. Further investigation revealed a blood-soaked terry cloth bathrobe on the floor in the little dining room that separated the living room and kitchen. At the end of the kitchen was a door that led downstairs to what looked like a laundry room; there were bloody footprints on the rickety wooden steps.

I went through the apartment looking for the murder weapon and found nothing, no sharp instruments of any kind. I checked the victim again. She was a pretty brunette and looked to be in her middle twenties. She had a slender body and very light green eyes. She was wearing dark red toenail polish and lipstick that matched perfectly the color of her dried blood. Her body was sprawled in what seemed like reluctant acceptance of death, but her face, with its open mouth and bulging eyes, seemed to be screaming, No!

I went through the rooms again, looking for more details that might mean something. I found a bloody partial fingerprint on the hallway wall near the bedroom door. I circled it with my pen. There was a telephone stand in the living room with no phone on it, just an ornate crystal ashtray filled with matchbooks. One of them caught my eye—a colorful orange job with three stars on it, all arranged around a martini glass. The Silver Star. I poked in the ashtray. All the matchbooks were from bars and night spots in the central L.A.-Hollywood area. I looked around for smoking materials—pipes, cigarettes, or tobacco. Nothing. Maybe the woman was a bar hopper or matchbook collector.

I heard loud footsteps thumping up the stairs. It was Wacky, followed by two plainclothes cops and an old guy I knew to be an assistant medical examiner. I nodded them in the direction of the bedroom. They went in ahead of me. I heard whistles, moans, disgusted snorts, and declarations of awe:

"Oh, God. Oh, shit," the first detective said.

"Holy Jesus," the second detective said.

The medical examiner just stared and exhaled slowly, then walked over and knelt beside the dead woman. He poked and prodded at her skin, then ran a thumbnail over the caked blood on her legs. "Dead at least twenty-four hours, fellas," he said. "Cause of death asphyxiation, although the stomach and breast wounds could have been fatal. Look at her eyes and tongue, though. She died gasping for breath. Look for a switchblade knife—and a fucking lunatic."

"Who found the body?" the first detective asked. He was a tall, burly guy I had seen around the station.

"I did," Wacky said.

"Name and shield number?" he asked.

"Walker, five eighty-three."

"Okay, Walker. I'm DiCenzo, my partner's name is Brown. Let's get out of here, stiffs depress me. Brownie, call the lab guys."

"I did, Joe," Brown said.

"Good."

We all walked into the living room, except for the doctor, who stayed with the body, sitting on the bed and rummaging through his black bag.

"Okay, Walker, tell me about it," DiCenzo said.

"Right. My partner and I were at the market around the corner when the lady who lives in the downstairs apartment comes running in, hysterical. She leads us back here. That's it. After we discovered the stiff and called you guys, I got the dame calmed down. She said she had a feeling something was wrong. The stiff was a friend of hers, and she didn't show up at work yesterday or today. They both work at the same place. She's got a key to the stiff's apartment, because sometimes the stiff went away for the weekend and she fed her cat. Anyway, she had this feeling and went up and unlocked the apartment. She found the stiff and went running for the cops. The woman's name is June Haller, the stiff's name is Leona Jensen. She was employed as a secretary at the Auto Club downtown. She was twenty-four. She's got parents someplace up north, near 'Frisco."

"Good, Walker," DiCenzo nodded. We were interrupted by a team of three guys from the crime lab. They were in plainclothes and were carrying cameras and evidence kits.

Brown pointed toward the bedroom. "In there, guys. The doc's waiting for you."

DiCenzo started scanning the living room, notebook in

hand. I tapped him on the shoulder and motioned him to the kitchen. "Holy shit," he said when he saw the blood-splattered linoleum floor.

"Yeah," I said. "He sliced her in here, then got her into the bedroom and strangled her. She resisted as he dragged her through the living room—that accounts for the over-turned furniture and broken glass. There's a door leading downstairs at the end of the kitchen. There are bloody foot-prints going down. He had to have come and gone that way. There's a bloody fingerprint in the hall near the bed-room. I circled it. What do you think?"

DiCenzo was nodding along with me. "What's your name?" he asked.

"Underhill," I said.

"You a college man, Underhill?"

"Yes, Sergeant."

"Well, I'd say that nothing you learned in college is gonna help us with this here homicide. Unless that print is complete and belongs to the killer. That's college stuff—scientific. It looks to me like a botched-up burglary. When we find out what the lab report says, which ain't gonna mean much, we're gonna get stuck with hauling in every known burglar, dope addict, and degenerate in Los Angeles. What I'm hoping is that the dame was raped—rape-o-burglar is a rare M.O. Not too many of those bastards around. Is this your first murder victim?"

"Yes."

"Is it getting to you?"

"No."

"Good. You and your partner go back to the station and write your reports."

"Right, Sergeant."

DiCenzo winked at me. "It's a shame, ain't it, Under-hill? That tomato had it all, you know what I mean?"

"Yeah, I know."

I found Wacky in the bedroom. Flash bulbs were popping and he was writing in his notebook, shielding his eyes from the glare, casting occasional glances at the late Le-ona Jensen. He was getting angry looks from the lab men, so I pulled him into the hallway.

"Let's go. We've got to get back to the station and write our reports."

Wacky continued scribbling in his notebook. "There," he said. "I'm finished. I wrote a poem about the stiff. It's a masterpiece. It's dedicated to John Milton. It's called 'Piece of Ass Lost.' "

"Forget it, Wacky. Let's just get out of here."

We drove north on Hoover in silence.

"You think they'll find the guy who croaked her?" Wacky finally asked.

"DiCenzo thinks there's a chance."

"Frankly, I'm pessimistic."

"Why?"

"Because death is going to be the new fad. I can feel it. It's going to replace sports. I'm writing an epic poem about it. All forty-eight states are going to have the atom bomb and drop them on each other. L.A. is going to drop the A-bomb on 'Frisco for stealing tourists. The Brooklyn Dodgers are going to A-bomb the New York Giants. I can feel it."

"You're crazy, Wack."

"No, I'm a genius. Freddy, you gotta call Big Sid. I loved Hillcrest. I want to play it. It's a shot-maker's course. I could shoot sixty-eight there."

I laughed. "That's a riot. You just want to throw the salami to Siddell again. Tell me, Wack, did you ever get to finish with her?"

"Yeah, but I've been calling her to try to fix up another date, and every time I call some maid answers and says, 'Miz Siddell ain't at home, officer.' I think she's giving me the bum's rush."

"Maybe, but don't worry. There's lots of other fat girls around."

"Yeah, but not like Siddell; she's class. Listen, partner, I need a favor. Will you talk to Siddell? Sound her out on how she feels about me? You're in tight with Big Sid, you can do it."

I hesitated, then felt my wheels start to turn. "Sure, Wack, I'll drop by Big Sid's place sometime next weekend. He gave me carte blanche for visits. I'm his new gravy train."

Wacky punched me in the arm. "Thanks, pard. When

I'm dodging flaming arrows down in Nigger Gulch and you're king of Wilshire Vice I'll remember this moment."

We pulled into the parking lot of the station. I started to offer a snappy rejoinder as token resistance, but couldn't. Instead, I walked upstairs to the detective's squad room and typed up my report.

I drove to Beverly Hills early Saturday evening, getting honest with myself en route: I could invent all the pretexts I wanted, but I knew I was going to Big Sid's home for only one reason: to search out Lorna Weinberg and attempt, somehow, to satisfy my curiosity about her. The house was on Canon Drive, just south of Sunset. I was expecting some outrageous pretensions to class and was surprised: the large white Colonial edifice with the well-tended front lawn was understated, almost somber.

I knocked on the door and a Negro maid answered, informing me that "Mr. Big Sid ain't at home, Miz Siddell be up in her room takin' a nap."

"What about Lorna?" I blurted.

The withered old woman looked at me as if I were nuts. "Miz Lorna done moved out years ago."

"Sorry," I said, peering through the crack in the door, scanning a living room furnished in old wood and rich fabrics. Somehow I felt that the place might be a treasure trove of wonder, even in Lorna's absence. I paused, then said forcefully, "Wake up Siddell, will you, please? I have an important message from a friend of hers."

The old woman eyed me suspiciously, then opened the door and gestured toward the living room. "You waits here," she said, "I get Miz Siddell."

The maid trotted upstairs, leaving me alone in the richly appointed room. I noticed some framed photographs above the red brick fireplace, and went over and looked at them. They were individual portraits of Big Sid, Siddell, and Lorna. Sid beamed proudly, Siddell looked as slender-faced as a good photographer could make her, and Lorna looked grave and abstracted, wearing a graduation gown and cap. There was another, larger photo of the family trio: Big Sid clutching his omnipresent cigar, Siddell looking sullen, and Lorna leaning on a cane. I noticed that her right leg was withered and deformed, and felt a nervous flush come over me. I shook my head to clear it, then recalled: Lorna had remained seated during our one meeting. But where was *Mother* Weinberg?

Lost in my reverie, I felt a sharp tug at my coat sleeve and turned to find Siddell Weinberg pushing herself against me. "I know what you must think of me," she was saying, "but I don't do those kinds of things all the time . . ."

I held the feverish-looking woman at arm's length and took a stern tack, the better to secure the information I now *had* to have. "Well, I do, Miss Weinberg, so it's not really a big issue. But you should call Wacky. He's fond of you, and wants to see you again."

"I know, but I can't! You have to tell Herbert not to call me here. Daddy thinks that anyone interested in me is just out for his money. Besides, I'm engaged."

"Does Big Sid approve of your fiancé?"

"No, not really, but at least he's Jewish, and he's in graduate school. He's got a future."

"And policemen don't have futures?"

"I didn't mean that!" Siddell wailed. "Daddy likes you, but he thinks Herbert is crazy."

I led Siddell to a plush red leather couch next to the fireplace. "Your father is right," I said. "He is. Are you in love with this guy you're going to marry?"

"Yes, no! I don't know!"

"Then call Wacky. He's in the phone book—Herbert L. Walker, 926 South St. Andrews, L.A. All right?"

"All—all right. I'm going out of town next week, but I'll call Herbert when I get back."

"Good." I patted Siddell's hand, then started fishing around for conversational lead-ins to get to the real purpose of my visit. Finally, I got one: "This is a hell of a nice house, Siddell. Your mother obviously puts a lot of time into it."

Siddell lowered her head. "Mama is dead," she said.

"I'm sorry. Was it recently?"

"No, it was in 1933. I was nine and Lorna was thirteen."

"That's a long time ago."

"Yes and no."

"You mean you still feel it?"

"Y—Yes . . . but mostly, Lorna does." Siddell's voice

had taken on the resonance of a person explaining a profound truth.

I prodded gently. "What do you mean, Siddell?"

"Well, Mama died and Lorna got crippled at the same time, so Lorna hates and loves Mama at the same time. They were driving down Sunset. Mama was pregnant again. It was raining, and Mama skidded into a tree. Her stomach hit the steering wheel. She lost the baby, but aside from that she wasn't hurt. Lorna went through the windshield. Her pelvis was crushed, that's why she walks so funny, and why her right leg is so skinny—all the nerve endings got torn up. Anyway, Mama wanted another baby, really badly. She knew Daddy wanted a son. She held the baby in there; she wouldn't believe it was dead. She was supposed to go to the hospital to get labor induced, but she didn't. The baby infected her stomach, and she ran away. They found her dead, up in the Hollywood Hills. She had made a little nest for herself up there, with all these baby clothes she bought from Bonwit Teller. She couldn't believe the baby was dead."

It was almost more than I wanted to know.

Siddell sensed this: "Don't be sad," she said. "It was a long time ago."

I nodded. "And your father never remarried?"

Siddell shook her head. "Daddy hasn't touched another woman since the day Mama died."

I got up to leave. By way of farewell, Siddell said, "Tell Herbert I'll call him. Tell him I like him."

"I will."

I walked out to my car, looking up at the sky and hoping for rain. As I hit the ignition, the wonder caught me, and the irony—my adopted family were orphans, too.

5

Wacky was out with the flu Monday and Tuesday, and Beckworth bought it because Wacky hardly ever used his sick leave. In reality, he was juiced up and working on his new "epic" poem and waiting by the phone for a call from Siddell Weinberg.

Early Wednesday morning as we swung out of the station parking lot, I put his fears to rest: "She's going out of town for a week or so. She's going to call you when she gets back."

"Really?"

"Yeah. We had a nice chat. She's engaged to some Jewish guy, but she isn't in love with him."

"And she's hot for some un-kosher meat on the side?" Wacky was almost drooling.

"I think so. She thinks you're the cat's meow."

Wacky celebrated the good news by hanging a U-turn in heavy traffic, hitting the siren and flooring the gas pedal for a good five minutes, cutting in and out of the quiet residential streets that bordered the station. When he finally returned to normal driving speed and cut the siren we were all the way down on Adams and Seventh Avenue, and he was grinning like a sated lover. "Thanks, partner," he said.

"For what?"

"For everything. Don't ask me to explain, I'm feeling elliptical today."

"That reminds me," I said, "I got you a present. It's back in my locker. A poetry anthology. But beware—I've looked through it pretty well, and the next time we play Name the Poet, I'm going to kick your ass."

"That'll be the day. Hot dog! I feel good today. You want coffee and doughnuts? I'm buying."

"You're on."

We drove to a Cooper's doughnut joint at Twenty-third and Western, where we got a dozen fresh glazed and coffee. We ate and drank in silence.

I took a seat that faced out toward the street and let my mind drift with prosaic wonder: a cold, sunny, winter's day. My city. The propriety born of my special, inside knowledge.

Across the street on Western, in front of the liquor store, a high school kid was convincing a wino to go in and buy him some booze. When the wino went inside the kid ogled the mulatto prostitute standing next door in front of the cabstand. She caught him looking at her and snorted her amusement. The wino came back out a few moments later and surreptitiously handed the kid a paper bag. The kid took off, practically running, hurling some kind of remark at the prostitute, who flipped him the finger. The wino walked off in the opposite direction, sucking on a short-dog of muscatel that the kid had bought him for his services.

A patrol car cruised by slowly, driven by my colleague, Tom Brewer. The wino stuck the bottle hurriedly into his back pocket, looking around guiltily. Brewer just drove on by, not noticing the little dance of fear. Even if he had, he wouldn't have cared. His father was a drunk, and he had loved his father, so he left drunks alone. Tom had told me about his father one night at a softball game at the Academy when he was half drunk himself.

My city. My wonder.

Three hours later, we were driving south on Berendo when a white Ford pickup passed us going in the opposite direction. I craned my neck and saw that there were two Mexicans in the cab. They turned right at the corner, out of my vision, and I *knew*. "Stop the car, partner," I said.

Wacky noted the gravity of my voice and pulled to the curb.

"We got a hot one, Wacky," I said. "There's a little market around the corner in back of us. The two Mexican heisters in the Ford truck just turned the corner . . ." I didn't have to finish. Wacky nodded and very slowly pulled the black-and-white around in a U-turn to the opposite side of the street, stopping just short of the intersection.

We got out very slowly, in perfect synchronization. We looked at each other, nodded and unholstered our guns, then inched our way along the front of a dry-cleaning place until we were at the corner. The Ford pickup was double-parked further down the block in front of the market.

"Now, partner," I whispered, as we flattened ourselves up against the corner building and worked our way toward the market three doors down.

We were within a few yards of it when two gunmen came running out with guns drawn. They saw us almost immediately and wheeled and aimed their .45s haphazardly, just as Wacky and I opened fire. I squeezed off three shots, and the first gunman spun to the pavement, dropping what looked like a bag full of money as he fell. Wacky sent off two wild shots at the other man, who spun and fired at me.

We were at very close range, but some kind of calm grabbed me and I returned his fire, hitting him in the chest and knocking him into the gutter. Wacky fired twice more at the man on the pavement, advancing toward him slowly. He was lying on his stomach, arms outstretched, fingers still curled around his gun.

Wacky was almost on top of him when I saw the gunman in the gutter take aim. I shot him twice, and was moving toward him to get his gun when I heard another shot. I turned and saw Wacky staggering backward, stunned, grasping at his chest. He dropped his gun and screamed, "Freddy!" and then fell over backward.

I screamed. The man on the pavement raised his automatic and got off four shots, wild, sending them into the front of the building above my head, the last one narrowly missing me. I ducked into the market and reloaded. There was screaming coming from behind me—an old man and woman.

I looked outside. Wacky lay on the sidewalk, motionless. The gunman in the gutter looked dead. The one who had shot Wacky was crawling toward the curb and the truck. He had his back to me, so I rushed out and pulled Wacky to safety. Inside the market I ripped open his blood-covered uniform, then put my ear to his chest. Nothing.

"No, no, no, no, no," I muttered. Trembling, I grabbed his wrist and felt for a sign of life. Nothing. I looked at Wacky's face. His eyes were shut. I pulled the lids up. His eyes were frozen, rigid in their final vision of terror and disbelief.

I lifted Wacky up to embrace him. As I started to cradle his head his mouth dropped open, sending a torrent of blood onto my chest. I screamed and ran outside.

The surviving gunman was still crawling toward the street when I came up behind him and spun him around, kicking the .45 out of his hand. I aimed my gun at him, and he screamed. I fired six shots into his chest, and the sound of my gunfire dissolved into the sound of my own screams. I screamed until a dozen black-and-whites poured into the street and four cops threw me into the back of an ambulance with Wacky, and I think I was still screaming at the hospital when they tried to take him away from me.

I got a week off with full pay to recover from the shock, at the insistence of the doctor who examined me at the hospital. I got a commendation and a standing ovation at roll call when I returned to duty.

Wacky got a hero's funeral, and his academy graduation photograph was blown up and framed behind glass and hung in the entrance hall at Wilshire Station. Taken a scant four years before, Wacky looked whimsical and very young. There was a little metal plaque beneath the frame. It said: "Officer Herbert L. Walker. Appointed May, 1947. Shot and killed in the line of duty, February 18, 1951."

The shooting made the L.A. papers in a big way, with pictures of Wacky and myself. They made a big deal out of the Medal of Honor Wacky had won. They called him "a true American hero," and his death "a call for all Americans to seek the path of courage and duty." It was too ambiguous for me; I didn't know what they were talking about.

Wacky's mother and sister flew in from St. Louis for the funeral. I had telephoned them with the news of his death and met them at the airport. They were polite, but very detached. Their remoteness was stupefying. They thought that Wacky "should have gone into the insurance business, like his dad." After determining that they had absolutely no inkling as to who Wacky was, I left them and went home to grieve in private.

I grieved, and fought being guilty over the way I had treated Wacky during his last weeks. I thought of his fatalistic acceptance of all the things of life and of death. I thought of our last tour of duty together and wept, knowing that my absolution was immediate and tendered with love.

High dark clouds were gathering on the day of the funeral. I drove out to the mortuary in Glendale anxious for the whole thing to be over.

The service was held in a roped-off area on a high grassy knoll in the middle of the cemetery. Hundreds of cops in uniform were there, from patrolmen to high brass. Wacky was eulogized by a half-dozen officers who didn't know him. There was no minister or mention of God. Wacky had left specific instructions about that with an old police chaplain several years before.

I was one of the pallbearers. The other five were cops I had never seen before. As we lowered Wacky into the ground, the police rifle team fired a twenty-one-gun salute and a bugler played "Taps." Then I saw Wacky's mother and sister being hustled off in the direction of a long black limousine. I could see a group of newsmen and photographers waiting by the limousine to descend on them.

Beckworth caught me in the parking lot. "Freddy," he called to me.

"Hello, Lieutenant," I said.

"Let's go over to my car and talk, Fred. We need to."

We walked over to where his car was parked, next to a walkway with statues of Jesus kneeling among friendly little animals.

Beckworth put a fatherly hand on my shoulder, and straightened the knot in my tie with his other one. He gave me a fatherly look and sighed. "Freddy, it may sound cruel, but it's over. Walker is dead. You have a commendation and a clean double-bandit killing on your record. Years from now that will look even better. Brass hats who have never drawn their guns will be impressed with that as you move up the ladder."

"No doubt. When do I go to Vice?"

"This summer. As soon as Captain Larson retires."

"Good."

"It all worked out, Freddy. I know you wanted the best for Walker. In a sense, he got it. He was a true hero. A Medal of Honor in the war and a hero's death in the war against crime. I'm sure he died knowing that. And it's funny, Freddy. Although I've spoken harsh words about Walker, I think that, somehow, I knew he was a true hero, and that he had to die."

Beckworth lowered his voice for dramatic effect and tightened his grip on my shoulder. I knew what I had to do. "You're full of shit, Lieutenant. Wacky Walker was a fucked-up crazy drunk, and that's all. And I didn't care, I loved him. So don't romanticize him to me. Don't insult my intelligence. I knew him better than anyone, and I didn't understand him, so don't tell me you did."

"Freddy, I—"

I shrugged my shoulder free of his grasp. "You're full of shit, Lieutenant."

Beckworth went beet red, and started to tremble. "Do you know who I am, Underhill?" he hissed.

"You're a fuck for the city," I said, and flipped his necktie up into his face.

It had started to rain by the time I got to Wacky's apartment. His landlady, intimidated by my uniform, let me in.

The living room was in a shambles. I found out why—Night Train had been left alone there since Wacky's death, and had torn the sofa and chairs apart looking for food. I found him in the back yard. The resourceful Labrador had chewed his way through a screen door and was now lying under a large eucalyptus tree munching on the carcass of a cat.

He came to me when I called him. "Wacky's dead, Train," I said. "He shuffled off this mortal coil, but don't worry, you can live with me if you don't shit in the house." Night Train dropped the dead cat and nuzzled my legs.

I went back into the apartment. I found Wacky's poetry bin: three large metal filing cabinets. Wacky was messy about everything and his apartment was completely disordered, but his poetry was immaculately kept—filed, dated, and numbered.

I carried his life's work out to my car and locked it in the trunk, then went back inside and found his golf clubs in the heavy leather bag he loved so much and brought them out, too.

Night Train hopped into the front seat with me, giving me quizzical looks. I found some raucous jazz on the radio and turned up the volume. Night Train wagged his tail happily as I drove him to his new home.

I found a safe, dry spot in my hall closet for the three filing cabinets. I cooked Night Train some hamburger and sat down to write a short biography of Wacky, one to send out to publishers with samples of his poetry.

I wrote: "Herbert Lawton Walker was born in St. Louis, Missouri, in 1918. In 1942 he enlisted in the United States Marine Corps. He was awarded the Congressional Medal of Honor in 1943, while serving in the Pacific theater. In 1946 he moved to Los Angeles, California, and in 1947 joined the Los Angeles Police Department. He was shot and killed by a holdup man on February 18, 1951. He wrote poetry, unique in its humorous preoccupation with death, from 1939 to the time of his own death."

I sat back and thought: I could cull the files and look for what I thought to be Wacky's best. I could also look for poetry authorities and pay them to go through the filing cabinets and select what they thought were his best works, then send them off to publishers and poetry journals. Maybe Big Sid had some friends in the publishing racket he could fix me up with. If all else failed, I could have Wacky's complete opus printed up and distributed by a vanity press. It had to be done.

But it didn't seem enough. I needed to do penance. Then it hit me. I got my golf bag out of the bedroom and hauled it, along with Wacky's, out to my car.

Still wearing my uniform, I drove all the way out to East L.A. and stopped at the edge of the concrete sewage sluice known affectionately as the Los Angeles River. I looked down into it, some thirty feet below me. The water was five or six feet deep all the way across and flowing south very swiftly. I waited for a break in the rain to give me time to reminisce and try to savor the wonder that Wacky had said was there in death. I waited a long time. When the rain finally abated it was getting dark. I hauled the two golf bags to the edge of the cement embankment and dumped them into the garbage-strewn water, then watched the tangle of iron, wood, and leather move south out of my vision, carrying with it a thousand dreams and illusions. It was the end of my youth.

II

DEATH BY STRANGULATION

6

Wacky Walker never made it to Seventy-seventh Street Division, Watts, L.A.'s heart of darkness, but I did.

Beckworth bided his time and in June, when Captain Larson retired, to muted fanfare, after thirty-three years on the job, I got my orders: Officer Frederick U. Underhill, 1647, to Seventy-seventh Street Division to fill manpower shortage.

Which was a joke: the ranks at Seventy-seventh Street were swelled to bursting. The ancient red brick building that served the hottest per capita crime area in the city was pitifully overstaffed with cops, and undersupplied with every crime-fighting provision from toilet paper to fingerprinting ink. There was a shortage of chairs, tables, floor space, lockers, soap, brooms, mops, and even writing implements. There was no shortage, however, of prisoners. There was an unsurpassed daily and nightly parade of burglars, purse snatchers, dope addicts, drunks, wife beaters, brawlers, pimps, hookers, perverts, and cranks.

The fifteen four-man cells held at least twice their capacity every day, and weekends were the worst. The drunks were kicked out on the street, usually to return several hours later, and the other misdemeanor offenders were released on their own recognizance—which left the tiny, sweltering jail filled with a minimum of a hundred howling felons, with more coming in every hour.

Standing at my first evening roll call I felt like a pygmy at a reunion of the Paul Bunyan family. At six feet two and a hundred ninety pounds, I was a shrimp, a dwarf, a Lilliputian compared to the gland cases I served with. They were all cut from the same mold: World War II combat vets

from the South or Midwest with low academy test scores
and extensive body-building experience who all hated Negroes and who all seemed to possess a hundred esoteric
synonyms for "nigger."

Physically, they were splendidly equipped for fighting
crime, what with their great size and illegal dumdum bul-
lets, but there their efficacy ended. They were sent to the
Seventy-seventh to hold down the lid of a boiling cauldron,
by scaring or beating the shit out of suspects real and
imagined, and that was it. They had no capacity for wonder, only a mania for order. Knowing that, and knowing I
would pass the sergeant's exam with very high marks in
less than a year, I decided to make the most of Watts and to
throw myself into police work as I never had before. Actually, that would be easy. Night foot patrol would put the
kibosh on chasing women and let me observe the wonder
close up.

After roll call the station commander, a harsh-looking
old captain named Jurgensen, called me into his office. I
saluted and he pointed me to a chair. He had my personnel
file open on his desk, and I could tell he was baffled: in a
sense that was good; it meant that he wasn't a buddy of
Beckworth's and that they hadn't conspired together on
my transfer.

Jurgensen gave me a handshake that matched his face
in sternness, then got right to the point: "You have an excellent record, Underhill. College man. Top-flight marks
at the academy. Killed two holdup men who killed your
partner. Excellent fitness reports. What the hell are you
doing here?"

"May I be candid, sir?" I asked.

"By all means, Officer."

"Sir, Captain Beckworth, the new commander of Wilshire Station, hates my guts. It's personal, which is why no
dissatisfaction with my performance is reflected on my fitness reports."

Jurgensen considered this. I could tell he believed me.
"Well, Underhill," he said, "that's too bad. What are your
plans regarding the department?"

"Sir, to go as far as I can as fast as I can."

"Then you have the opportunity to do some real police
work. Right here in this tragic sinkhole."

"Sir, I'm looking forward to it."

"I believe you are, Officer. Every man who comes to this division starts out the same way, walking a beat at night in the heart of the jungle. Sergeant McDonald will fix you up with a partner."

Jurgensen motioned his head toward the door, indicating dismissal. "Good luck, Underhill," he said.

When I met my new partner in the crowded, sweltering muster room, I knew I was going to need luck—and more. His name was Bob Norsworthy. He was from Texas and he chewed tobacco. He fingered his Sam Browne belt and rotated his billy club out from his right hip in a perfect circle as the desk sergeant introduced us. Norsworthy was six and a half feet tall and weighed in at about two-thirty-five. He had black hair cut extra close to his flat head and blue eyes so light that they looked like he sent them out to be bleached.

"Yo there, Underhill," he said to me as Sergeant McDonald walked away from us. "Welcome to the Congo."

"Thanks," I said and stuck out my hand, instantly regretting it as Norsworthy crushed it in his huge fist.

He laughed. "You like that old handshake of mine? I been workin' on it with one o' them hand-squeezer babies. I'm the champeen arm wrestler of this station."

"I believe you. What are we going to do on the beat tonight, Norsworthy?"

"Call me Nors. What should I call you?"

"Fred."

"All right there, Fred. Tonight we're gonna take a long walk up Central Avenue and let our presence be known. They got call boxes every two blocks, and we call the station every hour for instructions. Old Mac at the desk lets us know where there's trouble brewin'. I gotta key for the call boxes. Them boxes is ironclad. If we don't keep 'em all sealed up, them delinquents'd be bustin' into 'em and makin' all kinds of funny noises.

"We break up lots o' unlawful assemblies. An unlawful assembly is two or more niggers hangin' around after dark. We lean on known troublemakers, which is just about every wise-ass on the street. We check out the bars and liquor stores and haul out the bad jigaboos. That's.

where this job gets to be fun. You like to whomp on nig-gers, Fred?"

"I've never tried it," I said. "Is it fun?"

Nors laughed again. "You got a sense of humor. I heard 'bout you. You dispatched two taco-benders to the big fri-jole patch in the sky when you was workin' Wilshire. You a genuine hero. But you gotta be some kind of fuck-up or you wouldn't a got transferred here. You my kind of cop. We gonna be great buddies."

Norsworthy impulsively grabbed for my hand and crushed it again. I pulled it away before he could break any bones. "Whoa, partner," I said, "I need that hand to write reports with."

Norsworthy laughed. "You gonna be needin' that right hand for lots more'n writin' reports in this here division, white boy," he said.

If Norsworthy was less than sensitive, then he was more than instructive. Grudgingly, despite his racism and crudeness, I started to like him. I expected him to be bru-tal, but he wasn't: he was stern and civil with the people we dealt with on the street, and when violence was re-quired in subduing unarmed suspects his method was, by Seventy-seventh Street standards, mild—he would grasp the person in a fierce bear hug, squeeze them until their limbs took on a purple sheen, then drop them to the pave-ment, unconscious. It worked.

When we patrolled Central Avenue south of 100th Street, an area Norsworthy called "Darkest Africa," no-body save the far-gone drunks, hopheads, and the unknow-ing would give us anything but frightened nods. Nors-worthy was so secure in his knowledge of how dangerous he was that he granted the Negroes whom he privately maligned a stern respect, almost by rote. He never had to raise his voice. His gargantuan, tobacco-chewing presence was enough, and I, as his partner, caught the edge of the awed, fearful respect he received.

So our partnership jelled—for a while. We walked the beat and made lots of arrests for drunkenness, possession of narcotics, and assault. We would go into bars and arrest brawlers. Usually, Norsworthy would quell an incipient brawl just by walking in and clearing his throat, but sometimes we would have to go in with billy clubs flying and beat the brawlers to the ground, then handcuff them and call for a patrol car to take them to the station.

The "unlawful assemblies" that Norsworthy had told me about were easy to disperse. We would walk coolly by them, Nors would say, "Good evening, fellows," and the group would seem to vanish into thin air.

Thus the job went. But it started to bore me, and I started to resent my partner. His constant stream of talk—about his service in Italy during the war, his athletic prowess, the size of his dick, "niggers," "kikes," "grease-balls," and "gooks"—vexed and depressed me and undercut the wonder and strangeness of life in Watts. I wanted to be free of the awesome and fearful presence of my partner to be able to pursue the wonder in peace on my own, so I concocted a plan: I convinced Norsworthy that we could be twice as effective patrolling separately, on opposite sides of the street, within sight and earshot of each other. It took a lot of convincing, but finally he bought it, on the proviso that since it was against the rules, we get together once an hour to compare notes and deliberate on potential hot spots that might require the both of us.

So I was freed, somewhat, to let my mind drift and wander with fragments of the dusky neon night music. I grieved less and less for Wacky, and my once-rampant curiosity about Lorna Weinberg abated.

When I became more comfortable with solitary patrol, I would ditch out on Norsworthy completely and hit the numbered side streets off Central—tawdry rows of small, white-framed houses, tar-paper shacks, and overcrowded tenement buildings. I bought three pairs of expensive binoculars and secreted them on the rooftops of buildings on my beat. Late at night, I would scan lighted windows with them, looking for crime and wonder. I found it. The whole gamut, from homosexuality—which I didn't bother with—to wild jazz sessions, to heated lovemaking, to tears. I also found dope addiction—which I did act on, always relaying my information on reefer smoking and worse to the dicks, never trying to grandstand and make the collar myself. I wanted to prove I was a team player, something I never was at Wilshire, and I wanted class-A fitness reports to go with the sergeancy that would be mine shortly after my twenty-eighth birthday.

And I made collars, good ones. I found myself a cracker-jack snitch, a crazy-acting old shoeshine man who hated hopheads and pushers. Willy saw and retained everything, and he had the perfect cover. The neighborhood pimps, lowlifes, and pushers came to him to "glaze their alligators," and they talked freely in front of him—he was considered to be a blubbering idiot, rendered that way by thirty years of sniffing shoe polish.

He went along with the act, working for peanuts at his shine stand and selling information to me for a sizable chunk of my pay. Through Willy I was able to effect the arrest of a whole slew of grasshoppers and heroin pushers, including a guy wanted on a murder warrant back east.

Norsworthy resented my successes, feeling that I had usurped his power, making his fitness reports look bad by comparison. I felt his resentment and his frustration building. I knew what he was going to do, and took immediate steps to circumvent it.

I went to the commander of the detective squad and leveled. I told him of the collars I had given his men, and how I obtained the information that led to them—I had been walking my beat, at night, alone, free of my intrusive patrol partner.

The grizzled, skinny old lieutenant liked this. He thought I was a tough guy. I told him old big-dick Bob Norsworthy was about to blow all this to hell, that he was pissed off and wanted to horn in on my action, and was about to rat on me to Captain Jurgensen for ditching out on the beat.

The old lieutenant shook his head. "We can't let that happen, can we, son?" he said. "As of now, Underhill, you are the only solitary foot patrolman in this station. God have mercy on your soul if you ever run into trouble, or if Norsworthy ever quits the department."

"Thanks, Lieutenant," I said, "you won't regret it."

"That remains to be seen. One word of advice, son. Watch out for ambition. Sometimes it hurts more than it helps. Now close the door behind you, I want to turn on my fan."

7

I was at home the following Wednesday frying Night Train his morning hamburger when he brought me the news that was to change my life forever.

My landlady, Mrs. Gates, had been complaining about Train chewing up her plants, shrubs, garden chairs, newspapers, and magazines. She was a dog lover, but frequently told me that Night Train was more "voodoo beast" than dog, and that I should have him "fixed" to curb his rambunctiousness. So when I heard a shrill, "Mr. Underhill!" coming from the front lawn, I put on my widest smile and walked outside ready to do some placating.

Mrs. Gates was standing above Night Train, swatting him with a broom. He seemed to be enjoying it, rolling in the grass on his back with the morning paper wedged firmly between his salivating jaws.

"You give me my paper, voodoo dog!" the woman was shouting. "You can chew it up when I'm finished reading it. Give it to me!"

I laughed. I had come to love Night Train in the months since Wacky's death, and he never failed to amuse me.

"Mr. Underhill, you make that evil dog stop chewing my newspaper! Make him give it to me!"

I bent down and scratched Night Train's belly until he dropped the paper and started to nuzzle me. I flipped it open to show Mrs. Gates that no damage had been done, then caught the headlines and went numb.

"Woman Found Strangled in Hollywood Apartment" it read. Below the headline was a photograph of Maggie Cadwallader—the same Maggie with whom I had coupled in February, shortly before Wacky's death.

I pushed Train and the caterwauling Mrs. Gates away, then sat down and read:

A young woman was found strangled to death in her Hollywood apartment late Monday night by curious neighbors who heard sounds and went to investigate. The woman, Margaret Cadwallader, 36, of 2311 Harold Way, Hollywood, was employed as a bookkeeper at the Small World Import-Export Company on Virgil Street in Los Angeles. Police were summoned to the scene, and the woman's body was removed pending an autopsy. However, assistant L.A. County medical examiner David Beyless was quoted as saying, "It was a strangulation, pure and simple." Detectives from the Hollywood Division of the Los Angeles Police Department have sealed the premises, and are looking at burglary as the motive.

"I think the woman was killed when she awakened to her apartment being ransacked. The state of the apartment confirms this. That will be the starting point of our investigation. We expect a break at any time," said Sgt. Arthur Holland, the officer in charge.

The victim, originally from Waukesha, Wisconsin, had been a resident of the Los Angeles area for two years. She is survived by her mother, Mrs. Marshall Cadwallader, of Waukesha. Friends from her place of employment are tending to the funeral arrangements.

I put the newspaper down and stared at the grass.

"Mr. Underhill? Mr. Underhill?" Mrs. Gates was saying. I ignored her and walked back to my apartment and sat on the couch, staring at the floor.

Maggie Cadwallader, a lonely woman, dead. My one-night conquest, dead. Her death was not unlike that of the woman whose body Wacky and I had discovered. Probably the deaths were unrelated, yet there was the slightest bit of physical evidence linking them: I had met Maggie at the Silver Star. Her first time, she told me. But she may well have returned, frequently. I wracked my brain for the name of the woman whose body Wacky and I had found, and came up with it: Leona Jensen. She had had matches from the Silver Star in an ashtray filled with matchbooks. It was slight, but enough.

I changed clothes, putting on my light blue gabardine summer suit, made coffee and mourned for Maggie—thinking more of her little boy in the orphanage back east who would never see his mother. Maggie, so lonely, so much in need of what I and probably no man could have given her. It was a sad night I had spent with her. My curiosity and her loneliness had been left unresolved, anger on her part and self-disgust the only resolution on mine. And now this, leaving me feeling somehow responsible.

I knew what I had to do. I had three quick cups of coffee and locked Night Train in the apartment with a half-dozen big soup bones, then got my car and drove to my old home, Wilshire Station.

I parked in the Sears lot a block away and telephoned the desk, asking for Detective Sergeant DiCenzo. He came on the line a minute later, sounding harried. "DiCenzo here, who's this?"

"Sergeant, this is Officer Underhill. Do you remember me?"

"Sure, kid, I remember you. You got famous right after I met you. What's up?"

"I'd like to talk to you briefly, as soon as possible."

"I'm gonna get lunch in about five minutes, across the street at the Shamrock. I'll be there for the better part of an hour."

"I'll be there," I said, then hung up.

The Shamrock was a bar-lunch joint specializing in corned beef sandwiches. I found DiCenzo at the back, wolfing a "special" and chasing it down with a beer. He greeted me warmly. "Sit down. You look good, college man. Too bad about your partner. Where you been? I ain't seen you around."

I filled him in as quickly as I could. He seemed satisfied, but surprised that I liked working in Watts.

"So what do you want, kid?" he asked finally.

I tried to sound interested, yet offhand. "You remember that dead woman my partner and I found on Twenty-eighth Street?"

"Yeah, a beautiful young dame. A real pity."

"Right. I was wondering what the upshot of your investigation was. Did you ever find the killer?"

DiCenzo looked at me curiously. "No, we never did. We rousted a lot of burglars, but no go. We checked out the dame's personal life, which was nothing hot—no enemies, all her friends and relatives had alibis. That print you circled on the wall belonged to the dame herself. We got a couple of dozen crazies who confessed, but they were just nuts. It's just one of those things, kid. You win some, you lose some. How come you're interested?"

"The woman looked like an old girlfriend of mine. Finding her dead got me, I guess." I lowered my head, feigning disbelief at the awesomeness of death.

DiCenzo bought it. "You'll get over these things," he said. Lowering his voice, he added, "You'll have to, if you wanna stay on the job."

I got up to go. "Thanks, Sergeant," I said.

"Anytime, kid. Be good. Take care of yourself." DiCenzo smiled heartily and went back to devouring his lunch.

I drove up to Hollywood Station on Wilcox just south of Sunset and lucked out, walking brazenly through the entrance hall, nodding at the desk sergeant and walking straight upstairs to the detective squad room, where a briefing on Maggie Cadwallader's murder had just begun.

The small room was packed with at least twenty dicks standing and sitting at desks, listening as a portly older cop explained what he wanted done. I stood in the doorway, trying to blend in like just another off-duty officer. No one seemed to notice me.

"I think we got burglary," the older cop was saying. "The woman's apartment was ransacked but good. No prints—the only prints we got belong to the victim and her landlady she used to play cards with. The man from downstairs who found the body left some, too. They've been questioned and are not suspects. We got no recent murders on the books that match this. Now here's what I want: I want every burglar known to use violence brought in and questioned. There was no rape, but I want all burglars with sex offenses on their rap sheets brought in anyway. I want all burglary reports in the Hollywood area for the past six months that resulted in arrest and dismissal

checked out. Phone the D.A.'s office for disposition of all
cases. I want to know how many of these shitheads we
caught are back out on the street, then I want all of them
brought in and questioned.

"I've got two men talking to neighbors. I want to know
about what valuables this Cadwallader dame owned.
From there we can lean on fences and check out the pawn-
shops. I want all the dope addicts on the boulevard brought
in and leaned on hard. This is probably a panic killing, and
a hophead looking for a fix might strangle a dame and
then leave without taking anything. I've got two men
questioning people in the neighborhood about that night.
If anyone saw or heard anything, we'll know about it.
That's it for now. Let's break it up."

That was my cue to leave. I checked my watch. It was
two-forty. I had three hours before I had to report to duty.

I walked out to my car amidst a tangle of grumbling detectives. I lowered the top and sat in the front seat and
thought. No, not burglary, I kept saying to myself; not this
time. Maybe the Jensen woman, maybe the matches were
coincidental, but Maggie Cadwallader had a strangeness
about her, almost an aura of impending doom, and when
she saw my gun she had screamed, "Please, no! I won't let
you hurt me! I know who sent you! I knew he would." She
had been a strange woman, one who had wrapped her
small world tightly about herself, yet let frequent strangers in.

The Silver Star bar was the place to start, but it was
useless to hit it in the daytime, so I drove to a phone booth
and got the address of the Small World Import-Export
Company: 615 North Virgil. I drove there, exhila-
rated—and feeling slightly guilty about it.

The Small World Import-Export Company was in a large
warehouse in the middle of a residential block specializing
in rooming houses for students at L.A. City College a few
blocks away. Every house on the block advertised "Student Housing," and "Low Rates for Students." There were
a lot of "students" sitting on their front porches, drinking
beer and playing catch on their beat-up front lawns. They
were about my age, and had the superior look of G.I. Bill
recipients. Two wars, Underhill, I thought, and you

avoided them both and got what you wanted. Now here you are, a patrolman in Watts imitating a detective in Hollywood. Be careful.

I was. I entered the warehouse through its ratty front door stenciled with a ratty-looking globe by a guy who obviously didn't know his geography very well. But the receptionist knew a cop and a badge when she saw them, and when I inquired about friends of Maggie Cadwallader she said, "Oh, that's easy." She dialed a number on her desk phone, saying, "Mrs. Grover, our head bookkeeper, was a good friend of Maggie's. They had lunch together almost every day." Into the phone she said, "Mrs. Grover, there's a policeman here to talk to you about Maggie." The receptionist put down the phone and said, "She'll be out in a minute." She smiled. I smiled back.

We were exchanging about our eighth and ninth smiles when an efficient-looking woman of about forty came into the waiting room. "Officer?" she asked.

"Mrs. Grover," I answered, "I'm Officer Underhill, Los Angeles Police Department. Could I talk with you?"

"Certainly," she said, very businesslike. "Would you like to come to my office?"

I was enjoying my role but her brusque manner was unnerving. "Yeah, sure," I replied.

We walked down a dingy hallway. I could hear great numbers of sewing machines whirring behind closed doors. Mrs. Grover sat me down in a wooden chair in her sparsely furnished office. She lit a cigarette, settled behind her desk, and said, "Poor Maggie. What a godawful way to die. Who do you think did it?"

"I don't know. That's why I'm here."

"I read in the papers that you people think it was a burglar. Is that true?"

"Maybe. I understand you and Maggie Cadwallader were good friends."

"In a sense," Mrs. Grover replied. "We ate together every workday, but we never saw each other socially."

"Was there a reason for that?"

"What do you mean?"

"What I mean, Mrs. Grover, is that I'm trying to get a handle on this woman. What kind of person was she? Her habits, her likes, dislikes, the people she associated with, that kind of thing?"

Mrs. Grover stared at me, smoking intently. "I see," she said. "Well, if it's helpful I can tell you this: Maggie was a very bright, disturbed woman. I think she was a pathological liar. She told me stories about herself and later told stories that contradicted the earlier ones. I think she had a drinking problem, and spent her nights alone, reading."

"What kind of stories did she tell you?"

"About her origins. One day she was from New York, the next day the Midwest. She once told me she had a child out of wedlock, from a 'lost love,' then the very next day she tells me she's a virgin! I sensed that she was very lonely, so once I tried to arrange a dinner date for her with a nice bachelor friend of my husband's. She wouldn't do it. She was terrified. She was a cultured person, Maggie, and we had many lovely conversations about the theater, but she told me such crazy things."

"Such as?"

"Such as the nonsense about the baby back east. She showed me a photo once. It broke my heart. She had obviously clipped it from a magazine. It was so sad."

"Do you know of any men in her life, Mrs. Grover?"

"No, Officer, none. I really do believe she died a virgin."

"Well," I said, standing up, "thank you for your time, Mrs. Grover. You've been very helpful."

"She deserved so much better, Officer. Please find her killer."

"I will," I said, meaning it.

I wasn't much good on the beat that night. My mind was elsewhere. I knew I would need a very fast transfer to day watch in order to continue my investigation at night. I thought over my options—requests to Jurgensen? To the head of the Detective squad? Going on sick leave? All too chancy.

The following morning I drove to the station and knocked on Captain Jurgensen's door. He greeted me warmly, surprised to see me in the daytime. I told him what I wanted: I had a very sick friend from my orphanage days who needed someone to look after him at night while his wife went to work at Douglas Aircraft. I wanted day watch temporarily, to help out my friend, and to better acquaint myself with the area I was serving in.

Jurgensen put down his copy of *Richard III* and said, "Starting today, Underhill. We've got a man on vacation. No solo, though. No golden boy stuff. Just walk the beat with a partner. Now go to work."

At eleven-thirty that night I committed my first crime as an adult. I drove up to Hollywood, parked in a gas station lot and walked up to Maggie Cadwallader's apartment on Harold Way. Wearing gloves, I picked the lock on the door and made my way through the dark apartment to the bedroom. I carried a pocket flashlight, and by risking using it every few seconds I could tell that all of Maggie's personal belongings had been cleaned out, presumably to better show the apartment to prospective new tenants when the publicity of her death died down.

In the bedroom, holding the flashlight awkwardly, I unscrewed the bedpost that had contained Maggie's "priceless love gift." It was gone. I replaced the post and unscrewed the other one: nothing there. The two remaining ones were solid, melded into the bedstead. It was as I had hoped. Still, there was double-checking to be done.

I drove to Hollywood Station, parked, walked in and showed my badge to the desk sergeant. "I'm with Seventy-seventh dicks," I told him. "Is there anyone upstairs I can talk to?"

"Give it a try," he replied, bored.

The squad room was deserted, except for a tired old cop writing reports. I walked in like I owned the place, and the old-timer looked up only briefly from his paper work. When I didn't see what I wanted lying around in plain sight, I cleared my throat to get his attention.

He looked up again, this time displaying bloodshot eyes and a weary voice. "Yes?" he said.

I tried to sound brisk and older than my years. "Underhill, Seventy-seventh Street dicks. I'm working South Central pawnshop detail. The loot told me to come up here and check the property report on that dead dame, Cadwallader. We find a lot of stuff pawned down in the

Seventy-seventh that got clouted in Hollywood and West
L.A. The lieutenant figured maybe he could help you out."

"Shit," the old-timer said, getting up from his chair and
walking to a row of filing cabinets. "That was no burglary
caper, if you ask me. My partner and I wrote that report."
He handed me a manila folder containing three typewrit-
ten pages. "There was nothin' missin', accordin' to the
landlady, and she knew the stiff good. Could be the guy
panicked. Don't ask me."

The report was written in the usual clipped department
style, and everything from cat food to detergent was listed—but no mention was made of a diamond brooch, or any
other jewelry.

There was a signed statement from the landlady, a Mrs.
Crawshaw, stating that although the apartment had been
in complete disarray, nothing seemed to be missing. She
also stated that Maggie Cadwallader, to her knowledge,
had not owned jewelry or stocks and bonds, nor had she secreted in her apartment large sums of money.

The old cop was looking at me. "You want a copy of
that?" he asked wearily.

"No," I said, "you were right, it's a dull report. Thanks a
lot, I'll see you."

He looked relieved. I felt relieved.

It was twelve-forty-five and I knew I couldn't sleep now
even if I wanted to. I wanted to think, but I wanted it to be
easy, not filled with panicky speculation over the dangerous risks I was taking. So I decided to break my silent vow
of abstinence and drove out to Silverlake, where I knocked
on the door of an old buddy from the orphanage.

He was mildly glad to see me, but his wife wasn't. I told
them it wasn't a social call, that all I wanted was the loan
of his golf clubs. Incredulous, he turned them over. I promised to return them soon, and to repay him for his favor
with a good restaurant dinner. Incredulous, his wife said
she'd believe it when she saw it, and hustled her husband
back to bed.

I checked the clubs. They were good Tommy Armours,
and there were at least fifty shag balls stuffed into the
pockets of the bag. I went looking for a place to hit them,
and to think.

I drove home and picked up Night Train. He was glad to

see me and hungry for exercise. I found a few cold pork chops in the ice box and threw them at him. He was gnawing the bones as I attached his leash and slung the golf bag over my shoulder.

"The beach, Train," I said. "Let's see what kind of Labrador you really are. I'm going to hit balls into the ocean. Little chip shots. If you can retrieve them for me in the dark, I'll feed you steak for a year. What do you say?"

Night Train said "Woof!" and so we walked the three blocks down to the edge of the Pacific.

It was a warm night and there was no breeze. I unhooked Night Train's leash and he took off running, a pork chop bone still in his mouth. I dumped the balls onto the wet sand and extracted a pitching iron from the bag. Hefting it was like embracing a long-lost beloved friend. I was surprised to find I wasn't rusty. My hiatus from golf hadn't dulled that sharp edge my game has always had, almost from the first time I picked up a club.

I hit easy pitch shots into the churning white waves, enjoying the synchronization of mind and body that is the essence of golf. After a while the mental part became unnecessary, my swing became me, and I turned my mind elsewhere.

Granted: I had passed myself off as a detective twice, using my own name, which might cost me a suspension if it were discovered. Granted: I was going strictly on hunches, and my observations of Maggie Cadwallader were based on her behavior during one evening. But. But. But, somehow I *knew*. It was more than intuition or deductive logic or character assessment. This was my own small piece of wonder to unravel, and the fact that the victim had given me her body, tenuously, in her search for something more, gave it weight and meaning.

I whistled for Night Train, who trotted up. We walked back to the apartment and I thought, Wacky was right. The key to the wonder is in death. I had killed, twice, and it had changed me. But the key wasn't in the killing, it was in the discovery of whatever led to it.

I felt strangely magnanimous and loving, like a writer about to dedicate a book. This one's for you, Wacky, I said to myself; this one's for you.

8

It was strange to be sitting in a bar looking for a killer rather than a woman.

The following night, free of the obsession that usually brought me to such places, I sat drinking watered-down Scotch and watched people get drunk, get angry, get maudlin and pour out their life stories to perfect strangers in alcoholic effusiveness. I was looking for men on the prowl, like myself, but the Silver Star on that first night held nothing but middle-aged desperation played to the tunes of the old prewar standards on the jukebox.

I closed the place, walking out at 1:00 A.M., asking the bartender if the place ever picked up.

"Weekends," he said. "This joint really hops on weekends. Tomorrow night. You'll see."

The barman was right. I got to the Silver Star at seven-forty-five Saturday evening and watched as the joint started to hop. Young couples, servicemen on leave—easily recognizable by their short haircuts and plain-toed black shoes—elderly juiceheads, and single men and women casting lonely, expectant glances all competed for bar and floor space.

The music was livelier this evening, and tailored for a younger clientele; upbeat arrangements of show tunes, even a little jazz. A good-looking woman of about thirty asked me to dance. Regretfully I turned her down, offering a bad leg as an excuse. She turned to the guy sitting next to me at the bar, who accepted.

I was looking for "operators," "lover-boy" types, "wolves"—men who could gain a woman's confidence as well as access to her bed with surpassing ease. Men like myself. I spent three hours, sitting, changing seats from bar-side to table-side, sipping ginger ale, always looking. I began to realize that this might be a long, grueling surveillance. For all my eyeball activity, I didn't see much.

I was starting to get depressed and even a little angry when I noticed two definite lowlife types approach the bar and lean over to speak in undertones to the bartender, whose face seemed to light up. He pointed to a door at the rear of the place, next to a bank of phone booths and cigarette machines. Then all three walked off in that direction, the barman leaving the bar untended.

I watched as they closed the door behind them, then waited two minutes. I went over to the door and knelt down, sniffing at the crack where it met the floor. Reefer smoke. I smiled, then transferred my gun from its holster to the pocket of my sports coat, flipped open my badge's leather holder and very casually but forcefully threw my right shoulder into the doorjamb, splintering the wood and throwing the door wide open.

The noise was very sharp and abrupt, like an explosion. The three grasshoppers were standing against the back wall next to a ceiling-high collection of whiskey crates, and they jumped back and threw up their hands reflexively when they heard the noise and saw my badge and gun.

I looked back into the bar. No one seemed to have noticed what had happened. I closed the door behind me, softly. "Police officer," I said very quietly. "Move over to the left-hand wall and place your hands on it, above your heads. Do it now."

They did. The smell of the marijuana was rank and sensual. I patted the three men down for weapons and dope, but came up with nothing except three fat reefers. All the guys were shaking and the bartender started to blubber about his wife and kids.

"Shut up!" I snapped at him. I pulled the other two guys back by their shirt collars, then shoved them in the direction of the door. "Get the hell out of here, you goddamn lowlife," I hissed, "and don't ever let me see you in here again."

They stumbled out the door, casting worried glances at the barman.

I secured the door by placing a crate of gin bottles against it. The bartender cowered against the wall as I walked toward him. He fumbled in his pockets for cigarettes, looking at me imploringly for permission.

"Go ahead, smoke," I said. He lit up. "What's your name?" I asked.

"Red Julian," he said, eyeing the door.

I eased his fears. "This won't take long, Red. I'm not going to bust you, I just need a little help."

"I don't know no sellers, honest, Officer. I just light up once in a while. Fifty cents a throw, you know."

I smiled sardonically. "I don't care, Red. I'm not with narcotics. How long have you worked here?"

"Three years."

"Then you know what goes in this place—all the regulars, the con artists . . ."

"This is a good clean room, Officer, I don't let no—"

"Shut up. Listen to me. I'm interested in pickup artists—pussy-hounds, guys who score regular here. You help me out and I'll let you slide. You don't and I'll bust you. I'll call for a patrol car and tell the bulls you tried to sell me these three reefers. That's two to ten at Quentin. What's it gonna be?"

Red lit another cigarette with the butt of his old one. His hands were shaking. "We get hotshots, they come and go," he said. "We got one guy who comes and goes, but comes regular when he's in town. A good-lookin' guy named Eddie. That's the only handle I got on him, honest. He picks up here all the time." Red backed away from me again.

"Is he here tonight?" I asked.

"Naw, he comes in when it's quieter. A real smoothie. Flashy dresser. He's not here tonight, honest."

"Okay. Listen to me. You've got a new regular here. Me. What nights are you off?"

"Never. The boss won't let me. I work six to midnight, seven days a week."

"Good. Has Eddie been coming in lately? Scoring?"

"Yeah. A real smoothie."

"Good. I'll be coming back, every night. As soon as Eddie comes in, you let me know. If you try to tip him off, you know what'll happen." I smiled and held the three reefers under his nose.

"Yeah, I know."

"Good. Now get out of here—I think your customers are getting thirsty."

I closed the bar again that night. No Eddie.

First thing Sunday morning I went to a drugstore in Santa Monica that did one-day photo processing. I left four newspaper photographs of Maggie Cadwallader, telling the man, who shook his head dubiously, that I wanted his best reproduction blown up to snapshot size, six copies by six o'clock that evening. When I waved a twenty-dollar bill under his nose, then stuck it in his shirt pocket, he wasn't so dubious. The photos I picked up that afternoon were more than adequate to show to potential witnesses.

Red was nervously polishing a glass when I took a seat at the bar early Sunday night. It was sweltering hot outside, but the Silver Star was air-conditioned to a polar temperature.

"Hello, Red," I said.

"Hello, mister . . ."

"Call me Fred," I said magnanimously, sliding the blowup of Maggie Cadwallader across the bar to him. "Have you ever seen this woman?"

Red nodded. "A few times, yeah, but not lately."

"Ever see her with Eddie?"

"No."

"Too bad. Slow house tonight, eh?" I said, looking around the almost empty bar.

"Yeah. Daylight saving time kills it this early. People don't think it's right to drink before dark. Except boozehounds." He pointed toward a bloated couple mauling each other on one of the lounge sofas.

"I know what you mean. I had a friend once who liked to drink. He said he only liked to drink when he was alone or with people, in the daytime or the nighttime. He was a philosopher."

"What happened to him?"

"He got shot."

"Oh, yeah? That's a shame."

"Yeah. I'm going to have a seat on one of those sofas facing the door. If our buddy shows up, you come and let me know, capische?"

"Yeah."

By eight o'clock the bar was filled to half its capacity, and by ten the sustained darkness had me feeling like a bat in the Carlsbad Caverns.

At around eleven o'clock, Red walked over and nudged me. "That's him," he said, "at the bar. The guy in the Hawaiian shirt."

I motioned Red away and sauntered past the man on my way to the men's room, taking the stool next to him when I returned and catching a heady whiff of his lilac cologne. I called to Red loudly and ordered a double Scotch, in order to get a reaction from Eddie. He turned toward me, and I committed to memory a handsome face, delicate and arrogant at the same time, well-tanned, with curly, rather long brown hair, and soft, deep-set brown eyes. Eddie turned back quickly, engrossing himself in his martini and the woman sitting next to him, a skinny brunette in a nurse's uniform who was courteously feigning interest in his conversation.

". . . So it's been good lately. The trotters, especially. Don't believe what you read. There are systems that work."

"Oh, really?" the brunette said, bored.

"Really." Eddie leaned into the woman. "What did you say your name was?"

"Corrinne."

"Hi, Corrinne, I'm Eddie."

"Hi, Eddie."

"Hi. You like the ponies, Corrinne?"

"Not really."

"Oh. Well, you know it's really just a question of getting to know the game. You know?"

"I guess so. I don't know, it just bores me. I've got to go. Nice meeting you. Bye."

The brunette got up from her stool and left. Eddie sighed, then finished his drink and walked back in the direction of the men's room, stopping and standing in front of the full-length mirror on the wall and going through an elaborate ritual of smoothing his hair, brushing lint off his shirt, checking the crease in his trousers and smiling at himself several times from different angles. He seemed satisfied, as he should have been: he was the very proto-type of the smooth-talking L.A. lounge lizard, designed to charm, manipulate, and seduce. For a split second, I felt re-vulsion at my own womanizing, before telling myself that my motives were certainly entirely different.

I moved to another seat at the back of the room that afforded me a view of the whole bar. I watched as Eddie un-successfully tried to put the make on three young women. I could feel his disgust and desperation as he paid his bill, killed his last martini and stormed out. Quickly I exited, and followed him down a side street. He got into a '46 Olds sedan. My car was parked on the other side of the street, pointed in the opposite direction, so as Eddie drove off I sprinted for it. I gave him a thirty-second lead, then hung a U-turn and tailed him. Eddie turned left on Wilton then right on Santa Monica a mile later. He was easy to follow: his right taillight was out and he drove smoothly in the middle lane.

He led me to West Hollywood. I almost lost him crossing La Brea, but when he finally pulled to the curb at Santa Monica and Sweetzer, I was right behind.

After carefully locking his car, Eddie walked into a bar called the Hub. I gave him a minute's lead, then walked in myself, expecting it to be a lively off-the-Strip pickup joint. I was dead wrong: it was a pickup joint, but there were no women in the bar, just anxious-looking men.

I braced myself and walked to the bar. The bartender, a fat bald man, appeared and I ordered beer. He sashayed away from me to get it and I looked for Eddie.

I spotted him first, then heard him. He was in a booth in the back, arguing with another man—a handsome, decid-edly masculine man in his mid fifties. I couldn't hear their conversation, but was momentarily troubled any-way—what was he doing here? I had thought he was a woman-chaser. The argument grew more heated, but I still couldn't hear any words.

Finally, the other man shoved what looked like a large manila envelope at Eddie, got up, and walked out the back door of the bar. Out of the corner of my eye, I watched Ed-die sitting very still in his booth, then he suddenly bolted for the front door. I hunched over my beer as he passed by, then chased after him.

As I was flinging open the door of my car, Eddie hung a tire-screeching turn north onto Sweetzer, heading up the steep hill to the Strip. I peeled rubber in pursuit and finally caught up with him as he was signaling a left-hand turn onto Sunset. I stayed right behind him for about a half mile until he turned right on a little street called Horn Drive and parked almost immediately. I continued on and parked some fifty yards in front of him, getting out of my car just in time to see him cross the street and enter the court of a group of Spanish-style bungalows.

I ran across the street, hoping to catch Eddie as he entered one of the units, but was out of luck. The cement courtyard was empty. I checked the bank of mailboxes on the front lawn, looking for Edward, Edwin, Edmund, or at least the initial "E." No luck—the tenants of the fifteen bungalows were all designated by their last names only.

I went back to my car and pulled over to the other side of the street, directly in front of the entrance of the court, deciding to wait Eddie out. My curiosity about him was peaking; he was a volatile night owl and might well be leaving soon on another run.

I was wrong. I waited, and waited, and waited, almost dozing off several times, until nine-thirty the next morning. When Eddie finally emerged, immaculately dressed in a fresh Hawaiian shirt, light blue cotton slacks, and sandals, I felt my enervation drop like a rock. I studied his face and body movements as he walked to his car, searching for clues to his sexual makeup. There was a self-conscious disdainfulness about him that wasn't quite right, but I put it out of my mind.

Eddie drove fast and aggressively, deftly weaving through traffic. I stayed close behind, letting a few cars get between us. We drove this way all the way downtown to the Pasadena Freeway, out that tortuous expressway to South Pasadena, then east to Santa Anita racetrack in Arcadia.

Entering the racetrack's enormous parking lot, I felt relieved and hopeful. It was a brilliantly clear day, not too hot, and the parking lot was already filled with cars and plenty of people to hide me as I tailed my suspect. And I remembered what an old Vice cop had once told me: race-tracks were good places to brace people for information—they felt sinful and somehow guilty about being there, and cowered fast when confronted with a badge.

I parked and sprinted to the entrance turnstiles. I paid my admission, then lounged, eyes downcast, next to a souvenir stand and waited for Eddie to show up. He did, a good ten minutes later, flashing a pass at the ticket-taker and getting a big smile in return. As he passed me, consulting his racing form, I turned my back.

The giant entranceway and passages leading up to the grandstand were filling up fast, so I let a solid throng of horseplayers get between us as we maneuvered toward the escalators that led to the betting windows. Eddie was going first-class: the fifty-dollar window. He was the only one in line there. He got a warm welcome from the man in the cage, and I could hear him plainly as I stood by the ten-dollar window a few yards away.

"Howsa boy, Eddie?" the guy said.

"Not bad, Ralph. How's the action? You got any hot ones for me?" Eddie's voice seemed strained under the ritualistic overtones.

"Naw, you know me, Eddie. I like 'em all. That's why I'm working here and not bettin' here. I love 'em all, too much."

Eddie laughed. "I hear you. I got the system though, and I feel lucky today." He handed the man a sheet of paper and a roll of bills. "Here, Ralph, that's for the first four races. Let's take care of it all now. I want to check out the scenery."

The man in the cage scooped up the scratch sheet and money and whistled. He detached a row of tickets and handed them to Eddie. He shook his head. "You might be takin' a bath today, kid."

"Never, pal. Seen any lookers around? You know my type."

"Hang out at the Turf Club, kid. That's where the class dames go."

"Too ritzy for me. I can't breathe in there. I'll be back for my money at the end of the day, Ralph. Have it ready for me."

Ralph laughed. "You bet, kid."

* * *

I followed Eddie to his seat in one of the better sections of the grandstand. He bought a beer and peanuts from a vendor and settled in, reading his racing form and fiddling with a pair of binoculars in a leather case.

I was wondering what to do next when an idea struck me. I waited for the first race to start, and when the passageways cleared and the crowd started to yell, I made my way back down to the souvenir stand, where I bought the current issues of three magazines: *Life, Collier's,* and *Ladies' Home Journal.*

I took them into the men's room, locked myself into a stall and thumbed through them, finding what I wanted almost immediately—five black-and-white photographs of rather ordinary women, taken from the neck up. I tore them out, left the rest of the magazines on the floor and placed the blowup photo of Maggie Cadwallader in the middle of the tear-outs.

Then I went looking for Ralph, the man at the fifty-dollar window. He wasn't in his cage, so I strolled aimlessly through the now-deserted passageways until I spotted him walking out of the radio broadcasters' booth, smoking a cigar and holding a cup of coffee.

He spotted me too, and some sort of recognition hit him even before I showed him my badge. "Yes, Officer," he said patiently.

"Just a few questions," I said. I pointed across the hall to a snack stand that had tables and chairs.

Ralph nodded patiently and led the way. We sat facing each other across a grease-stained metal table; I was brusque, even a little bullying.

"I'm interested in the man you were talking to at the window about a half hour ago. His first name is Eddie."

"Yeah. Eddie."

"What's his last name?"

"Engels. Eddie Engels."

"What's his occupation?"

"Gambler. Punk. Wise guy. I don't think he has a job."

"I'm interested in the women he runs around with."

"So am I! Ooh, la la!" Ralph started cracking up at his own wit.

"Don't be funny; it's not amusing." I fanned the six pho-

tographs on the table in front of him. "Ever see Eddie with
any of these women?"

Ralph scrutinized the photos, hesitated a moment, then
placed a fat index finger square on the picture of Maggie
Cadwallader. My whole body lurched inside and my skin
started to tingle.

"Are you sure?" I asked.

"Yeah," he said.

"How are you sure?"

"This tomato is a dog compared to some of the babes I
seen Eddie with."

"When did you see them together?"

"I don't know—I think it was a couple of months ago.
Yeah, that's right, it was the day of the President's
Stakes—in June."

I gathered up my photos and left Ralph with a stern
warning. "You don't breathe a word of this to Eddie. You
got that?"

"Sure, Officer. I always figured Eddie wasn't quite on
the up and—"

I didn't let him finish. I was out the door, looking frantically for a pay phone.

I called L.A.P.D. R & I, gave them my name and badge
number and told them what I wanted. They got back to me
within five minutes: there was no Edward, Edwin, or Edmund Engels, white male, approximately thirty years old
with a criminal record in Los Angeles. I was about to hang
up, then got another idea: I told the clerk to go through the
automobile registration files for the last four years. This
time he hit pay dirt: Edward Engels, 1911 Horn Drive,
West Hollywood, owned two cars: the green '46 Olds sedan
I had tailed him in, and a '49 Ford convertible—red with
white top, license number JY 861. I thanked the clerk,
hung up and ran out to my own car.

My next stop was Pasadena, where I looked for Ford and
Oldsmobile dealerships. It took a while, but I found them
and got what I wanted: advertising stills of their '46 and
'49 models. Next I drove to a five and dime on Colorado
Boulevard and bought a box of kiddie crayons. In the parking lot I went to work on my visual aids, coloring the Olds
sedan a pale sea green and the Ford a bright fire engine

red with a pristine white top. The results were good.

By this time it was one-forty-five and getting very humid. I needed a shave and a change of clothes. I drove home, showered, shaved, and changed. I got out my diary and destroyed all the pages pertaining to my encounter with Maggie Cadwallader. Then I stretched out on the bed and tried to sleep.

It was no good. My brain wouldn't stop running with plans, schemes, contingencies, and expectations. Finally I gave up, shooed Night Train out to the back yard, locked up, and drove to the Sunset Strip.

I timed it just right, parking my car in the lot of a gas station on Sunset and Doheny and starting off on foot. The nightclubs were just opening, gearing up for another evening of high-life, and the barmen, waiters, and parking attendants I wanted to talk to were fresh faced and had plenty of time to answer my questions.

I was developing a theory about Eddie Engels; that he was arrogant, cocky to an extreme, loudmouthed, and rather stupid—just stupid enough to bring women he was planning to harm or even kill into his own back yard to wine and dine. It seemed logical. He lived within walking distance of the hottest night spots in the city, and he clearly loved to be seen with women.

So I theorized, and walked east, showing my photograph of Maggie Cadwallader to parking lot attendants, doormen, maitre d's, and waiters. I hit every nightclub and juke joint on both sides of Sunset from Doheny to La Cienega—with no luck. I was about to admit defeat when I decided to start checking out restaurants, as well.

At my third one, I got my first confirmation. It was an Italian place and the garrulous old waiter nodded in recognition as I showed him the photo. He remembered Maggie from several weeks before, and was about to embark on a long discourse about the food she ate when I hissed at him, *"Did she have an escort?"*

Startled, the old guy smiled, said "sure," and described Eddie Engels. He went on to tell me of all the "nicea-looking bambinas" the "nicea-looking young man" brought to eat there. It was enough confirmation, but I wanted proof. I wanted it covered thoroughly from every angle, so that

when I presented my case to my superiors it wouldn't leak
an ounce of water.

I hit four more restaurants, all within five blocks of Eddie Engels's apartment on Horn Drive, and got three more
positive identifications from waiters who recalled Eddie as
an extravagant tipper who talked loudly of his racetrack
winnings. They remembered Maggie Cadwallader as
being quiet, clinging to Eddie and drinking a lot of rum
and Cokes.

I took down the names and home addresses and phone
numbers of all my witnesses and ran back to my car. It was
eight-thirty, which gave me, I figured, about two hours before most people would be in bed.

I drove to Hollywood and started knocking on doors. The
people I spoke to weren't surprised: other officers had been
around the week before asking questions. When I showed
them my colored photos of the two cars, they were surprised. The other cops hadn't asked anything about
that—just about "strange things," "funny stuff " that
they might have seen or heard on the night of the murder. One after another they shook their heads. No one
had noticed the '46 Olds or '49 Ford ragtop. I covered all of
Harold Way and turned onto De Longpre, getting discour-
aged. Lights were starting to go off; people were going to
bed.

On the corner of De Longpre and Wilton, I ran into three
high school boys playing catch by the light of a streetlamp.
I played it very palsy with them, even letting them look at
my gun. With their confidence gained, I showed them my
pictures.

"Hey!" the biggest of the three kids exclaimed. "What a
sharp drop-top! Man, oh, man!"

One of his pals grabbed the photo and scrutinized it silently. "I seen a car like that. Right here. Just down the
street," he said.

"When?" I asked quietly.

The kid thought, then looked to the big kid for support.
"Larry," he said, "you remember last week, I snuck out
and came over. Remember?"

"Yeah, I remember. It was Monday night. I had to go
to—"

I interrupted, keeping my voice stern and fatherly,

"And the car was red and white like the one in this picture?"

"Yeah," the kid said, "Exactly. It had a foxtail on the antenna, real sharp."

I was ecstatic. I took down their names and phone numbers and told them they were on their way to becoming heroes. The kids were somber with the gravity of their heroism. I solemnly shook hands with all three of them, then took off.

I found a pay phone on Hollywood Boulevard and got Eddie Engels's telephone number from Information. I dialed it, and let it ring fifteen times. No answer. Night owl Eddie was on the prowl.

I drove back to the Strip, turned north on Horn Drive and parked across the street from his bungalow court. I dug around in my trunk for some makeshift burglar tools and found some old college drafting stuff—including a metal T-square with thin edges that looked as if it could snap a locking mechanism. Equipped with this and a flashlight, I walked toward the darkened courtyard.

This time I knew to look for "Engels" on Number 11. It was three bungalows down, on the left-hand side. All the lights were off. I pulled open a flimsy screen door, looked in both directions, then covertly flashed my light on the inner door and studied the mechanism. It was a simple snap-bolt job, so I got out my T-square, transferred the flashlight to the crook of my left arm, wedged the metal edge between lock and doorjamb and pushed. It was hard, but I persisted, almost snapping the blade of the T-square. Finally, there was a loud metallic *ka-thack,* and the door opened.

I walked in quickly, and closed the door behind me. I ran the flashlight along the walls looking for a light switch, found one, and flipped it on, momentarily illuminating a living room tastefully furnished with Persian carpets, modern blond bentwood furniture, and, on all four walls, oil paintings of horses in racing colors.

I turned the light off, and headed for the hallway. I switched on another light and almost knocked over a telephone stand. The stand had three drawers, and I went through them hoping to find some kind of personal phone book. There was nothing—the three drawers were empty.

I flipped off the light and maneuvered my way into the

bedroom. My eyes were getting accustomed to the darkness, so it was easy to pick out objects in the room—bed, dresser, bookshelves. The window was covered by heavy velvet curtains, so I decided to risk leaving a light on while I did my searching. I turned on a table lamp, lighting up a room that was strangely sedate—just a simple bed with a plaid bedspread, a bookshelf crammed with picture books on horse racing, and bullfight posters and framed prints of a beautiful palomino on the walls. There was a deep walk-in closet behind the bed, crammed with clothes. At least fifty sport coats on hangers, thirty or forty pairs of slacks, scores of dress shirts and sport shirts. The floor of the closet was lined with shoes, from somber wingtips to sporty loafers, all shined and arranged neatly. Eddie the dude. It wasn't enough. I wanted evidence pointing to Eddie the degenerate—Eddie the killer.

I went through the dresser drawers, four of them, very thoroughly and very carefully, looking for phone books, journals, photographs, anything to link Eddie Engels to Maggie Cadwallader or Leona Jensen. There was nothing. Just gold silk underwear, but that was not enough to hang a man on.

I went back into the big closet and felt inside the jacket pockets. Nothing. Finished with the bedroom, I turned out the light and went back to the living room, shining my flashlight in corners, into bookshelves, under chairs and sofas. Nothing. Nothing personal. Nothing to indicate that Eddie Engels was anything but a spiffy dresser who loved horses.

There was a liquor cabinet with one bottle each of Scotch, bourbon, gin, and brandy. There were no photographs of family or loved ones. It was a maddeningly impersonal habitat, the home of a phantom.

I went into the kitchen. It was as I expected, compact and very tidy; a breakfast nook, a sink that held no dishes, a refrigerator with nothing but a cold-water bottle inside, and a 1950 calendar tacked to the wall with no notations on any of its pages.

Which left the bathroom. Maybe old Eddie cut loose in there. Maybe the bathtub would be filled with mermaids or alligators. No such luck—the bathroom was pink tile, spotless, with a giant mirror above the sink, and a full-length mirror on the inside of the door. Eddie, the narcissist.

Above the toilet was a medicine cabinet. I opened it, expecting to find toothpaste and shaving gear, but found instead a half-dozen tiny shelves holding rolled-up neckties. Eddie, the sartorially splendid, used the full-length mirror to ensure a perfect Windsor knot. I ran a hand over the collection of silk, arranged according to color and style. What a mania for order; what a mania for small perfections. Then I noticed what seemed like a strange anomaly—one silk tie, a green one, was sticking out further than the others. I poked at it with a finger, and felt something solid inside. I pulled the tie out carefully and unrolled it. Maggie Cadwallader's diamond brooch fell into my hand.

I stared at it for long moments, shocked. After a minute or so, my calm flew out the window and my mind started churning with plans. I rolled the brooch back into the tie and replaced it in the little cabinet exactly as I had found it. I turned the bathroom light off and walked through the dark apartment to the front door. I locked it behind me, checking the jamb for signs of entry. There were none.

All the lights in the courtyard were off. I stood there a few moments, savoring the wonder of the night and what I had just discovered, then walked behind the bungalows. There was a corrugated overhang that sheltered the tenants' cars. The car on the end, shiny in the moonlight, was a bright red '49 Ford with a white ragtop. A foxtail dangled from the radio antenna. I flicked it with my finger.

"You killed Maggie Cadwallader and God knows who else, you degenerate son of a bitch," I said, "and I'm going to see that you pay."

9

My case. My suspect. My revenge? My collar? My glory and gravy train? All these thoughts went through my head the following day as I walked my beat on sun-beaten Central Avenue.

A decision was due, and I would have to act either rationally or quixotically. I gave my options more thought, and as my tour ended I made a decision—a humbling, but safe one. I changed back into my civvies and knocked on Captain Jurgensen's door.

"Enter," he called through it. I walked in and saluted. Jurgensen dog-eared his paperback *Othello* and looked at me. "Yes, Underhill?" he said.

"Sir," I said, "I know who killed that woman who was found strangled in Hollywood last week. He may have killed others. I can't make the collar myself. I need to turn my evidence over to someone who can formalize an investigation, so I came to you."

"Perdition, catch my soul," Jurgensen said, then sighed and drew a pipe and pouch from his desk drawer. I stood at parade rest while he took his time packing the pipe and lighting it. He seemed to have forgotten I was there. I was about to clear my throat when he said, "For Christ's sake, Underhill, sit down and tell me about it."

It took me twenty minutes, by the electric clock on the captain's wall.

I covered everything, except my coupling with Maggie Cadwallader. I told him of the similarities between the two killings. I told him of my noticing the matches in Leona Jensen's apartment last February, and how that was the link that drew me to the Silver Star. I omitted my knowledge of the diamond brooch.

During the course of telling my story, I watched Jurgensen's normally stoic expression veer between curiosity, anger, and some kind of bitter amusement. When I finished he stared at me in silence. I stared back, sensing that phony contrition for the liberties I had taken wouldn't be believed. We stared at each other some more.

The captain looked very grave. He started to tamp his pipe bowl into his palm very slowly and deliberately. "Underhill," he said, "you are a supremely arrogant young man. In the course of what you arrogantly call your 'investigation,' you have committed infractions of departmental regulations that could end your career; you have committed two felonies that could send you to San Quentin; and implicitly you have held the detectives of two divisions and the Homicide Bureau up to ridicule—"

"Sir, I—"

"Don't interrupt, Underhill! I am a captain and you are a patrolman, and don't forget it." Jurgensen's face was very red, and there was an angry blue vein throbbing in his neck.

"Sir, I apologize."

"Very well. I could crucify you for your arrogance, but I won't."

"Thank you, sir."

"Don't thank me yet, Officer. You are a very gifted young man, but your arrogance supersedes your gifts. Arrogance cannot be tolerated in police officers; to tolerate it would be to promote anarchy. The Los Angeles Police Department is a superbly structured bureaucracy, one you have sworn allegiance to. Your actions have reviled the department. Know that, Underhill. Know that your ambition is threatening to kill you as a policeman. Do you understand me?"

I cleared my throat. "Sir, I do believe I acted rashly, and I apologize to you—and to the department—for that. But I think my motives were sound. I wanted justice."

Jurgensen snorted and shook his head. "No, Underhill, you didn't. I would accept that from many young officers, but not from you. Beyond self-aggrandizement, I'm not sure that even you know what you want, but it certainly isn't justice. You laugh at the penal code of this state, and tell me you want justice? Don't insult my intelligence."

Jurgensen's anger was winding down. I tried to deflect his attack. "Sir, with all due respect, what do you think of my case?"

"Your 'case'? I think that as of this moment you have nothing but a strong suspect and an incredible gift of intuition. This man Engels is so far nothing but a gambler and a womanizer, neither of which is criminal behavior. He's also probably a homo, which doesn't make him a murderer. You have no hard evidence. I don't think much of your 'case.' "

"And my intuition, Captain?"

"I trust your intuition, Underhill, or I would have suspended you from duty half an hour ago."

"And, sir?"

"And . . . what do you *want,* Underhill?"

"I want to be part of the investigation, and I want to go to the Detective Bureau when I pass the sergeant's exam later this year."

Jurgensen laughed bitterly. He reached into his desk, pulled out a scratch pad, and wrote something on it, ripping the page free and handing it to me. "This is my home address, in Glendale. Be there tonight at eight-thirty. I want you to tell your story to Dudley Smith. He'll decide the course of this investigation. Now leave me alone."

When he said the words "Dudley Smith," Jurgensen's cold blue eyes had bored into me like poison darts, waiting for me to show fear or apprehension. I didn't.

"Yes, sir," I said, then got up and walked out the door without saluting.

Dudley Smith was a lieutenant in the homicide bureau, a fearsome personage and legendary cop who had killed five men in the line of duty. Irish-born and Los Angeles-raised, he still clung tenaciously to his high-pitched, musical brogue, which was as finely tuned as a Stradivarius. He often lectured at the academy on interrogation techniques, and I remembered how that brogue could be alternately soothing or brutal, inquisitive or dumbfounded, sympathetic or filled with pious rage.

He was over six feet tall and broad as a ceiling beam. He was an immense brownness—brown hair cut close, small brown eyes, and always dressed in a baggy brown vested suit. There was a frightening set to his face, regardless of the interrogation technique he was explaining. He was a master actor with a huge ego who was adept at changing roles at the drop of a hat, yet who always managed to impart purity of personality to the part he was currently playing.

I was at the academy when the Black Dahlia investigation was going on. Smith was in charge of rounding up all known sex criminals in Los Angeles. After finishing his lecture, applause-loving actor that he was, he told us about the kind of "human scum" with which he was dealing. He told us that he had heard things and seen things and done things in his search for the killer "of that tragic, thrill-seeking colleen, Elizabeth Short" that he hoped we, the "cream of Los Angeles manhood," about to enter "the grandest calling on God's earth" would never have to hear or see or do. It was brilliantly elliptical. Speculation on the sternness of Smith's measures was the number one topic of conversation at the academy for weeks. I asked one of my instructors, Sergeant Clark, about him.

"He's a brutal son of a bitch who gets the job done," he said.

Elizabeth Short's killer was never found—which meant that Dudley Smith was human, and fallible. I pumped myself up with logic as I drove out Los Feliz to Glendale that evening. I went over my story from all possible angles, knowing I could not betray any personal knowledge of Maggie Cadwallader. I was prepared for a master performance myself, prepared to kiss the big Irishman's ass, to butt heads with him, to run profane, run subservient, run any way but stupid with him in my effort to be part of the investigation that brought down Eddie Engels.

Captain Jurgensen lived in a small wood-framed house on a treeless side street off of Brand Avenue near downtown Glendale. As I walked up the steps a dog started barking and I heard Jurgensen shush him: "Friend, Colonel, friend. Now, hush." The dog whimpered and trotted over to greet me, going straight for my crotch.

Jurgensen was sitting inside the screened porch on a lawn chair. "Hello, Underhill," he said, "sit down." He pointed to the wicker armchair next to him. I sat down.

"About this afternoon, Captain—" I started to say.

Jurgensen shushed me as he had the dog. "Forget it, Fred. Enough said. As of now you are temporarily attached to the detective bureau. Lieutenant Smith will tell you about it. He'll be here in a few minutes. Would you like iced tea? Or a beer?"

"Beer would be fine, sir."

The captain brought it, in a coffee cup, just as I saw an old prewar Dodge pull up to the curb. I watched as Dudley Smith carefully locked the car, hitched up his trousers and walked across the front lawn toward us.

"Don't be scared, Fred," Jurgensen said, "he's only human."

I laughed and sipped my beer as Dudley Smith knocked loudly on the flimsy wooden frame of the porch. "Knock, knock," he said broadly in his musical, high-pitched brogue. "Who's there? Dudley Smith, so crooks beware." He laughed at his own poetry, then walked in and stuck out a huge hand to Captain Jurgensen. "Hello, John. How are you?"

"Dudley," the captain said.

Smith nodded in my direction. "And this is our brilliant young colleague, Officer Frederick Underhill?"

I got up to shake the big cop's hand, noting with satisfaction that I was two inches taller than he. "Hello, Lieutenant," I said, "it's a pleasure to meet you."

"The pleasure is entirely mine, lad. Why don't we all sit down? We have grave matters to discuss, and we should relax our bodies while we tax our brains."

Smith folded himself into the only padded chair on the porch. He stretched out his long legs and smiled charmingly at Jurgensen. "Beer, please, John, in a bottle, and please take your time getting it."

The ranking officer walked dutifully away while the big Irishman stared at me with beady brown eyes, hugely offset by his blunt red face. After a moment, he spoke.

"Officer Frederick U. Underhill, twenty-seven years old, college graduate, not a veteran. Exceedingly high marks at the academy, excellent fitness reports at Wilshire and

Seventy-seventh Street. Killed two men in the line of duty. I am suitably impressed, and I don't give a damn what vigilante actions you have taken lately. John is an excitable, traditional cop. I am not. I applaud you for your actions and congratulate you on your intelligence in taking your investigation to a superior officer. Enough horseshit. Talk to me of dead women and killers. Take your time, I'm a good listener."

The little brown eyes had never left my own, and they remained on target while Dudley Smith fished in his trouser pockets for cigarettes and matches, then lit up and blew smoke at me.

I cleared my throat. "Thank you, sir. In February, I was working Wilshire Patrol. My partner and I were summoned by a distraught woman to a murder scene. The victim was a young woman named Leona Jensen. She had been strangled and stabbed to death in her apartment; the place had been ransacked. I called the dicks. They came and said it looked as if the woman had interrupted a burglar. I noticed a book of matches from the Silver Star bar on a table, but didn't think anything about it.

"Last week another woman was strangled in her apartment in Hollywood; I read about it in the papers. Her name was Margaret Cadwallader. I started thinking about the similarities between the two murders. The Hollywood dicks put this one off as a burglary killing, too, and they were basing their entire investigation on that thesis. I had an intuition about it, though. It wouldn't let me sleep. I trust my intuitions, sir, which is why my record of felony arrests is so good.

"Somehow I knew the two deaths were connected. I broke into the Cadwallader woman's apartment"—I slowed down as I got ready to drop my first outright lie—"and found a book of matches for the selfsame bar under the corner of the living room carpet." I paused for effect.

"Go on, Officer," Dudley Smith said.

"All right. Now I knew that the Cadwallader dame had gone to the Silver Star, at least once. I wangled my way onto day watch so I could go there at night, too. I had a hunch that the Jensen woman and Margaret Cadwallader had been picked up there by a lover-boy type. I enlisted the aid of the bartender, who told me about 'Eddie,' a real smooth operator who picked up a lot of women at the joint. Eddie came in the following night. The barman pointed him out to me. He tried putting the make on several women, who turned him down. He left, and I tailed him to a queer bar in West Hollywood, where he had an argument with a guy. Then I followed him to his apartment off the Strip. He stayed there all night. The next morning, I tailed him to Santa Anita racetrack. From his conversation with the man at the fifty-dollar window, I determined he was a heavy gambler who frequently brought women to the track.

"I showed a photograph of Margaret Cadwallader to the window man. He told me that Eddie's last name was Engels, and that Eddie had brought the woman to the track in June for the President's Stakes. He positively identified her. I had mixed the photo in with several others, so I know he was certain.

"Next I called R&I and got some info on Engels's record and car ownership. No record; two cars. I went to car dealers and got pictures of the models he owns, then colored them in the appropriate colors. Next I went to every night-club on the Sunset Strip. Four people remembered seeing Eddie Engels with Margaret Cadwallader. I got their names and addresses. Then I drove to Hollywood. A high school kid remembered seeing Engels's '49 Ford convertible parked around the corner from the Cadwallader apartment on the night of the murder. He described it as having a foxtail on the radio antenna. Later that night I broke into Engels's bungalow. I found no evidence linking him to anything criminal, but I did see his '49 Ford. It had a foxtail on the aerial. That's it, Lieutenant."

I expected Dudley Smith to fix me with a stern, probing look. He didn't. He just smiled crookedly and lit another cigarette. He exhaled smoke and laughed heartily.

"Well, lad," he said, "you've got us a killer. That's for damn sure. The Cadwallader dame, a certainty. The other woman, what was her name?"

"Leona Jensen."

"Ahhh, yes. Well, there I'm not so sure. What was the cause of death, do you know?"

"The M.E. at the scene said asphyxiation."

"Ahhh, yes. Who handled it for Wilshire dicks?"

"Joe DiCenzo."

"Ahhh, yes. I know DiCenzo. Freddy, lad, what are your feelings about this degenerate Engels?"

"I think he knocked off Cadwallader ahd Jensen and God knows who else."

"God knows? Are you a religious man, lad?"

"No, sir, I'm not."

"Well, you should be. Ahhh, yes. Divine Providence is certainly at work in this case."

Captain Jurgensen came onto the porch holding a beer.

"Ahhh, John. Thank you," the lieutenant said. "Give us ten more minutes, will you, lad?"

The captain muttered, "Sure, Dud" and retreated again.

"I was about to say, lad," Dudley Smith went on, "that I concur wholeheartedly with you. How old are you? Twenty-seven, isn't it?"

"Yes, sir."

"Don't call me sir, call me Dudley."

"All right, Dudley."

"Ahhh, grand. Well, lad, I'm forty-six, and I've been a cop for half my life. I was in the O.S.S. during the war. I was a major in Europe and I came back to my sergeancy in the department, expecting to rise very fast. I caught a lot of killers, and I killed a few myself. I made lieutenant, and I expect I'll always be a lieutenant. I'm too tough and smart and valuable to be a captain and sit on my ass all day and read Shakespeare like our friend John."

Dudley Smith leaned toward me and clamped his huge right hand over my knee. He lowered his tenor voice a good three octaves, and said, "In Ireland, the brothers taught me an abiding love and respect for women. I've been married to the same woman for twenty-eight years. I've got five daughters. There's a lot of the beast in me, lad, God knows. What gentleness there is I owe to the brothers and the women I've known. I hate killers, and I hate woman-killers more than I hate Satan himself. Do you share my hatred, lad?"

It was his first test, and I wanted to pass it with honors. I tightened my whole face and whispered hoarsely, "With all my heart."

Smith tightened his grip on my knee. He wanted me to show pain in acquiescence, so I winced. He released my knee, and I rubbed it gingerly. He smiled. "Ahhh, yes," he said. "Grand. He's ours, Freddy. Ours. He's claimed his last victim, God mark my words."

Smith leaned back and slouched bearlike into his chair. He picked up his bottle of beer and drained it. "Ahhh, yes. Grand. Detective Officer Underhill. Do you like the sound of that, lad?"

"I like it fine, Dudley."

"Grand. Tell me, lad, how did you feel after you gunned down those two pachucos who killed your partner?"

"I felt angry."

"Did you weep, later?"

"No."

"Ahhh, grand."

"When do we start, Dudley?"

"Tomorrow, lad. There'll be four of us. Two fine young protégés of mine from the bureau, and us. As of now, John is out. As of now, I am your commanding officer. During the war, we in the O.S.S. had a word we used to describe our activities: clandestine. Isn't that a grand word? It means 'in secret.' That's what our investigation is going to be—in secret. Just the four of us. I can get hold of anything, any file we need from within the department or any other police agency. The case is all ours, the glory all ours, the plaudits all ours, the commendations and advancements to be earned, all ours—once we get an airtight case and a confession from this monster Eddie Engels."

"And then?"

"Then we go to the grand jury, lad, and let the people of our grand Republic of California decide the fate of handsome Eddie, which, of course, will be to send the dirty son-of-a-whore to the gas chamber."

"He's as good as in the little green room right now, Dudley."

"Indeed he is, lad. Now you listen. Our command post will be at the Havana Hotel, downtown at Eighth and Olive. I've already rented us a room, number sixteen. You be there tomorrow morning at eight sharp. Wear civvies. Get a good night's sleep. Say your prayers. Thank God that you're free, white, twenty-one and a splendid young cop—

per. You go home now. John will be miffed at not being in on this, and I want to soft-pedal his pride. Now, shoo."

I got up and stretched my legs. I stuck out my hand to Dudley Smith. "Thanks, Dudley," I said. "This means a lot to me."

Smith shook my hand firmly. "I know it does, lad. I can tell we are going to be grand friends. God bless you. When you say your prayers, send one up for old Dudley."

"I will."

Smith laughed. "No, you won't," he said, "you'll go out and find yourself some grand piece of tail and show her your badge and tell her you're the next chief of police. Ha-ha-ha! I know you, lad. Now go and leave me to placate old John."

I walked back to my car feeling touched by madness and wonder. Mad, wonderful laughter trailed after me as I drove off.

Mad laughter filled my sleep that night. Nagging doubts tore at me in the form of Wacky Walker and Dudley Smith twirling nightsticks and shouting obscene poetry at each other. Reuben Ramos watched, honking on his sax and offering cryptic comments like a hophead Greek chorus. Captain Bill Beckworth was there too, offering his two cents' worth—"Caution, Freddy. Improve my putting stroke and I'll make you the king of Wilshire Division. All the pussy and wonder you can stomach! I'll bring back Walker from the dead and make him a nobel laureate. Trust me!"

I woke up with a headache and the certainty that Dudley Smith was going to screw me out of all the plaudits to be earned from the Eddie Engels case. He was the ranking officer, the decision maker, the one who would file with the district attorney's office when Engels was arrested. I needed an insurance policy, and I knew exactly who to call.

I took my time dressing and eating breakfast. I fried Night Train a pound of hamburger. He wolfed it down greedily and licked the inside of his dish. I threw him a soup bone as dessert. He gnawed it while I called Information and got the number of the office of the district attorney, city of Los Angeles. It was still early. I hoped someone would be there.

I dialed. "District attorney's office," a woman's singsong voice answered.

"Good morning," I said, "may I speak to Miss Lorna Weinberg, please?"

"Your name please, sir?"

"Officer Fred Underhill."

"One moment, Officer. I'll ring."

Lorna Weinberg came on the line a moment later, sounding harried. "Hello," she said.

"Hello, Miss Weinberg. Do you remember me?"

"Yes, I do. Is this something about my father?"

"No, it's not. It's both personal and professional. I need to speak to you, as soon as possible."

"What is it?" Lorna snapped.

"I can't discuss it on the phone."

"What is this, Mr. Underhill?"

"It's something important. Something I know that you'll think is important. Can I meet you tonight?"

"All right. Briefly. How about outside city hall, the Spring Street entrance, at five o'clock? I can give you fifteen minutes."

"I'll be there."

"Good day, Officer," Lorna Weinberg said, hanging up before I could deliver the witty remark I had prepared.

It was a hot, smoggy day, and it didn't faze me in the least. I drove downtown feeling buoyant with anticipation, and parked in front of the Havana Hotel, an old, one-story red brick building with a rickety elevator in its small entrance foyer. It was 7:59 by my watch, so I leaped the stairs three at a time, knocking on the door of room 16 at exactly eight o'clock.

A stocky blond man in a short-sleeved white shirt and a shoulder holster opened it. I held out my badge to gain entrance and he nodded me inside. Dudley Smith and another man were in the middle of the dingy little room, hunched over a folding card table.

Smith looked over his shoulder and greeted me. "Freddy! Laddy! Welcome! Let me make the introductions—gentlemen, this is Officer Fred Underhill, my newest protégé. Fred, meet Sergeant Mike Breuning," he nodded toward the stocky blond man. "And Officer Dick

Carlisle," he nodded toward the other man, a tall, thin, sallow-faced man with wire-rimmed glasses. I shook hands with my new colleagues and exchanged pleasantries with them until Dudley Smith cleared his throat loudly and called for our attention.

"Enough horseshit," he said. "Freddy, tell Mike and Dick your story. Omit nothing. Here, stand up in back of this table like a good toastmaster. Ahhh, yes, that's grand."

Breuning and Carlisle pulled up chairs while I assumed my position behind the folding table. Smith sat on the bed, smoking and sipping coffee and smiling at me. It took me fifteen minutes to recount my tale. I could tell that Breuning and Carlisle were impressed. They looked to Dudley Smith for confirmation, almost doglike in their deference to the big cop.

He smiled at them. "Ahhh, yes. A real live degenerate woman-killer. Comments, lad? Questions?"

Carlisle and Breuning shook their heads.

"Freddy?" Smith asked.

"Only one, Dudley. When do we start?"

"Ha-ha-ha! Grand! We start now, lad. Now listen: here are your assignments. Mike, you will go immediately to Horn Drive. You will tail Eddie Engels. You will go with him all day and all night until he returns home to sleep. If he picks up any women, you will stay very close. Do you get my meaning, lad? This beast must claim no more victims. Freddy, you will go to Horn Drive, too. You will question people on that street about their degenerate neighbor. I want names and addresses for any eyewitnesses to violence or abuse on Engels's part. Take the whole day on this. Dick, you go to Wilshire Station and talk to Sergeant Joe DiCenzo. Talk to him about the Leona Jensen killing. Tell Joe that I'm working on this investigation on my own time—he'll understand. Read the reports on the caper—coroner, dicks' log sheets, property, everything. Take notes. I'll be doing the digging into Eddie-boy's background myself. We'll meet here tomorrow, same time. Now go to work and God be with you!" Dudley Smith clapped his big hands, thunderously indicating dismissal.

Breuning and Carlisle filed out the door, looking grim-

ly determined. I was about to follow them when Dudley
Smith grabbed my arm. "You call me this afternoon at the
bureau, lad. About four o'clock."

"Sure, Dudley," I said.

Smith squeezed my arm very hard, then gently shoved
me out the door.

Breuning was standing on the sidewalk, apparently
waiting for me. "Since we're both going out to the Strip, I
thought I could follow you," he said.

"Sure," I said. "Where's your car?"

"Around the corner." Breuning was doing a little nervous shuffle.

I could tell there was something he wanted to say. I tried
to make it easy for him. "How long have you been on the
job, Mike?"

"Eleven years. You?"

"Four."

"That must have been a tough nut, shooting those two
Mexicans."

"I don't think about it too much."

"I was wondering. Dudley likes you, you know that?"

"I guess so. Why do you mention it?"

Breuning's stolid German face darkened. "Because I noticed the way you were looking at him. Studying him like
he was kind of a crazy man. A lot of people think Dudley's
nuts, but he's not. He's nuts like a fox."

"I believe you. He's just an actor, and a damn good one.
He's good at firing people up. That's his gift."

"Right. He wants this guy Engels, though. Bad."

"I know. He told me. He hates woman-killers."

"It's more than that. You have to know Dudley. I know
him real well. Since I was a rookie. He's still pissed off
about the Dahlia. He told me the Engels case is his penance for not catching the guy who sliced her."

I gave that some thought. "He wasn't in charge of the
entire investigation, Mike. The whole L.A.P.D. and sheriff's department couldn't find the killer. It wasn't
Dudley's fault."

"I know, but he took it that way. He's a religious man,
and he's taking the Engels thing real personal. The reason
I'm bringing all this up is that Dudley wants to make you

his number one man. He says you've got the stuff to go all the way in the department. That's no skin off my ass, I like being a sergeant in the bureau. But you've got to play it Dudley's way. I can tell you're not scared of him, and that's bad. If you cross him, he'll fuck you for real. That's what I wanted to tell you."

I smiled at the admonition. It increased my respect for Dudley Smith, and my respect for Mike Breuning for mentioning it. "Thanks, Mike," I said.

"You're welcome. Now let's hotfoot it over to the Strip. I'm getting itchy to start."

Mike got his car and pulled up behind me. I drove straight out Wilshire, hoping that Eddie Engels was still a late sleeper, so that Mike would have someone to tail. I turned north on La Cienega. Mike was right behind me as I turned onto the Strip ten minutes later. Horn Drive came up, and I pulled over to the curb and pointed out Engels's bungalow and Olds sedan. Mike smiled and gave me the thumbs-up sign. I waved and drove up the hill, parked the car and set out on foot to do my questioning.

I knocked on the doors of bungalow huts, well-tended cottages, French chateau walk-up apartments, artist's dives, and miniature Moorish castles and got a succession of blank looks, yawns, and bored shakes of the head. "Sorry, I can't help you, Officer." Eddie the phantom. This consumed five hours. At two o'clock I walked down to the diner on the corner of Horn and Sunset and ordered two cheeseburgers, French fries, a salad, and a jumbo pineapple malt. I was famished—and nervous about my meeting with Lorna Weinberg.

The man who served me at the counter looked like a jaded soda jerk out of hell. He slouched in front of me while I tore into my salad, alternately picking his teeth and his nose. We were obviously destined to converse—it was only a question of who would speak first. It was me, out of necessity. "Get me some ketchup, will you?"

"Sure, buddy," the counterman said, handing me a bottle of Heinz's and leaning over to breathe on me. "You with the sheriff's?" he asked. That was interesting.

"L.A.P.D.," I said. "You an ex-con?"

"I been clean for six years. Topped out my parole, knock wood." The guy made an elaborate show of rapping his knuckles on the counter top.

"I congratulate you," I said. "How long have you been working this joint?"

"Two years on the job. Knock wood."

"You know the locals pretty well?"

"Local yokels or regular customers?"

"Very astute. I mean people who live in the neighborhood who frequent this place."

"Oh." The man's eyes narrowed into a con-wise squint. "You got any particular locals in mind?"

"Yeah. A guy named Eddie. A handsome guy about thirty. Curly brown hair. Brown eyes. Sharp dresser. A lover-boy. Always a good-looking tomato in tow. You know him?"

The counterman's eyes remained impassive. When I finished, he nodded, almost imperceptibly. "Yeah, I think so."

I came on strong. "I'm a police officer and a big tipper. Tell me."

He looked around for prying ears. There weren't any. "Okay—you got it right. Smooth boy. Lover-boy. I should get the dames I seen that bastard with. Listen, Officer—"

I reached into my coat pocket for my photograph of Maggie Cadwallader. "Her?" I said. "This tomato?"

The counterman scrutinized the photo and shook his head. "Naw, lover-boy would never be seen with a beast like this. Ugh. What a—"

"Shut up. Tell me about the women you have seen him with."

Chastened, he went on, his voice low: "Just movie star material. Real beauts. Class-A poontang hangin' on to him like there's no tomorrow."

"Do you know any of these women? Are any of them regular customers?"

"Naw, I think he just brings 'em in for a quick burger, 'cause he lives around here."

"How do you know that?"

"That's kinda funny. Once he was in here with this good-lookin' blond. She was teasin' him about somethin'. He didn't like it. She had her hand on the counter top. Eddie started squeezin' it, real hard. The dame had tears in her eyes. She was hurtin' bad. She said, 'Not now, baby. You can give it to me good at the apartment, but not here. We'll be back there in a minute. Please, baby.' She looked scared, but kind of excited, too, you know?"

"When was this?" I asked.

"I dunno. Months ago."

"Have you seen this woman again, with or without Eddie?"

"I don't think so."

"Did you see Eddie exhibit violence toward any other women?"

"Naw. But I wouldn't call that violence."

"Shut up." I handed him a slip of paper from my notebook. "Write down your name and address," I said.

The ex-con did it, his jaw quavering slightly. "Look, Officer . . ." he started.

"Don't worry," I said, smiling. "You're in no trouble. Just keep it zipped about what we talked about. Capische?"

"Yeah."

"Good." I put the slip of paper into my pocket and dropped a five-spot on the counter. "Keep the change," I said.

I found a pay phone in the parking lot and called Dudley Smith downtown. It took some moments for him to come onto the line and I waited in the sweltering booth, lost in thought, the receiver jammed to my ear. Smith's loud high-pitched brogue suddenly hit me.

"Freddy, lad! How nice to hear from you!"

I recovered fast, speaking calmly: "Good news, Dudley. Our boy was seen at a local diner with a woman some months ago. The counterman said he abused her physically and she enjoyed it. I got a statement from him." Dudley Smith seemed to be considering this—he was silent for the better part of a minute. In my eagerness, I broke the silence: "I think he's a sex sadist, Dudley."

"Ahhh, yes. Well, lad, I think our pal is a lot of things. I've got some interesting stuff, too. Now, Freddy, tomorrow you will be the straight man to greatness. You pick me up at my house at nine A.M., 2341 Kelton Avenue, Westwood. Wear a light-colored suit, and be prepared to learn. Have you got that?"

"Yes."

"Ahhh . . . grand. Was there anything else you wished to tell me, lad?"

"No."

"Grand. Then I'll see you tomorrow."

"Goodbye, Dudley."

I drove home and showered and changed clothes. I shaved for the second time that day. I drove downtown fighting a tingling anticipation that was half nerves and half a thigh-warming sexual flush. I parked in the lot for city employees on Temple Street, showing the attendant my badge in lieu of a parking sticker. I combed my hair several times, checking in my rearview mirror to see that the part was straight.

At exactly five o'clock, I was stationed directly in front of the Spring Street entrance to city hall, waiting for Lorna Weinberg.

Lorna came out the broad glass doors a few minutes later, limping with one foot kicked out at almost a right angle. She guided her way with a thick, rubber-tipped black wood cane. She carried a briefcase in her left hand, and had an abstracted look on her face. When she saw me she frowned.

"Hello, Miss Weinberg," I said.

"Mr. Underhill," she returned. She moved her cane to her left hand and offered me her right. We shook, the handshake an implicit reminder that this was a civil meeting of two professional people.

I said, "Thank you for agreeing to see me. I know you're a busy woman."

Lorna nodded brusquely and shifted her weight to her good leg. "And you're a busy man. We should find a place to go and talk. I'm very curious to hear what you have to say." Catching herself being almost friendly, she added, "I trust you wouldn't waste my time." When I didn't acknowledge that, she asked, "Would you?"

I gave Lorna Weinberg my widest, most innocent smile. "Maybe. So much for the amenities. Do you eat dinner?"

Lorna frowned again. "Yes, Officer, I do. Do you?"

"Yeah. Every night. An old childhood habit. You know any decent places around here?"

"Not that I can walk to."

"If your bum leg acts up we can rest or I can carry you. Or we can drive somewhere."

Lorna winced against my comments, curling her lip reflexively. "We can drive," she said, "in my car."

I was more than willing to concede the point.

We walked the half-block to Temple very slowly, saying very little. Lorna limped steadily, easily throwing the dead leg forward in almost perfect rhythmic grace. If she was in pain she didn't show it, only her bare arm holding the cane betrayed any sign of tension.

I tried to think of something to say, but all my one-liners seemed fatuous or abrasive. As we crossed the street I grabbed her elbow to steady her and she withdrew it angrily.

"Don't," she snapped, "I can manage myself."

"I'm sure you can," I said.

The car was a late model Packard with an automatic shift and a specially constructed stirrup to hold Lorna's bad leg. Without consulting me, she drove north to Chinatown. She was a good, efficient driver, maneuvering the big car deftly through the heavy evening traffic on North Broadway. Squeezing effortlessly into a tight parking space and setting the hand brake with a flourish, Lorna turned to face me. "Is Chinese all right?" she asked.

The restaurant interior was a marvel of papier-mâché architecture. All four walls were shaped like mountain ranges, with cascading waterfalls dropping into a trough filled with giant goldfish. The room was bathed in a bluish-green light that imparted an underwater effect.

An obsequious waiter guided us to a booth at the back and handed us menus. Lorna made a great show of studying hers while I formulated my thoughts into a useful brevity. I stared at her as she perused her menu. Her face was very strong and very beautiful.

She looked up from her menu and caught my gaze. "Aren't you going to eat?" she asked.

"Maybe," I said. "If I do, I know what I'll have."

"Are you that rigid? Don't you like to try new things?"

"Lately, yes. Which is why I'm here."

"Is that a double-entendre, Officer?"

"It's a cross between a proposition and a statement of purpose."

"Is *that* a double-entendre?"

"It's a cross between a paradox and a logical fallacy."

"And the part I—"

I interrupted, "The paradox is murder, counselor, and the fact that I intend to profit from the capture of the murderer. The logical fallacy is that—well, in part I'm here because you are a very handsome and interesting woman." Lorna opened her mouth to protest, but I raised my voice to drown her out. "Pardon my language, but, as a colleague of mine says, 'Enough horseshit.' Let's eat, then I'll tell you about it."

Lorna glowered at me, speechless. I could tell she was mustering her resources for a wicked return salvo. Fortunately for me, our waiter glided up silently and said, "You order now?"

Before Lorna could start again I took a sip of green tea and began the story of Freddy Underhill, rogue cop, and his incredible intuition and persistence. She started to question me several times, but I just shook my head and continued. She changed expressions only once during my monologue, when I mentioned the name of Dudley Smith. Then her rapt look changed to one of anger. By the time I finished, our food had come. Lorna looked from me to her plate, then pushed it away and made a face.

"I can't eat now," she said. "Not after what you've told me."

"Do you believe me?"

"Yes. It's circumstantial, but it fits. What exactly do you want from me?"

"When the case is airtight, I want to file my depositions with you personally. The truth: Smith is going to try to screw me out of this; I can tell. I don't trust the bastard. Frankly, I want the glory. Are you still preparing cases for the grand jury?"

"Yes."

"Good. Then as soon as I have enough evidence, or as soon as we arrest Engels, I'll come to you. You prepare the case and the grand jury will indict Engels."

"And then, Officer?" Lorna asked sarcastically.

"And then we both have the satisfaction of knowing Eddie Engels is on his way to the gas chamber. Your career will be aided, and I'll go to the detective bureau." Lorna was morosely silent. I tried to cheer her up. "Which will make your job easier. I'll be filing lots of cases with you—but only ones where I'm sure my arrestee is guilty." I smiled.

"Dudley Smith is going to crucify you for this," Lorna said.

"No, he isn't. I'll be too big. The case will make the papers. I'll have too much support—from the press, plus from within the department. I'll be untouchable."

Lorna poked her chopsticks at her fried rice.

"Will you help me?" I asked.

"Yes," she said. "It's my job, my duty."

"Good. Thank you."

"You're very, very cocky."

"I'm very, very good."

"I don't doubt it. My father talks of you often. He misses you. He told me you don't play golf anymore."

"I gave it up last winter, shortly after I met you."

"Why?"

"My best friend got killed, and I killed two men. Golf didn't seem important anymore."

"I read about it in the papers. My sister was very upset. It bothered me, too. I wondered how you were affected. Now I can tell that you weren't, really. You were cocky then and you're more cocky now. You're a hard case."

"No, I'm not. I'm a nice guy and I'm flattered that you thought of me."

"Don't be. It was purely professional."

"Yeah, well purely unprofessionally, I've been thinking about you ever since we met. Nice, warm, unprofessional thoughts."

Lorna didn't answer—she just blushed. It was a purely feminine, unprofessional blush.

"Are you finished eating?" I asked.

"Yes," Lorna said softly.

"Then let's leave."

Ten minutes later we were back at the parking lot on

Temple Street. I got out of the car and walked around to the driver's side.

"Please smile before we say good night, Lorna," I said.

Lorna grudgingly obliged, parting her lips and gritting her teeth.

I laughed. "Not bad for a neophyte. Will you have dinner with me tomorrow night? I know a place in Malibu. We can take a seaside drive."

"I don't think so."

"That's right, don't think."

"Look, Mr.—"

"Call me Freddy."

"Look, Freddy, I . . ." Lorna's voice and resistance trailed off, and she grimaced and smiled again, unsolicited.

"Good," I said buoyantly. "Silence implies consent. I'll meet you in front of city hall at six o'clock."

Lorna stared at the steering wheel, unwilling to meet my eyes. I leaned into the car window and gently turned her head to face me, then kissed her softly on her closed mouth. Her hand came off the wheel and closed tightly on my arm. I broke the kiss.

"Don't think, Lorna. Tomorrow at six."

I ran off in the direction of my car before she could answer.

10

Dudley Smith and his female brood lived in a modest, spacious house a mile south of Westwood Village. I pulled up in front of it with five minutes to spare, wearing my only light-colored suit, which was somewhat wrinkled and soiled. I rang the doorbell and heard myself announced by several girlish giggles:

"Daddy, he's here!"

"Daddy, your policeman is here!"

"Daddy, visitor, Daddy!"

Curtains were pulled back in the picture window adjoining the doorway. A freckle-faced little girl was staring at me. She stared until I grinned and waved to her. Then she stuck out her tongue and retreated.

Dudley Smith threw open the door a moment later. As usual, he was wearing a brown vested wool suit. In September. The freckle-faced little girl was atop his shoulders, in a pink cotton dress. She giggled down at me.

"Freddy, lad, welcome," Dudley said, bending over and lowering the little girl to floor level. "Bridget, darling, this grand-looking young gentleman is Officer Fred Underhill. Say hello to Officer Fred, darling."

"Hello, Officer Fred," Bridget said, and curtsied.

"Hello, fair Bridget," I said, bowing.

Dudley was laughing loudly. It almost seemed genuine. "Oh, lad, you're a heartbreaker, you are. Bridget, get your sisters. They'll be wanting to meet the young gentleman."

Bridget scampered off. I felt the momentary loss I sometimes do around big families, then pushed it aside. Dudley seemed to notice my slight change in mood. "A family is something to cherish, lad. You'll have yours in time, I expect."

"Maybe," I said, glancing around at the warmly appointed living room. "Why the light-colored suit, Dudley?"

"Symbolism, lad. You'll see. Let's not talk about it here. You'll find out soon enough."

Bridget returned with her sisters in tow, all four of them. The girls ranged in age from six to about fourteen. They all wore identical pink cotton dresses and they all looked like soft, pretty versions of Dudley. The Smith girls lined up behind Bridget, the youngest.

Dudley Smith announced proudly, "My daughters, Fred. Bridget, Mary, Margaret, Maureen, and Maidred."

The girls all curtsied and giggled. I bowed exaggeratedly.

Dudley threw a rough arm around my shoulders. "You mark my words, lassies, this young man will be chief of police someday." He tightened his grip and my shoulder started to numb. "Now, say goodbye to your old dad and Officer Fred, and wake up your mother, she's slept long enough."

"Bye, Daddy. Bye, Officer Fred."

"Bye-bye, Mr. Officer."

"Bye-bye."

The girls all rushed to their father and hugged at his legs and pulled his suit coat. He blew them kisses and shooed them gently inside as he shut the door behind us. Walking across the lawn to my car, Dudley Smith said matter-of-factly, "Now do you know why I hate woman-killers worse than Satan, lad?"

"Drive, lad, and listen," Dudley was saying. "Yesterday I sent out some queries on handsome Eddie. Edward Thomas Engels, born April 19, 1919, Seattle, Washington. No criminal record, I checked with the feds. Navy service in the war, '42–'46. Good record. Honorable discharge. Our friend was a pharmacist's mate. I called the L.A. Credit Bureau. He financed two cars with a finance company, and they checked him out. He listed two credit references. That's who we're going to see now, lad, known intimates of handsome Eddie."

We pulled up to the light at Pico and Bundy. I looked to
Dudley for some clue to our destination.

"Venice, lad," he said. "California, not Italy. Keep driving due west."

"Why the light suit, Dudley?" I tried again.

"Symbolism, lad. We're going to play good guy–bad guy.
This fellow we're going to see, Lawrence Brubaker, is an
old chum of handsome Eddie's. He owns a bar in Venice. A
queer joint. He's a known homo with a lifetime of lewd-
conduct arrests. A surefire degenerate. We'll play with
him like an accordion, lad. I'll browbeat him, you come to
his rescue. Just follow my lead, Freddy lad. I trust your instincts."

I turned left on Lincoln then right on Venice Boulevard,
headed for the beach and my first real interrogation. Dudley Smith smoked and stared out the window in abstracted
silence. "Pull up to the curb at Windward and Main," he
said finally as we came in view of the ocean. "We'll walk to
the bar, give us time to talk."

I pulled up and parked in the lot of an American Legion
meeting hall, got out, stretched my legs and gulped in
the bracing sea air. Dudley got out and clamped me on the
back.

"Now listen, lad. I've been checking the files for unsolved murders of women that fit handsome Eddie's M.O. I
found three, lad, all choke jobs, as far back as March, 1948.
One was found three blocks from here, strangled and
beaten to death in an alley off Twenty-seventh and Pacific.
She was twenty-two, lad. Keep that in mind when we brace
this degenerate Brubaker."

Dudley Smith smiled slowly, a blank-faced, emotionless
carnivore smile, and I knew that this was the real man, de-
void of all his actor's conceit. I nodded. "Right, partner," I
said, feeling myself go cold all over.

Larry's Little Log Cabin was a block from the beach, a
pink stucco building with phony redwood swinging doors
and a sign over them posting its hours—6:00 A.M. to 2:00
A.M., the maximum allowed by law.

Dudley nudged me as we entered. "It's only a queer joint
at night, lad. In the daytime it's strictly a hangout for local
riffraff. Follow my lead, lad, and don't upset the locals."

The room was very narrow, and very dimly lit. There were hunting scenes on the walls and sawdust on the floor. Dudley nudged me again. "Brubaker changes the decor at night, lad, muscle-boy paintings all over the walls. A sergeant from Venice Vice told me."

There were a half-dozen elderly juiceheads sitting at the log-shaped bar, slopping up brew. They looked dejected and meditative at the same time. The bartender was dozing behind the counter. He looked like countermen everywhere—jaded even in sleep. Dudley walked over to the bar and slammed two huge hands down on the wooden surface. The bar reverberated and the early morning drinkers snapped out of their reverie. The bartender's head jerked back abruptly and he started to stutter: "Y-y-yess, s-s-s-sir?"

"Good morning!" Dudley bellowed musically. "Could you direct me to the proprietor of this fine establishment, Mr. Lawrence Brubaker?"

The barkeep began a stuttering sentence, then thought better of it and pointed to a doorway at the back of the bar. Dudley bowed to the bartender, then propelled me before him in that direction, whispering, "We're cop antagonists, lad. I'm the pragmatist, you're the idealist. Brubaker's a homo and you're a fine-looking young man. He'll go for you. If I have to get rough with him, you touch him gently. We have to go about this in a roundabout way. We can't let him know this is a murder investigation."

I nodded my head and twisted free of Dudley's grasp. I felt myself getting very keyed up.

Dudley knocked softly on the door and spoke in an effete American voice, the last syllables strained and upward intoned. "Larry, open up, baby!" A moment later the door was opened by an almost totally bald, blue-eyed, very skinny mulatto who stood there staring at us for a brief instant before cowering backward almost reflexively.

"Knock, knock," Dudley bellowed in his brogue. "Who's there? Dudley Smith, so queers beware. Ha-ha-ha! Police officers, Brubaker, here to assure our constituency that we are on the job, ever vigilant!"

Lawrence Brubaker stood in the middle of the office, his thin body trembling.

"What's the matter, man?!" Dudley screamed. "Have you nothing to say?"

I took my cue. "Leave the gentleman alone, Dud. He's no queer, he's a property owner." I slapped Dudley on the back, hard. "I think that Vice sergeant had it wrong. This is no homo hangout, is it, Mr. Brubaker?"

"I don't ask my customers for their sexual preferences, Officer," Brubaker said. His voice was light.

"Well put. Why should you?" I said. "I'm Detective Underhill and this is my partner Detective Smith." I clapped Dudley's broad back again, this time even harder. Dudley winced, but his brown eyes twinkled at me in silent conspiracy. I pointed to a sofa at the back of the little office. "Let's all sit down, shall we?"

Brubaker shrugged his frail shoulders and took the chair facing the sofa, while Dudley sat on his desk, dangling one leg over the edge and banging his heel against the wastebasket. I sat on the couch and stretched out my long legs until they were almost touching Brubaker's feet.

"How long have you owned this bar, Mr. Brubaker?" I asked, taking out a pen and note pad.

"Since 1946," he said sullenly, his eyes moving from Dudley to me.

"I see," I went on. "Mr. Brubaker, we've had numerous complaints about your bar being used as a pickup place for bookmakers. Plainclothes officers have told us this is a hangout for known gamblers."

"And a homo den of iniquity!" Dudley bellowed. "What was the name of that flashy-dressing gambler we rousted, Freddy?"

"Eddie Engels, wasn't it?" I asked innocently.

"That's the pervert!" Dudley exclaimed. "He was taking bets at every queer joint in Hollywood."

Brubaker's eyes went alive with recognition when I mentioned Engels's name, but no more. He was holding his ground stoically.

"Do you know Eddie Engels, Mr. Brubaker?" I asked.

"Yes, I know Eddie."

"Does he frequent your bar?"

"Not really, not for a while."

"But he did in the past?"

"Yes."

"When?"

"The first few years I owned the Cabin."

"Why did he quit coming here?"

"I don't know. He moved out of the area. He broke up with the woman he was living with. She used to come here frequently, and when they broke up Eddie stopped coming around."

"Eddie Engels used to live here in Venice?" I asked mildly.

"Yes, he and Janet lived in a house near the canals, around Twenty-ninth and Pacific."

I let my breath out slowly. "When was this?"

"The late forties. From sometime in '47 to early '49, as I recall. Why all this interest in Eddie?" Brubaker inched his feet closer to my outstretched legs so that they touched my ankles. I felt a queasy sort of revulsion come up, but I didn't move.

Out of the corner of my eye I saw Dudley swivel his neck. "Enough horseshit!" he bellowed. "Brubaker, are you and Eddie Engels lovers?"

"What the world, are you—" Brubaker exclaimed.

"Shut up, you goddamned degenerate! Yes or no?"

"I don't have to—"

"The hell you say. This is an official police investigation, and you will answer our questions!"

Dudley got up and advanced toward Brubaker, who fell over in his chair, got up and backed himself into the wall, trembling.

I came between them as Dudley closed his hand into fists. "Easy, Dud," I said, pushing him gently at the shoulders. "Mr. Brubaker is cooperating, and we're investigating bookmaking, not homosexuality."

"The hell you say, Freddy, I want to get a handle on this degenerate Engels. I want to know what makes him tick."

I sighed, and released Dudley. Then I sighed again. I took Brubaker by the arm and led him to the couch. He sat down and I sat down beside him, letting our knees touch lightly. "Mr. Brubaker, I apologize for my partner, but he has a point. Could you tell us about your association with Eddie Engels?"

Brubaker nodded assent. "Eddie and I go back to the

war. We were stationed together down at Long Beach. We became friends. We went to the races together. We stayed friends after the war. Eddie is a very popular guy at the racetrack, and he brought lots of people here to the Cabin. Lots of beautiful women, gay and straight. I introduced him to Janet, Janet Valupeyk, and they moved in together, here in Venice. He still comes by here once in a while, but not so much since he broke it off with Janet. We're still friends. That's about it."

"And he likes boys, right?" Dudley hissed.

"That's none of my business, Officer."

"You tell me, Brubaker, now!"

"He's a switch-hitter," Brubaker said, and stared into his lap, ashamed at divulging that intimacy. Dudley snorted in truimph and cracked his knuckles.

"What does Eddie do for a living, Mr. Brubaker?" I asked gently.

"He gambles. He gambles big and he usually wins. He's a winner."

Dudley caught my eye and nodded toward the door. Brubaker continued to stare downward.

"Thank you for your cooperation, Mr. Brubaker. You've been very helpful. Good day." I got up from the sofa to leave.

Dudley got in a parting shot: "You don't breathe a word of this to a soul; you got that, you scum?"

Brubaker moved his head in acquiescence. I gave his shoulder a gentle squeeze as I followed Dudley out the door.

Walking back to my car, Dudley let out a big whoop. "Freddy, lad, you were brilliant! As was I, of course. And we got solid evidence—handsome Eddie was living two blocks away when that tragic young woman was croaked in '48. Just think, lad!"

"Yeah. Are we going to put someone on that?"

"We can't, lad. Mike and Dick are tailing Engels twenty-four hours a day. There's just the four of us on this investigation, and besides, the trail's too cold—three and a half years cold. But don't worry, lad. When we pop Eddie for Margaret Cadwallader, he'll confess to all his sins, don't you fear."

"Where to now?"

"This Janet Valupeyk bimbo. She lives in the Valley. She was the other credit reference for handsome Eddie. We can mix business with pleasure, lad; I know a great place on Ventura Boulevard—corned beef that melts in your mouth. I'm buying, lad, in honor of your stellar performance."

With our guts full of corned beef and cabbage, Dudley and I drove to Janet Valupeyk's house in Sherman Oaks.

"Let's just hope old queer Larry didn't call her ahead. Kid gloves with this one, lad," he said, pointing at the large, white, one-story ranch-style house. "She's obviously got dough and she's got no record at all. It's no crime being charmed by a lounge lizard like charming Eddie."

We knocked and a handsome, full-bodied woman in her late thirties threw open the door. She was blurry eyed and wearing a wrinkled yellow summer dress.

"Yes?" she said, slurring slightly.

"We're police officers, ma'am," Dudley said, showing her his badge. "I'm Lieutenant Smith, this is Officer Underhill."

The woman nodded at us, her eyes not quite focusing. "Yes?" She hesitated, then said, "Come in . . . please."

We took seats uninvited, in the large air-conditioned living room. The woman plopped down in a comfortable armchair, looked at us and seemed to draw on hidden resources in an effort to correctly modulate her voice: "I'm Janet Valupeyk," she said. "How can I help you?"

"By answering a few questions," Dudley said, smiling. "This is an absolutely charming home, by the way. Are you an interior decorator?"

"No, I sell real estate. What *is* it?"

"Ahhh, yes. Ma'am, do you know a man named Eddie Engels?"

Janet Valupeyk gave a little tremor, cleared her throat and said calmly, "Yes, I knew Eddie. Why?"

"Ahhh, yes. You said 'knew.' You haven't seen him recently, then?"

"No, I haven't. Why?" Her voice was steady, but her composure seemed to be faltering.

"Miss Valupeyk, are you all right?" I asked.

"Shut up," Dudley snapped.

I went on, "Miss Valupeyk, the purpose of our—"

"I said, shut up!" Dudley roared, his high-pitched brogue almost breaking.

Janet Valupeyk looked like she was about to break into tears.

Dudley whispered, "Wait for me in the car. I won't be long."

I walked outside and waited, sitting on the hood of my car and wondering what I had done to irk Dudley.

He came out half an hour later. His tone was conciliatory, but firm; his voice very low and patient, as if explaining something to an idiot child. "Lad, when I tell you to shut up, do it. Follow my lead. I had to play that woman very slowly. She was on dope, lad, and too confused to follow the questions of two men."

"All right, Dudley," I said, letting the slightest edge of pride go into my voice. "It won't happen again."

"Good, lad. I got more confirmation, lad. She lived with handsome Eddie for two years. She paid the bills for that no-good gigolo. He used to beat her up. Once he tried to choke her, but came to his senses. He's a longtime cunthound, lad. He used to pick up girls even when he was living with lonely Janet. She was in love with him, lad, and he treated her like dirt. He bought whores and paid them to stand abuse. And he's queer, lad. Queer as a three-dollar bill. Boys are his passion, and women his victims."

I was amazed. "How did you get that out of her?"

Dudley laughed. "When I realized she was on dope, rather than booze, I checked out her medicine cabinet. There was a doctor's precription bottle of codeine pills. A hophead, lad, but a legal one. So I played on her fear of losing that prescription, and it all came out: Eddie jilted her for some muscle boy. She loves Eddie and she hates him and she loves codeine most of all. A tragedy, lad."

Without being told, I took the long way back to downtown L.A. Laurel Canyon Boulevard, with its rustic, twisting streets would give me plenty of time to probe the man who was growing before my eyes in several different directions.

Dudley Smith was a wonder broker, but a brutal one, and I felt a very strange ambivalence about him. He was

too sharp for elliptical games, so I came right out with it:
"Tell me about the Dahlia," I said.

Dudley feigned surprise. "The Dahlia? What Dahlia?"

"Very funny. *The* Dahlia."

"Oh. Ahhh, yes. The *Dahlia*. What precisely was it you
wanted to know, lad?"

"How far you had to go in your investigation, what you
saw, what you had to do." I turned to give Dudley a look
that I hope conveyed equal parts interest and tight-lipped
allegiance. He smiled demonically and I felt another little
chill go through me.

"Watch the road, lad, and I'll tell you. You've heard
tales, have you?"

"Not really."

"Then hear one now, from the horse's mouth: I have
seen many, many crimes on women, lad, and the crime on
Elizabeth Short exceeded them all by a country mile—the
atrocities committed on her defied even Satan's logic. She
was systematically tortured for days, and then sawed in
half while she was still alive."

"Jesus Christ," I said.

"Jesus Christ, indeed, lad. The investigation was three
weeks old when I was called in. I was given a special assignment: check out all the psycho confessors that were being held without bail as material witnesses; the ones the
dicks thought could actually have done it. There were
thirty of them, lad, and they were the scum of the
earth—degenerate mother-haters and baby-rapers and animal fuckers. I eliminated twenty-two of them right away.
Breaking an arm here and a jaw there, I confronted them
with intimate facts about lovely Beth's wounds. I gauged
their reactions as I hit them and made them fear me more
than Satan himself. None of them did it; they were guilty, filthy degenerates who wanted to be punished, and I
obliged them. But none of them were guilty of the crime
against lovely Beth."

Dudley paused dramatically and stretched, waiting for
me to ask him to continue.

I obliged: "And the other eight?"

"Ahhh, yes. My hard suspects; the ones whose reactions
old Dudley wasn't quite astute enough to gauge. Well,
lad, I was astute enough to know that those eight had one

thing in common: they were stark raving insane, slobbering, frothing-at-the-mouth lunatics capable of anything, which made them rather difficult to deal with. I was sure their insanity was of such an intensity that they could withstand any degree of physical duress. Besides, they thought they actually *had* croaked lovely Beth; they'd confessed to it, hadn't they?

"The dicks I'd talked to told me they figured the killer had hung lovely Beth from a ceiling beam; there were rope burns on her ankles. That got me to thinking. I needed to shock these degenerate lunatics. I needed to break through their insanity. First I rented a friend's warehouse. A big, grand, deserted place it was. Then I procured a fine-looking young female stiff from a pathologist at the morgue who owed old Dudley a favor. A big one, lad—old Dudley looked the other way for this fellow, and he belonged to old Dudley for life.

"Dick Carlisle and I snuck the stiff over to the warehouse late one night. I dyed her hair jet black, like the Dahlia's. I stripped her nude, and tied her ankles with a rope, and Dick and I hoisted her up feet first and hung her from a low ceiling beam. Then Dick went and got our eight degenerates from the Hall of Justice jail. We let them view her, one at a time, lad, with appropriate props. One scum was a knife man; he had scores of arrests for knife fighting. I handed him a butcher knife and made him slice the corpse. He could hardly do it. He didn't have it in him. Another filth was a child molester, recently paroled from Atascadero. His M.O. was asking little girls if he could kiss their private parts. I made him kiss the dead girl's private parts, smell that dead sex flesh up close. He couldn't do it. And on and on. I was looking for a reaction so vile, so unspeakable that I would *know* that this was the scum that killed Beth Short."

I was stunned. Speechless. I felt my hands gripping the steering wheel so hard that I thought I would push it through the front of the car. My voice was breaking when I finally got it out: "And?"

"And, lad, I kept them there through the night, making them look at the corpse. I hit them, and Dick hit them, and we made them kiss the dead girl and fondle her while we questioned them."

"And?"

"And, lad, none of them killed lovely Beth."

"Jesus Christ," I said.

"Ahhh, yes. Jesus Christ. I didn't get the fiend who killed the Dahlia, lad. I know in my heart of hearts that no one ever will. I took the young dead woman back to the morgue to be cremated. She was a lonely Jane Doe, who unknowingly served justice by her death. I went to confession the next morning. I told the father what I had done and asked for absolution. I got it. Then I went home and prayed to God and to Jesus and to the Blessed Virgin to let me have the strength to do it again and again, if I had to, in the name of justice and the church."

We were coming down into Hollywood. I pulled over to the curb at Crescent Heights and Sunset. I stared at Dudley's florid, demonic face. He stared back.

"And, lad?" he said, mimicking my tone.

"And what, Dudley?" I managed to get out, my voice steady.

"And do you think Dudley's a lunatic, lad?"

"No, I think you're a master actor."

"Ha-ha-ha! Well said. Is 'actor' a euphemism for 'madman,' lad?"

"No, I just think sometimes you're not sure what role you're playing."

Tiny brown predator eyes bored into me. "Lad, all my roles are in the name of justice and all my roles are me. Don't you forget that."

"Sure, Dudley."

"And, lad, don't think I don't know you. Don't think I don't know how smart you think you are. Don't think I didn't notice how you relished giving me guff in front of Brubaker. Don't think I don't know what a son of a bitch you think I am. Ha-ha-ha! Enough sorrow and contention, lad. Drive me downtown and take the rest of the day off."

I dropped Dudley downtown in front of Central Division headquarters on Los Angeles Street. He stuck his big hand out and we shook. "Tomorrow, lad. Eight A.M. at the hotel. We'll go over our evidence and decide when we'll snatch handsome Eddie."

"Right, Dudley."

He squeezed my hand until I rewarded him with a

wince, then he winked and left me to contemplate madness and salvation.

I had over four hours to kill before my date with Lorna. I drove home and wrote out a detailed report on my involvement in the Margaret Cadwallader case. I put it in a large manila envelope and sealed it shut. I fed Night Train, changed clothes, and shaved again.

On my way downtown I stopped at a florist's shop, where I bought Lorna a dozen long-stemmed red roses. Somehow they made me think of the dead girl whose eternal sleep Dudley Smith had so viciously interrupted. I started to get a little scared, but the thought of Lorna kiboshed my fear and turned it into some strange symbioses of hope and the odd amenities of justice.

I waited impatiently, red roses in hand, outside the Spring Street entrance to city hall until six-thirty.

Lorna was standing me up. I jogged over to the parking lot on Temple. Her car was in its space. Angry, I walked back to city hall and entered. I checked out the directory in the vestibule: the office of the district attorney occupied two whole floors. Nervously, I took the elevator, although I wanted to run the nine flights of stairs. I walked down the deserted ninth floor corridors, poking my head in open doorways, checking empty conference rooms. I even ducked my head into the ladies' can. Nothing.

I heard the clack-clacking of a typewriter in the distance. I walked down the hallway to a glass door with "Grand Jury Investigations" lettered on it in flat black paint. I knocked softly.

"Who is it?" Lorna's voice called testily.

I disguised my voice: "Telegram, ma'am."

"Shit," I heard her mutter. "It's open."

I pushed in the door. Lorna looked up from her typewriter, noticed me and jumped toward the door in an attempt to block my entrance. I sidestepped her, and she crashed to the floor.

"Shit. Oh, shit. Oh, God!" she said, pushing herself up into a sitting position against the wall. "What the hell are you doing with me?"

"Stalking your heart," I said, tossing the roses onto her desk. "Here, let me help you up."

I squatted down and grabbed Lorna under her arms and gently lifted her to her feet. She made feeble motions toward pushing me away, but her heart wasn't in it. I embraced her tightly and she didn't resist.

"We had a date, remember?" I whispered into her soft brown hair.

"I remember."

"Are you ready to go?"

"I don't think so."

"I told you last night, don't think."

Lorna disengaged herself. "Don't patronize me, Underhill," she hissed. "I don't know what you want, but I know you underestimate me. I've been around. I'm thirty-one years old. I've tried promiscuity and I've tried true love, and they're like my dead leg: they don't work. I don't need a charity lover. I don't need a deformity-lover. I don't need compassion—and above all, I don't need a cop."

"But you need me."

"No, I don't!" She raised her hand to slap me.

"Do it, counselor," I said. "Then I'll file on you for a 647-f, assault on a police officer. You'll have to investigate it yourself and then be in the incongruous position of being defendant, investigator, and defense attorney all at once. So go ahead."

Lorna lowered her hand and started to laugh.

"Good," I said. "I drop all charges and grant parole."

"In whose custody?"

"In mine."

"Under what conditions?"

"For starters, that you accept my flowers and have dinner with me tonight."

"And then?"

"That will depend on your probation reports."

Lorna laughed again. "Will I get time off for good behavior?"

"No," I said, "I think it's going to be a life sentence."

"You're out of your bailiwick, Officer, as you once said to me."

"I'm above the law, counselor, as *you* once said to me."

"Touché, Freddy."

"A standstill, Lorna. Dinner?"

"All right. The flowers are lovely. Let me put them in water, then we can go."

We headed for the beach and the Malibu Rendezvous, a classy seaside eatery I had catalogued in my mind since the "old days" when I dreamed of the "ultimate" woman. Now, years later, I was driving there, an adult, a policeman, with a crippled Jewish attorney sitting beside me blowing smoke rings and casting furtive glances at me as I drove.

"What are you thinking?" I asked.

"You told me not to think, remember?"

"I retract it."

"All right. I was thinking that you're too good looking. It's disarming and it probably makes people underestimate you. There's a side to you that could take advantage of that underestimation very easily."

"That's very perceptive. What else were you thinking?"

"That you're too good to be a cop. No—don't interrupt, I didn't mean it quite that way; I'm glad you're a cop. Eddie Engels would be free to kill with impunity if you weren't. It's just that you could be anything you want, literally. I was also thinking that I don't want to be fawned over in a fancy restaurant; I don't want to go clumping through there getting a lot of pitying looks."

"Then why don't we eat on the beach? I'll have the restaurant fix us up with a picnic basket and a bottle of wine."

Lorna smiled and blew a smoke ring at me, then tossed her cigarette out the window. "That's a good idea," she said.

I parked in the blacktopped area adjoining the restaurant, about a hundred yards away from the beach. Lorna waited in the car while I went to fetch our feast. I ordered three orders of cracked crab and a bottle of chablis. The waiter was hesitant about boxing an order "to go," but changed his tune when I whipped a five-spot on him, even popping the cork on the wine bottle and throwing in two glasses.

Lorna was standing outside the car, smoking, when I returned. When she saw me she stared up at the warm summer sky and pointed her cane heavenward. I looked up,

too, and committed the twilight sky and a low-hanging
cloud formation to memory.

There was a flight of rickety wooden steps leading down
to the sand. I carried our picnic and Lorna limped by my
side. The stairs were barely wide enough for the two of us,
so I threw an arm around Lorna and she huddled into my
chest and hopped on her good leg all the way down, laughing, out of breath when we reached the bottom.

We found a nice spot to sit on a rise. The sun was a de-
parting orange ball, and it lovingly caught strands of Lorna's light brown hair and burnished them into gold.

We sat on the sand, and I laid out our food on top of the
brown paper bag it had come in. Not standing on ceremony, we polished off all three crustaceans in short order
without saying a word. The sun had gone down while we
ate, but the light from the big picture window of the restaurant cast an amber glow that allowed us a muted view
of each other.

Lorna lit a cigarette as I poured us each a glass of wine.
"To September 2, 1951," I said.

"And to beginnings." Lorna smiled and we clinked
glasses. I didn't quite know what to say. Lorna did. "Who
are you?" she asked.

I gulped my wine and felt it go to my head almost
immediately. "I'm Frederick Upton Underhill," I said.
"I'm twenty-seven years old, I'm an orphan, a college graduate and a cop. I know that. And I know that you've caught
me at the most exciting time of my life."

"Caught you?" Lorna laughed.

"No, more correctly, I caught you."

"You haven't caught me."

"Yet."

"You probably never will."

" 'Probably' is an equivocation, Lorna."

"Look, Freddy, you don't know me."

"Yet."

"All right, yet."

"But in a sense, I do. I went over to your dad's house last
winter. I saw some photographs of you. I talked to Siddell
about you, and she told me about the accident and your
mother's death, and I felt I knew you then, and I still feel
it."

Lorna's eyes glittered with anger and she spoke very coldly: "You had no right to pry into my life. And if you pity me, I will never see you again. I will walk up to that restaurant and call a cab and ride out of your life. Do you understand me?"

"Yes," I said. "I understand. I understand that I don't know what pity is, never having felt it for myself. I pity some of the people I meet on the job, but that's easy; I know I'm never going to see them again. No, for what it's worth I don't give a damn if you've got a bad leg, or two, or three. When I met you in February I *knew,* and I still know."

"Know what?"

"Don't make me say it, Lorna. It's too early."

"All right. Will you hold me for a while, please?"

I moved to Lorna and we embraced clumsily. She held me around the small of my back and nuzzled her head into my chest. I rested my hand on the knee of her bad leg until she took it and cupped it to her breast, holding it tightly there. We stayed that way for some time, until Lorna said in a very small voice, "Will you drive me back to my car, please?"

An hour later we were embracing again, this time standing in the parking lot on Temple Street. We kissed, alternately soft and hard. A patrol car cruised by, shined its light on us and departed, the cop shaking his head. Lorna and I laughed.

"Do you know him?" she asked.

"No, but I know you."

"All right, you know me, and I'm starting to know you."

"Dinner tomorrow night?" I asked.

"Yes, Fred. Only I don't want to go out, I want to cook for you myself."

"That sounds wonderful."

"My address is 8987 Charleville, in Beverly Hills. Can you remember that?"

"Yes. What time?"

"Seven-thirty?"

"I'll be there. Now kiss me so I can let you go."

We kissed again, this time quickly.

"No protracted farewells," Lorna muttered as she broke from my arms and limped over to her car.

11

We assembled at the Havana Hotel at 8:00 A.M., Wednesday, September 3. Dudley Smith was stern-faced and businesslike as he called for our reports and our conclusions.

Dudley reported first, telling of our questioning of Lawrence Brubaker and Janet Valupeyk. He volunteered his information on the three unsolved strangulation homicides in the West L.A.-Venice area, with special emphasis on the woman fround in the alley near the Venice canals in March of '48.

Breuning and Carlisle whistled in awe at these new offshoots of the case. Mike raised his hand and interjected, "Dud, Dick's got absolutely nothing to tie our boy to the Leona Jensen homicide. I've got a pal on the Venice dicks who could give me access to their files. If Engels was living two blocks away at the time of the killing, there could well be something in their files that point to him."

Dudley shook his head patiently. "Mike, lad, we have this fiend cold for the Cadwallader snuff. Cold, lad. I'm thinking now that the Jensen killing was unrelated. Freddy, you discovered the stiff, what do you think?"

"I don't know, Dudley," I said, measuring my words carefully. "Of course, if I hadn't discovered those matches at the death scene we wouldn't be here today. But I'm beginning to think it was just an incredible coincidence, and that Engels didn't snuff Leona Jensen. Engels is a strangler, and although the Jensen woman was strangled, she was also stabbed all over. I've got a picture of Engels as a very competent, fastidious homosexual. Someone who hates women, but abhors blood. I agree with Dudley—forget the Jensen killing; it's the wrong M.O."

136

Dudley laughed. "There's a college boy for you—brains all the way. Mike, you've been tailing handsome Eddie. What have you got?"

Stolid Mike Breuning cleared his throat and gave Dudley Smith a toadying look. "Skipper, I agree with Underhill. Engels is too immaculate. But he's been chasing skirts and taking home a different tomato every night for three nights running. I've been hiding out in the carport next to his bungalow listening for signs of violence. No such luck. The dames all left in the morning, without a mark on them. I tailed all three of them back to their cars. Engels gives them cab fare to get back to their cars, which were all parked next to cocktail bars. I tailed them all to juke joints in Hollywood. I got the license numbers of the cars the dames got into, in case we need them as witnesses."

"Fine work, Mike," Dudley said, reaching over from his straight-backed chair to give Breuning a fatherly pat on the shoulder. "Dick, lad, what have you to say?"

The cold-eyed, bespectacled Carlisle said resolutely, "All I know is that Engels is a cold-blooded killer and a smart son of a bitch. I say we grab him before he gets smart and knocks off another dame."

Dudley surveyed all of us in the tiny hotel room. "I think we all concur on that, don't you, men?" he said. We all nodded. "Are there any questions then, lads?"

"When do we file our reports with the D.A.?" I asked.

Breuning and Carlisle laughed.

"When Eddie Engels confesses, lad," Dudley said.

"What jail are we booking him into, then?"

Dudley looked to his more experienced underlings for support. They looked at me and shook their heads, then looked back to Dudley in awe.

"Lad, there will be no official police sanctions or paper work until Eddie Engels confesses. Tomorrow morning at five-forty-five A.M., we will rendezvous in front of handsome Eddie's courtyard. I will drive my car. Mike, you will pick up Dick and Freddy. Mike and Dick, you will carry shotguns. Freddy, bring your service revolver. At five minutes of six we will kick in Eddie's door. We will subdue him, and put the fear of God into any colleen or homo who might be sharing his bed, then send them on their way. I

have an interrogation place set up, an abandoned motel in
Gardena. Freddy, Dick, Engels, and I will travel in my car.
Mike will follow in his. This is apt to be a long interrogation, lads, so spend some time with your loved ones tonight and tell them you may not be seeing them for a
while. Now, stand up, lads."

We did, in a little semicircle.

"Now all put your hands on top of mine."

We did.

"Now, lads, say a little silent prayer for our clandestine
operation."

Breuning and Carlisle closed their eyes reverently. I
did, too, for a brief moment. When I opened them I saw
Dudley staring straight ahead past all of us to some distant termination point.

"Amen," he said finally, and winked at me.

Lorna's apartment was a block south of Wilshire near
the Beverly Hills business district, and it was a perfect tes-
tament to her pride and competence; a neat, one-bedroom
affair with subdued, expensive furnishings that reflected
the things she held close—a sense of order and propriety,
and a nonhysterical concern for the great unwashed. The
place was a clearinghouse for her professional interests:
the shelves were crammed with law texts and volumes and
volumes of statute books for both California and the rest of
the nation. There was a big cherry-wood desk placed diagonally into the corner of the living room that held her giant
dictionary as well as scores of official-looking papers separated neatly into four piles.

The apartment was also a clearinghouse for wonder, and
I tingled with pride as Lorna took me on a guided tour and
gave me rundowns on the wonder-filled framed prints that
hung on her walls. There was a Hieronymus Bosch painting that represented insanity—hysterical grotesque creatures in an undersea environment importuning God—or
someone—for release from their madness. There was a
Van Gogh job that featured flowery fields juxtaposed
against brown grass and a somber sky. There was Edward
Hopper's "Nighthawks"—three lonely people sitting in an
all-night diner, not talking. It was awesome and filled with
lonely wonder.

I took Lorna's hand and kissed it. "You know the wonder, Lorna," I said.

"What's the wonder?"

"I don't know, just the wonderful elliptical, mysterious stuff that we're never going to know completely."

Lorna nodded. She knew. "And that's why you're a cop?"

"Exactly."

"But I want justice. The wonder is for artists and writers and other creative people. Their vision gives us the compassion to face our own lives and treat other people decently, because we know how imperfect the world is. But I want justice. I want specifics. I want to be able to look at the people I send to court and say, 'He's guilty, let the will of the people reflect that guilt' or 'He's guilty with mitigating circumstances, let the will of the people reflect the mercy I recommend' or 'He's innocent, no grand jury trial for him.' I want to be able to see the results, not wonder."

We moved to a large, floral-print couch and sat down. Lorna stroked my hair tentatively. "Do you understand, Fred?"

"Yes, I do. Especially now. I want justice for Eddie Engels. He'll get it. But the grand jury system is predicated on people, and people are imperfect and wonder-driven; so justice is no kind of absolute—it's subservient to wonder."

"Which is why I work so hard. Nothing is perfect, even the law."

"Yeah, I know." I paused and fished in my coat pocket for a large manila envelope. "We're arresting Eddie Engels tomorrow, Lorna." I handed her the sealed envelope. "This is my report as the arresting officer."

She looked into my eyes and squeezed my hand. "You look worried," she said.

"I'm not, really. But I need a favor."

"What?"

"Don't open that envelope until I call you. Just forget about this case until I call you. And when Dudley Smith files with you, know this: my report is the truth. If there are discrepancies, see me. *We'll* build the case for the grand jury. All right?"

Lorna hesitated. "All right. You're putting yourself out on a big limb, Freddy."

"I know."

"And you want Engels more for your career than for justice."

"Yes." I said it almost apologetically.

"I don't care. I care about you, and Engels is guilty. You see to your career and I'll see to justice and we'll both get what we want."

I laughed nervously at the imperfect logic of it. Lorna took my hand. "And you're afraid of Dudley Smith."

"He's out of his mind. He's got no business being a policeman."

"Ha! The imperfection, the wonder, remember?"

"Touché, Lorna."

"Where are you booking Engels?"

Lorna saw my face cloud over. "I don't know," I said.

We stared at each other, and I knew she knew. Her whole body stiffened and she painfully hoisted herself to her feet and said, "I'll get dinner started."

Lorna hopped the ten or so steps to the kitchen without her cane. I stayed on the couch. I heard the refrigerator door open and shut and the clatter of cooking utensils being pulled out of cupboards. There was a nervous silence, and when I couldn't take it any longer I went into the kitchen, where Lorna stood leaning against the sink, distractedly fingering a saucepan. I wrenched it out of her hands. She resisted, but I was stronger. I hurled it against the wall where it clattered and fell to the floor. Lorna threw herself at me in a fierce embrace. She pummeled my shoulders with her fists and moaned deeply. I pried her chin from my chest and kissed her, lifting her off her feet. She started to resist, banging my shoulders even harder, but then thought better of it and stopped. I carried her into the bedroom.

Afterward, after the coupling, sated and aware of a new beginning, I started to search for words to make the future right, to make it multiply endlessly on this moment. "About Eddie En—" was all I got out before Lorna pressed gentle fingertips to my mouth to stop me.

"It's all right, Fred. It's all right."

We held each other, and I played with Lorna's big, soft breasts. She held me there, wanting to play mother, but I had other ideas. I kissed my way down her stomach toward the scar tissue that covered her pelvis. Lorna pulled away from me. "No, not there," she said, "next you'll be telling me how you love me for it, and how you love my bad leg. Please, Freddy, not that."

"I just want to see it, sweetheart."

"Why?!"

"Because it's part of you."

Lorna twisted in the darkness. "That's easy for you to say, because you're perfect. When I was a girl, all the boys who wanted to play with my big tits tried to get at them through my leg. It was very ugly. My leg is ugly and my stomach is ugly and I've got no uterus, so I can't have children."

"And?"

"And I used to cover my stomach with a towel when I slept with men so they couldn't touch me there. If there was a way I could have covered my leg I would have done that, too." Lorna started to cry. I kissed away her tears and bit at her neck until she started to laugh.

"Is it Freddy and Lorna now?" I whispered.

"If you want it to be," Lorna said.

"I do."

I got up from the bed and went into the living room. I found the phone and called Mike Breuning at his home. I told him not to pick me up in the morning, that I would meet everyone on Sunset and Horn at the specified time. He gave me an "Oh, you kid" chuckle and hung up.

I went into the kitchen and opened the refrigerator. I found a bag of ice in the freezer compartment and extracted a half-dozen cubes. I walked back to the bedroom. Lorna was lying on her stomach, very still. I approached the bed and dropped the ice cubes onto her shoulders. Lorna shrieked and threw herself backwards.

I leaped onto her, burying my head in the dead flesh of her abdomen. "I love you," I said. "I love you, Lorna, I love you, I love you."

Lorna squirmed and twisted to extricate herself. Her dead leg flopped uselessly in her efforts. I grabbed it and encircled it tightly with both my arms. "I love you, Lorna. I love you, Lorna. I love you. I love you."

Gradually, Lorna relinquished her fight and began to

sob softly. "Oh, Freddy. Oh, Freddy. Oh, Freddy." Then
she pressed both her hands to the back of my head and held
me strongly to that part of herself she hated so terribly.

Morning and dark reality came too quickly.

Lorna had dozed off, nuzzled into my shoulder, but I had
remained awake, savoring the feel of her next to me, but
unable to stop thinking of Eddie Engels and Dudley Smith
and shotguns and justice and my career in the new light of
the woman I loved.

At four-thirty by the luminous dial of Lorna's bedside
alarm clock I gently slid out of her embrace, kissed her
neck and went into the living room to dress.

When I put on my shoulder holster and fingered my
leather encased .38 service revolver I went chilly all over.
Justice, I kept thinking as I drove up to the Sunset Strip,
justice. Justice, not wonder. Not this time.

I barely had time to get coffee before meeting the others
at Sunset and Horn.

Mike Breuning was already there, parked directly in
front of the entranceway to Engels's courtyard. He waved
at me as I parked across the street. I walked over and
we shook hands through the driver's side window. Mike's
badge was pinned to the lapel of his coat, and there was a
pump shotgun beside him on the seat.

"Morning, Fred," he said, "nice day for it."

"Yeah. Where are Dudley and Dick?"

"They're taking a walk around the block. Engels is
alone; Dick tailed him all night. I'm glad for that."

"So am I."

"Are you a little nervous?"

"Maybe a little."

"Well, don't be. Dudley has this thing all worked out."
Breuning craned his head out the window. "Here they
come now," he said. "Pin your badge to your coat."

I did, as Dudley Smith and Dick Carlisle crossed the
street in our direction.

"Freddy, lad," Dudley hailed. "Top of the morning!"

"Good morning, skipper, good morning, Dick," I said.

"Underhill," Carlisle said, blank-faced.

"Well, lad, are you ready?"

"Yes."

"All right, then. Grand. Mike?"

"Ready, Dudley."

"Dick?"

"Ready, boss."

Dudley reached into the back seat of Breuning's car and handed Carlisle a double-barreled 12-gauge. Mike squeezed out his passenger door holding the Ithaca pump. I unholstered my service revolver and Dudley pulled out a .45 automatic from his waistband.

"Now, gentlemen," he said.

We walked rapidly into the courtyard, our weapons pointing to the ground. My heart was beating very fast and I kept stealing sidelong glances at Dudley. His tiny brown eyes were glazed over with something that went far beyond acting. This was the real Dudley Smith.

As we came to Engels's front door I whispered to him, "Let me go in first. I've been here before; I know where the bedroom is."

Dudley nodded assent and motioned Breuning and me to the front. "Kick it in," he hissed.

Mike raised his shotgun to chest level and I held my .38 above my head as we raised right feet in unison and simultaneously kicked the smooth surface. The lock gave way and the door burst inward. I ran straight for the bedroom, my gun in front of me, Smith, Breuning and Carlisle close behind. The bedroom door was open, and in the darkness I could glimpse a shape on the bed.

I flicked on the overhead light, and just as Eddie Engels stirred to life I placed the muzzle of my gun at his temple and whispered, "Police officers! Don't make a move or you're dead."

Engels, his eyes wide with terror, started to scream. Dick Carlisle jumped from behind me onto the bed and twisted his head into his pillow and started to strangle him with it. Breuning was right behind, stripping off the blue silk sheets and yanking Engels's hands behind his back.

"Goddamnit, Freddy, think! Sit on his legs!" Dudley shouted.

I threw myself onto the twisting form and put all my weight on the lower half of Engels's body as Mike managed to apply his handcuffs. Carlisle was still twisting the pillow-encased head of Eddie Engels.

"Stop it, Dick," Dudley screamed, "or you'll kill him!"

Carlisle let go and Engels went inert. We all got off the bed and looked at one another in shock. Dudley had gone red-faced in anger. He bent over and ripped open Engels's purple silk pajama top, placed an ear to his chest and started to laugh. "Ha-ha-ha! He's still alive, lads, thanks to old Dudley. He'll be all right. Let's get him the hell out of here. Now."

Carlisle lifted Engels up, and I slung him over my shoulder. He didn't seem to weigh much. I carried him through the dark apartment and out the door, my three colleagues forming a cordon around me. Covering our tracks, we carefully shut the door behind us. I ran toward my car, the unconscious killer bumping up and down on my back. My heart was beating faster than a trip-hammer and my eyes kept darting in all directions, looking for witnesses to the kidnapping. Dudley threw open the car door and I tossed Engels in a heap into the back seat. He came awake with a stifled scream and Dudley slammed him in the jaw with the butt end of his .45

"Get in back with him, lad," he whispered. I did, pushing Engels headfirst onto the floorboards. Dick Carlisle got in the driver's seat and hit the ignition. Dudley got in the passenger side and said very calmly: "You know where to go, Dick. Freddy, keep handsome Eddie out of sight. Lift his head up so he can breathe. Ahhh, yes. Grand." He reached an arm out the window and gave Mike Breuning the thumbs-up sign. "Gardena, lads," he said.

We took surface streets to the Hollywood Freeway. Mike was right behind us all the way. Dudley and Carlisle talked nonchalantly of major league baseball. I stared at the bloody swollen face of Eddie Engels and inexplicably thought of Lorna.

We took the Hollywood Freeway to Vermont, and Vermont south. As we passed the U.S.C. campus, Engels started to regain consciousness, his lips blubbering in mute terror. I placed a finger to them. "Ssshhh," I said.

We stayed that way, Engels pleading with his eyes, until Dudley craned his head around and said, "How's our friend, lad?"

"He's still unconscious."

"Ahhh, yes. Grand. We'll be there in a few minutes. It's a safe place, deserted. But I don't want to take any chances. When Dick pulls over, you wake Eddie up. Put your badge back in your pocket. Keep your gun out of sight. We're going to walk him in like he's a drunken pal of ours. You got the picture, lad?"

"I've got it."

"Grand."

Eddie Engels and I stared at each other. Some minutes passed. We threaded our way in and around the early morning traffic. When Dick Carlisle stopped the car completely I pretended to wake up Engels. He understood, and played along. "Wake up, Engels," I said. "We're police officers and we aren't going to hurt you. We just want to ask you some questions. Do you understand?"

"Y-yes," Engels said, breathing shallowly.

"Good. Now I'll help you out of the car. You're going to be weak, so hang on to me. Okay?"

"O-okay."

Carlisle and Smith threw open the doors of the car. I pulled Engels into a sitting position on the back seat. I removed his handcuffs and he rubbed his wrists, which had gone almost blue, and started to sob.

"Quiet now," Dudley whispered to him. "We'll have none of that, you understand?"

Engels caught the maniacal look in the big Irishman's face and understood immediately. He looked at me imploringly. I smiled sympathetically, and felt vague power stirrings: if justice was the imperative, and good guy–bad guy was the method of interrogation, then we were already well on our way.

Mike Breuning pulled up in back of us and tooted his horn. I took my eyes off Engels and checked out the surroundings. We were parked in a garbage-strewn alley in back of what looked like a disused auto court.

"Freddy," Dudley said, "you go with Mike and open up the room. Make sure no one's around."

"Right, skipper."

I got out of the car, stretching my cramped legs. Mike Breuning clapped me on the back. He was almost feverish in his excitement and praise of Dudley: "I told you old Dud thought of everything, didn't I? Look at this place," he said, leading me in through a narrow walkway to a one-story L-shaped collection of tiny connected motel rooms, all painted a faded puke green. "This is great, isn't it? The place went under during the war, and the guy who owns it won't sell. He's waiting for the value to go up. It's perfect."

It *was* perfect. Chills briefly overtook me. A perfect impressionist representation of hell: the L-shaped wings fronted by dead brown grass covered with empty short dog bottles and condom wrappers. "Keep Out" signs painted over with obscenities posted every six feet. Dog shit everywhere. A dead, towering palm tree standing sentry, keeping the parking lot of an aircraft plant across the street at bay.

"Yeah, it's perfect," I said to Mike. "Does it have a name?"

"The Victory Motel. You like it?"

"It does have a ring to it."

Mike pointed me toward room number 6. He unlocked the door, and a large rat scurried out. "Here we are," he said.

I surveyed our place of interrogation: a small, perfectly square, putrid-smelling room with a rusted bedstead holding a filthy mattress on bare springs. A desk and two chairs. A cheap oil painting of a clown, unframed, above the bed. A magazine photograph of Franklin D. Roosevelt pinned to a doorway leading into a bathroom where the bathtub and fixtures were covered with rodent droppings. Someone had drawn a Hitler mustache on F.D.R. Mike Breuning pointed to it and giggled.

"Go get our suspect, will you, Mike?" I said. I wanted to be alone, if only for a moment, if only in a hovel like this.

Dudley, Breuning, and Carlisle entered the tiny room a minute later, propelling our pajama-clad suspect in front of them. Carlisle threw Engels down on the bed and handcuffed his hands in front of him. He was trembling and starting to sweat, but I thought I noted the slightest trace of indignation come into his manner as he squirmed to find a comfortable posture on the urine-stained mattress.

He looked up at his four captors hovering over him and said, "I want to call a lawyer."

"That's an admission of guilt, Engels," Carlisle said. "You haven't been charged with anything yet, so don't fret about a shyster until we book you."

"If we book him," I interjected, assuming my role of "good guy" without being told.

"That's right," Mike Breuning said. "Maybe the guy ain't guilty."

"Guilty of what?" Eddie Engels cried out, his voice almost breaking. "I haven't done a goddamned thing!"

"Hush now, son," Dudley said in a fatherly tone. "Just hush. We're here to see to justice. You tell the truth and you'll serve justice—and yourself. You've got nothing to fear, so just hush."

Dudley's softly modulated brogue seemed to have a calming effect on Engels. His whole body seemed to slump in acceptance. He swung his legs over the side of the mattress. "Can I smoke?" he asked.

"Sure," Dudley said, reaching into his back pocket and pulling out a handcuff key. "Freddy, unlock Mr. Engels, will you?"

"Sure, Dud."

I unlocked the bracelets, and Engels smiled at me gratefully. Playing my unassigned role, I smiled back. Dudley tossed him a pack of Chesterfields and a book of matches. Engels's hands shook too badly to get a light going, so I lit his cigarette for him, smiling as I did it. He wolfed in the smoke and smiled back at me.

"Dick, Freddy," Dudley said, "I want you lads to make the run to the liquor store. Eddie, lad, what's your poison?"

Engels looked bewildered. "You mean booze? I'm not much of a drinker."

"Are you not, lad? Barhopper like yourself?"

"I don't mind gin and Coke once in a while."

"Ahhh, grand. Freddy, Dick, you heard the man's order. Hop to it; there's a liquor store down the street."

When we were outside, Carlisle outlined the plan for me. "Dudley says the key word is 'circuitous.' He says it means 'roundabout.' First off we're going to get Engels drunk, get him to talk openly about himself. You're supposed to be with the feds, which means you're an attorney. You and Dudley are going to good guy–bad guy the shit out of him.

We'll keep him up all night, stretch him thin. We've got the room next door all cleaned up. We can take naps there. And don't worry: Dudley's got pals on the Gardena force —they'll leave us alone."

I smiled, again warming to Dudley Smith as a pragmatic wonder broker. "What are you and Mike going to do?"

"Mike's going to take it all down in shorthand, then edit it after Engels confesses. He's a whiz. I'm going to play bad guy along with Dudley."

"What if he doesn't confess?"

"He'll confess," Carlisle said, taking off his glasses and polishing them with his necktie.

When we returned from the liquor store with a quart of cheap gin, three bottles of Coke, and a dozen paper cups, Dudley was regaling Eddie Engels with stories of his life in Ireland around the time of World War I, and Mike Breuning was in the room next door, making sandwiches and brewing coffee.

Mike came into the interrogation room bearing a half-dozen stenographic pads and a fat handful of sharp pencils. He pulled up a chair next to the bed and smiled at Engels. Engels's eyes went back and forth from Mike's affable blond face to his .38 in its shoulder holster. Eddie was putting up a brave front, but he was scared. And curious about how much we knew, of that I was sure. He had killed at least one woman, but was obviously involved in so much illegal activity that he didn't know *why* we had busted him. But he didn't act like a trapped killer—there was an effete arrogance that cut through even his fear. He had sailed on his good looks and charm for some thirty years and obviously considered himself a naturally superior being. His self-sufficient masquerade was about to end, and I wondered if he knew.

Dudley got the proceedings started, banging his huge hands on the little wooden table that held Mike's stenographic pads.

"Mr. Engels," he said, "you are probably wondering exactly who we are, and why we brought you here." He paused and poured gin and Coca-Cola, mixed half and half, into a paper cup and handed it to Engels, who took it and sipped dutifully, dark intelligent eyes glancing around at the four of us.

Dudley cleared his throat and continued. "Let me introduce my colleagues," he said, "Mr. Carlisle, Los Angeles Police Department; Mr. Breuning, of the district attorney's office; I am Lieutenant Dudley Smith of the L.A.P.D.; and this gentleman"—he paused and inclined his head toward me—"is Inspector Underhill of the F.B.I." I almost laughed at my big new promotion, but kept a straight face. "If you have any legal questions, you ask the inspector. He's an attorney, he'll be glad to answer them."

I butted in, somehow wanting to calm Engels before the onslaught of brutality I knew would be coming. "Mr. Engels, you may not know it, but you are acquainted with some people who exist on the edges of the L.A. crime world. We want to question you about these people. Our methods are roundabout, but they work. Just answer our questions and I assure you everything will be all right."

It was a well-informed, ambiguous stab in the dark, and it hit home. Engels believed me. His features relaxed and he gulped the rest of his drink in relief. Dudley poured him another immediately, this one a good two-thirds gin.

Eddie took two healthy slugs of it and when he spoke, his voice had gone down considerably, almost to the baritone range. "What do you want to know?" he asked.

"Tell us about yourself, lad," Dudley said.

"What about me?"

"Your life, lad, past and present."

"Exactly what do you mean, Lieutenant?"

"I mean *everything,* lad."

Engels seemed to consider this. He seemed to draw into his memory, and guzzled his gin and Coke to speed his thought processes.

I looked at my watch. It was 7:00 and already getting hot in the sordid little room. I took off my suit coat and rolled up my shirtsleeves. I felt tired, having gone more than twenty-four hours without sleep. Almost as if in answer, Mike Breuning switched on a portable fan and handed me a cup of lukewarm coffee. Dudley poured Engels a cupful of pure gin.

"Your life story, lad," he said. "We're all dying to hear it."

"Mom and Dad were good people," Eddie began, his voice taking on the stentorian tone of one explaining profound intrinsic truth. "They still are, I guess. I'm from Seattle. Mom and Dad were born in Germany. They came here before the First World War. They—"

"Were you a happy youngster, Eddie?" Dudley interrupted.

Engels sipped his gin, wincing slightly at the full-strength bitterness. "Sure, sure, I was a happy kid. A good sport. An ace gent. I had a dog, I had a treehouse, I had a bike. Dad was a good guy. He never hit me. He was a pharmacist. He never sent Ma or me to the doctor. He fixed us up with this stuff from the pharmacy. Sometimes it had dope in it. Once Ma took some and had these religious hallucinations. She said she saw Jesus walking Miffy—that's another dog we had who got run over. She said Miffy could talk and wanted her to become a Catholic and work at this pet cemetery outside of town. Dad never gave Ma any more of the stuff after that; he hated Catholics. Dad was an ace guy with me but he was tough as nails with my sister, Lillian. He wouldn't let her date guys, he was always prowling around this flower shop where she worked to make sure no mashers were trying to date her. Dad was an old-fashioned Kraut. He hated guys who chased tail. He didn't want me to chase tail, he wanted me to marry some Kraut bimbo and go to pharmacist school."

Engels paused and downed the rest of his gin. His body shook and I could see that he was getting drunk, smiling crookedly, his face glazing over with sentiment. Dudley refilled his cup.

"But you wanted to chase tail, right, Eddie?" I said.

Engels laughed and guzzled gin. "Right," he slurred, "and I wanted out of that fucking dead-dog town, Seattle. Nothing but rain and dead dogs and pharmacies and ugly tail. U-u-u-gly! Woo! I had the best tail Seattle had to offer and it was worse than the lowest piece of Hollywood ass. U-u-ugly!"

"So you moved to L.A.?" Mike interjected.

"Fuck, no! The fucking Japs bombed Pearl Harbor and I

got drafted. The navy. Dad said I looked like Donald Duck in my uniform. I said he looked like Mickey Mouse in that smock he wore at the pharmacy. He didn't want me to go. He tried to fix it so I could stay in Seattle. He tried to hand the appeals board this hardship caper, but it didn't work. But Dad got poetic justice. They made me a pharmacist's mate. He called me Doctor Duck."

Eddie Engels doubled over with laughter on the mattress, then jolted up and vomited on the floor, his head between his knees, his hands hanging limply by his sides. He had knocked over his glass of gin, and when he looked up he banged a drunken hand all over the mattress looking for it. He found the glass on the floor in a pool of vomit, picked it up and waved it at Dudley.

"Gimme a refill, Lieutenant. Pharmacist's Mate Engels, 416-8395 requests a fucking drink on the double!"

Dudley gladly obliged him, this time filling the glass half-full. Engels grabbed it and bolted the liquid, falling back onto the mattress and muttering, "Lotsa tail, lotsa tail," before he passed out.

Eddie Engels woke up some six hours later, panicked and dehydrated to the bone. His eyes were feverish and his voice tremulous and raspy.

Dudley had outlined his plan while Engels was passed out: good guy–bad guy, with modifications. He had gotten a list of known bookmakers, homosexuals, and fences from the dicks at Hollywood Division, figuring Engels would have to know some of them. Throwing these names at Eddie would keep him from guessing why he was really in custody. It sounded like a good, if time-consuming, plan. I had rested during the afternoon and was up for it. But I wanted it to be over, and fast: I wanted to be with Lorna.

As Engels came awake, Mike Breuning was just returning with two big paper bags stuffed with hamburgers, French fries, and coffee in paper cups. We dug in and ignored our prisoner on the mattress.

"I have to go to the bathroom," he said meekly. No one answered him. He tried again. "I have to go to the bathroom." We ignored him again. "I said I have to go to the bathroom!" This time his panicked voice intoned upward sharply.

"Then go to the bathroom, for Christ's sake!" Dudley bellowed.

Engels got up from his resting place and wobbled into the filthy lavatory. We could hear the sound of him vomiting into the toilet bowl, then running water and urinating. He came came back a moment laer, having discarded his vomit-soaked pajama top. His lean, muscular torso had been given a quick washing. He shivered in the late afternoon heat of the smelly little room.

"I'm ready to answer your questions, officers," he said. "Please let me answer them so I can go home."

"Shut up, Engels," Dudley said. "We'll get to you when we're damn good and ready."

"Ease off, Lieutenant," I said. "Don't worry, Mr. Engels, we'll be right with you. Would you like a hamburger?" Engels shook his head and stared at us.

We finished our dinner. Dick Carlisle announced that he was going for a walk, and got up and left the room. Mike, Dudley, and I arranged three chairs around the mattress. Engels had backed himself up against the wall. He sat Indian-style, with his hands jammed under his knees to control their trembling. We took our seats facing him and stared at him for a long moment before Dudley spoke: "Your name?"

Our prisoner cleared his throat: "Edward Engels."

"Your address?"

"1911 Horn, West Hollywood."

"Your age?"

"Thirty-two."

"Your occupation?"

Engels hesitated. "Real estate liaison," he said.

"What the hell is a 'real estate liaison'?" Dudley barked. Engels groped for words. "Come on, man!" Dudley shouted.

"Ease off, Lieutenant," I said. "Mr. Engels, would you explain your duties in that capacity?"

"I . . . I . . . uh, help close real estate deals."

"Which entails?" I asked.

"Which entails fixing up buyers with real estate people."

"I see. Well, could you—"

Dudley cut in. "Horseshit, Inspector. This guy is a

known gambler. I've got reports on him from bookies all over Hollywood. In fact, I've got several witnesses who say he's a bookie himself."

"That's not true," Engels cried. "I bet the ponies, but I don't book any action with bookies or make book myself, and I'm clean with the cops! I've got no criminal record!"

"The hell you say, Engels! I know better!"

I raised my hands and called for order. "That's enough! That's enough from both of you! Now, Mr. Engels, betting the horses is not illegal. Lieutenant Smith just got carried away because he hasn't picked any winners lately. Would you call yourself a winning gambler?"

"Yes, I'm a winner."

"Do you earn more at gambling than at your real estate job?"

Engels hesitated. "Yes," he said.

"Do you list these winnings on your income tax returns?" I asked.

"Uh . . . no."

"What did you file as your total income on this year's return?"

"I don't know."

"What about 1950?"

"I don't know."

"1949?"

"I don't know."

"1948?"

"I don't remember."

"1947?"

"I don't know!"

"1946?"

"I don't . . . I was in the navy then . . . I forget."

Dudley butted in: "You do pay income tax, don't you, Engels?"

Engels hung his head between his legs. "No," he said.

"You realize that income tax evasion is a federal crime, don't you, Engels?" Dudley continued, pressing.

"Yes."

"I pay income tax, so does the inspector, so do all good law-abiding citizens. What the hell makes you so special that you think you don't have to?"

"I don't know."

"Ease off, Lieutenant," I said. "Mr. Engels wants to co-operate. Mr. Engels, I'm going to name some people. Tell me of your association with them."

Engels nodded dumbly. Dudley handed me a carefully typed slip of paper broken down into three columns headed: "Gamblers," "Bookmakers," and "Hollywood Vice offenders." I started with the gamblers. Mike Breuning got out his steno pad and poised his pencil over it. Dudley lit a cigarette for himself and one for Engels, who accepted it gratefully.

"Okay, Mr. Engels, listen carefully: James Babij, Leslie 'Scribe' Thomas, James Gillis, Walter Snyder, Willard Dolphine. Any of those names sound familiar?"

Engels nodded confidently. "Those guys are high rollers, big spenders at Santa Anita. Entrepreneurs, you know what I mean?"

"Yes. Are you intimate with any of them?"

"What do you mean 'intimate'?" Engels narrowed his eyes suspiciously.

"I mean have you gambled with any of these men? Have you entertained any of them in your home?"

"Oh, no. I just see those guys at the track, maybe they buy me a drink at the Turf Club, maybe I buy them one. That kind of thing."

"All right," I said, smiling and going to the list of the bookies. "William Curran, Louis Washington, 'Slick' Dellacroccio, 'Zoomer' Murphy, Frank Deffry, Gerald 'Smiler' Chamales, Bruno Earle, Duane 'The Brain' Tucker, Fred 'Fat Man' Vestal, Mark 'The Gimp' McGuire. Ring any bells, Mr. Engels?"

"Lotsa bells, Inspector. Those bimbos are all West L.A. handbooks. Cocktail lounge sharpies. Mark 'The Gimp' pimps nigger broads on the side. They're all small potatoes, strictly from nowhereville." Engels smiled at his captors cockily. He was starting to feel confident of our purpose. All three of us gave him a deadpan. It made him nervous. "Freddy Vestal pushes reefers, I heard talk," he blurted out.

I gave Engels a winning smile. "All right now, let's try these: Pat Morneau, 'Scooter' Coleman, Jack Foster, Lawrence Brubaker, Al Bay, Jim Waldleigh, Brett Caldwell, Jim Joslyn."

Engels went ashen-faced. He swallowed several times, and, recovering quickly, threw out a smile that was pure charm, pure bravado. "Don't know those guys, Inspector, sorry."

Dudley went on the attack, saying very softly, "Do you know who those men are, Engels?"

"No."

"Those men are known degenerates—pansies, sissies, nancy boys, queers, homos, faggots, pederasts, and punks. They all have long rap sheets with the vice squads of every police agency in L.A. County. They all frequent queer bars in West Hollywood. Places we know you frequent, Engels. Half of those men have identified you from photographs. Half—"

"What photographs?!" Engels screeched. "I'm clean! I ain't got a police record. This is all a lie! This is—"

I entered the fray: "Mr. Engels, just let me ask you once, for our official records: are you homosexual?"

"Fuck, no!" Eddie Engels practically screamed.

"All right. Thank you."

"Inspector," Dudley said calmly, "I don't buy it. We know for a fact that he's tight with this homo, Lawrence Brubaker. We know—"

"Larry Brubaker was an old navy buddy! We were stationed together at the Long Beach yard during the war!" Engels was sweating, his face and torso were popping sweat from every pore. I handed him a glass of water. He gulped it down in one second flat, then looked to me for support.

"I believe you," I said. "You used to live near his bar in Venice, right?"

"Right! With a woman. I was shacked with her. I tell you I dig women. Ask Janet, she'll tell you!"

"Janet?" I asked innocently.

"Janet Valupeyk. She's the dame I do the real estate gig with. She'll tell you. We shacked together for two years, she'll tell you."

"All right, Mr. Engels."

"Not all right, Inspector," Dudley said, his voice rising in pitch and timbre, "not all right at all. We have witnesses who place this degenerate at known queers bars like the Hub, the Black Cat, Sergio's Hideaway, the Silver

Star, the Knight in Armor, and half the homo hangouts in
the Valley."

"No, no, no!" Engels was shaking his head frantically in
denial.

I raised my voice and glared sternly at Dudley. "This
time you've gone too far, Lieutenant. You've been badly
misinformed. The Silver Star isn't a homosexual hangout—I've been there myself, many times. It's just a conge-
nial neighborhood cocktail lounge."

Engels grabbed at what he thought was a life raft.
"That's right! I been there myself, lotsa times."

"To place bets?" I interjected.

"Hell no, to chase tail. I picked up lots of good stuff
there." Unaware that he was hanging himself, Engels
rambled on, squirming on the now sweat-drenched mattress. "I scored in half the juke joints in Hollywood. Queer,
shit! Somebody's been feeding you guys the wrong dope!
I'm a veteran. Larry Brubaker's queer, but I just used him,
borrowed money from him. He didn't try no queer stuff
with me! You ask Janet. You ask her!" Engels was
addressing all his remarks to me now. It was obvious he
considered me his savior. Out of the corner of my eye I saw
Dudley draw his finger across his throat.

"Mr. Engels," I said, "let's take a break for a while,
shall we? Why don't you take a rest?"

Engels nodded. I went into the bathroom and wet a paper napkin in the sink. I tossed it to him and he swabbed
his face and upper body with it.

"Rest, Eddie," I said, smiling down at the handsome
killer.

He nodded again and hid his face in his hands.

"I'm going for a walk," I announced to Dudley and Mike
Breuning. I grabbed a container of cold coffee and a cold
hamburger and walked outside.

A Santa Ana wind had come up, and the shabby front
lawn was littered with a fresh array of debris. Palm fronds
had blown out onto the sidewalk. The wind had cleared all
traces of smog from the air, and the twilight sky was a
pure light blue tinged with the remnants of a pink sun.

I tried to eat my burger, but it was too greasy and cold,
and my nervous stomach balked. I threw the sandwich to

the ground and sipped my coffee, pondering the rituals of justice.

Dudley came out a minute later. "Our friend is asleep, lad," he said. "Mike slipped him a Mickey Finn. He'll wake up in about four hours or so with a devilish headache. Then I'll go to work on him."

"Where's Carlisle?"

"He's going through handsome Eddie's apartment. He should be back soon. How do you feel, lad?"

"Expectant. Anxious for it to be over."

"Soon, lad, soon. I'm going to have at that monster for a good long time. You stay out until I take off my necktie. Then you intervene. Meet force with force, lad, be it verbal or physical. Do you follow?"

"Yes."

"Ahhh, grand. You are a brilliant young policeman, Freddy. Do you know that?"

"Yes, I do."

"I've wanted a protégé like you for a long time, lad. Mike and Dick are good cops, but they've got no brains, no imagination. You have a spark, a brilliant one."

"I know."

"Then why do you look so glum?"

"I'm wondering how I'll like the detective bureau."

"You'll like it fine. It's the cream of the department. Now get some rest."

I went into the room adjoining the interrogation room and lay down on a saggy army cot that was a good half foot too short for me. I got up and walked to the bathroom. It was relatively clean; almost clean enough to use. I looked at myself in the cracked mirror above the sink. I needed a shave and hadn't thought to bring a razor.

I lay back down on my cot. Exhaustion grabbed me before I could remove my shoes or shoulder holster. I fought sleep for brief moments, managing to mutter, "Lorna, Lorna, Lorna" until sleep triumphed.

I awoke to someone jostling me. I bolted upright and went for my gun. Dick Carlisle materialized and pinned my arms. The light from the overhead bulb was glinting off his steel-rimmed spectacles.

I swung my legs over the edge of the cot and suddenly realized that I didn't like Carlisle. There was something sullen and animalistic about him. And he was plainly keyed up.

"Look at this," he said, digging into his coat pocket and pulling out Maggie Cadwallader's diamond brooch.

"Jesus!" I said. "Where the hell did you get that? Is it real?"

"Dudley says so. He knows a lot about this kind of stuff, and he says it's legit. I found it at Engels's apartment hidden away in a tie rack."

"Jesus," I said, feigning awe, my wheels turning. "Jesus. When I searched the Cadwallader dame's apartment, I found a little photograph of her. She was wearing a brooch just like this one!"

"Christ, Underhill! What did you do with it?"

"I lost it when I had the newspaper photo reprinted."

"Shit. I'll tell Dudley."

Carlisle disappeared through the door that connected the two rooms, and I busied myself throwing water on my face and combing my hair. When I entered the interrogation room Dick Carlisle was slapping Eddie Engels awake, and Dudley and Mike Breuning were huddled in conversation. Seeing me, Dudley waved me toward him.

"Freddy, you're sure you saw a brooch like this one in that photograph you found?" He held it up for me to see.

"I'm positive, Dud."

"Grand, another confirmation. You sit back, lad. Remember your cue."

Carlisle went back to rousing Engels. "Wake up, wake up, you goddamned degenerate!" he shouted, then gave up in frustration, and stripped his belt from his trousers and lashed it across Eddie's bare back.

Engels, coming out of his doped stupor, curled himself into a fetal ball, his arms covering his face. "No, don't hit me, you can have it. You can have it all, don't hit me!" he shrieked.

Carlisle shrieked back: "We want the truth, you homo! The truth!"

"I'm not a homo!"

"Prove it!" Carlisle flailed Engels again with his belt.

The heavy brass buckle catch ripped shreds of flesh loose from his shoulder blades, and Eddie threw himself onto his back to protect himself.

Dudley wrenched the belt from Carlisle and wrapped it around his broad right fist. "Ask Janet!" Eddie pleaded.

"I did, lad. Shall I tell you what she said?"

Engels faltered. "Tell me," he whispered.

Dudley Smith moved to the bed, picked up Engels under his arms and threw him across the room. He landed in a wild tangle of arms and legs and screamed. I gasped at the feat of strength. Dudley walked to Engels and jerked him to his feet with his left hand, then slammed a leather-encased right hand into his stomach. Engels screamed again, and doubled over, still held erect by the hand Dudley had dug into his shoulder.

"Janet told me that you were a dirty, cock-sucking degenerate," Dudley said, "who spurned her bed for the bed of a muscle-bound nancy boy. Is that true, Eddie?"

"No!"

"No?" Dudley dug his hand into Engels's shoulder until little geysers of blood shot out. "No, Eddie?"

Eddie Engels screamed, "No!"

"No?"

"No!"

"No?" Blood was trickling down Engels's chest, combining with his sweat. Dudley gritted his teeth and dug his hand in full force. "No?" he screeched, his brogue almost breaking. He released his hand and Engels fell to his knees, sobbing.

"Yes," he blubbered.

"Good, lad. Now answer a few more questions for me. Do you pay income tax?"

"No."

"Ahhh, yes. Do you take bets on the ponies?"

"Yes." Engels pawed at his shoulder. It was a giant purple swelling with deep puncture wounds.

"Get to your feet, lad," Dudley said. Engels managed to bring himself upright, and Dudley swung a huge roundhouse right at his midsection. Engels stifled a scream and fell to the floor, clutching his stomach. "More questions, lad. Janet told me you hit her. Is that true?"

"No!" Engels elbowed his way toward the wall, drawing his arms protectively over his head. "No! No! No! No!" he shrieked, drawing himself tighter into a ball with each screaming repeat of the word.

Dudley smiled menacingly. "No?"

"Yes," Engels said softly.

"Ahhh, grand. Did you hit her often, lad?"

"Yes."

"And other women?"

"Yes."

"Why? You filthy scum-sucker!"

"I . . . I . . . I don't know!"

"You . . . don't . . . know." Dudley tried the words on his palate like a connoisseur tasting a fine wine. "Tell me about the muscle boy, lad."

I looked around the room. Dick Carlisle was sipping a beer by the bathroom door, Mike Breuning was writing rapidly on his steno pad, and Dudley Smith was inching himself slowly toward the prostrate form of Eddie Engels. He squatted next to him and said softly, "Do you believe in God, lad?"

Engels nodded his head. "Yes."

"Then don't you think God wants you to be rid of your guilt, like a good believer?"

"Yes . . ." Engels said, his voice surprisingly calm.

"Good, lad. Tell me about the muscle boy."

"His name was Jerry. I met him at Larry's Log Cabin. He was on dope. He needed help and I helped him."

"Did he like to hit women, too?"

"No!"

"Did the two of you prowl for lonely young women to beat up, then go home and commit sodomy with each other?"

"No! Please God, no, please God!" Engels wailed.

Dudley reached behind him and grabbed his arms and pulled him to his feet. Engels pliably submitted and stared at him impassively, until Dudley's right hand crashed into his solar plexus. He vomited, spraying a gush of pink goo that smelled like gin onto Dudley's shirtfront. Dudley's face contorted and his whole body twitched, but he just stood there, staring down at the woman-killer he hated so much.

There was complete silence in the room. Nobody moved.
Engels remained perfectly still on the floor, arms wrapped
around his devastated midsection. There was a straight-
backed wooden chair directly behind him. Dudley lifted
Engels into it. He pulled up another chair for himself and
drew it up so that his knees almost touched Eddie's.

"Now, Eddie, we know that you like to hit women, don't
we?"

"Y-yes."

"A handsome lad like yourself has no trouble finding
young ladies, isn't that true? You said you go to cocktail
bars. Is that correct?"

"Yes."

"And you pick up young ladies there?"

"Uh . . . I . . . yes."

"For what purpose?"

"What? To fuck. To sleep with. I'm no fag!"

"Easy, lad. We know you like boys."

"No! No!"

Dudley slapped him.

"No, no, no, no!" he continued.

Dudley slapped him again, this time harder. Blood was
flowing out of his nose, dripping into his mouth. He licked
it off his lips and started to cry. Dudley sighed and handed
Engels a handkerchief. "Maybe you aren't queer, lad.
Maybe you do like tail. After all, the inspector said he saw
you at that place, what was the name of it? The Silver
Star? That place is no homo hangout."

Engels started to shake his head, spraying Dudley with
blood and sweat. "I'm no fag. I've had more tail than any
cop in L.A."

"Tell me about it, Eddie," Dudley said, lighting him a
cigarette and placing it between his lips.

The cocky ladies' man came briefly to life, cutting
through all his terror and fatigue. "They love me, they
can't leave me alone. I'm a virtuoso. I just snap my fingers.
Every bartender in Hollywood knows me—"

Dudley interrupted: "The barman at the Silver Star
says you're a sissy. He says you hate women. You hate
them, so you fuck them to make them like you, then you
hurt them, right, Eddie? Right, Eddie? Right, Eddie,
right? Queer, cock-sucking Eddie, Right . . . ?"

Engels threw himself on Dudley, knocking his chair over and falling on top of him, trying to smother him with his battered body. Breuning and Carlisle watched for stunned seconds, then ran over and grabbed Eddie by his flailing arms and legs and pinned him against the wall. Engels was screaming as Dick Carlisle began to slam him with both fists in the groin and rib cage. Breuning mashed his face into the wall until Engels bit into the palm of his hand. Breuning screamed and backed off, and Carlisle wrapped his hands around Engels's neck and started to choke him. Engels relinquished Breuning's hand and started to make gurgling sounds.

I jumbed up and grabbed Carlisle by the shoulders, flinging him backward onto the mattress. Breuning was trying to get at Engels with his good hand, holding his bitten one between his legs to stanch the pain. I flattened myself against Engels, trying to push the two of us through the wall to another reality. Breuning pulled at my shoulders.

Finally Dudley screamed, "Stop it, all of you. Stop it. Stop it now!"

Breuning let go of me. I moved away from Engels, who fell to the floor, unconscious.

"You filthy traitor," Carlisle hissed at me. I advanced toward him, my fists cocked.

Dudley planted himself in front of me. "No, lad."

I flopped down into the chair that had held Engels. I was exhausted and shaking from head to foot. Breuning, Carlisle, Dudley, and I all stared at one another in ugly silence.

Finally Dudley smiled. He drew a hypodermic needle and a little vial out of his pants pocket. He inserted the needle into the vial and drew out some clear liquid, then knelt beside the unconscious Engels, checked his pulse, nodded and stuck the needle into his arm just above the elbow. He pushed the plunger and held it in for a few seconds, then lifted Engels onto the mattress.

"He'll sleep," Dudley said. "He needs it. You men do, too. We all do. So rest, lads. We'll start over in the morning."

We did. Fueled by a night's sleep—mine fitful, Engels's drugged—we began at nine o'clock the following day. Dudley had roused me at seven-thirty, presenting me with a razor and a fresh short-sleeved shirt. The ritual of shaving and bathing restored me somewhat.

I was still shocked by what had happened. Dudley knew it, and assuaged my fears. "No more violence, lad. He can't take much more. I've sent Dick Carlisle home; he might get carried away. We'll play it kid gloves from here on in." All I could do was nod dumbly. I couldn't even try to play protégé to the insane Irishman—he was a loathsome object to me now.

I walked down the street to a diner that served a boisterous, good-humored aircraft-worker clientele. The rough-hewn camaraderie of the men who sat beside me at the counter restored me further. I ate a big breakfast of sausage, eggs, and potatoes, chased by about a gallon of coffee. I bought a triple order of poached eggs and two chocolate malts for Eddie Engels. Ordering it boxed "to go" made me sad and angry. This was beyond the bailiwick of wonder and justice, reaching toward some kind of knowledge of the human condition that for once I didn't want to know.

There was a pay phone at the back of the diner. I almost gave in to an impulse to call Lorna, but didn't. I wanted it to be over first.

When I got back to the room, Eddie Engels was still passed out on the filthy mattress, his face contorted in terror even in repose.

Dudley, Breuning, and I watched him wake up. For long moments he didn't seem to know where he was. Finally, his brain clicked into reality, and when his eyes focused on Dudley he began to twitch spastically, shutting his eyes and trying to scream. No sound came out.

Dudley and I looked at each other. Mike Breuning fiddled with his steno pad, his eyes downcast, ashamed. I motioned to Dudley. He followed me into the adjoining room. "Let me have him," I said. "He's too terrified of you. Let me talk to him. Alone. I'll bring him around."

"I want a confession, lad. Today."

"You'll have it."

"I'll give you two hours, lad. No more."

I led Engels gently into the other room. I told him he could take his time using the halfway clean bathroom. He did, closing the door behind him. I waited while Engels cleaned himself up. He came back out and sat down on the edge of one of the cots. His torso was badly bruised, and the welt on his shoulder where Dudley had dug in his fingers had swollen to the size of an orange.

I lit him a cigarette and handed it to him. "Are you scared, Eddie?" I asked.

He nodded. "Yeah, I'm real scared."

"Of what?"

"Of that Irish guy."

"I don't blame you."

"What do you want? I'm just a small-time gambler."

"And an abuser of women." He lowered his head. "Look at me, Eddie." He raised his head and met my eyes. "Have you hurt a lot of women, Eddie?" He nodded. "Why?" I asked.

"I don't know!"

"How long have you been doing this?"

"A long time."

"Before you left Seattle?"

"I . . . yes."

"Do your parents know about it?"

"No! Leave them out of this!"

"Sssshhh. Do you love your parents?"

Engels snorted, then looked at me as if I were crazy. "Everyone loves their parents," he said.

"Everyone who knows them. I never knew mine. I grew up in an orphanage."

"That's so sad. That's really sad. Is that why you became a cop, so you could track them down?"

"I never thought about it. You're a lucky fellow, though, to have a nice family."

Engels nodded, his frightened features softening for a moment.

"Are you close to your sister, Lillian?" I asked. Engels didn't answer. "Are you?" Still no response. "Are you, Eddie?"

Engels's face went beet red. "I hate her!" he screamed. "I hate her, I hate her, I hate her!" He slammed his hands into the edge of the cot in frustration. The outburst was over as quickly as it had started, but Eddie's personality had changed again. "I . . . hate . . . Lillian." He said it very softly, with great finality, one word at a time.

"Did she hit you, Eddie?" I asked.

A shake of the head in answer.

"Did she make fun of you?"

No response.

"Did she have power over you?"

"Yes," Engels whimpered. He bit his lip.

"What did she do to you?" I said gently.

Eddie Engels said, quite calmly: "She brought me out. She was lez and she didn't want me to love any other girls but her."

"And?" I whispered.

"And she dressed me up, and made me up . . ."

"And?"

"And . . . fixed me up, and made me do her in front of her girlfriend . . ." Engels's sad voice trailed off.

I cleared my throat. My own voice sounded strange and disembodied. "And you hate her for it?"

"And I hate her for what she made me, Officer. But I love her, too. And I'd rather be what I am than be what *you* are."

His words hung in the air, poisonous, like atomic fallout. I handed Engels the paper sack containing the eggs and malted milks. "Eat your breakfast," I said. "Rest for a little while, and soon you'll find out why we brought you here."

Making sure the windowless room was locked from the outside, I left Engels alone to contemplate my threat, then went and reported to Dudley Smith.

"You should have been a headshrinker, lad," was his only comment.

At one-thirty that afternoon we brought Eddie Engels back into the interrogation room. He was fed and rested, but looked weary and ready to accept anything. I sat him down on the mattress, and Dudley, Breuning, and I arranged our chairs, allowing him nothing to look at but three oversized cops. Dudley placed an ashtray, matches, and an open pack of Chesterfields on the mattress next to him. Engels helped himself, warily.

Dudley kicked it off: "Of course you know what this is all about, don't you, Engels?"

Engels gulped and shook his head. "No," he said.

"Lad, were you living on Twenty-ninth and Pacific in Venice in March of 1948?"

"Y-yes," Engels said.

"A young woman was found strangled to death two blocks from the house you shared with Janet Valupeyk. Did you kill her?"

Engels went white and screamed, "No!"

"Her name was Karen Waters. She was twenty-two."

"I said, no!"

"Very well. I have here the names of two other young women, lonely young women who met untimely deaths by strangulation. Answer if the names ring a bell, will you, lad? Mary Peterson?"

"No!"

"Jane Macauley?"

"I said, no!"

Dudley sighed, feigning exasperated patience: "So you did," he said. "Well, lad, Janet Valupeyk says otherwise. She positively identified all three of those dead women as conquests of yours. She remembers them well. She—"

"She couldn't have! Janet was a hophead! She was on dope all the time we lived together—"

Dudley swung his hand in a quick arc, catching Engels on the cheek. Stunned, Engels just stared at him like a reprimanded child.

"I thought you picked up lots of women, lad."

"I did. I mean, I do."

"Then how do you know you didn't pick up one of these women?"

"I . . . I don't . . ."

"Have you killed that many, Eddie?"

"I never killed any—"

Dudley swung his open hand, this time harder, opening up facial cuts inflicted the night before. Engels flailed his arms but remained in a sitting position. His face had shown uncomprehending fear and anger, but now it moved into outright grief. He knew we were closing in.

"Leona Jensen, remember her?" Dudley asked.

Engels hung his head and shook it. Dudley loosened his tie. I moved to the mattress.

"I called Seattle this morning," I said. "I talked to your

dad. I told him we suspected you of killing five women. He said you didn't have it in you. He said you were a good boy. I believed him, and I believe you. But Lieutenant Smith doesn't. I've told him that there's no hard evidence to link you to those women he mentioned. I think there's only one case against you, and I think we can close that one out if you answer the lieutenant's questions truthfully."

Engels took his chin off his chest and looked at me dolefully, like a dog waiting to be praised or hit. When he spoke his voice had gone effete again: "Did you really talk to Dad?"

"Yes."

"What did he say?"

"That he loves you. That your mother loves you, that Lillian loves you most of all."

"Oh, God . . ." Engels started to sob.

Dudley spoke up. "All righty, *Mr.* Engels. Does the name Margaret Cadwallader mean anything to you?"

Eddie's whole face started to spasm. He brought his voice down to baritone and said, "No," tremulously.

"No? We have a dozen eyewitnesses who placed the two of you together at the racetrack and at nightclubs on the Sunset Strip."

Engels shook his head frantically.

"The truth, Eddie," I said. "For your family's sake."

"We da-dated," Engels said.

"But you broke up?" I continued for him.

"Y-yes."

"Why, killer?" Dudley bellowed. "Because she wouldn't let you hit her?"

"I never killed anybody!"

"Nobody said you killed her, homo! Did you hit her?"

"I didn't wa— she wasn't . . ."

"You didn't what? You fucking degenerate!" Dudley reached his arm back and swung it at Engels in slow motion.

I caught it in mid-swing, grabbing Dudley's wrist and holding it above my head. "I told you no more of that, Smith!"

"Goddamnit, Inspector, this punk is guilty and I know it!"

"I'm not so sure. Eddie, one thing troubles me. Your Ford convertible was seen parked on Margaret Cadwallader's street on the night she was strangled."

Engels moaned, "Oh, God."

I continued: "What was it doing there?"

"I . . . lent it to her."

"How did you get it back?" Dudley interjected.

"I . . . I . . ."

"Did you ever fuck her at her apartment, lover-boy?" Dudley bellowed.

"No!"

"That's funny, we got your fingerprints from her bedroom."

"That's a lie! I never been fingerprinted!"

"You're the liar, lover-boy. You were fingerprinted when the Ventura cops raided a homo hangout you were drinking at."

"*That's* a lie!"

Dudley went into a laughing attack. Perfectly modulated, his musical laughter rose and fell, diminuendoed and crescendoed like a Stradivarius in the hands of a master. "Ho-ho-ho! Ha-ha-ha!" Tears were streaming down his red face. It went on and on while Engels, Breuning, and I stared at him, dumbstruck. Finally, Dudley's laughter metamorphosed into a huge, expansive yawn. He looked at Breuning. "Mike, lad, I think it's time to set lover-boy straight, don't you?"

"Yes, I do, Lieutenant."

With all eyes on him, Dudley Smith dug into his coat pocket and pulled out Maggie Cadwallader's diamond brooch. There was absolute stillness in the sordid little room. Dudley smiled demonically and Eddie Engels's face broke out into a network of throbbing blue veins. He placed his head in his hands and sat very still.

"Do you know where we got that, Eddie?" I asked.

"Yes," he said, his voice gone high.

"Did you get it from Margaret Cadwallader?"

"Yes."

"Did you pay for it?"

Engels stated to laugh—high, feminine laughter. "Baby, did I pay for it! Oh, baby! Pay and pay and pay!" he shrieked.

Dudley butted in: "I'd say Margaret paid for it, lover-boy—with her life. You beat 'em, you kill 'em—and now you steal from 'em. Do you desecrate their corpses, lover-boy?"

"No!"

"You just kill them?"

"Ye— No!"

"What were you going to do with that brooch, you filth? Give it to your lezbo sister?"

"Aaarrugh!" Engels screeched.

"Did your unholy sister teach you to eat cunt, lover-boy? Did you hate her for it? Is that why you hate women? Did she piss on you? Did she make you lap her on your knees? Is that why you kill women?"

"Yes, yes, yes, yes, yes," Engels screamed, his voice a shrieking, cacophonous soprano. "Yes, yes, yes, yes, yes!"

Dudley threw himself on Engels, lifted him from the bed and slammed his back repeatedly into the wall. "Tell me how you did it, killer! Tell me how you croaked lovely Margaret and we won't tell your mommy and daddy about the others. Tell me!"

Engels went limp as a rag doll in Dudley's hands. When Dudley finally released him he crumpled to the bed and moaned hideously.

Dudley pointed to the bathroom. I followed him in. There was a giant cockroach crawling out of the filthy bathtub. "Cock-sucking cockroaches," he said. "They sneak into your bed at night and suck your blood. Dirty cocksuckers." He bent down and let the bug crawl onto his hand, then he closed his fist around it and squashed it into a greenish-yellow pulp. He rubbed the oozy remains on his trouser leg and said to me: "He's about to crack, lad."

"I know that," I said.

"You'll be the one to give him the final push."

"How?"

"He likes you. He's queer for you. His voice goes queer whenever you're close to him. You're his savior, but you're about to become his Judas. When I loosen my tie, I want you to hit him." I looked into Dudley's mad brown eyes and hesitated. "It's the only way, lad."

"I . . . I can't."

"You can and you will, Officer," Dudley hissed in my

face. "I've had enough pretty-boy prima donnaism from you! You want a piece of this collar and you'll crack that fucking pervert in the face, hard! Do you understand, Underhill?"

I went cold all over. "Yes," I said.

We reassembled in the little room that now looked as battered as Eddie Engels himself. Dudley gestured to Mike Breuning's steno pad: "Every word, Mike."

"Right, skipper."

I brought Engels a glass of water. Knowing what I had to do, I didn't compound it by being nice to him. I just handed him the water, and when he gave me a smile, I gave him a deadpan in return.

"All right, Engels," Dudley said. "You admit to knowing Margaret Cadwallader?"

"Yes."

"And being intimate with her?"

"Yes."

"And hitting her?"

"No, I couldn't. She . . . look, I could turn snitch for you." Eddie tried desperately. "I know lots of people I could turn over. Dope addicts, pushers. I know some stuff from my navy time."

Dudley slapped him. "Hush, handsome Eddie. It's almost over now. We're going to fly your lovely sister, Lillian down here. She wants to talk to you about lonely Margaret. She wants you to confess and spare your family the anguish of an indictment on five counts of murder."

"No, please," Engels whimpered.

"Lieutenant, I won't have it," I said angrily. "We've got no evidence. All we've got is the Cadwallader croaking. We can indict on that."

"Oh shit, Inspector. We can get indictments on at least five counts. We can go the whole hog! Let's get Lillian Engels down here, she'll drum some sense into little Eddie's head, like she's always done!"

"Please, no," Engels whimpered.

"Eddie," I said, "do your parents know you're homosexual?"

"No."

"Do they know that Lillian is a lesbian?"

"No. Please!"

"You don't want them to find out, do you?"

"No!" He screeched the word, his voice breaking. He wrapped his arms around himself and rocked back and forth.

"We can spare them, Eddie," I said. "You can confess to Margaret, and we won't file with the grand jury on the others. Listen to me, I'm your friend."

"No . . . I don't know!"

"Sssshhh. Listen to me. I think there were mitigating circumstances. Did Margaret taunt you?"

"No . . . yes!"

"Did she remind you of Lillian? Of all the bad things in the past?"

"Yes!"

"Evil things? Dreadful, awful things that you hate to think about?"

"Yes!"

"Do you want it to be over?"

"Oh, God, yes," he blubbered.

"Do you trust me?"

"Yes. You're nice. You're a sweet person."

"Then tell me about Margaret."

"Oh, God. Oh, please, God."

I put my hands on Engels's knee. "I care, Eddie. I really do. Tell me."

"I can't!"

Out of the corner of my eye I saw Dudley loosen his necktie. I steeled myself, then got up and faced Engels. He looked up at me, beseeching me with wide brown eyes. I curled my hand into a fist and swung it full force at the side of his nose. It cracked, and blood and cartilage fragments burst into the air. Engels grabbed at his bloody face and fell back on the mattress.

"Confess, you goddamned murderer!" Dudley screamed.

I stood there, shaking. Engels rolled to his side on the mattress and blew out a noseful of blood. When he spoke his voice was resigned and sorrowful. "I killed Maggie. No one else. It was all mine. No one else's. I killed her and now I have to pay. She didn't deserve it, but she had to pay, too. We all have to pay." Then he passed out.

Breuning was scribbling furiously, Dudley was grinning

like a sated lover, and I stood there trying to drum up some exhilaration for my compromised victory.

No one spoke, and then I realized I had to move fast to salvage even this compromised glory. I left the room abruptly, then ran across the street and found a pay phone. I dialed Lorna at work.

"Lorna Weinberg," she answered.

"This is Fred, Lorna."

"Oh, Freddy. I—"

"He confessed, Lorna. To Margaret Cadwallader. We're taking him in. Probably to the Hall of Justice jail. I don't think it's a grand jury case. I think he'll plead loony. Will you get the papers ready?"

"I can't until I have the arrest report. Freddy, are you all right?"

"I do . . . yes, sweetheart, I'm fine."

"You don't sound fine. Will you call me when Engels is booked?"

"Yes. Can I see you tonight?"

"Yes, when?"

"I don't know. I might be wrapped up tonight writing reports."

"Just come over when you're finished, all right?"

"Yes."

"Freddy?"

"Yes?"

"I . . . I'll . . . tell you when I see you. Be careful."

"I will be."

Engels was in handcuffs when I got back to the interrogation room. He was wearing tan slacks, sandals, and a Hawaiian shirt that Carlisle had brought from his apartment.

Breuning was taking down his statement: ". . . And I panicked. I thought I heard noises from upstairs. I hopped out the kitchen window. I was afraid to get my car. I ran to some bushes by the freeway ramp. I hid out for . . . hours . . . then I took a cab home . . ." Engels's voice trailed off. He looked at me and spat blood on the floor. His nose was purple and hugely swollen, and both his eyes were black.

"Why, Engels?" Breuning asked.

"Because someone had to pay. It shouldn't have been someone as sweet as Maggie, but it just happened."

Dudley clapped me on the back. "Mike and I are taking Engels to the H.O.J.J. You go home. We have to corroborate on our statements. You were brilliant, lad, brilliant. The sky's the limit for you once this thing has been sorted out."

"Wrong, Dudley," I said, making my move at last. "I'll go with you. It's my collar. You can file your report, and Engels's confession, but it's my collar. I filed my report with the D.A.'s office the day before we arrested Engels. It tells the truth from the beginning. You've been meaning to fuck me out of this collar and I won't have it. You try, and I'll go to the papers. I'll tell them your little Dahlia story and how you kidnapped Engels and beat the shit out of him. I'll throw my career down the toilet if you try to take this collar away from me. Do you understand?"

Dudley Smith had gone beyond red to a trembling purple. His big hands twitched at his sides. His eyes were tiny pinpoints of hatred. Spittle formed at the corners of his mouth, but he didn't utter a sound.

I beat them downtown.

The steps at the Hall of Justice were already jammed with reporters. Old Dudley, in true ham fashion, had prepared them for his arrival.

I parked on First off Broadway and stationed myself on foot on the corner to wait for my colleagues and our prisoner. They rounded the corner a minute later, and stopped for the light. Breuning glowered at me from the driver's seat. I opened the door and got in; Dudley and Engels were sitting in the back.

Dudley said, "You're through, Judas," and Engels hissed at me through gritted teeth.

I ignored them both and said, bluff-hearty in an imitation of Dudley's brogue: "Hi, lads! Just thought I'd drop by for the booking. I see the press is here. Grand! I've got a lot to tell them. Dudley, have you heard of the latest anthropological discovery? Man descended not from the ape, but from the Irishman! Ho-ho-ho! Isn't that grand?"

"Judas Iscariot," Dudley Smith said.

"Wrong, Dud. I'm the Irish Santa Claus. Beggora!"

We pulled to the curb in front of the maze of reporters, and I pinned my badge to the lapel of my wrinkled suit coat. Dudley shoved the handcuffed Engels out the door of the car, and we both grabbed his arms and led him up the steps to the Hall of Justice. Someone yelled, "Here they are!" and a mob of shirt-sleeved newshawks descended on us like vultures, throwing questions indiscriminately amidst the explosion of flash bulbs.

"Dudley, how many did he get?" "Did he confess, Dudley?" "Smile, killer! This is for the L.A. *Daily News!*" "Tell us about it, Dud!" "Hey, it's the cop who killed those two Mexican gunsels. Talk to us, Officer!"

We waded through them. Engels kept his head down, Dudley beamed for the cameras and I kept it stoical. We were met in the vestibule of the building by the head jailer, a sheriff's lieutenant in uniform. He led us to an elevator, where a deputy shackled Engels's legs. We rode up to the eleventh floor in silence. We watched as Engels was uncuffed and shackled, issued county jail denims, and led to a one-man security cell. Safely locked in, he stared at me one last time and spit on the floor.

The lieutenant spoke: "You men are wanted immediately at Central Division. The chief of detectives himself called me."

Dudley nodded, stone-faced. I excused myself, took the steps down to street level, and walked out the front door, to be mobbed by reporters. Some recognized me from my previous notoriety and hurled questions as I made for the sidewalk.

"Underhill, whose arrest is it?" "What happened?" "Dudley says this guy's a loony. Can you make him for any unsolved jobs on the books?"

I ignored them and pushed myself free as we hit the sidewalk. I ran all the way to Central Division headquarters on Los Angeles Street, four blocks away. Sweating, I tore through corridors, stopping for a moment to compose myself before I knocked on the door of Thad Green, the chief of detectives. His secretary admitted me to his waiting room. Dudley Smith was already there, sitting on the couch, smoking. We stared at each other until the buzzer on the secretary's desk rang and he said, "You can go in now, Lieutenant Smith."

Dudley walked into the pebble-glass-doored inner sanctum, and I waited nervously, furiously thinking of Lorna in an effort to quiet my mind. Dudley emerged half an hour later, walked right past me and out the door.

A voice from within the chief's office called, "Underhill" and I went in to meet my fate. The chief sat behind his huge oak desk. He acknowledged my salute with a brisk nod of his iron gray head. "Report, Underhill," he said.

When I finished, still standing, the chief said, "Welcome to the detective bureau, Underhill. I'll issue a statement to the press. The D.A.'s office will be in touch with you. I want a full written report in two hours. Don't talk to any reporters. Now go home and rest."

"Thank you, sir," I said. "Where will I be assigned?"

"I don't know yet. To a squad somewhere, probably." He consulted his calendar. "You report back to me one week from today, at eight o'clock. That will be Friday, September 12. We'll have found a suitable assignment for you then."

"Thank you, sir."

"Thank you, Officer."

I wrote my report down the hall in a vacant storage room and left it with the chief's secretary, then retrieved my car and drove home to Night Train, a shower, and a mercifully dreamless sleep.

12

A sparkling twilight found me waiting for the evening papers at a newsstand on Pico and Robertson. They came and the headlines screamed "Korea" rather than "Murder in L.A." I was disappointed. I was curious to see how the department's press release would jibe with Dudley Smith's press handout.

After checking the second and third pages for a flash update, I started to feel relieved: I had Dudley by the balls, and the day's reprieve the press was giving us would help smooth out what might be a tense evening with Lorna.

As I parked on Charleville I could see Lorna in her living room, smoking abstractedly and staring out her window. I rang the bell, and all my anger and enervation dropped like a rock. I started to feel a delicious anticipation.

The buzzer that unlocked the door sounded, and I sprinted up the stairs to find Lorna standing in the middle of the living room, leaning on her cane. She wore pink lipstick and a trace of mascara, and her burnished light brown hair had been set in a new style—swept up and back on the sides. It gave her a breathless look. She was wearing a tartan skirt and a man's French-cuffed dress shirt that perfectly outlined her large breasts.

She smiled blankly when she saw me, and I walked to her slowly and embraced her, cradling the new hairdo gently.

"Hello," was all I could think of to say.

Lorna dropped her cane and held me around the waist. "It's not going to the grand jury, Freddy," she said.

"I didn't think it would. He confessed."

"To how many?" I started to release Lorna, but she held on. "To how many?" she persisted.

"Just to Margaret Cadwallader. Let's not talk about it, Lor."

"We have to."

"Then let's sit down."

We sat on the couch.

"I looked for you at the Hall of Justice. I figured you'd be there for the booking," Lorna said.

"I got summoned to see the chief of detectives. I imagine Smith went back and booked Engels. I was dog tired. I went home and slept. Why?" Lorna's face darkened angrily. "Why?" I repeated. "What the hell's going on?"

"I was there, I got a jail pass. The D.A. was there. He and Dudley Smith were talking. Smith told him that the Cadwallader killing was just the tip of the iceberg, that Engels was a mass murderer."

"Oh, God."

"Don't interrupt me. He was booked on just the one count. Cadwallader. But Smith kept repeating, 'This is a grand jury job, there's no telling how many dames this maniac's bagged!' The D.A. seemed to go along with it. Then the D.A. saw me and mentioned to Smith that I read potential grand jury cases. Smith notices that I'm a woman, and starts to lay on the blarney. Then he asks me what I'm doing here, and I tell him that you and I are friends. Then he goes livid and starts to shake. He looked insane."

Shaken, I said: "He is insane. He hates me, I crossed him."

"Then *you're* insane. He could ruin your career!"

"Hush, sweetheart. No, I've been promoted. Smith reported first, I reported afterward. I'm going to the detective bureau. To a squad room somewhere. Thad Green told me himself. Whatever Smith told Green jibes with my report to you and my official arresting officer's report, which is the truth. What Smith told the D.A. is just hyperbole. All I—"

"Freddy, you told me there was no hard evidence to connect Engels to any other murders."

"That's absolutely true. But . . ."

Lorna was getting more red-faced and agitated by the

second: "But nothing, Freddy. I *saw* Engels. He was beaten terribly. I asked Smith about that and he handed me some baloney about how he tried to resist arrest. I kept saying to myself, Good God, could my Freddy have had anything to do with that? Is that justice? What kind of man have I gotten involved with?"

I just stared at the Hieronymous Bosch print on the wall.

"Freddy, answer me!"

"I can't, counselor. Good night."

I drove home, steadfastly quelling all speculation regarding Lorna, woman-killers, and lunatic cops. I tried out my new rank: Detective Frederick U. Underhill. Detective Fred Underhill. The dicks. At twenty-seven. I was probably the youngest detective in the Los Angeles Police Department. I would have to find out. In November, the sergeant's exam. Detective Sergeant Frederick Underhill. I would have to buy three new suits and a couple of sports jackets, some neckties and a half dozen pair of slacks. Detective Fred Underhill. But. It kept rearing its beautiful, burnished brown head. Lorna Weinberg, counselor at law. Lorna Weinberg.

Be still, I said to myself, trying to heed my own advice —just don't think.

At home, after a roughhouse session with Night Train, some kind of nameless future-fear hit me and to combat it I dug out some textbooks.

I tried to engross myself, but it was useless; the words flew by undigested, almost unseen. I couldn't stop thinking.

I was about to give it up when my doorbell rang. Not daring to guess, I flung the door open. It was Lorna.

"Hello, Officer," she said. "May I come in?"

"I'm a detective now, Lorna. Can you accept what I had to do to get there?"

"I . . . I know I convicted you of an unknown crime on insufficient evidence."

"I would have filed a writ of habeas corpus, counselor, but you would have beat me in court."

"I would have appealed, in your behalf. Did you know that you are the only Frederick U. Underhill in all the L.A. area phone books?"

"No doubt. What are you doing here, Lorna?"

"Stalking your heart."

"Then don't stand in the doorway, come in and meet my dog."

Many joyful hours later, sated and engulfed with each other, too tired to sleep or think and unable to relinquish each other's touch, I had an idea. I dug out my meager collection of corny ballads, formerly used to seduce lonely women. I put "You Belong to Me" by Jo Stafford on the phonograph and turned the volume up so that Lorna could hear it in the bedroom.

She was laughing when I returned to her. "Oh, Freddy, that's so . . ."

"Corny?"

"Yes!"

"My sentiments, too. But, needless to say, I feel romantic tonight."

"It's morning, darling."

"I stand corrected. Lorna?"

"Yes?"

"May I have the next dance?"

"Dance? Freddy, I can't dance!"

"Yes, you can."

"Freddy!"

"You can hop on your good leg. I'll hold you up. Come on!"

"Freddy, I can't!"

"I insist."

"Freddy, I'm naked!"

"Good. So am I."

"Freddy!"

"Enough said, Lor. Let's hit it!"

I scooped the naked, laughing Lorna into my arms and carried her into the living room and deposited her on the couch, then put Patti Page singing "The Tennessee Waltz" on the phonograph. When she began to intone the syrupy introduction, I walked to Lorna and extended my hands.

She reached for them and I pulled her to me and held her close, encircling her at the buttocks and lifting her slightly off the floor so that her bad leg was suspended, and her

weight was stationed on her good one. She held me tightly
around my back, and we moved awkwardly in very small
steps as Patti Page sang.

"Freddy," Lorna whispered into my chest, "I think I—"

"Don't think, Lor."

"I was going to say . . . I think I love you."

"Then think, because I know I love you."

"Freddy, I don't think this record is corny."

"Neither do I."

We drove to Santa Barbara Saturday afternoon, taking
the Pacific Coast Highway. The blue Pacific was on our
left, brown cliffs and green hills were on our right. There
was hardly a cloud or a trace of smog. We cruised along
with the top down in comfortable silence. Lorna kept her
hand on my leg, giving me playful squeezes from time to
time.

We hadn't talked about the case all morning, and it hovered benignly on some back burner of my mind. By silent
agreement we had not turned on the radio. The present
was too good, too real, to be marred by intimation of the
harsh reality we both worked in.

So we drove north, on our first outing together. Lorna
inched her hand, broadly in a parody of stealth, up my leg
until I went, "Garrr! What the hell are you doing?"

She laughed. "What do you think?"

I laughed. "I think it feels good."

"Don't think, just drive." Lorna removed her hand.
"Freddy, I was thinking."

"About what?"

"I just realized that I don't know a damn thing about
what you do—I mean, with your time."

I considered this, and decided to be candid. "Well, before
Wacky was killed I used to spend a lot of time with him. I
don't really have any friends. And I used to chase women."

Surprisingly, Lorna laughed at this. "Strictly to get
laid?"

"No, it was more than that. It was partly for the wonder,
but that was B.L."

"B.L.?"

"Before Lorna."

Lorna squeezed my leg and pointed to the shoulder. "Pull over, please."

I did, alarmed at the darkly serious look on Lorna's face. I framed that face with both my hands. "What is it, sweetheart?" I asked.

"Freddy, I can't have children," Lorna blurted out.

"I don't care," I said. "I mean, I do care, but it doesn't make a goddamned bit of difference to me. Really, I—"

"Freddy, I just had to say it."

"Because you think we have a future together?"

"Y-yes."

"Lorna, I couldn't even consider a future without you." She twisted away from me and bit at her knuckles. "Lorna, I love you, and we're not leaving here until you tell me you believe what I've just told you."

"I don't know. I think so."

"Don't think."

Lorna burst out laughing, tearfully. "Then I believe you."

"Good, now let's get the hell out of here, I'm hungry."

We timed our arrival perfectly, Santa Barbara opening up before us, muted in the twilight like a heaven-sent reprieve from the humid, smog-bound commonness of L.A.

We found our weekend haven on Bath Street, a few blocks off State: the Mission Bell Hotel, a converted Victorian mansion painted a guileless bright yellow. We registered as Mr. and Mrs. Frederick Underhill. The desk clerk started to look askance at our lack of luggage, but the sight of my badge when I pulled out my billfold to pay for the room calmed him down.

Giggling conspiratorially, I took Lorna's arm as we walked to the elevator. Our room had bright yellow walls festooned with cheap oil paintings of the Santa Barbara Mission, bay windows fronting the palm-lined street, and a big brass bed with a bright yellow bedspread and canopy.

"I'll never eat another lemon," Lorna said.

I kissed her on the cheek. "Then let's not have fish tonight. I left my shaving kit in the car. I'll be right back."

I took the yellow carpeted stairs down to street level. The clerk, a skinny, middle-aged man with incongruous

bright red hair, started to fidget when he saw me walk
through the foyer. I had the feeling he wanted to ask me
something. He put out his cigarette and approached me.

I made it easy for him. "What's up, doc?" I asked.

The man slouched in front of me, his hands jammed into
his trouser pockets. He hemmed and hawed, then blurted
it out: "It ain't none of my business, Officer," he said, looking around in all directions and lowering his voice, "but
when they say 'degenerate' do they really mean 'queer'?"

"What the—" I started to say, then realized the source of
the crazy non sequitur and sighed. "You mean it made the
Santa Barbara papers?"

"Yes, sir. You're a big hero. *Is* that what it means?"

"I'm not at liberty to discuss it," I said, leaving the clerk
alone in the yellow foyer contemplating semantics.

I trotted down to State Street and found a newsstand,
where I bought copies of the L.A. *Times* and the Santa Barbara *Clarion*. It was on the front page of both papers, big
headlines complete with photos. I started with the *Times:*

GAMBLER CONFESSES
TO KILLING OF
HOLLYWOOD WOMAN!

Linked to at Least
Six Other Murders!

LOS ANGELES Sept. 7: Police today arrested a
suspect in the August 12 strangulation murder of
Margaret Cadwallader, 36, of 2311 Harold Way, Hollywood. The suspect was named as Edward Engels, 32,
of Horn Drive, West Hollywood. Shortly after his arrest, Engels, a gambler with no visible means of support, confessed to L.A.P.D. detectives Dudley Smith,
Michael Breuning, and Frederick Underhill, saying,
"I killed Maggie! She treated me like dirt, so I returned her to the dirt."

Miss Cadwallader, who worked as a bookkeeper at
the Small World Import-Export Company in Los Angeles, was believed to have been killed by a burglar

she interrupted in the early morning hours of August 12. Police had been carrying their investigation along those lines, questioning burglars known to use violence and getting no results, until the intervention of Detective Underhill, who was then assigned to patrol duties.

In a formally signed statement to the press, Detective Underhill, 27, said: "When I was working Wilshire Patrol earlier this year, my partner and I discovered the body of a young woman. She had been strangled. When the Cadwallader case made the papers, I noted similarities between the two deaths. I began an investigation of my own, and brought my evidence, which at this time I cannot discuss, to Lieutenant Dudley Smith. Lieutenant Smith headed the investigation, which led to the arrest of Edward Engels."

Lieutenant Smith praised Underhill for his "grand, splendid police work" and went on to say, "We got Engels through dogged police work; long stakeouts at the many bars where he went looking for lonely women. His arrest is a victory for justice and a moral America."

Links to More Victims Sought

In his rich brogue, the Irish-born L.A.P.D. lieutenant, 46, with 23 years on the force, continued: "I believe the tragic Miss Cadwallader is just the tip of the iceberg. Engels is a known degenerate who has frequented bars catering to his kind in the Hollywood area for many years. We know for a fact that he picks up women in cocktail lounges and pays them to be beaten. I strongly believe Engels to be responsible for at least half a dozen strangulation killings of women over the past five years throughout Southern California. I hope to persuade the district attorney to launch a massive investigation along these lines."

I couldn't think for my sudden anger. Hurriedly, I read through the front pages of the Santa Barbara paper. There was nothing new, they copied the *Times* almost verbatim.

Dudley Smith, the fat-mouthed glory-monger, was pulling out all the stops in his monomania. I was covered, but he was out to hang fresh victims on the head of a one-time murderer.

I ran back to the hotel, bursting through the foyer and taking the stairs three at a time. The door to our room was open, and Lorna was sitting in an armchair, smoking contentedly and reading a Santa Barbara tourist brochure.

I flung the newspapers at her lap. "Read these, Lorna," I said.

She did, after giving me a long, concerned look. I watched her read. When she finished, she said, "It's nothing I didn't expect."

"What do you mean?"

"I knew Smith would milk it for all it was worth."

"You don't know him, Lor. Not like I do. He'll try to pin everything from the Johnstown flood to World War II on Engels. He's out of his goddamned mind!"

Lorna smiled and took my hands. "Freddy, did Eddie Engels kill Margaret Cadwallader?"

"Yes, but—"

"Be still. Then he's in custody where he belongs. And you put him there, not Dudley Smith. If you're worried about Smith starting some insane, far-flung investigation that would involve you, forget about it. The D.A. would never authorize it."

I calmed down, slightly. "Are you sure?"

"Yes. He would never spend the money. He believes in letting sleeping dogs lie. You think Engels is innocent of those other killings?"

"Yes. He killed Cadwallader, and that's it."

Lorna took my face in her hands and kissed it several times, softly. "You are beginning to care about justice, darling," she said, "and it's a wonderful thing to see."

"I'm not sure of that."

"I am. Did you read the story on the twelfth page of the *Times?*"

"No."

"Good. Then I'll read it to you." Lorna put out her cigarette and cleared her throat. "The title is 'Hailing a True-Life Hero,' and the subtitle is 'Policeman Is a One-Man Crimestopper Wave!' Here we go: 'Detective Frederick U.

Underhill, twenty-seven, is the youngest officer to achieve that rank in the history of the Los Angeles Police Department. He is not your average cop. He is a 1946 graduate of Loyola College who didn't want to be a college man. He fought tenaciously to enter the service during World War II, petitioning the draft board several times to let him enlist, despite his punctured eardrum. He was refused, and made the most of his college years, graduating magna cum laude with a degree in history. Detective Underhill is an orphan, and possessed the highest grade point average ever achieved at the St. Brendan's Home for Children. Monsignor John Kelly, principal of St. Brendan's High School, where Underhill attended, said, "Fred's recent successes as a police officer don't surprise me at all. He was a hard-working, devout boy who I knew was destined for great things."

" 'But what things! Underhill has said, "I have never wanted to be anything but a cop. It's the only life I have ever considered."

" 'And we, the citizens of Los Angeles, are the lucky benefactors of Fred Underhill's boyhood decision to seek the selfless life of a police officer. Item: while working as a patrolman in the Wilshire Division, Fred Underhill had more felony arrests to his credit than any officer at the station. Item: Fred Underhill had one of the highest academic averages ever to come out of the Police Academy. Item: Captain William Beckworth, Underhill's former watch commander at Wilshire called him "The greatest natural policeman I have ever encountered." Heady praise indeed, but backed up by fact: in February of this year, Officer Fred Underhill shot and killed the two armed robbers who had just robbed a market. His partner died in the shootout. Now the cracking of the baffling Margaret Cadwallader case, both within one year.

" 'The Korean War rages on. Overseas we are at a standstill with the communist enemy. On the homefront, the war against crime wages on. It is a war that will regrettably always be with us. Thank God men like Detective Fred Underhill will always be with us.' "

Lorna finished with a flourish and swooned in a parody of lovestruck awe. "Well, Officer Fred?" she said.

"They forgot to say I was tall, handsome, intelligent,

and charming. That would have been the truth. However, they opted for horseshit—it reads better. They couldn't very well have said that I was an atheist draft dodger and, before you, a pussy-chaser on the prowl . . ."

"Freddy!"

"It's the truth. Oh, shit, Lorna, I'm so goddamned tired of this thing."

"Are you really, dear?"

"Yes."

"Then will you do me two favors?"

"Name them."

"Don't mention the case for the rest of the weekend."

"Okay. And?"

"And make love to me."

"Double okay." I reached for Lorna, and we fell laughing onto the bed.

Sometime later, we called room service for two trout dinners that arrived on a linen-covered pushcart, delivered by a bellboy who rapped discreetly on the door and called out softly, "Supper, folks!"

After eating, Lorna lit a cigarette and eyed me with warmth and much humor. Somehow it brought forth in me a huge rush of curiosity, and I said, "Turnabout, Lorna?"

"Turnabout?"

"Right. You wanted to know about the missing hours in my life . . ."

"All right, darling, turnabout. After the accident, much self-pity: feeling trapped, a saintly dead mother, a fat sister, a buffoon for a father, and all the goddamned operations—and false hopes and speculations and guilt and self-hatred and anger. And the detachment. That was the worst of all. *Knowing* I was not of this time and place—or any time and place. Then learning to walk all over again, and feeling joyous until the doctor told me I could never have children. Then awful, awful bitterness and the little lessons in acceptance."

"What do you mean, Lor?"

"I mean never knowing when my bad leg would go out completely, and I'd fall on my ass. It always seemed to happen when I was wearing a white dress. Learning to take stairs. Having to leave early for class when I knew there would be stairs to climb. The awful, gentle people who wanted to help. The men who thought I'd be an easy lay because I was crippled. They were right, you know. I was an easy lay."

"So was I, Lor."

"Anyway, then college, and law school, and books and painting and music and a few men and some kind of reconciliation with my family, and finally the D.A.'s office."

"And?"

"And *what*, Freddy?" Lorna's voice rose in exasperation. "You are so goddamned persistent! I know you want me to talk about the 'wonder'—whatever the hell it is—but I just don't *feel* it."

"Easy, sweetheart. I wasn't prying."

"You were and you weren't. I know you want to know everything about me, but give it time. I'm not the wonder."

"Yes, you are."

"No, I'm not! You want to control the wonder. That's why you're a cop. Freddy, I want to be with you, but you can never control me. Do you understand?"

"Yes, I understand that you're still afraid of things. I'm not anymore."

"Don't be oblique, goddamnit!"

"Shit," I said, feeling suddenly the weight of my carefully thought-out life collapse from three weeks of tension and expectation. "Wonder, justice, horseshit. I just don't know anymore."

"Yes, you do," Lorna said. "There's me. I'm not wonder or justice."

"What are you?"

"I'm your Lorna."

That night and early morning we didn't go sight-seeing on State Street or take a romantic walk on the beach, or tour historic Santa Barbara Mission. We went dancing—in our lemon-colored room—to the music, on the radio, of the Four Lads, the McGuire Sisters, Teresa Brewer, and the immortal big band of the late Glenn Miller.

We found a station that played requests, and I called in and importuned them to play a host of old standards that were suddenly dear to me in the light of Lorna. The disc jockey obliged, and Lorna and I held each other close and moved slowly across the room to the soft beat of "The Way You Look Tonight," "Blue Moon," "Perfidia," "Blueberry Hill," "Moments to Remember," "Good Night, Irene" and, of course, Patti Page singing "The Tennessee Waltz.'

At dawn on Monday morning, we got up and reluctantly drove back to L.A. and the administration of justice.

13

I was sound asleep in my apartment when the telephone rang. It was two o'clock Monday afternoon. I had been asleep a scant three hours.

It was Lorna. "Freddy, I have to see you right away. It's urgent."

"What is it, Lor?"

She sounded gravely worried. There was a timbre to her voice I had never heard before. "I can't talk about it on the phone."

"Did they arraign Engels?"

"Yes. He pleaded not guilty. Dudley Smith was there with the assistant D.A. and Engels started screaming. The bailiffs had to restrain him."

"Jesus. Are you at your office?"

"Yes."

"I'll be there in forty-five minutes."

It took me fifty-five, dressing hurriedly and highballing my Buick at ten miles over the speed limit. I flashed my badge at the parking attendant at the lot on Temple and he nodded crisply, placing an official-looking piece of paper under my windshield wiper. Two minutes later I was barging through the door of Lorna's office.

Lorna had company, and they looked grave. Both were smartly tailored men in their early forties. One of them, the more impressive looking of the two, seemed familiar. He was sitting on Lorna's green leather couch with his long legs stretched out and crossed at the ankles. He fingered a leather briefcase stationed next to him on the floor. He was intimidating even in this casual posture. The other man was sandy-haired and plump, and wearing an ascot

189

and a cashmere sweater on a day when the temperature promised to reach ninety-five. He was licking his lips repeatedly and moving his eyes back and forth from the briefcase man to me.

Lorna made the introductions as I pulled up a wooden chair next to her desk. "Detective Fred Underhill, this is Walter Canfield." She pointed to the man with the briefcase. "And this is Mr. Clark Winton." She nodded in the direction of the man with the ascot. Both men acknowledged my presence with stares—Canfield's hostile, Winton's nervous.

"What can I do for you, gentlemen?" I said.

Canfield started to open his mouth, but Lorna spoke first in a voice that was all business: "Mr. Canfield is an attorney, Fred. He represents Mr. Winton." She hesitated, then said haltingly, "Mr. Canfield and I have worked together in the past. I trust him." She looked at Canfield, who smiled grimly.

"I'll be brief, Officer," he said. "My client was with Eddie Engels on the night Margaret Cadwallader was murdered." He waited for my reaction. When all he got was silence he added, "My client was with Engels all night. He remembers the date very well. August 12 is his birthday."

Canfield looked at me triumphantly. Winton was staring into his lap, kneading his trembling hands.

I felt my whole body go rigid with a pins-and-needles sensation. "Eddie Engels confessed, Mr. Canfield," I stated carefully.

"My client has informed me that Engels is a disturbed man who carries a great deal of guilt with him for certain events in his past."

Winton interjected: "Eddie is a troubled man, Officer. He was in love with an older man when he was in the navy. The man made him do awful things, and made Eddie hate himself for being what he was."

"He confessed," I repeated.

"Come, Officer. We both know that confession was obtained under physical duress. I saw Engels at his arraignment this morning. He has been severely beaten."

"He was restrained through force when he tried to resist arrest," I lied.

Canfield snorted. In different surroundings he would

have spat. I met his contemptuous look with one of my own, then transferred it to Clark Winton. "Are you homosexual, Mr. Winton?" I asked, already certain of the answer.

"Freddy, goddamnit!" Lorna blurted.

Winton swallowed and looked to his attorney for support. Canfield started to whisper into his ear, but I interrupted them: "Because if you are, and you are planning to come forth with this information, the police will want signed statements regarding your relationship with Engels and a detailed account of your activities with him on the night of August 12. Are you prepared for that?"

"Eddie and I were lovers," Winton said calmly, with great resignation.

I gathered my argument and spat it out: "Mr. Winton, we have a signed confession. We also have eyewitnesses who will testify to having seen Engels's car on Harold Way on the night of the murder. You are opening yourself up to an accessory rap if you go public with your story."

Canfield eyed me coldly. Out of the corner of my eye I saw Lorna sitting rigid, fuming. "My client is a man of courage, Officer," Canfield said. "Edward Engels's life is at stake. Thad Green is an old friend of mine, as is the district attorney. Mr. Winton's affidavit will be delivered this afternoon. Mr. Winton realizes the police will have many questions for him; I will be present at the questioning. Mr. Winton is a prominent man; you will not beat any confession out of him. I came here to talk to you only because Lorna is an old friend and I respect her judgment of people. She told me you were concerned with justice, and I believed her . . ."

"I *am* concerned with justice, and . . ."

I couldn't finish. My resistance crumbled in a heap, and I felt my vision darken at the corner of my eyes. I picked up a heavy quartz bookend from Lorna's desk and hurled it at the glass part of her office door. The glass shattered outward and the bookend landed on the corridor floor with a loud bang. My hands were aching to hit something, so I mashed them together and closed my eyes, fighting tears and tremors. I heard Canfield say goodbye to Lorna, and heard footsteps as he ushered his client out the half-destroyed door.

"I believe Winton," Lorna said finally.

"So do I," I said.

"Freddy, Dudley Smith convinced the D.A. to let him head an investigation into a half-dozen unsolved homicides. He wants to pin them on Eddie Engels."

"Jesus, crazy Dudley. Is this guy Canfield a hotshot? He looks familiar."

"He's one of the finest, highest-paid criminal lawyers on the West Coast."

"And Winton has got money?"

"Yes, he's very wealthy. He owns two textile plants in Long Beach."

Still looking for outs, I persisted. "And Canfield is buddies with Thad Green and the D.A.?"

"Yes."

"Then Engels will go free and Dudley Smith and I will be up shit's creek without a paddle."

I looked through the gaping glass hole in the door, searching for something that would stop up the now-gaping hole in my life. "I'm sorry about the door, Lorna," was all I could think of.

Lorna pushed her swivel chair over to where I was sitting. "Are you sorry for Eddie Engels?" she asked.

"Yes," I said.

Lorna kissed me softly on the lips. "Then let justice be done. It's out of your hands now."

I pushed Lorna away from me. I didn't want to believe her. "And what about Maggie Cadwallader?" I shouted. I turned around to look at the hole in the door. Three men in suits were looking in on us.

"You okay, Lorna?" one of them asked.

Lorna nodded. They departed, looking skeptical. I could hear glass being swept up.

"What *about* Maggie Cadwallader?" Lorna asked. "Did you want revenge for her, or was this whole crusade just an exercise in wonder that went bad?"

Suddenly I wanted to hurt Lorna as I had never wanted to hurt anyone before. "I fucked Maggie Cadwallader on the same day I met you. I picked her up at the Silver Star bar and took her to her apartment and fucked her. That was how I got involved in this thing, how I knew where to look for evidence. I knew if I found the killer my career would skyrocket. I wanted you from the first moment I saw you. I wanted to have you, to fuck you, to make you mine. That was why I involved you in this; it was just another seduction in a whole fucking long line of them."

I didn't wait for Lorna to respond. I walked out of her office, not looking back.

I drove aimlessly, the way I had on the night I had met Maggie Cadwallader. I bought a copy of the L.A. *Mirror.* Engels's arraignment was on the front page. " 'I Am Not A Homo!' Killer Screams." Yellow journalism at its best. The account revealed that Engels had had to be restrained and dragged out of the courtroom by three muscular bailiffs after submitting his plea of not guilty.

I threw the paper out the car window and drove east. Near San Bernardino I glimpsed from the freeway a large, well-set-up municipal golf course. I got off at the next exit, found the golf haven, parked in the deserted lot, bought two dozen balls, and rented a set of beat-up clubs from the pro shop. After paying my green fee, I ducked past the starter's cubicle and walked straight into the heart of the course.

I thought and thought—and thought. I tried not to think. I succeeded and I failed. I sailed a half-dozen well-hit 2 irons into deep nowhere and felt nothing.

Mea culpa, I said to myself. What went wrong? What really happened? What will happen next? Will the department back me up? Will I go back to patrol in Watts, humbled, singled out as a maverick destined to go nowhere? Logical fallacies. Post hoc, ergo propter hoc: after this, therefore because of this. Circumstantial evidence. A guilty man. Guilty not of murder, but of guilt. Poor queer Eddie. Gallant queer Clark Winton. Mea maxima culpa. Forgive me, father, for I have sinned. What father? Eddie Engels? Dudley Smith? Thad Green? Chief Parker? God? There is no God but the wonder. I tried to harden my heart against Lorna, and failed. Lorna, Lorna, Lorna.

I slammed a furious succession of 3 irons straight into a grove of trees, hoping they would ricochet back and knock me dead. They didn't; they just disappeared, never to be seen again, sacrifices to a golf god I had ceased to believe in.

* * *

I drove home. I could hear my phone ringing as I pulled into the driveway. Thinking it might be Lorna, I ran for it.

The ringing persisted as I unlocked my front door. I picked up the receiver. "Hello?" I said warily.

"Underhill?" a familiar voice queried.

"Yes. Captain Jurgensen?"

"Yes. I've been calling you since six o'clock."

"I've been out. I drove out to San Berdoo."

"I see. Then you haven't heard?"

"Heard what?"

"Eddie Engels is dead. He committed suicide in his cell this afternoon. He was about to be released. Evidence came up to point to his innocence."

"I . . . I . . ."

"Underhill, are you there?"

"Y-yes."

"The chief himself asked me, as your last commanding officer, to inform you."

"I . . . don't . . ."

"Underhill, you are to report downtown at eight tomorrow morning. Central Division, room 219. Underhill, did you hear me?"

"Yes, sir," I said, letting the receiver slip out of my shaking hands and fall to the floor.

14

There were three of us present in room 219. The two cops, my interrogators, were named Milner and Quinn. Both were sergeants from Internal Affairs and both were burly and sunburned and middle-aged. They had both doffed their suit coats as they had ushered me into the crowded little room. I strangely relished their fatuous attempt at intimidation, and was certain I could best them at any form of psychological warfare.

We were all wearing Smith and Wesson .38 police specials in shoulder holsters, which gave the proceedings a ritualistic air. I was nervous, high on adrenaline and phony righteous indignation. I was prepared for anything, including the end of my career, and that strengthened my resolve to defeat these two obdurate-looking policemen.

I pulled up a chair, propped up my feet on a ledge of recruiting posters, and smiled disarmingly while Quinn and Milner dug cigarettes and Zippo lighters out of their suitcoats and lit up. Milner, who was the slightly taller and older of the two, offered the pack to me.

"I don't smoke, Sergeant," I said, keeping my voice clipped and severe, the voice of a man who takes trouble from no one.

"Good man," Quinn said, smiling, "wish I didn't."

"I quit once, during the Depression," Milner said. "I had a good-looking girlfriend who hated the smell of tobacco. My wife don't like it either, but she ain't so good looking."

"Then why'd you marry her?" Quinn asked.

" 'Cause she told me I looked like Clark Gable!" Milner snorted.

Quinn got a big bang out of that. "My wife told me

195

I looked like Bela Lugosi and I slugged her," he said.

"You should have bit her neck," Milner cracked.

"I do, every night." Quinn guffawed, blowing out a huge lungful of smoke and pulling up a chair facing me. Milner laughed along and opened a tiny window at the back of the room, letting in rays of hazy sunshine and a flood of traffic noise.

"Officer Underhill," he said, "my partner and I are here today because doubts have been raised about your fitness to serve the department." Milner's voice had metamorphosed into a precise professorial tone. He started a dramatic pause, drawing on his cigarette, and I answered, mimicking his inflections:

"Sergeant, I have grave doubts about the brass hats who sent you here to question me. Has Internal Affairs questioned Dudley Smith?"

Milner and Quinn looked at each other. Their look was informed with the humorous secret knowledge of longtime partners.

"Officer," Quinn said, "do you think we are here because a queer slashed his wrists in County Jail yesterday?" I didn't answer. Quinn continued: "Do you think we're here because you initiated, illegally, the arrest of an innocent man?"

Milner took over. "Officer, do you think we're here because you have brought great disgrace on the department?"

He took a folded up newspaper out of his back pocket and read from it: " 'Hero cop quick on the trigger? L.A.P.D. in hot water? Thanks to crack legal beagle Walter Canfield and a courageous anonymous witness, Eddie Engels almost walked out the door of County Jail a free man. Instead, humiliated and tortured by his ordeal of false arrest, he left under a sheet. Canfield and the man with whom Engels spent the night of August 12—the night he was alleged to have murdered Margaret Cadwallader —tragically got to the authorities too late with their information. Eddie Engels slashed his wrists with a contraband razor blade in his cell on the eleventh floor of the Hall of Justice yesterday afternoon, the victim of gunslinger justice.

" 'Our Seattle correspondent contacted the victim's fa-

ther, Wilhelm Engels, a pharmacist in suburban Seattle.
"I can't believe that God would do such a thing," the
white-haired old gentleman said. "There must be an investigation into the policemen who arrested my Edward.
Edward was a gentle, lovely boy who never hurt anyone.
We must have justice." Mr. Engels told our correspondent
that Walter Canfield has offered his services, free of
charge, in filing suit for false arrest against the Los Angeles Police Department. "Mr. Engels will have his justice," Canfield told reporters shortly before he learned of
Engels's death, "the justice his son was denied. This is
clearly a case of a quick-on-the-trigger young cop out to
make a name for himself." ' "

Milner paused. My vision was starting to darken at the
edges, but I shook my head and it cleared.

"Go on," I said.

Milner coughed and continued. " 'Officer Frederick U.
Underhill, canonized within the L.A.P.D. and by Los Angeles newspapers earlier this year for killing two holdup
men, brought the same rash justice to his investigation of
Eddie Engels. Veteran L.A.P.D. Detective Lieutenant
Dudley Smith told our reporter: "Fred Underhill is an am-
bitious young man out to make chief of police in record
time. He caught myself and several others up in his crusade to get Eddie Engels. I admit I went along with it. I admit I was at fault. Last night I lit a candle for poor Eddie's
family. I also lit one for Fred Underhill and prayed that he
learns a lesson from this tragedy he perpetrated." ' "

I started to laugh. My laughter sounded hysterical to
my own ears. Milner and Quinn didn't think it was funny.
Quinn snapped: "This article, which was in the L.A. *Daily
News*, goes on to call for your resignation and an investigation into the entire department. What do you think about
that, Underhill?"

I calmed myself and stared at my inquisitors. "I feel that
that article was written in a very poor prose style. Convo-
luted, hysterical, hyperbolic. Hemingway would disap-
prove of it. F. Scott Fitzgerald would turn over in his
grave. Shakespeare would be dismayed. That's what I
think."

"Underhill," Milner said, "you know the department
takes care of its own, don't you?"

"Sure. Witness that lunatic Dudley Smith. He'll come out of this thing smelling like a rose and probably make Captain. Ahhh, yes. Grand!"

"Underhill, the department was prepared to stand by you until we did a little checking up on you."

I started to go cold in the hot, smoky room. The traffic noise on Los Angeles Street sounded alternately very loud and very soft.

"Oh, yeah?" I said. "Come up with anything interesting?"

"Yes," Quinn said, "we did. Let me quote. 'Sarah had high full breasts with cone-shaped dark brown nipples. Coarse hairs surrounded them. She was an experienced lover. We moved well together. She anticipated my motions and accommodated them with fluid grace.' Want some more, Underhill?"

"You filthy bastards," I said.

"Did you know that Sarah Kefalvian is a Communist, Underhill? She's listed in the rolls of five organizations that have been classified as Commie fronts. Did you know that?" Milner leaned over me, his knuckles white from grasping the table. "Do you fuck a lot of Commies, Underhill?" he hissed.

"Are *you* a Communist, Freddy?" Quinn asked.

"Go fuck yourself," I said.

Milner leaned over further; I could smell his tobacco breath. "I think you *are* a Communist. And a filthy pervert. Decent men don't write about the women they fuck. Decent men don't fuck Commies."

I stuck my hands under my thighs to control their shaking and to keep myself from hitting someone. My head was pounding and my vision blurred from the blackness throbbing behind my eyes. "You forgot to mention I've got red upholstery on my car. You forgot to mention I also fuck Koreans, Republicans, and Democrats. When I was in high school I had a redheaded girlfriend. I've got a red cashmere sweater, you forgot to mention that."

"There's one thing *you* didn't forget to mention," Quinn said. "Listen: 'I told Sarah about dodging the draft in '42. She is the only person besides Wacky to know that. Telling her made me feel strangely free.' "

Quinn spat on the floor. "I served in the war, Underhill.

I lost a brother at Guadalcanal. All good Americans served. Anyone who dodged the draft is a no-good Commie traitor, and not worthy to carry a badge. You have brought disgrace to the department. The chief himself has been told of what we found in your diary. He ordered this investigation. We only had a little time to search your apartment. God knows what other Commie degeneracy we would have found, if we had had more time. You have two choices: resign, or face departmental trial on charges of moral turpitude. If you don't resign, we will take your diary to the feds. Draft-dodging is a federal offense."

Milner took a typed form out of his suit coat pocket. He placed it on the table along with a pen; then he and his partner walked out of the room.

I stared at the resignation form. The print blurred before my eyes. Tears welled in them, and I willed the effort to stanch their flow. It took a minute, but they stopped before they could burst out of me. I walked to the window and looked out. I marked the time and committed the scene to memory, then took off my shoulder holster and laid it on the table. I placed my badge next to it and signed away my access to the wonder.

Camera-wielding reporters were stationed in front of my apartment as I turned onto my block. I couldn't face them, so I drove around the corner and cut through the alley, then parked and hopped fences, entering my apartment through the back door. I filled a suitcase with clean clothes, hitched Night Train to his leash and walked back out to the alley and around the block to my car.

I drove north, with no destination in mind. Night Train chewed golf balls in the back seat. It was easy not to think of my future; I didn't have one.

Hugging the coast road reminded me of my recent jaunt with Lorna, which suddenly brought the future back to me in a blinding rush of schemes and contingencies.

I looked at the telephone poles lining the Pacific Coast Highway and contemplated sweet, instant oblivion. When the tall wooden spires began to look like the ultimate scheme, I let out a muffled, dry sob and swung my Buick inland through some insignificant dirt canyon trail, moving upward through green scrub country until I came down forty-five minutes later in the San Fernando Valley.

I headed north again, catching the ridge route in Chatsworth and moving up it toward the Grapevine and Bakersfield. I wanted to find someplace barren and bereft of beauty, a good flat place to walk my dog and arrive at decisions without the distractions of picturesque surroundings.

Bakersfield wasn't the place. At three-thirty P.M., the temperature was still close to one hundred degrees. I stopped at a diner and ordered a Coke. The Coke cost a nickel and the ice that accompanied it a quarter. The counterman was giving me the fisheye. He handed me my Coke in a paper cup and opened his mouth to speak. I didn't let him; I slammed some change on the counter top and walked quickly back to my car.

Some hundred and fifty miles north of Bakersfield, I realized I was entering Steinbeck country, and I almost sighed with relief. Here was a place to light, filled with the nuances and epiphanies of my carefree college reading days.

But it didn't happen. My mind took over and I knew that being surrounded by verdant farmland and picaresque, hard-drinking Mexicans would bring back the wonder full force, along with a barrage of guilt, shame, self-loathing, and fear that spelled only one thing: it is over.

I pulled to the edge of the roadside. I let Night Train out and he ran ahead of me into a seemingly endless sea of furrowed irrigation trenches. I walked behind him, listening to his happy bays. We walked and walked and walked, kicking up dust clouds that soon covered my trouser legs with a rich, dark brown soil. I walked all the way into a spot where the world seemed eclipsed in all directions. All my horizons were a deep dark brownness.

I sat down in the dirt. Night Train barked at me. I scooped up a handful of soil and let it slip through my fingers. I smelled my hands. They smelt of feces and infinity.

Suddenly the irrigation pipes that surrounded me broke into life, spraying me with water. I got up reflexively and started running in the direction of my car. Night Train did too, quickly passing me. Some unseen timing device was at work, and the sprinklers kept popping on in perfect succession, right behind me. I ran and I ran and I ran, barely staying ahead of the ten-foot-high geysers of water. Exhausted, I came to a halt at the edge of the blacktop, trying to catch my breath. Night Train barked happily, his chest heaving also. My shoes, socks, and trouser legs were soaking wet and smelled of manure. I got clean clothes out of the suitcase in the back seat, and changed right there on the roadway.

By the time I had finished dressing and had regained my breath, an eerie stillness had come over me. It held me there and wouldn't let me move or think. After a few moments I started to weep. I wept and I wept and I wept, standing there on the dusty roadside, my hands braced against the hood of my car. Finally my sobbing stopped, as abruptly as the stillness had begun. I took my hands from the car and stood upright as tenuously as a baby taking his first steps.

It took me a solid four hours of lead-footed driving to make it back to Los Angeles. After dropping Night Train with my mystified landlady, I drove to Lorna's apartment.

I could hear her radio blaring from the living room window as I pulled to the curb. Her electrically operated front door was propped open with a stack of telephone books. She had left the light on in the stairway, and I could see the glow of candlelight illuminating her living room at the top of the stairs.

I cleared my throat repeatedly to prepare her for my coming as I took the stairs slowly, one at a time. Lorna was lying on her floral-patterned couch, with one arm dangling over the side holding a wineglass. The light from candles placed strategically throughout the room on lamp tables, bookshelves, and windowsills encased her in an amber glow.

"Hello, Freddy," she said as I entered the room.

"Hello, Lor," I returned. I pulled an ottoman up alongside the sofa.

Lorna sipped her wine. "What will you do now?" she asked.

"I don't know. Who told you?"

"The four-star edition of the L.A. *Examiner*. 'Under-hill Resigns in Wake of False Arrests Suits. Communist

Ties Cited.' Do you want me to read you the whole thing?"

I reached for her arm, but she pulled it away. "I'm sorry for yesterday, Lorna, really."

"For my office door?"

"No, for what I said to you."

"Was it the truth?"

"Yes."

"Then don't apologize for it."

Lorna's face was an iron mask in the candlelight. Her expression was expressionless, and I couldn't decipher her feelings. "What are you going to *do*, Freddy?"

"I don't know. Maybe I'll paint my car red. Maybe I'll dye my hair red, too. Maybe I'll enlist in the North Korean Army. I've never done anything half-assed in my life, so why be a half-assed Commie?"

Lorna lit a cigarette. The smoke she exhaled cast her in a second halo within the amber light. Her mask was starting to drop. She was starting to get angry, and that gave me heart. I threw out a line calculated to compound that anger. "The wonder got me, I guess."

"No!" Lorna spat out. "No, you bastard. The wonder didn't get you; *you* got you! Don't you know that?"

"Yes, I do. And do you know the only thing I'm sorry for?"

"Eddie Engels and Margaret Cadwallader?"

"The hell with them. They're dead. I'm only sorry I took you with me."

Lorna laughed. "Don't be sorry. I fell for circumstantial evidence and the brightest, brashest, handsomest man I'd ever met. What will you *do* now, Freddy?"

I took Lorna's hand, holding it tightly so she couldn't withdraw it. "I don't know. What will you do?"

Lorna wrenched her hand free and began twisting her head sideways, banging it back and forth violently on the couch. "I don't know, I don't know, I don't know, for Christ's fucking sake, I don't know!"

"Will you stay with the D.A.'s office?"

Lorna shook her head again. "No. I can't. I mean, I could if I wanted to, but I can't. I can't go on with justice and cops and criminal law. When you called me and told me Engels confessed, I went straight to the D.A. Maybe I gushed about you, I don't know, but he had my number, and when

Canfield brought Winton to see him and we talked afterward, I knew that I was through in the office. With Engels dead, it's final. I don't even *want* to be there now. Freddy, will you try to get another policeman's job?"

The naive question was a challenge. I shook my head. "Not unless it's in Russia. Maybe I could be a deputy commissar in Leningrad, something like that. Write parking tickets for bobsleds in Siberia."

Lorna stroked my hair: "What do you *want*, Freddy?"

"I want you. That's all I know. Will you marry me?"

Lorna smiled in the candlelight. "Yes," she said.

We decided not to lose our momentum. Lorna hurriedly packed a suitcase while I put the top up on the car. We left immediately for the border, cracking jokes and singing along with the radio and playing grab-ass as we highballed it south on Route 5.

Coming into San Diego, Lorna started to cry as the realization hit her that she had lost her secure old life and had gained an uncertain new one. I held her tightly with one arm and continued driving. We crossed the border into Mexico at three in the morning.

We found an all-night wedding chapel on Revolución, the main drag of Tijuana. A fat, smiling Mexican priest married us, took the ten-dollar wedding fee and typed our marriage license, assuring us all the while that it was lawful and binding before man and God.

We drove through the impoverished Tijuana streets until we spotted a hotel that looked clean enough to spend our wedding night in.

I paid for three days in advance and carried our bags to a rickety elevator that took us up to the top floor. Our room was simple: clean, polished wood floors; clean, threadbare carpeting; a clean bathroom; and a big clean double bed.

Lorna Underhill undressed, lay down on the bed and fell asleep immediately. I sat in a chair and watched my wife sleep, believing that the steadfastness of my love for her would cover all the contingencies of life without the wonder.

III

TIME, OUT OF TIME

15

Years passed. Years of regret and introspection; years of hitting hundreds of thousands of golf balls, of reading, of long walks along the beach with Night Train; years of trying to live like other people. Years of looking for something to which I could commit my life. Years of learning what works and what doesn't. But mostly, years of Lorna.

Lorna. Lorna Weinberg Underhill. My wife, my lover, my confidante, my anodyne, my substitute for the wonder. Actually, my definition of the wonder—the synthesis of absolute knowledge and continual surprise. My tender, mercurial, brittle Lorna. The very prototype of love's efficacy: if it doesn't work, try something else. If that doesn't work, try something else again. If that fails, review your options and search out your errors. Just keep going, Freddy; sooner or later, by choice or chance or rote, you will find something that will move you as much as being a policeman did.

Did? From late 1951 through late 1954 there was virtually not one moment when I wouldn't have rather been cruising Central Avenue, or Western or Wilshire or Pico or any L.A. street in a black-and-white, armed for bear and high on illusion.

When we returned from our three-day Mexican honeymoon, Korea had once again taken over as front page news, and Lorna and I moved into a big rambling house in Laurel Canyon. There was a yard for Night Train, a big bedroom with a balcony and a rustic view, and a sunken living room with French windows that would have done a chateau in Burgundy proud.

We played house for a month, reading poetry aloud and playing Scrabble and making love and dancing to "The Tennessee Waltz." But Lorna tired of it before I did and took the first law job she could get her hands on: legal counsel for Weinberg Productions, Inc. She didn't last long; she was constantly at loggerheads with her father on matters of money, morality, and the administration of movie "justice."

In May of '52 she quit and went to work for the Adlai Stevenson campaign. She was afire with the spirit of the intellectual Illinois governor, and even managed to wrangle a paying job as the campaign's legal adviser. The job lasted until it came to light that she was married to a "Communist" ex-cop. Saddened, but no less justice-minded, she joined a Beverly Hills law firm that specialized in personal injury cases. My Lorna, champion of the poor bastard who got his thumb caught in the drill press.

Those first months of our marriage were very good. Big Sid accepted his goy son-in-law with a surprising magnanimity. He showed moral courage in bringing me out to Hillcrest to play golf at a time when I was still notorious. We played for money, and I made more than enough to hold up my half of the expenses of the Laurel Canyon love nest.

Lorna and I never discussed the Eddie Engels case. It was the pivotal event in both our lives, always hanging over us, but we never talked about it.

On our first night in the new house I broached the subject, in the interest of clearing the air. "We paid for it, Lor. We paid for what we did."

"No," Lorna said. "I was just an infatuated pencil-pusher. I got off easy. *You* paid, and it's a life sentence. I never want to discuss it again."

Mercifully for me, Canfield and the Engels family never sued either the L.A.P.D. or me for false arrest or anything else. I waited for months, fearfully expecting a summons that would result in the opening of the whole filthy can of worms to public scrutiny, but it never came.

In February of 1955 I found out why, from a drunken, resentful Mike Breuning. I ran into him in the bar of a restaurant in Hollywood. Passed over again for lieutenant, he was waxing profane about the department and his mentor, Dudley Smith. He told me, between effusive apologies, that Dudley was the one who snatched my diary, and who put Internal Affairs onto Sarah Kefalvian the very day that Eddie Engels "confessed." Dudley was also the one who flew up to Seattle and dug through local police files and came up with a rap sheet on Lillian Engels that showed a dozen drunk arrests at lesbian bars in the Seattle area. He went straight to Wilhelm Engels with this and coerced him into dropping his lawsuit. The elder Engels had died of a heart attack sometime the following year.

From time to time I would suddenly realize that I was terrified, and that I had no control over my terror. Blinding memories of the bloody face of Eddie Engels would take me over and would not let me go, even as I rambled on about the weather to Lorna. Gradually the image would shift, and Engels's face would change into my own, and then it would be Dudley Smith and Dick Carlisle hitting *me,* while I myself watched sipping coffee in room number 6 of the Victory Motel. I wouldn't cry or talk or move; just tremble as Smith and Carlisle bludgeoned me. Sometimes Lorna would hold me, and I would dig myself deeper into her as each blow crashed into my mind.

So the dead hovered over my wife and me, solidifying their presence as Lorna and I lived on. For years we loved, and it was worth the price in sorrow that my blind ambition had exacted from me and so many others. For a long while I wanted nothing that I didn't have, and I was moved beyond movement by Lorna's willingness to give it to me. When I thought and thought and thought about it, and tried to reduce it to words, Lorna would read my mind and place fingertips to my lips and whisper softly the words I had once told her: "Don't think, darling, please don't try to hurt it." She always *knew* when the wonder was creeping into my consciousness, and she always circumvented it with love tinged with the slightest bit of fear.

That fear ran concurrent with our love; an undertow of guilt, a clandestine transit of many restive dead souls that seemed to give an almost spiritual weight to our lives—as though our joy were a communion for Eddie and Maggie and a vast constituency of the dead. We both felt this, but we never talked about it. We were both afraid that it would kill the joy for which we had worked so hard.

For a long time our destiny *was* manifest joy—joy in each other, in the sharing of our separate solitudes, in the spirit of loving contention that would end our arguments with us laughing in bed, Lorna's hands clamped over my mouth while she shrieked, "No, no, tell me a story instead!"

I told her stories and she told me stories, and gradually the distinctions between my stories and Lorna's receded until they became one vast panorama of experience and more than a little fantasy.

Because somehow, in our fusion, we lost sight of ourselves as the separate entities that we were, and somehow, very strangely, that made us easy prey for the long unmentioned dead.

16

It started getting bad with Lorna gradually, so that there was no place to look for causes and no one to blame. It was just a series of smoldering resentments. Too much giving and too much taking; too much time spent away from each other; too much investing of fantasy qualities in each other. Too much hope and too much pride and too little willingness to change.

And too much thinking on my part. Early in '54 I told Lorna that. "Our brains are a curse, Lor. I want to use my muscles and not my brain." Lorna looked up from her breakfast coffee and scratched my arm distractedly. "Then go ahead. You used to tell me 'Don't think,' remember?"

Construction work and later brick-laying was mindless and exhilarating. The men I worked with and drank beer with were vital and raw. But Lorna was aghast when I stuck to this kind of work for eight months, liking it more each day. She thought I was wasting the overactive brain that I was trying so hard to quiet. And her resentment grew. She couldn't stand the anomaly of a successful attorney married to a laborer husband. An ex-cop accused Communist, yes; a working stiff, no. I noted the contradiction of a champion of the "working man" disdaining the very same in her own household.

"I didn't marry a hod carrier," Lorna said coldly.

I was beginning to wonder who she did marry. I began to wonder who I married. I started to feel a hollowness, a depression that was fifty times worse than fear. But I held on: rigorously continuing to earn through construction

211

work and golf hustling at least as much as Lorna did as an attorney.

We split the household expenses fifty-fifty, and each contributed monthly stipends to our joint savings and checking accounts. At the end of each month when we did our bookkeeping, Lorna would shake her head at the sad equity of it. We had a running gag at these sessions. We would split the expenses fifty-fifty, but I would pay for everything connected with Night Train. Lorna was mildly amused by him, but considered my noble link to Wacky and the past an obscene object. She thought dogs belonged on farms. "And the beast is your burden," she would say as we concluded our paperwork.

One day early in '55, she didn't crack her usual jokes. She was drawn and cross that day. When I looked to her to deliver her line she flung a sheaf of papers at me and screamed, "It's so goddamned easy for you! Goddamnit, how can you live with yourself? Do you know how hard I work to make the money I do? Do you, Freddy, goddamnit? Don't you think it's sad that I went to school for eight years to become a lawyer and help people, while all you do is swing a hammer and hit golf balls? Goddamn you, you Renaissance bum!"

For the first time I felt my marriage vows begin to impinge me. I began to feel that I couldn't ever be the man Lorna wanted me to be. And for the first time I didn't care, because the Lorna of 1955 was not the Lorna I married in 1951. I started to get itchy to break the whole thing up, to blow it all sky high.

As my love for Lorna entered this awful, angry stasis, I felt stirrings of what I could only call the wonder. Wonder.

Years had passed. With the end of the Korean War and the discrediting of Joe McCarthy, a slightly more sane political climate was emerging. Time seemed to be opening new wounds in my present and healing the old ones in my past. If Lorna was the replacement for the wonder, maybe now it was time to reverse the situation.

Knowing I could never be hired as a police officer, I applied for a state of California private investigator's license, and was refused. I applied for positions as insurance investigator with over thirty insurance companies, and was rejected by each one.

So I hit more thousands of golf balls, recalling the trinity of my youth: police work, golf, and women. Women. The very word bit at me like a jungle carnivore, filling me with a venomous guilt and excitement.

One night I went to a bar in Ocean Park and picked up a woman. The old small talk and moves were still there. I took her to a motel near my old apartment in Santa Monica. We coupled and talked. I told her my marriage was shot. She commiserated; it had happened to her, too, and now she was "playing the field."

In the morning I drove her back to where her car was parked, then drove home to Laurel Canyon and my wife, who didn't ask me where I had spent the night. She didn't have to.

I did it again and again, savoring the mechanics, the art of briefly touching another lonely life. Lorna knew, of course, and we settled down to a quiet war of attrition: conversations of exaggerated politeness, awkward attempts at lovemaking, silent recriminations.

Inexplicably, my womanizing stopped as abruptly as it had begun. I was sitting in a bar in the Valley nursing a beer and eyeing the cocktail waitresses, when I was hit by the same eerie stillness that had come over me in the irrigation field on the day I had quit the cops. I didn't break down this time, I just became flooded with some incredible nonverbal feeling of what I can only think of as vastness.

I tried to explain it to Lorna: "I can't explain it, Lor. It's just a feeling of, well, mystery, of truth and illusion, of something much bigger than us or anything else. It's a feeling of commitment to something very vague, but decent and good. And it's not the wonder."

Lorna snorted. "Oh, God, Freddy. Are you getting religious on me?"

"No, it's not that. It's entirely different."

I searched for words and gestures, but none came. I looked at Lorna, who shrugged, with some contempt.

The following week I found out that Lorna had a lover. He was an older man, a senior partner in her law firm. I saw them holding hands and cooing at each other in a Beverly Hills restaurant. My peripheral vision blackened as I strode toward their booth. Unreasonable as it was, I pulled the man to the floor by his necktie, dumped a pitcher of water on his face and followed it with a plate of lobster thermidor.

"Sue me, counselor," I said to the shocked Lorna.

I moved my dog, my golf clubs and my few belongings to an apartment in West L.A. I paid for three months' rent in advance, and wondered what the hell I was going to do.

Lorna ferreted out my address and sent me a petition for divorce. I tore it up in the presence of the process server who had handed it to me. "Tell Mrs. Underhill never," I told him.

Lorna discovered my phone number and called me, threatening, then begging for release from our marriage.

"Never," I told her. "Tijuana marriages are lifetime contracts."

"Goddamn you, Freddy, it's over! Can't you see that?"

"Nothing's ever over," I screamed back, then threw the phone out my living room window.

I wasn't entirely under control, but I was right. It was a prophetic remark. Three days later was June 23, 1955. That was the day I heard about the dead nurse.

IV

THE CRIME AGAINST MARCELLA

17

The initial newspaper accounts were both lurid and disinterested. Just another murder, the reports seemed to be saying.

From the Los Angeles *Herald Express*, June 23, 1955:

NURSE FOUND MURDERED IN EL MONTE

Strangulation Death for Attractive Divorced Mother

Scouts and Their Leader Make Grisly Discovery

EL MONTE, June 22—A Boy Scout troop and their leader made a grisly discovery early Sunday morning when returning from an overnight camping trip in the San Gabriel Mountains. When passing Arroyo High School on South Peck Road, one of the Scouts, Danny Johnson, age 12, thought he saw an arm poking out of a line of scrub that runs along the fence on the school's south side. He called this to the attention of his troop leader, James Pleshette, 28, of Sierra Madre. Pleshette went to investigate and discovered the nude body of a woman. He called El Monte police immediately.

Description Broadcast

Police went to the scene and immediately sent out a description of the woman to all Los Angeles TV and

radio stations. Response to the broadcast was gratify-
ingly quick. Mrs. Gaylord Wilder, an El Monte resident, thought the description fit her tenant, Mrs.
Marcella Harris, who had been gone since Friday
night. Mrs. Wilder was brought to the morgue,
where she positively identified the dead woman as
Mrs. Harris.

Good Mother

Mrs. Wilder started to sob upon viewing the body.
"Oh, God, what a tragedy!" she said. "Marcella was
such a good woman. A good mother, devoted to her
son." Mrs. Harris, 43, was divorced from her husband,
William "Doc" Harris, several years ago. They have a
nine-year-old son, who was spending the weekend
with his father. When notified of the death, Harris
(who has been eliminated as a suspect) said, "I have
every hope the police will quickly catch my wife's
killer." Nine-year-old Michael, distraught, is now living with his father in Los Angeles. Mrs. Harris
worked as head nurse at the Packard-Bell Electronics
plant in Santa Monica. Both the El Monte Police Department and the Los Angeles County Sheriff's Department have mounted a full-scale investigation.

I sat and thought, feeling strangely calm, yet engulfed
by a prickly sensation when I put down the newspaper. It
was too long after the facts, I told myself, too far away, too
prosaic a form of murder. Strictly a non sequitur. I didn't
want to catch myself up in another logical fallacy.

I needed statistics, and the only person I knew who could
furnish them was a crime-buff law clerk in Lorna's firm. I
called the office and got him. The receptionist recognized
my voice and gave me the cold shoulder, but put me
through anyway. After several minutes of amenities, I
popped my question: "Bob, what are the statistics on strangulation murders of women, where the killer is not a
known intimate of the victim?"

Bob didn't have to think: "Commonplace, but they usually catch the killer fast. Barroom jobs, drunks strangling

prostitutes, that kind of thing. Very often the killer is re-
morseful, confesses, and cops a plea. Is this an academic
question, Fred?"

"Yeah, strictly. How about premeditated strangulation
murders of women?"

"Including psychopaths?"

"No, presupposing relative sanity on the part of the
killer."

"Relative sanity, that's a hot one. Very rare, kid, very
rare indeed. What's this all about?"

"It's about an ex-cop with time on his hands. Thanks a
lot, Bob. Goodbye."

I watched TV that night, but television coverage of the
murder was scant. The dead woman's face was flashed
on the screen, a photograph taken some twenty years before upon her graduation from nursing school. Marcella
Harris had been a very handsome woman: high, strong
cheekbones, large widely spaced eyes, and a determined
mouth.

The somber-voiced announcer called on all concerned
citizens "who might be able to help the police" to call the
detective bureau of the Los Angeles County Sheriff's Department. A phone number was flashed across the bottom
of the screen for a few brief seconds, before the announcer
started a used-car commercial. I turned the TV off.

I started collecting all the newspaper articles I could
find about the murder. By Tuesday the Harris murder had
been relegated to the third page. From the Los Angeles
Times, June 24, 1955:

LAST HOURS OF DEAD NURSE
RECONSTRUCTED

LOS ANGELES, June 24—Marcella Harris, who
was found strangled in El Monte Sunday morning,
was last seen alive in a cocktail lounge on nearby Valley Boulevard. Police revealed today that eyewitnesses placed the attractive redheaded nurse at
Hank's Hot Spot, a bar at 18391 Valley Boulevard in
South El Monte, between the hours of 8:00 and 11:30
Saturday night. She left alone, but was seen huddling

in conversation with a dark-haired man in his forties and a blond woman in her late twenties. Police artists are now at work assembling composite drawings of the pair, who at this time are the only suspects in the grisly strangulation murder.

Father and Son Together

"Michael will always bear the scars, of that I am sure," William "Doc" Harris, a handsome man in his late fifties, said yesterday. "But I know that I can make up for the love he has lost in losing his mother." Harris ruffled his nine-year-old son's hair fondly. Michael, a tall, bespectacled youngster, said, "I just hope the police get the guy who killed my mom."

It was a peaceful but sad scene at the Harris apartment on Beverly Boulevard. Sad because police are powerless in dealing with the grief of a motherless nine-year-old boy. El Monte police spokesman Sergeant A.D. Wisenhunt said, "We're doing everything within our power to track down the killer. We have no idea where Mrs. Harris was killed, but we figure that it had to be in the El Monte area. The coroner places the time of her death at between 2:00 A.M. and 5:00 A.M., and the Scouts found her at 7:30 A.M. We have detectives and uniformed officers out circulating composite drawings of the two people Mrs. Harris was last seen talking to. We have to be patient—only diligent police work will crack this case."

Half of me felt crazy for even following newspaper accounts of this "case," but the other half of me screamed inside when the words "cocktail lounge" jumped out at me from the printed page. I hemmed and hawed, and pounded myself internally for several hours, until I realized there would never be a moment's peace until I gave it a whirl. Then I picked up the phone and called Sergeant Reuben Ramos at Rampart Division.

"Reuben, this is Fred Underhill."

"Jesus H. Christ on a crutch, where the hell have you been?"

"Away."

"That's for sure, man. Jesus Christ, did *you* get fucked! What happened? I heard tons of rumors, but nothing that sounded like the straight dope."

I sighed. I hadn't counted on recalling the past to a former colleague. "I got the wrong man, Rube, and the department had to make me look bad to take the onus off them. That's it."

Reuben didn't buy it. "I'll settle for that, man," he said skeptically, "but what's up? You need a favor, right?"

"Right. I need you to run someone through R&I for me."

Reuben sighed. "You got some amateur gig going?"

"Kind of. Are you ready?"

"Hit me."

"Marcella Harris, white female, forty-three years old."

"Isn't she that dead dame from—"

"Yeah," I cut in. "Can you run her and get back to me as soon as possible?"

"You crazy fuck," Reuben said as he hung up.

The telephone rang forty-five minutes later, and I leaped at it, catching it on the first ring.

"Fred? Reuben. Grab a pencil."

I had one ready. "Hit it, Rube."

"Okay. Marcella Harris. Maiden name DeVries. Born Tunnel City, Wisconsin, April 15, 1912. Green and red, five feet seven inches, one hundred forty. Nurse, U.S. Navy 1941-1946, discharged as a Wave lieutenant commander. Pretty impressive, huh? Now dig this: arrested in '48, possession of marijuana. Dismissed. Arrested in '50 on suspicion of receiving stolen goods. Dismissed. Arrested for drunk twice in '46, once in '47, three times in '48, once in '49 and '50. Nice, huh?"

I whistled. "Yeah. Interesting."

"What are you planning on doing with this information, man?"

"I don't know, Rube."

"You be careful, Freddy. That's all I'm gonna say. Some bimbo gets choked in El Monte, and well . . . Freddy, it's got nothing to do with the other. That's dead history, man."

"Probably."

"You be careful. You ain't a cop no more."

"Thanks, Rube," I said, and hung up.

The following morning I got up early, put on a summer suit and drove out to El Monte, taking the Santa Monica Freeway to the Pomona, headed east.

I went from smog-shrouded L.A. past picturesque, seedy Boyle Heights and a succession of dreary semi-impoverished suburbs, growing more expectant as each new postwar boom community flew by. This was new territory for me, well within the confines of L.A. County, yet somehow otherworldly. The residential streets I glimpsed from my elevated vantage point seemed sullen in their sameness, the big boom in postwar disappointment and malaise.

El Monte was smack in the middle of the San Gabriel Valley, enclosed by freeways in all directions. The San Gabriel Mountains, awash in smog, bordered the northern perimeter.

I got off at the Valley Boulevard exit and cruised west until I found Hank's Hot Spot, described by the papers as a "convivial watering hole." It didn't look like that; it looked like what it more probably was: a meeting place for lonely juiceheads.

I pulled up to the curb. The place was open at eight-thirty in the morning. That was encouraging. It went along with the scenario I was composing in my mind: Maggie Cadwallader and Marcella Harris, lonely juiceheads. I kiboshed the thought: don't think, Underhill, I said to myself as I locked the car, or this thing—which is probably only coincidence—will eat you up.

I hastily prepared a cover story as I took a seat at the narrow, imitation-wood bar. The place was deserted, and a lone bartender who was polishing glasses as I entered approached me guardedly. He nodded at me as he placed a napkin on the bar.

"Draft beer," I said.

He nodded again and brought it to me. I sipped it. It tasted bitter; I wasn't cut out to be a morning drinker.

I decided not to waste time with small talk. "I'm a reporter," I said. "I write crime stuff laced with the human interest angle. There's a double sawbuck in it for anybody who can give me some interesting lowdown on this Marcella Harris dame who got croaked last weekend." I pulled out my billfold, packed with twenties, and fanned the cash in the bartender's face. He looked impressed. "The real lowdown," I added, waggling my eyebrows at him. "The barfly tidbits that make bartending such an interesting profession."

The barman swallowed, his Adam's apple rotating nervously in his wiry neck. "I already told the cops everything I know about that night," he said.

"Tell *me*," I said, taking a twenty out of my billfold and placing it under my cocktail napkin.

"Well," the barman said, "the Harris dame came in around seven-thirty that night. She ordered a double Early Times old-fashioned. She practically chugalugged it. She ordered another. She sat here at the bar by herself. She played some show tunes on the jukebox. Around eight-thirty this greasy-lookin' guy and this blond dame with a ponytail come in. They get in some kind of conversation with the Harris dame and they all go to a booth together. The guy drinks red wine and the ponytail drinks Seven-Up. The Harris dame left before them, around eleven. The greasy guy and the ponytail left together around midnight. That's it."

I fingered an inch or so of the twenty out from its hiding place. "Do you think Marcella Harris already knew these people, or do you think they just met one another?"

The barman shook his head. "The cops asked me the same thing, buddy, and it beats me."

I tried another tack: "Was Marcella Harris a regular here?"

"Not really. She came in once in a while."

"Was she a pickup? Did she leave with a lot of different men?"

"Not that I ever noticed."

"Okay. Was she a talker?"

"Not really."

"Did you ever talk with her at length?"

"Sometimes. I don't know, once or twice."

"I see. What did you discuss?"

"Just small talk. You know . . ."

"Besides that."

"Well . . . once she asks me if I've got kids. I say yes. She asks me if I ever have trouble with 'em, and I say yeah, the usual stuff. Then she starts tellin' me about this wild kid she's got, how she don't know how to handle him, that she's read all these books and still don't know what to do."

"What was the problem with the kid?" I asked.

The bartender swallowed and shuffled his feet in a little dance of embarrassment. "Aw, come on, mister," he said.

"No, you come on." I stuffed the twenty into his shirt pocket.

"Well," he said, "she said the kid was gettin' into fights, and talkin' dirty . . . and . . . exposing himself to all the other little kids."

"Is that it?"

"Yeah."

"Did you tell the police about this?"

"No."

"Why?"

"Because they never asked me."

"That's a good reason," I said, then thanked the man and walked back outside to my car.

I looked through the L.A. papers I had been collecting and found Marcella Harris's home address in Monday's *Mirror*: 467 Maple Avenue, El Monte. It took me only five minutes to get there.

I surveyed El Monte as I drove. The residential streets were unpaved, and the residences that fronted them were ugly cubelike apartment buildings interspersed with sub-divided farmhouses and auto courts held over from the not too distant time when this was open country.

I parked on the dirt shoulder at the corner of Claymore and Maple. Number 467 was right there on the corner, directly across from my parking spot. Two small frame houses stood in a large front yard encircled by a shoulder-high stone wall. Both houses looked well cared for, and a beagle puppy cavorted in the yard.

I didn't want to attempt the landlady—she had probably been frequently questioned by the police on her former tenant—so I just sat in the car and thought. Finally it hit me, and I dug a briefcase out of my trunk and went walking. School had recently let out for the summer, and the kids playing in their dirt front yards looked happy to be free. I waved to them as I walked down Maple, getting slightly suspicious looks in return. My crisp summer suit was obviously not standard El Monte garb.

Maple Avenue dead-ended a hundred yards or so in front of me, where a kids' softball game was in progress. The kids probably knew the Harris boy, so I decided to brace them.

"Hi, fellows," I said.

The game stopped abruptly as I walked through their makeshift infield. I got suspicious looks, hostile looks, and curious looks. There were six boys, all of them wearing white T-shirts and blue jeans. One of the boys, standing by home plate, threw the ball to first base. I dropped my briefcase, ran and made a daring leaping catch. I fumbled the ball on purpose and crashed to the pavement. I made a big show of getting to my feet. The kids surrounded me as I brushed off my trousers.

"I guess I'm not Ted Williams, fellows," I said. "I must be getting old. I used to be a hotshot fielder."

One of the boys grinned at me. "That was still a pretty swell try, mister," he said.

"Thanks," I returned. "Geeze, it's hot out here. Dusty, too. You guys ever get the chance to go to the beach?"

The boys started jabbering all together: "Naw, but we got the municipal pool." "The beach is too far and it's full of beer cans. My dad took us once." "We play baseball." "I'm gonna pitch like Bob Lemon." "Wanna see my fastball?"

"Whoa, whoa! Hold on there," I said. "What about the Scouts? Don't any of you guys go on field trips with them?"

Quiet greeted my question. There was a general reacting of down-turned faces. I had hit a nerve.

"What's the matter, fellows?"

"Aw, nothin' really," the tall first baseman said, "but my mom got real down on our troop for somethin' that wasn't even our fault."

"Yeah." "Yeah." "What a crummy deal!" the other boys chimed in.

"What happened?" I asked innocently.

"Well," a tall boy said, "it was our troop that found the dead lady."

I tossed the battered softball into the air and caught it. "That's a shame. You mean Mrs. Harris?"

"Yeah," they all said practically at once.

I waded in cautiously, although I knew that the boys wanted to talk. "She lived here on this street, didn't she?"

This brought forth a huge response: "Ooh! Yeah, you shoulda seen her, mister. All naked. Ooh!" "Yeachh, really sickening." "Yeah, ugh."

I tossed the ball to the quietest of the boys. "Did any of you boys know Mrs. Harris?" There was an embarrassed silence.

"My mom told me not to talk to strangers," the quiet boy said.

"My dad told me not to say bad things about people," the first baseman said.

I yawned, and feigned exasperation. "Well, I was just curious," I said. "Maybe I'll get a chance to talk to you guys later. I'm the new baseball coach at Arroyo High. You guys look pretty good to me. In a few years you'll probably be my starting lineup." I pretended to leave.

It was the perfect thing to say, and it was followed by a big volley of excited "oohs" and "aahs."

"What's so bad about Mrs. Harris?" I asked the first baseman.

He stared at his feet, then looked up at me with confused blue eyes. "My dad says he saw her a whole bunch of times down at Medina Court. He said no good woman would have anything to do with a place like that. He said that she was an unfit mother, that that was why Michael acted so strange." The boy backed away from me, as if the specter of his father was right there with us.

"Hold on, partner," I said, "I'm new in this territory. What's so bad about Medina Court? And what's wrong with Michael? He sounded like a pretty good kid from what I read in the papers."

A redheaded boy clutching a catcher's mitt answered me frankly. "Medina Court is Mex Town. Wetbacks —mean ones. My dad says never, ever, ever go there, that they hate white people. It's dangerous there."

"My dad delivers the mail on Medina," the first baseman said. "He said he's seen Mrs. Harris do nasty things there."

A chill went over me. "What about Michael?" I asked.

No one answered. My expression and manner must have changed somehow, alerting some sixth sense in the youthful ballplayers.

"I gotta go," the quiet boy said.

"Me, too," another one piped in.

Before I knew it they were all running off down Maple Avenue, casting furtive glances at me over their shoulders. They all seemed to disappear into dusty front yards just moments later, leaving me standing in the street wondering what the hell had happened.

Medina Court was only one block long.

A tarnished brass plaque inlaid in the cracked sidewalk at the entrance to it said why: the street and the four-story tenements that dominated it had been constructed for the housing of Chinese railroad workers in 1885.

I parked my car on the dirt shoulder of Peck Road—the only access lane to Medina Court—and looked around. The buildings, obviously once painted white, were now as grayish-brown as the plague of smog that stifled the summer air. A half-dozen had burned down, and the charred detritus of the fires had never been removed. Mexican women and children sat on the front steps of their peeling, sunbaked dwellings, seeking respite from what must have been ovenlike interiors.

Garbage covered the dusty street through Medina Court and prewar jalopies lay dead along both sides of it. Mariachi music poured forth from inside some of the tenements, competing with high-pitched Spanish voices. An emaciated dog hobbled by me, giving me a cursory growl and a hungry look. The poverty and meanness of Medina Court was overpowering.

I needed to find the mailman-father of the first baseman, so I started by checking out the entranceways of the tenements to see if the mail had been delivered. The mailbox layout was identical in all of the buildings—banks of metal mail slots, rows and rows of them, bearing poorly printed Spanish surnames and apartment numbers. I checked out three buildings on each side of the street, getting a lot of dirty looks in the process. The mailboxes were empty. I was in luck.

Medina Court dead-ended at a combination weed patch–
auto graveyard where a throng of tattered but happy-look-
ing Mexican kids were playing tag. I walked back to Peck
Road feeling grateful that I didn't live here.

I waited for three hours, watching the passing scene: old
winos poking about in the rubble of the burned-out buildings, looking for shade to drink their short-dogs in; fat
Mexican women chasing their screaming children down
the street; a profusion of squabbles between men in
T-shirts, filled with obscenities in English and Spanish;
two fistfights; and a steady parade of pachucos tooling
down the street in their hot rods.

At one o'clock, as the sun reached its stifling zenith and
the temperature started to close in on one hundred degrees, a tired and dejected-looking mailman walked into
Medina Court. My heart gave a little leap of joy—he was
the very image of the blond first baseman. He walked into
the "foyer" of the first tenement on the south side of the
street, and I was waiting for him on the sidewalk when he
walked back out.

His tired manner perked up when he saw me standing
there, white and official-looking in my suit and tie. He
smiled; the nervous, edgy smile of someone hungry for
company. He looked me up and down. "Cop?" he said.

I tried to sound surprised: "No, why do you ask?"

The mailman laughed and swung his leather mail sack
from one shoulder to the other. "Because any white man
over six feet in a suit on a day like this in Medina Court
has gotta be a cop."

I laughed. "Wrong, but you're close. I'm a private investigator." I didn't offer any proof, because of course I didn't
have any. The mailman whistled; I caught a whiff of booze
on his breath. I stuck out my hand. "Herb Walker," I said.

The mailman grasped it. "Randy Rice."

"I need some information, Randy. Can we talk? Can I
buy you a beer? Or can't you drink on duty?"

"Rules are made to be broken," Randy Rice said. "You
wait here. I'll deliver this mail and see you in twenty minutes."

He was good to his word, and half an hour later I was in
a seedy bar near the freeway, listening politely to Randy

Rice expound on his theory of the "wetback problem plagu-
ing America."

"Yeah," I finally broke in, "and it's a tough life for the
white working man. Believe me, I know. I'm on this tough
case now, and none of the Mexicans I talk to will give me a
straight answer." Randy Rice went bug-eyed with awe. I
continued: "That's why I wanted to talk to you. I figured a
smart white man familiar with Medina Court ought to be
able to give me a few leads."

I ordered another beer for Rice. He gulped it, and his
face contorted into a broad parody of caginess. "What do
you wanna know?" he asked.

"I heard Marcella Harris used to hang out on Medina
Court. I think that's a hell of a place for a white woman
with a kid to be spending her time."

"I seen the Harris dame there," Randy Rice said, "lots of
times."

"How did you know it was her? Did you just recognize
her from her picture in the paper when she got knocked
off?"

"No, she lived on my block at home. I seen her leave for
work in the morning, and I seen her at the store, and I used
to see her walk her dog. I used to see her play catch with
that crazy kid of hers in her front yard, too." Rice swallowed. "Who hired you?" he blurted out.

"Her ex-husband. He's out for blood. He thinks one of
her boyfriends croaked her. Why do you say her kid is
crazy?"

"Because he is. That kid is poison, mister. For one thing,
he's only nine years old and he's at least six feet tall. He
hates the other kids, too. My boy told me that Michael was
always breakin' up the softball games at school, always
challengin' everyone to fight. He'd always get beat up—I
mean he's a gigantic kid, but he don't know how to fight
and he'd get beat up, then he'd start laughing like a madman, and . . ."

"And expose himself?"

". . . Yeah."

"You didn't seem surprised when I mentioned Marcella
Harris's boyfriends." With a flourish I ordered the now
red-faced Rice another beer. "Tell me about that," I said.

He leered and said, "I been seein' her around Medina for

months, drivin' in her Studebaker, hangin' out in Deadman's Park—"

"Deadman's Park?"

"Yeah, where Medina dead-ends. Dead dogs and dead
winos and dead cars. I seen her a coupla times hangin' out
with Joe Sanchez on his stoop, lookin' real cozy with him.
Him in his zoot suit and Harris in her nurse's uniform.
Once she walked out of Sanchez's apartment real glassy-
eyed, like she was walkin' on mashed potatoes, and nearly
knocked me over. Jesus, I said to myself, this dame is high
on dope. She—"

I halted Rice. "Does Sanchez sell dope?" I asked.

"Does he ever!" Rice said. "He's the number one pusher
in the San Gabriel Valley. I seen loads of hopheads leavin'
his dump like they was on cloud nine. The cops roust him
all the time, but he's always clean. He don't use the shit
himself, and he don't hide it at Medina. I heard lots of
young punks talk about what a smart vato he is. If you ask
me, scum like Sanchez should be sent straight to the electric chair."

I considered this latest information. "Have you talked to
the cops about this, Randy?" I asked.

"Hell no, it's none of my business. Sanchez didn't bump
off Harris, some loony did. That's obvious. I got my job to
consider. I gotta deliver mail to Medina. It's no skin off my
ass what Sanchez does."

"Is Sanchez tough, Randy?"

"He don't look tough, he just looks oily. Mexican-
smart."

"What's his address?"

"Three-one-one Medina, number sixty-one."

"Does he live alone?"

"I think so."

"Describe him for me, would you?"

"Well, five foot eight inches, one-forty, skinny, duck's-
ass haircut. Always wear khakis and a purple silk jacket
with a wolf's head on the back, even in the summer. I
guess he's about thirty."

I got up and shook Randy Rice's hand. He winked and
started in on another windy monologue on the wetback
problem. I cut him off with a wink of my own and a clap on

the shoulder. As I walked out of the bar I heard him giving his spiel to the other lonely booze-hounds.

Twenty minutes later I was back on Medina Court, sweltering in the vestibule of number 311. I scanned the bank of mailboxes for apartment 61, found it, and ripped the metal latch off to find the box stuffed with letters bearing Mexican postmarks.

Taking a chance on my rudimentary Spanish, I tore open three of the envelopes at random and read. The letters were scrawled illegibly, but I managed to discern one main theme after reading all three. Cousin Joe Sanchez was moving the Mexican wing of his family up to America, cautiously, one at a time, for a nominal charge. The letters were brimful of gratitude and hope for a good life in the New World. Cousin Joe was effusively praised, and monetary commitments were promised once the new Americans found work. I started to dislike Cousin Joe.

He showed up at six-thirty, just as the sun's hammer blows were starting to fall short of Medina Court. I watched from the steps of his tenement as a purple 1950 Mercury with fender skirts pulled to the curb and a skinny Mexican with a purple silk jacket and a sullen grin got out, locked the car carefully, and skipped up the steps in my direction.

I had my eyes locked into his face, waiting to read it for signs of fear or violence when he noticed my presence. But when he saw me Sanchez just threw up his hands in mock surrender and said, "You waiting for me, Officer?" grinning broadly all the while.

I grinned back. "I know you're clean, Joe. You always are. I just wanted to have a little talk with you."

Sanchez grinned again. "Why don't we go up to my crib, then?"

I nodded assent and let him walk into the steaming hallway ahead of me. We took the stairs up to the third floor. Sanchez fiddled with the double lock on his door, and when the door opened I slammed my right fist into the back of his neck, sending him sprawling into his immaculate, cheap-plush living room. He looked up at me from the

floor, his whole body trembling in anger. I closed the door
behind me, and we stared at each other. Sanchez recovered
quickly, getting to his feet and brushing off his silk jacket.

The sardonic grin returned. "This ain't happened in a
while," he said. "You with the sheriff's?"

"L.A.P.D.," I said, for old-times' sake. I dug the letters
out of my coat pocket, holding my coat closed so that Sanchez wouldn't know that I was unarmed. I tossed them in
his face. "You forgot your mail, Joe."

I waited for a reaction. Sanchez shrugged and plopped
into a sofa covered with Mexican souvenir blankets. I
pulled a chair up to within breathing distance of him.

"Dope and green cards, pretty nice," I said.

Sanchez shrugged, then looked at me defiantly. "What
do you want, man?" He spat at me.

"I want to know what a good-looking, middle-class white
woman like Marcella Harris was doing down here on Medina Court," I said, "besides buying dope from you."

Sanchez's manner seemed to crumple in relief, then
tense up in fear. It was bizarre. "I didn't kill her, man," he
said.

"I'm sure you didn't. Let's make this simple. You tell me
what you know, and I'll leave you alone—forever. You
don't tell me, and I'll have the Immigration cops and the
feds up here in fifteen minutes. *Comprende?*"

Sanchez nodded. "A friend of mine brought her around.
She wanted to buy some reefer. She kept coming back. She
thought Medina Court was kicks. She was a loca, a hot-
headed redhead. She liked to smoke reef and dance. She
liked Mexican music." Sanchez shrugged, indicating com-
pletion of his story.

It wasn't enough. I told him so: "Not good enough, Joe.
You make it sound like you just tolerated her. I don't buy
it. I heard she used to hang out with you and a bunch of
other pachucos down at the auto graveyard."

"Okay, man. I liked her. '*La Roja,*' I used to call her.
'The Red One.' "

"Were you screwing her?"

Sanchez was genuinely indignant: "No, man! She
wanted me to, but I'm engaged! I don't mess with no
gringas."

"Forgive me for mentioning it. Was she hooked on stuff?"

Sanchez hesitated. "She . . . she took pills. She was a nurse and she could get codeine. She used to get crazy and act silly when she was high on it. She said she could be . . ."

I leaned forward. "She said *what*, Joe?"

"She . . . she . . . said she could outfight any Mexican, and out-fuck and out-drink any *puta*. She said that she'd seen stuff that . . . that . . ."

"That *what?*" I screamed.

"That would have made our *cojones* fall off!" Sanchez screamed back.

"Did she hang out with any other guys here on Medina?" I asked.

Sanchez shook his head. "No. She was just interested in me. I told the others to leave her alone, that she was bad news. I liked her, but I had no respect for her. She used to leave her kid alone at night. Anyway, I started giving Marcella the cold shoulder. She took the hint and didn't come around no more. I ain't seen her in six months."

I got up and walked around the room. The walls were adorned with bullfight posters and cheap landscape prints. "Who introduced her to you?" I asked.

"My friend, Carlos. He used to work at that factory where she was the nurse."

"Where can I find Carlos?"

"He went back to Mexico, man."

"Did Marcella Harris ever bring anyone else around to see you?"

"Yeah, once. She knocks on my door at seven in the morning. She had this guy with her, she was hanging on to him real tight, like they been . . ."

"Yeah, I know. Go on."

"Anyway, she starts jabbering about the guy, how he just got promoted to graveyard foreman at the plant. I sold them some reef and they split."

"What did this guy look like?"

"Kind of fat and blond. Kind of like a *stúpido*. He had no thumb on his left hand. It kind of spooked me. I'm superstitious and I . . ."

I sighed. "And what, Joe?"

"And I knew that Marcella was gonna die mean. That she *wanted* to die mean."

"Ever see Marcella with a dark-haired man or a blond woman with a ponytail?"

"No."

I got up to leave. "Poor *roja,*" Joe Sanchez said as I walked out his door.

Mrs. Gaylord Wilder, Marcella Harris's landlady, had nervous gray eyes and a manner of barely controlled hysteria. I didn't know how to play her—impersonating a cop was too risky with a solid citizen, and intimidation might well bring repercussions from the real cops.

Standing in her doorway as she openly scrutinized me, I hit on it. Mrs. Wilder had an avaricious look about her, so I tried a wild gambit: I attempted to pass myself off as an insurance investigator, interested in the recent past of the late Marcella. Mrs. Wilder took it all in, wide-eyed, with a nervous hand on the doorjamb. When I said ". . . and there's a substantial reward for anyone who can help us," she swung the door open eagerly, and pointed to an imitation leather davenport.

She went into the kitchen, leaving me alone to survey the crammed living room, and returned in a moment with a box of See's candy. I popped a piece of sticky chocolate into my mouth. "That's delicious," I said.

"Thank you, Mr. . . ."

"Carpenter, Mrs. Wilder. Is your husband at home?"

"No, he's at work."

"I see. Mrs. Wilder, let me level with you. Your late tenant, Marcella Harris, had three policies with us. Her son, Michael, was the beneficiary on all of them. However, there has been a rival claim, filed out of nowhere. A woman who claims to be a dear friend of the late Mrs. Harris states, in an affidavit, that Mrs. Harris told her that *she* was the beneficiary on all three policies. Right now, I'm investigating to determine if this woman even *knew* Marcella Harris."

Mrs. Wilder's hands did a nervous little dance in her lap. Her eyes did a little dance of greed. "How can *I* help you, Mr. Carpenter?" she asked eagerly.

I gave that some mock concentration. "Mrs. Wilder, you can help me by telling me anything and everything you know about the friends of Marcella Harris."

Now the woman's whole body seemed to dance. Finally, her tongue caught up with her. "Well, to tell you the truth . . ." she began.

"You are *sworn* to tell the truth," I interjected sternly

She went for it. "Well, Mr. Carpenter, Marcella's friends were mostly men. I mean she was a good mother and all, but she had lots of men friends."

"That's no crime."

"No, but—"

I interrupted. "I heard Michael Harris was a wild boy. That he got into fights. That he exposed himself to the other kids in the neighborhood."

Mrs. Wilder went red and shrieked, "That boy was the devil! All he needed was horns! Then everyone would have known. A boy without a father is a sinful thing!"

"Well, Michael is with his father now."

"Marcella told me about *that* one! What a no-good, handsome, good-for-nothing he was!"

"About her men friends, Mrs. Wilder . . ."

"I thought you said a woman filed this claim you're investigating."

"Yes, but this woman claimed that Marcella didn't have any gentleman friends, that Marcella was a quiet career woman dedicated to her son."

"Ha! Women like Marcella attract men the way sweets attract flies. I know. I had my share of suitors before I got married, but I never carried on the way that hussy did!"

I let Mrs. Wilder catch her breath. "Please be specific," I said.

Mrs. Wilder continued, warily this time. "Well . . . when Marcella moved in I offered to throw a little get-together for her, invite some of the ladies in the neighborhood. Well . . . Marcella told me that she didn't want any women friends, that women were all right to have a cup of coffee with once in a while, but she'd take men any day. I told her, 'You're a divorcée. Haven't you learned your lesson?' I'll never forget what she said: 'Yes, I did. I learned to use men the way they use women, and keep it at that.' I don't mind telling you, Mr. Carpenter, I don't mind telling you I was shocked!"

"Yes, that is shocking. Did Marcella Harris ever talk about her ex-husband at length? Or any of her boyfriends?"

"She just told me that Doc Harris was a charming, good-for-nothing snake. And about her boyfriends? If I'd known they were sleeping over I would have put a stop to it right away! I don't put up with promiscuous goings on."

I was getting tired of Mrs. Wilder. "How did you finally find out about Mrs. Harris's goings on?" I asked.

"Michael. He . . . used to leave notes. Anonymous ones. Obscene ones. I don't—"

I came awake. "Do you still have them?" I blurted.

Mrs. Wilder shrieked again: "No, no, no! I don't want to talk about it. I knew she was bad from the moment she moved in. I require references, and Marcella gave me fake ones, fake all the way down the line. If you ask me, she—"

The telephone rang. Mrs. Wilder went into the kitchen to answer it. When she was out of sight, I gave the room a quick toss, checking out the contents of shelves and bookcases. On top of the television set I found a stack of unopened mail. There was a letter addressed to Marcella Harris. Someone, probably Mrs. Wilder, had written in pencil on the envelope: "Deceased. Forward to William Harris, 4968 Beverly Blvd., L.A. 4, Calif."

I heard the landlady jabbering away in the kitchen. I put the envelope into my pocket and quietly left her house.

It was almost dusk. I drove toward the freeway, stopping a few blocks from the on-ramp to check the letter. It was just an overdue dentist's bill, and I threw it out the window, but it fit in: Marcella Harris lived a fast life and neglected small commitments. I wondered what kind of nurse she had been. I headed back toward Santa Monica to see if I could find out.

The freeways that night were surreal; seemingly endless red and white glowing jet streams carrying travelers to home and hearth, work and play, lovers' rendezvous and unknown destinations. This was not my Los Angeles I was passing over, and the dead nurse was none of my business, but as the eastern suburbs turned into good old familiar downtown L.A., old instincts clicked into place and the excitement of being out there and on the track of the immutable yet ever-changing took me over. There was nothing happening in my life, and looking for a killer was as good a way as any to fill the void.

I willed myself to form the nude image of Maggie Cadwallader. For the first time in years I didn't gasp reflexively.

The Packard-Bell Electronics plant was on Olympic Boulevard in the heart of the Santa Monica industrial district.

There was a drive-in movie theater around the corner on Bundy, and when I parked my car I could see that they were screening a Big Sid horror extravaganza. That depressed me, but the anticipation of pursuit quashed the depression fast.

The plant was a one-story red brick building that seemed to run off in several directions. Adjacent to a shipping and receiving area were two parking lots, separated by a low chain link fence. The closer lot, situated next to the front entrance, was empty. It was well lighted and bordered by evenly spaced little shrubby plants. The other lot was larger, and strewn with cigarette butts, candy wrappers, and newspapers. It had to be the lower-echelon employees' lot.

I hopped the fence to give it a closer look. The cars that were parked diagonally across it were for the most part old and beat-up. Little metal signs on poles marked the parking assignments, which were set up according to prestige: the maintenance men parked the furthest from the entrance. Closer in were "shippers"; closer still were "assembly crew."

I found what I was looking for flush up against the poorly lighted shipping entrance: a single parking slot with "foreman" stenciled in white paint on the cement.

I checked the time—nine-twenty-three. The graveyard crew probably came on at midnight. All I could do now was wait.

It was late when I was rewarded. Over three hours of squatting in a darkened corner of the parking lot had put me in a foul mood. I watched as the night shift took off at precisely twelve o'clock, peeling rubber in my face. They seemed happy to be free.

The graveyard crew trickled in over the next half hour, seemingly not as happy. My eyes were glued to the parking space in front of the building, and at 12:49 a well-kept '46 Cadillac pulled in and parked in the foreman's space. A fat blond man got out. From my vantage point, I couldn't tell if he was missing any thumbs.

I waited five minutes and followed him inside. There was an employees' lunchroom at the end of a long, dimly lit corridor. I walked in and looked around. A youth in a duck's-ass haircut gave me a curious look, but none of the other goldbricking workmen seemed to notice me.

The fat blond foreman was sitting at a table, holding a cup of coffee in his right hand. I got a Coke from a machine and took my time drinking it. The foreman had his left hand in his pocket. He kept it there, driving me nuts. Finally, he took it out and scratched his nose. His thumb was missing—more than enough confirmation.

I walked back outside and found a rusty old coat hanger on the ground at the edge of the parking lot. I fashioned a hook device out of it and casually walked over to the foreman's Cadillac. The car was locked, but the wind wing on the driver's side was open. I looked in all directions, then slipped the bent coat hanger through the window and hooked it over the door button. The hanger slipped off once, but the second time it caught and I pulled the button up.

Quickly I got in the car and hunched down in the front seat. I tried the glove compartment. It was locked. I ran a hand over the steering column and found what I wanted: The car registration, attached in a leather holder, fastened on with buckles. I removed it and huddled even lower in the seat.

The plastic-encased official paper read: Henry Robert Hart, 1164¼ Hurlburt Pl., Culver City, Calif.

It was all I needed. I fastened the registration back on the steering column, locked Henry Hart's car and ran to my own.

Hurlburt Place was a quiet street of small houses a few

blocks from the M.G.M. Studios. Number 1164¼ was a garage apartment. I parked across the street and rummaged in my trunk for some makeshift burglar's tools. A screwdriver and a metal carpenter's rule were all I could come up with.

I walked slowly across the street and into the driveway that led back to the garage. No lights were on in the front house. The wooden steps that led up to Henry Hart's apartment creaked so loudly that they must have been heard all the way downtown, but my own heartbeat seemed to drown them out.

The lock was a joke: working the rule and screwdriver simultaneously snapped it easily.

When the door opened, I stood there hesitantly, wondering if I dared enter. My previous B&Es had been done as a policeman; this time I was a civilian. I took a deep breath and walked in, wrapping my right hand in a handkerchief as I fumbled for a light switch.

Stumbling in the darkness, I crashed into a floor lamp, almost knocking it over. Holding it at waist level, I turned it on, illuminating a dreary bedroom–living room: ratty chairs, ratty Murphy bed, threadbare carpet, and cheap oil prints on the walls—probably all inherited from previous tenants long gone.

Deciding to give myself one minute to toss the room, I stood the lamp up on its stand and rapidly scanned the place, picking out a card table covered with dirty dishes, a pile of laundry on the floor next to the bed, and a stack of lurid paperbacks—held upright by two empty beer bottles—resting against a windowsill, and several empty cigarette packs.

My minute was just about up when I spotted a stack of newspapers sticking out from under the bed. I pulled them out. They were all L.A. papers, and they all contained articles which detailed the killing of Marcella Harris.

There was handwriting along the borders; grief-stricken pleas and prayers: "God, please catch this fiend who killed my Marcella." "Please, please, please, God, make this a dream." "The gas chamber is too good for the scum who killed my Marcella." Next to a photo of the sheriff's detective who was heading the investigation were the words:

"This guy is a crumb! He told me to get lost, that the cops don't need no friends of Marcella to help. I told him this is a case for the F.B.I."

I flipped through the rest of the newspapers. They were arranged chronologically, and Henry Hart's grief seemed to be building: the last newspaper accounts were scrawled over illegibly and seemed to be stained by teardrops.

I checked my watch: I had left the light on for eight minutes. With the handkerchief still over my hand I rifled every drawer in the three dressers that lined one wall: empty, empty, empty; dirty clothes, phone books.

I opened the last one, and stopped and trembled at what I'd found: a pink, silk-lined dresser drawer. Black lace brassieres and panties were folded neatly in one corner. In the middle was a cigar-box filled with marijuana. Underneath it were black-and-white photographs of Marcella DeVries Harris, nude, her hair braided, lying on a bed. Her sensual mouth beckoned with a come-hither look that was both the ultimate come-hither look and a parody of all come-hither looks.

I stared, and felt my tremors go internal. There was the hardest, most knowing, most mocking intelligence in Marcella Harris's eyes that I had ever seen. Her body was a lush invitation to great pleasure, but I couldn't take my eyes off those eyes.

I must have stared at that face for minutes before I came back to earth. When I finally realized where I was, I replaced the cigar box, closed the silk-lined drawer, turned off the light, and got out of the little garage apartment before Marcella Harris weaved the same spell on me that she had on Henry Hart.

18

I came prepared for William "Doc" Harris, stopping by a printer's shop and getting a hundred phony business cards made up before I went to brace him. The cards read: "Frederick Walker, Prudential Insurance." Prudential's rock insignia was there in the middle, and underneath in official-looking italics was the single word, "investigator." A phony telephone number completed the pretense. The ink on the cards was hardly dry when I shoved them into my pocket and drove to 4968 Beverly Boulevard.

". . . And so you see, Mr. Harris, it's just a case of going through the past of your late wife so that I'll be able to tell the payment department conclusively that this claim is fraudulent. I think it is, and I've been a claims investigator for eight years. Nevertheless, the legwork has to be done."

Doc Harris nodded pensively, flicking my bogus calling card with his thumbnail and never taking his eyes from mine. Sitting across the battered coffee table from me he was one of the most impressive-looking men I had ever seen: six feet tall, close to sixty, with a full head of white hair, the body of an athlete and a chiseled face that was a cross between the finer elements of stern rectitude and rough humor. I could see what Marcella had seen in him.

He smiled broadly, and his features relaxed into infectious warmth. "Well, Mr. Walker," Doc Harris said, "Marcella had a knack for attracting lonely people and making them ridiculous promises that she had no intention of keeping. Be frank with me, please, Mr. Walker. What have you discovered about my ex-wife so far?"

"To be candid, Mr. Harris, that she was promiscuous and an alcoholic."

"No man has to lie when he talks to me," Harris declared. "I give and expect complete candor. So how can I assist you?"

I leaned back and folded my arms. It was an intimidation gesture, and it didn't work. "Mr. Harris—" I started.

"Call me Doc."

"All right, Doc. I need names, names, and more names. All the friends and acquaintances you can recall."

Harris shook his head. "Mr. Walker—"

"Call me Fred."

"Fred, Marcella picked up her lovers and her entourage of friends, if you can call them that, in bars. Bars were the sole focus of her social life. Period. Although you might try the people at Packard-Bell, where she worked."

"I have. They were evasive."

Harris smiled bitterly. "For good reason, Fred. They didn't want to speak badly of the dead. Marcella hit bars all over L.A. She didn't want to become familiar in any one place. She had a tremendous fear of winding up as a slatternly bar regular, so she moved around a lot. She had, I think, several arrests for drunk driving. What's the name of this phony claimant?"

"Alma Jacobsen."

"Well, Fred, let me tell you what I think happened: Marcella met this woman at some gin mill, drunk. She bowled her over with her personality and her nurse's uniform, and showed the woman, who was probably also half-gassed, some official-looking papers. Marcella then told the woman how desperately alone she was, and how she needed someone to carry on her antivivisectionist work in case of her death. Marcella was a big animal lover. Marcella, in her alcoholic effusion, then probably made a big show of getting the woman's name and address and made a big show of signing the papers. Marcella was a superb actress, and the woman undoubtedly went for it. When Marcella's death made the papers, Alma thought she had herself a gravy train. Sound plausible, Fred?"

"Completely, Doc. Lonely people will do strange things."

Harris laughed. "Indeed they do. What do you usually do, Fred?"

I made my laughter match Harris's perfectly. "I look for women. You?"

"I've been known to," Doc laughed.

I got serious again. "Doc, could I talk to your son about this? I think your theory is valid, but I want to touch all bases in the report I file. Maybe your son can tell me something that will disprove this Jacobsen woman conclusively. I'll be gentle with him."

Doc Harris considered my request. "All right, Fred. I think Michael is up at the park with the dog. Why don't we walk up there and talk to him? It's only two blocks from here."

It was three, and it wasn't much of a park; it was just a vacant lot overgrown with weeds. Doc Harris and I talked easily as we trod through knee-high grass looking for his son and his son's dog.

When we did find them we almost tripped over them. Michael Harris was lying on his back on a beach towel, his arms outstretched in a crucifixion pose. The beagle puppy I had seen in the yard on Maple Street in El Monte was chewing grass by his side.

"On your feet, Colonel!" Harris bellowed good-naturedly.

Michael Harris got to his feet, unsmiling, brushing the grass from his blue jeans. When he stretched to his full height I was astounded—he was almost as tall as I. The boy looked nervously at his father, then at me. Time froze for a brief instant as I recalled another brown-haired, fiercely bright boy of nine playing in the desolate back lot of an orphanage. It was over twenty years ago, but I had to will myself to return to the present.

". . . And this is Mr. Walker, Colonel," Doc Harris was saying. "He represents an insurance company. They want to give us some money, but there's a crazy old woman who says your mother promised it to her. We can't let that happen, can we, Colonel?"

"No," Michael said softly.

"Good," Harris said. "Michael, will you talk to Mr. Walker?"

"Yes."

I was starting to feel controlled, manipulated. Doc Harris's manner was unnerving. The boy was intimidated, and I was starting to feel that way myself. I had the feeling that Harris sensed I wasn't on the up-and-up. Intellectually, we were evenly matched, but so far his will was the greater, and it angered me. Unless I asserted myself I would only know what Harris wanted me to know.

I clapped Harris hard on the back. "Jesus," I said, "it's hot here! I noticed a drive-in down on Western. Why don't we go get cream sodas? My treat."

"Can we, Dad?" Michael pleaded. "I'm dying of thirst."

Doc didn't lose a second's worth of his considerable aplomb. He clapped me on the back, equally hard. "Let's go, amigos," he replied.

We walked the four blocks in the hot summer sun, three generations of American males united by darkness and duplicity. The dog trotted behind us, stopping frequently to explore interesting scents. I walked in the middle, with Doc on my left on the street side. Michael walked to my right, closed in against my shoulder by the hedges that ran along the sides of the homes on Beverly Boulevard. He leaned into me, seeming to relish the contact.

I queried Doc on his nickname, and he laughed and said, "Med school dropout, Fred. It was too bloody, too abstract, too time-consuming, too literal, too much."

"Where did you attend?"

"University of Illinois."

"Jesus, it sounds grim. Were there a lot of farm boys wanting to be country doctors?"

"Yes, and a lot of Chicago rich kids out to be society doctors. I didn't fit in."

"Why not?" I asked. It was a challenge.

"It was the twenties. I was an iconoclast. I realized that I'd be spending the rest of my life treating smug, small-town hicks who didn't know shit from Shinola. That I'd be prolonging the lives of people who would be better off dead. I quit in my final year."

I laughed. Michael did, too. Michael's prematurely deep voice went up a good two octaves in the process. "Tell him about the dead horse, Dad."

"That's the Colonel's favorite," Harris laughed. "Well, I used to have a racket going in those days. I knew some gangsters who ran a speakeasy. A real third-class dive where all the rich kids from school hung out. Cheap booze and cheaper food. The joint had one distinction: big juicy steaks for a quarter. Sirloin steaks smothered in onions and tomato sauce. Ha! They weren't steaks, they were fillet of horse. I was the butcher. I used to drive around the countryside with a stooge of mine and steal horses. We used to lure the nags into the back of our truck with oats and sugar, then we'd drive back to town to this warehouse and inject the nags with small quantities of morphine I'd stolen. Then I'd sever their neck arteries with a scalpel. My partner did the real dirty work, I had no stomach for it. He was the cook, too.

"Anyway, as events came to pass, business went bad. The owners tried to stiff me on my rustling dues. This was about the time I decided to give med school the big drift. I decided to go out in style. I knew the goombahs would never pay me, so I decided to give them a good fucking. One night there was a private party at the speak. My stooge and I got ourselves two broken-down old nags, put them in the truck and backed them up to the front door of the joint. We gave the password and the door opened and the nags ran right in. Jesus! What a sight! Tables destroyed, people screaming, broken bottles everywhere! I got out of town and Illinois and never went back."

"Where did you go?" I asked.

"I went on the bum," Harris said. "Have you ever been on the bum, Fred?"

"No, Doc."

"You should have. It's instructive."

It was a challenge. I took it. "I've been too busy being on the make—which is better than being on the bum, right, Michael?" I squeezed the boy around the shoulders, and he beamed at me.

"Right!"

Doc pretended to be amused, but we both knew that the gauntlet had been thrown down.

We took seats inside the Tiny Naylor Drive-In on Beverly and Western. It was air-conditioned, and Michael and

Doc seemed to crash in relief from the heat as we all stretched our long legs out under the table.

Michael sat down beside me, Doc across from us. We all ordered root beer floats. When they arrived, Michael gulped his in three seconds flat, belched, and looked to his father for permission to order another. Doc nodded indulgently and the waitress brought another tall glass of brown and white goo. Michael chugged this one down in about five seconds, then belched and grinned at me like a sated lover.

"Michael, we have to talk about your mother," I said.

"Okay," Michael said.

"Tell me about your mother's friends," I said.

Michael grimaced. "She didn't have any," he said. "She was a bar floozy."

I grimaced, and Michael looked to Doc for confirmation. Doc nodded grimly.

"Who told you that, Michael?" I asked.

"Nobody. I'm no dummy, I knew that Uncle Jim and Uncle George and Uncle Bob and Uncle What's-his-face were just pickups."

"What about women friends?"

"She didn't have any."

"Ever heard of a woman named Alma Jacobsen?"

"No."

"Was your mother friendly with the parents of any of your friends?"

Michael hesitated. "I don't have any friends."

"None at all?"

Michael shrugged. "The books I read are my friends. Minna is my friend." He pointed to the puppy, tethered to a phone pole outside the plate glass window.

I kicked this sad information around in my head. Michael leaned his shoulder against me and gazed longingly at my half-finished root beer float.

"Kill it," I said.

He did, in one gulp.

I opened up another line of questioning: "Michael, you were with your dad when your mother was killed, right?"

"Right. We were playing duckball."

"What's duckball?"

"It's catch. If you miss the ball, you have to get down on your knees and quack like a duck."

I laughed. "Sounds like fun. How did you feel about your mother, Michael? Did you love her?"

Michael went red all over. His long skinny arms went red, his neck went red, and his face went red all the way up to his soft brown crew cut. He started to tremble, then swept an arm across the tabletop and knocked all the glassware and utensils onto the floor. He pushed his way across me and ran outside in the direction of his beagle pup.

Doc stared at me, letting an alarmed waitress pick up the detritus of our root beer floats.

"Does that happen often?" I asked.

Doc nodded. "My son is a volatile boy."

"He takes after his dad." It was both a challenge and a compliment. Doc understood that.

"In some ways," he said.

"I think he's a wonderful boy," I added.

Doc smiled. "So do I."

I laid a five-dollar bill on the table. Doc and I got up and walked outside. Michael was playing tug-of-war with his dog. The dog held the leather leash in her jaws and strained happily against the pull of Michael's skinny arms.

"Come on, Colonel," Doc called. "Time to go home."

Michael and the dog ran ahead of us across Western Avenue and they remained a good forty yards in front as we walked west in the hot afternoon sun. Doc and I didn't talk. I thought about the boy and wondered what Doc was thinking. When we got to the apartment building on Beverly and Irving, I stuck out my hand.

"Thanks for your cooperation, Doc," I said.

"It was a pleasure, Fred."

"I think you've been a big help. I think you've proven conclusively that this Jacobsen woman's claim is a phony."

"I didn't know Marcella had a policy with Prudential. I'm surprised she didn't tell me about it."

"People do surprising things."

"What year did she take out the policy?"

"In '51."

"We were divorced in '50."

I shrugged. "Stranger things have happened."

Doc shrugged too. "How true," he said. He reached inside his pants pocket and pulled out the business card I had given him earlier. He handed it to me. The ink on it was smudged. Doc shook his head. "A smart young insurance bulldog like you should get his cards printed at a better place."

We shook hands again. I felt myself start to go red. "So long, Doc," I said.

"You take care, Fred," Doc returned.

I walked to my car. I had the key in the door when suddenly Michael ran to me and grabbed me in a fierce hug. Before I could respond, he shoved a wadded-up piece of paper into my hand and ran away. I opened up the paper. "You are my friend" was all it said.

I drove home, moved by the boy and puzzled by the man. I had a strange sensation that Doc Harris knew who I was and somehow welcomed my intrusion. I had another feeling, equally strange, that there was a bond building between Michael and me.

When I got home I called Reuben Ramos and begged for some favors. Reluctantly, he did what I wanted: he ran Doc Harris through R&I. No record in California. Next he came up with the addresses Marcella Harris had given at the time of her many arrests: in 1946, nine years ago, she lived at 618 North Sweetzer, Los Angeles. In 1947 and '48, 17901 Terra Cotta, Pasadena. In 1949, 1811 Howard Street, Glendale. At the time of her last drunk arrest in 1950, she was living at 9619 Hibiscus Canyon, Sherman Oaks.

I wrote it all down and spent a long time staring at the information before going to bed. I slept fitfully, waking up repeatedly, expecting to find my bedroom inhabited by ghosts of murdered women.

The following day, Friday, I went out to retrace the past of Marcella DeVries Harris. I went first to shady, tree-lined Sweetzer Avenue in West Hollywood, and got the re-

sults I expected: no one at the 618 address, a Spanish-style
walk-up apartment building, recalled the redheaded nurse
or her then-infant son. I inquired with people in the neighboring houses and got puzzled shakes of the head. Marcella
the cipher.

At Terra Cotta Avenue in Pasadena the results were the
same. There Marcella had rented a house, and the current
tenant told me that the previous owner of the house had
died two years ago. The people on the surrounding blocks
had no recollection of Marcella or her little boy.

From Pasadena I drove to nearby Glendale. It was hot
and smoggy. I took care of 1949 in short order: the bungalow court Marcella had lived in that year had been
recently demolished to make way for a modern apartment
complex. "Marcella Harris, good-looking red-haired nurse
in her late thirties with a three-year-old son?" I asked two
dozen Howard Street residents. Nothing. Marcella, the
phantom.

I took the Hollywood Freeway to Sherman Oaks. A gas
station attendant near the freeway off-ramp directed me to
Hibiscus Canyon. It took me five minutes to find it; nestled
in a cul-de-sac at the end of a winding street, lined, appropriately, with towering hibiscus bushes. Number 9619 was
a four-story walk-up, in the style of a miniature Moorish
castle.

I parked the car, and was walking across the street toward 9619 when my eyes were riveted to a sign stuck into
the front lawn of the house next to it. "For Sale. Contact
Janet Valupeyk, Valupeyk Realty, 18369 Ventura Blvd.,
Sherman Oaks."

Janet Valupeyk. Former lover of Eddie Engels. The
woman Dudley Smith and I had questioned about Engels
back in '51. I felt myself go prickly all over. I forgot all
about 9619 Hibiscus Canyon and drove to Ventura Boulevard instead.

I remembered Janet Valupeyk well. She had been
nearly comatose when Smith and I had interviewed her
four years ago.

She had changed; I could tell that immediately as I
looked at her through the plate glass window of her real estate office. She was seated at a metal desk near the win-

dow, shuffling papers and nervously smoking a cigarette.
During the four years since I had last seen her she had
aged ten. Her face had gone gaunt and her skin had turned
a pasty white. One eyebrow twitched dramatically as she
fumbled with her paperwork.

I could see no one else within the office. I walked
through a glass door that set off little chimes as I entered.
Janet Valupeyk nearly jumped out of her skin at the noise.
She dropped her pen and fumbled her cigarette.

I pretended not to notice. "Miss Valupeyk?" I asked innocently.

"Yes. Oh, God, that goddamned chime! I don't know why
I put it in. Can I help you?"

"I'm interested in the house on Hibiscus Canyon."

Janet Valupeyk smiled nervously, put out her cigarette
and immediately lit another one. "That's a dandy
property," she said. "Let me get you the statistics on it."

She moved from her desk to a bank of metal filing cabinets, opening the top drawer and rummaging through the
manila folders. I joined her, watching her nervous fingers
dig through files that were arranged by street name and
subheaded by street address. She found Hibiscus Canyon
and started muttering, "9621, 9621, where the hell is that
little devil?"

My eyes were glued to the street numbers, and when
9619 came up I reached my hand into the cabinet and
yanked out the file.

Janet Valupeyk said, "Hey, what the hell!"

I shouted at her, "Shut up! Or I'll have Narcotics detectives here within fifteen minutes!" It was a stab in the
dark, but it worked: Janet Valupeyk collapsed in her
chair, her face buried in her hands. I let her sob and tore
through the file.

The tenants were listed in chronological order, along
with the amount of rent they had paid. The tenant list
went back to 1944, and as I thumbed through it the blood
rushed to my head and the periphery of my vision blackened.

"Who are you?" Janet Valupeyk choked.

"Shut up!" I screamed again.

Finally I found it. Marcella Harris had rented apart-

ment number 102 at 9619 Hibiscus Canyon from June,
1950, to September, 1951. She had been a resident there at
the time of Maggie Cadwallader's murder. Next to the list-
ing there were comments in a minute hand: "Mrs. Groberg's bro. to sublet 7/2/51-?" Next to that, a check mark
in a different color ink and the letters "O.K.-J.V."

I put down the file and knelt beside the quaking Janet
Valupeyk. Stabbing again, I asked, "Who told you to rent
to Marcella Harris, Janet?" She shook her head violently.
I raised my hand to hit her, then hesitated and shook her
shoulders instead. "Tell me, goddamnit, or I'll get the
heat!"

Janet Valupeyk began to tremble from head to toe. "Eddie," she said. "Eddie, Eddie, Eddie." Her voice was very
soft.

So was mine as I said, "Eddie who?"

Janet looked at me carefully for the first time. "I . . . I
know you," she said.

"Eddie who?" I screamed, shaking her by her shoulders
again.

"Eddie Engels. I . . . I know you. You—"

"But you broke up with him."

"He still had me. Oh, God, he still had me!"

"Who's Mrs. Groberg?"

"I don't know. I don't remember—"

"Don't lie to me. Marcella Harris is dead! Who killed
her?"

"I don't know! You killed Eddie!"

"Shut up! Who's Mrs. Groberg?"

"She lives at 9619. She's a good tenant. She wouldn't
hurt any—"

I didn't hear her finish. I left her sobbing for her past as I
ran to my car and rushed headlong back into mine.

Five minutes later I was parked crossways at the end of
the Hibiscus Canyon cul-de-sac. I ran down the street to
the Moorish apartment house, flung open the leaded glass
door, and scanned the mailboxes in the foyer. Mrs. John
Groberg lived in number 419. I took the stairs two at a
time to the fourth floor. I listened through the door to a TV
blasting out a game program. I knocked. There was no an-

swer. I knocked again, this time louder, and heard mild
cursing and the volume on the TV diminished.

Through the door a cranky voice called out, "Who is it?"

"Police officer, ma'am," I called out, consciously imitating Jack Webb of "Dragnet" fame.

Giggles answered my announcement. The door was
flung open a moment later, and I was confronted by the
adoring gaze of a gasbag matron. I quickly sized her up as
a crime buff and took my act from there.

Before the woman could ask me for my nonexistent
badge I said forcefully, "Ma'am, I need your help."

She fidgeted with her housecoat and the curlers in her
hair. She was on the far side of fifty. "Y-yes, Officer," she
said.

"Ma'am, a former tenant here was murdered recently.
Maybe you've heard about it; you look like a woman who
keeps abreast of the news."

"Well, I—"

"Her name was Marcella Harris."

The woman's hands flew up to her throat. She was
shaken, and I compounded her fear: "That's right, Mrs.
Groberg, she was strangled."

"Oh, no!"

"Oh, yes, ma'am."

"Well, I—"

"Ma'am, could I come in?"

"Oh, yes, Officer."

The apartment was hot, stuffy, and overfurnished. I took
a seat on the couch next to Mrs. Groberg, the better to bore
in quickly.

"Poor Marcella," she said.

"Yes, indeed, ma'am. Did you know her well?"

"No. To tell you the truth, I didn't like her, really. I
think she drank. But I doted on her little boy. He was such
a sweetheart."

I tossed her a ray of hope: "The boy is doing fine, Mrs.
Groberg. He's living with his father."

"Thank God for that."

"I understand that Marcella sublet her apartment to
your brother in the summer of '51. Do you recall that?"

The Groberg woman laughed. "Yes, I do! I set it up, and
what a mistake it was. My brother Morton had a drinking

problem, just like Marcella. He came out from Omaha to go to work at Lockheed and dry out. I lent him the money to come out here, and the money to rent the apartment. But he found Marcella's liquor and drank it all! He was swacked for three weeks."

"How long was Morton in the apartment?"

"For two months! He was on a bender, and he ended up in the hospital. I—"

"Marcella was gone that long?"

"Yes."

"Did she tell you where she was going?"

"No, but when she got back she said, 'You can't go home again.' That's the name of a book, isn't it?"

"Yes, ma'am. Had Marcella taken her son with her?"

"No . . . I don't . . . no, I know she didn't. She left the tot with friends. I remember talking with the child when Marcella came back. He didn't like the people he stayed with."

"Marcella moved out after that, didn't she?"

"Yes."

"Do you know where she went?"

"No."

"Did she seem upset when she returned from her trip?"

"I couldn't tell. That woman was a mystery to me! Who . . who killed her, Officer?"

"I don't know, but I'm going to find out," I said by way of farewell.

Barely controlling my exultation, I drove with shaky hands over the Cahuenga Pass into Hollywood. I found a pay phone and called Doc Harris. He answered on the third ring: "Speak, it's your dime."

"Doc, this is Fred Walker."

"Fred, how are you? How's the insurance game?" The bluff heartiness of his tone told me that he knew the game wasn't insurance, but that he wanted to play anyway.

"Fifty-fifty. It's a racket like any other. Listen, how would you and Michael like to go for a ride tomorrow? Out to the country somewhere, just get in my car and go. I've got a convertible."

There was silence on the other end of the line. Finally, Doc said, "Sure, kid. Why don't you pick us up at noon?"

"Until then," I said, and hung up.

I drove to Beverly Hills.

Lorna's office was in a tall building attached to the Stanley-Warner Theater on Wilshire near Beverly Drive. I parked down the street and walked there. I checked out the rear parking area first; I was afraid Lorna had already left for the day, but I was in luck: her '50 Packard was still in its space. Hardworking Lorna—still on the job at six-thirty.

The sky was turning golden, and people were already lining up for the first evening performance of "The Country Girl." I waited an hour by the parking entrance, until the sky turned a burnished copper and Lorna turned the corner onto Canon Drive, staying close to the building, jamming her heavy wooden cane into the space where the wall met the sidewalk.

When I saw her, I felt the old shakiness grip me. She walked head down, abstracted. Before she could look up and see me, I committed to memory the look on her face, her hunched posture and her light blue summer dress. When she did look up, she must have seen the love-struck Freddy Underhill of old, for her drawn face softened until she realized this was 1955, not 1951, and that walls had been constructed during the interim.

"Hello, Lor," I said.

"Hello, Freddy," Lorna said coldly. Her manner stiffened, she sighed and leaned against the marble of the building. "Why, Freddy? It's over."

"No, it's not, Lor. None of it."

"I won't argue with you."

"You look beautiful."

"No, I don't. I'm thirty-five and I'm putting on weight. And it's only been four months."

"It's been a lifetime."

"Don't do that with me, goddamn you! You don't mean it, and I don't care! I don't care, Freddy! Do you hear that?"

Lorna gave herself a shove and almost toppled over. I moved to steady her and she swatted at me clumsily with her cane. "No, goddamn you," she hissed. "I won't be charmed one more time. I won't let you beat up my friends, and I won't take you back."

She hobbled into the parking lot. I stayed behind, wondering if she would believe me, or think me insane, or even care. I let her get all the way to her car. I watched as she fished her keys out of her purse, then ran up and grabbed them out of her hand as she began to unlock the door. She started to resist, then stopped. She smiled patiently and put her weight on her cane. "You never listened, Freddy," she said.

"I listened more than you know," I countered.

"No, you didn't. You just heard what you wanted to hear. And you convinced me you were listening. You were a good actor."

I couldn't think of a retort, or a dig, or a plea, so I just said—moving a few steps backward to give myself objectivity—"It's on again. I've connected Eddie Engels to a woman who was murdered recently. I'm going to see it through, wherever it takes me. Maybe when it's all over we can be together."

Lorna was perfectly still. "You are insane," she said.

"It's been hanging over us like a plague, Lor. Maybe we can have some peace when it's over."

"You are insane."

"Lorna—"

"No. We can never be together again; and not because of what happened four years ago. We can never be together because of what you are. No, don't touch me and don't try to charm me or sweet-talk me. I'm getting in my car and if you try to stop me I will make you regret we ever met."

I handed Lorna the keys to her car. Her hand shook as she took them from me. She fumbled her way into the car and drove away, spewing exhaust fumes on my trouser legs.

"Nothing's ever over, Lorna," I said to the air. But I didn't know if I believed it.

We drove east on the San Bernardino Freeway with the top down, away from the stifling, sun-blinded L.A. streets, past successions of interconnected working-class communities spread through terrain ranging from desert sand flats to piny woods. I was at the wheel, Michael was beside me on the front seat, and Doc was sprawled in the back, his long legs propped up on the passenger-side doorjamb, where Michael wrapped a protective arm around his ankles and beat time to the big-band boogie-woogie coming from the radio.

The air that whizzed past us got hotter and thinner as we climbed the winding roads of a fir-covered forest. Lake Arrowhead was nominally our destination, but none of us seemed to care if we ever got there; we were lost in games of silence—Doc and I each knowing that the other *knew,* but knew what? And unwilling, as yet, to push it any further. And Michael, craning his long neck above the windshield, getting full blasts of summer air, gulping it in as fuel for what I knew had to be a brilliant imagination.

Lake Arrowhead came upon us abruptly at the end of a scrub-littered access road. It was shimmering light blue, miragelike in the heat and dotted with rowboats and swimmers. I stopped the car at the side of the road and turned to face my companions.

"Well," I said, "here or beyond?"

"Beyond!" they both exclaimed in unison, and I accelerated, skirting the blue oasis and driving a circuitous path through small mountain ranges piled up one on top of the other.

But soon my mind clicked in. We were miles from Los Angeles and I had work to do. I started getting itchy, looking around for a quiet, shady place for us to stop and eat the picnic lunch I had made. Almost as if in answer to my anxiety, it shot up in the near distance: "Jumbo's Animal Park and Rest Area." It looked like a set from a western movie: a single street of battered one-story frame buildings, and behind that a small wooded area crowded with picnic tables. A weatherbeaten sign at the entrance exclaimed: "Christmas in the Summertime! See Santa's Reindeer at Jumbo's."

I nudged Michael as I pulled into the parking area. "Do you believe in Santa Claus, Mike?"

"He doesn't like to be called Mike," Doc said.

"I don't mind," Michael retorted, "but Santa Claus sucks a big dick." He giggled at his own wit. I laughed along with him.

"A jaded lad," Doc piped in wryly from the back seat. "Like his dad?"

"Very much like his dad. In some respects. I take it this is our destination?"

"Let's vote. Mike?"

"Yes!"

"Doc?"

"Why not?"

I dug a big paper bag full of sandwiches and a large thermos of iced tea out of the trunk, and we strolled through the little town. I was right—the building facades *were* studio sets: Dodge City Jail, Miller's General Store, Diamond Jim's Saloon, Forty-niners Dance Hall. But only the roofs remained intact—the fronts had been ripped out and replaced with bars, behind which a scrawny assortment of wildlife reposed. The Dodge City Jail held two skinny lions.

"The king of beasts," Doc muttered as we passed by. "I'm king of the beasts," Michael countered, walking next to me ahead of his father.

Diamond Jim's Saloon held a bloated elephant. It lay comatose on a cement floor covered with feces.

"Looks like a certain Republican I could name," I said.

"Watch out!" Michael squealed. "Dad's a Republican, and he can't take a joke!" Michael started to giggle and leaned into me. I put my arm around him and held him tightly.

Our last stop before the picnic area was "Diamond Lil's Carny House and Social Hall," no doubt a B-movie euphemism for "whorehouse." Diamond Lil and her girls were not in residence. Ugly, chattering, pink-faced baboons were there instead.

Michael tore free from my arm. He started to tremble as he had in the drive-in two days before. He pulled large hunks of dirt from the ground and hurled them full force at the baboons.

"Dirty fucking drunks!" he screamed. "Dirty, filthy, goddamned, fucking drunks!" He let loose another barrage of dirt and started to scream again, but no words came out, and the jabbering of the creatures in the cage rose to a shrieking cacophony.

Michael was bending down to pick up more ammunition when I grabbed him around the shoulders. As he squirmed to free himself, I heard Doc say soothingly, "Easy, fellow. Easy, Michael boy, it's going to be okay, easy . . ."

Michael slammed a bony elbow into my stomach. I let go of him and he tore off like an antelope in the direction of the rest area. I let him get a good lead, then followed. He was fast, and sprinting full out, and I knew in his condition he would run until he collapsed.

We ran through the wooded area into a miniature box canyon laced with scrub pines. Suddenly there was no place left to run. Michael fell down at the base of a large pine tree and encircled it fiercely with his skinny arms, rocking on his knees. As I came up to him, I could hear a hoarse wail rise from his throat. I knelt beside him and placed a tentative hand on his shoulder and let him cry until he gradually surrendered his grip on the tree and placed his arms around me.

"What is it, Michael?" I asked softly, ruffling his hair. "What is it?"

"Call me Mike," he sobbed. "I don't want to be called Michael anymore."

"Mike, who killed your mother?"

"I don't know!"

"Have you ever heard of anyone named Eddie Engels?"

Mike shook his head and buried it deeper into my chest.

"Margaret Cadwallader?"

"No," he sobbed.

"Mike, do you remember living on Hibiscus Canyon when you were five?"

Mike looked up at me. "Y-yes," he said.

"Do you remember the trip your mother took while you were living there?"

"Yes!"

"Ssssh. Where did she go?"

"I don't . . ."

I helped the boy to his feet and put my arm around him. "Did she go to Wisconsin?"

"I think so. She brought back all this gooey cheese and this smelly sauerkraut. Fucking German squarehead bastards."

I lifted the boy's chin off his chest. "Who did you stay with while she was gone?"

Mike twisted away from me, looking at the ground at his feet.

"Tell me, Mike."

"I stayed with these fly-by-night guys my mom was seeing."

"Did they treat you all right?"

"Yeah. They were drunks and gamblers. They were nice to me, but . . ."

"But what, Mike?"

Mike screamed, "They were nice to me because they wanted to fuck Marcella!" His tears had stopped and the hatred in his young face aged him by ten years.

"What were their names?"

"I don't know, Uncle Claude, Uncle Schmo, Uncle Fucko, I don't know!"

"Do you remember the place where you stayed?"

"Yeah, I remember; 6481 Scenic Avenue. Near Franklin and Gower. Dad said . . ."

"Said what, Mike?"

"That . . . that he was going to fuck up Marcella's boyfriends. I told him they were nice, but he still said it. Fred?"

"Yes?"

"Dad was telling stories last night. He told me this story about this guy who used to be a cop. Did you used to be a cop?"

"Yes. What—"

"Michael, Fred, where the hell are you?" It was Doc's voice, and it was nearby. A second later we saw him. Michael moved away from me when Doc came into view.

He walked toward us. When I saw his face up close I knew that all pretense was gone. His expression was a mask of hatred; the hard, handsome features were drawn inward to the point where each plane melded perfectly in a picture of absolute coldness.

"I think we should go back to L.A.," Doc said.

No one said a word as we made our way back to Los Angeles via a labyrinthine network of freeways and surface streets. Mike sat in back, and Doc sat up front with me, his eyes glued straight ahead for the entire two hours.

When we finally pulled up to the house all three of us seemed to breathe for the first time. It was then that I smelled it, a musky, sweaty pungency that permeated the car even with the top down: the smell of fear.

Michael vaulted out of the back seat and ran without a word into his concrete back yard. Doc turned to face me. "What now, Underhill?" he said.

"I don't know. I'm blowing town for a while."

"And then?"

"And then I'll be back."

Harris got out of the car. He looked down at me. He started to smile, but I didn't let his cold face get that far.

"Harris, if you harm that boy, I'll kill you," I said, then drove off in the direction of Hollywood.

Scenic Avenue was a side street about a mile north of Hollywood Boulevard. Number 6481 was a small stone cottage on the south side. There was a small yard of weeds encircled by a white picket fence. It was deserted, as I knew it would be; all the front windows were broken and the flimsy wooden front door was half caved in.

I walked around the corner of the house. The back yard was the same as the front—same fencing, same high weeds. I found a circuit box next to the fence, attached to a phone pole, and wedged a long piece of scrap wood under the hinge, snapping the box open. I toyed with the switches for five minutes until the dusk shrouded inside of 6481 was illuminated as bright as day.

I brazenly walked across the wooden service porch and through the back door. Then I walked quietly through the entire house, savoring each nuance of the evil I felt there.

It was just an ordinary one-family dwelling, bereft of furniture, bereft of all signs of habitation, bereft even of the winos who usually inhabited such places; but it was alive with an unspeakable aura of sickness and terror that permeated every wall, floorboard, and cobweb-knitted corner.

On the oak floor of the bedroom near an overturned mattress I found a large splotch of dried blood. It could have been something else, but I knew what it was. I upended the mattress; the bottom of it was soaked through with brownish matter.

I found what I knew to be old blood in the bathtub, in the

living room closet, and on the dining room walls. Somehow each new sign of carnage brought forth in me a deeper and deeper sense of calm. Until I walked into the den that adjoined the kitchen and saw the crib, its railings splattered with blood, the matting that lined the inside caked thick with blood, and the teddy bear who lay dead atop it, his cotton guts spilling out and soaked with blood from another time that was reaching out to hold me.

Then I got out, knowing that this was the constituency of the dead that Wacky Walker had written about so many years before.

V

WISCONSIN DUTCH

19

I watched from my window as the propellers churned their way through a billowy cloud bank over the Pacific. The plane then arced left and headed inland for the long trip to a middle America I had never seen: first Chicago, then a connecting flight to southern Wisconsin, birthplace of Margaret Cadwallader and Marcella DeVries Harris.

As California, Arizona, and Nevada passed below me, I shifted my gaze from that arid landscape to the whirring propellers and became hypnotized by their circuitous motion. After a while a process of synchronization took over: my mind started to run in perfect circles, logically, chronologically, and in thematic unison: Marcella DeVries was born in Tunnel City, Wisconsin, in 1912. Tunnel City was eighty-five miles from Waukesha, where Maggie Cadwallader was born in 1914. Two years and eighty-five miles apart.

"I'm just a Wisconsin farm girl," Maggie had told me. She had also gotten hysterical when she'd seen my off-duty revolver. *"No, no, no, no!"* she had screamed. *"I won't let you hurt me! I know who sent you!"*

Six months later she was dead, strangled in the very bedroom where we had made love. The time of her death coincided with Marcella Harris's abrupt journey to parts unknown.

"You can't go home again," Marcella had told her neighbor, Mrs. Groberg.

"Gooey cheese and smelly sauerkraut" her son had remembered—ethnic foods from the German/Dutch/Polish-dominated state of Wisconsin.

A comely stewardess brought me coffee but got only a distracted grunt of thanks. I stared at the propeller closest to me, watching it cut the air, feeling a deepening symbiosis of past and present, and a further unfolding of logic. Eddie Engels and Janet Valupeyk had been lovers. Eddie had been intimate with Maggie Cadwallader. Eddie had told Janet in the early summer of '51 to rent Marcella Harris the apartment on Hibiscus Canyon. It *had to* be related, all of it. It was too perfect not to be.

When the plane landed in Chicago and I hit terra firma again, I decided to change my plans and rent a car to drive the hundred miles or so into Wisconsin. I picked up an efficient-looking Ford at a rental agency and set off. It was near dusk and still very hot. There was a breeze coming from Lake Michigan that did its best to cool things off, but failed.

I drove into the heart of the city, watching the early evening tourists and window shoppers, not knowing what I was looking for. When I passed a printer's shop on the near north side I knew that it was my destination. I went in and purchased five dollars' worth of protective coloration; two hundred phony insurance investigator business cards, these bearing my real name and a ritzy-sounding Beverly Hills address and phone number.

At a nearby novelty store I purchased three reasonably realistic-looking badges designating me "Deputy Sheriff," "Official Police Stenographer," and "International Investigator." When I scrutinized that last one more closely, I threw it out the window of my car—it had the distinct look of a kiddies' cereal box giveaway. But the others looked real, my business cards looked real, and the .38 automatic in my suitcase *was* real. I found a hotel room on the north side and went to bed early; I had a hot date with history, and I wanted to be rested for it.

Southern Wisconsin was colored every conceivable shade of green. I crossed the Illinois-Wisconsin border at eight o'clock in the morning and left the wide eight-lane interstate, pushing my '52 Ford sedan north on a narrow strip of blacktop through a succession of dairy farms interrupted every few miles or so by small lakes.

* * *

I almost missed Tunnel City, spotting the turn-off sign at the last moment. I swung a sharp right-hand turn and entered a two-lane road that ran straight through the middle of a giant cabbage field. After half a mile a sign announced "Tunnel City, Wis. Pop. 9,818." I looked in vain for a tunnel, then realized as I dropped down into a shallow valley that the town was probably named for some kind of underground irrigation system that fed water to the endless fields of cabbage that surrounded it.

The town itself was intact in every respect from fifty years ago: red brick courthouse, red brick grain and feed stores, red brick general store; white brick drugstore, grocery store, and public library. The focal point for the little community seemed to be the two tractor supply stores, glass-fronted, situated directly across the street from each other, their crystal-clear windows jammed with spanking-new farm machinery.

A few sunburned men in coveralls stood in front of each store, talking good-naturedly. I parked my car and joined one group on the sidewalk. It was very hot and very humid, and I immediately shed my suit coat. They spotted me for a city slicker right away, and I saw subtle signals pass between them. I knew I was going to be the butt of some jokes, so I resigned myself to it.

I was about to say "Good morning" when the largest of the three men immediately in front of me shook his head sadly and said, "Not a very good morning, young fellow."

"It is a big muggy," I said.

"You from Chicago?" a small beetle-browed man asked. His small blue eyes danced with the knowledge that he had a live one.

I didn't want to disappoint him. "I'm from Hollywood. You can get anything you want in Hollywood except good sauerkraut juice, so I came to Wisconsin because I couldn't afford a trip to Germany. Take me to your wisest cabbage."

This got a big laugh all around. I dug into my coat pocket and brought out a handful of my business cards, giving one to each man. "Fred Underhill," I said, "Amalgamated Insurance, Los Angeles." When the stolid-looking farmers didn't seem impressed, I dropped my bomb: "You men ever read the L.A. papers?"

"No reason to," the big man said.

"Why?" the beetle-browed man asked.

"What's it got to do with the price of cheese in Wisconsin?" another asked.

I took that as my cue: "A Tunnel City girl was murdered in Los Angeles last month. Marcella DeVries. Married name Harris. The killer hasn't been found. I'm investigating a claim and working with the L.A. police. Marcella was here four years ago, and she may have been back even later than that. I need to talk to people who knew her. I want the son of a bitch who killed her. I . . ." I let my voice trail off.

The men were staring at me blankly. Their lack of expression told me they knew Marcella DeVries and weren't surprised about her murder. Their immobile faces also told me that Marcella DeVries was an anomaly to them, far beyond the limits of their small-town bailiwick.

No one said a word. The other group of tractor worshipers had halted their conversation and were staring at me. I pointed across the street to a white three-story building that bore a sign reading "Badger Hotel—Always Clean Rooms."

"Are the rooms there really always clean?" I asked my rapt audience.

No one answered.

"I'll be staying there," I said. "If any of you want to talk to me, or know anyone who might, that's where I'll be."

I locked my car, got my suitcase out of the trunk, and walked to the Badger Hotel.

I lay on my clean bed for four hours, in my skivvies, waiting for an onslaught of farmers bent on detailing every aspect of the life of Marcella DeVries Harris. No one called or knocked on my door. I felt like the marshal summoned to clean up the rowdy town who finds that the townsfolk are unaccountably afraid of him.

I checked my watch: five-thirty. The heat and smothering humidity were starting to abate, so I decided to go for a walk. I dressed in slacks and sport shirt and strolled through the clean lobby of the Badger Hotel, getting a suspicious look from the clean desk clerk before entering the clean streets of Tunnel City, Wisconsin.

Tunnel City had one business thoroughfare, named, appropriately, Main Street. Every bit of Tunnel City commerce existed on that one street. The town's residential streets spread out from this commercial hub, pointing outward to the bordering farmland.

I walked south, toward the cabbage fields, feeling out of place. Every house I passed was white, with a perfectly tended front lawn bearing well-pruned trees and shrubs. Every automobile parked in every driveway was clean and glistening. The people who sat on the porches looked resolute and strong.

I walked all the way to where Tunnel City proper ended and Tunnel City's nourishing farmland began. Walking back to my hotel I knew why Marcella DeVries had had to get out—and why she had had to return.

I was strolling down Main Street looking for a place to eat when a man crossed the street toward me, coming from the direction of the hotel. He was a tall man in his forties, dressed in blue jeans and a checked sport shirt. There was something different about him, and when his gaze zeroed in on me I knew he wanted to talk.

When he hit the sidewalk he planted himself firmly in my path and stuck out a large bony hand for me to shake. I took it.

"I'm Will Berglund, Officer," the man said.

"Fred Underhill, Mr. Berglund, and I'm not a policeman, I'm an insurance investigator."

"I don't care. I knew Marcy DeVries better than anyone. I—" The man was obviously very moved.

"Where can we go to talk, Mr. Berglund?"

"I run the movie theater here in town." He pointed down Main Street. "The last show is over at nine-forty-five. Meet me there then. We can talk in my office."

When I walked into the lobby of the Badger Theater Will Berglund shooed the few remaining moviegoers out the door, locked it, and wordlessly led me to an upstairs office crowded with beat-up theater seats and inoperative movie projectors. "I like to tinker," he said by way of explanation.

I took a seat without being asked, and he took one across from me. My mind was jumping with questions that I never got the chance to ask—I didn't need to. Berglund opened all the windows in the room for air and began to talk.

He talked without interruption for seven hours, his manner by turns plaintive, morose, but above all else tragically accepting. It was an intimate story, a panorama of small-town life, small-town talk, small-town hope, and small-town retribution. It was the story of Marcella DeVries.

They had been lovers from the very beginning, first in spirit, then in flesh.

The Berglund family had emigrated from Norway the same year as the DeVries family had left Holland. A network of Old Country friends and cousins secured work for the two families in the stockyards of Chicago.

It was 1906, and work was plentiful. The hardy Berglund men became foremen, the quicker-witted DeVries men became master bookkeepers. The three Berglund brothers and Piet and Karl DeVries shared a dream common to immigrants—the dream of Old Country power, the dream of land.

All five men, then in their thirties, were impatient. They knew that the feudal power they so desperately desired could not be achieved by the attrition of begging, borrowing, scrimping, and slaughtering cattle with ten-pound sledgehammers. Time was not on their side, and history was not on their side. But brains and ruthlessness were, compounded by their Calvinist religious fervor, and the five men embarked on a career of crime, with only one goal in mind: the acquisition of twenty-five thousand dollars.

It took three years, and cost two lives, one from each family. The Berglunds and DeVrieses became burglars and armed robbers. Piet DeVries was the acknowledged leader and treasurer, Willem Berglund his adjutant. They were the planners, the shrewd overseers of impetuous Karl DeVries and the outright violent Hasse and Lars Berglund.

Piet was a romantic intellectual, and an ardent lover of Beethoven. He loved jewelry, and converted the cash

gleaned from the gang's burglaries into diamonds and ru-
bies that he sold in turn for a small profit on the commodi-
ties exchange, always keeping a few small gems for himself. He longed to be a jewel thief—for the romance of it as
well as for the profit—and he planned the strong-arm theft
of an elderly, jewel-bedecked Chicago matron known to attend the opera unescorted. His brother Karl and Lars
Berglund were to do the job. It was 1909, and the money
from the robbery would put them well over their twenty-
five-thousand mark.

The woman traveled to and from her home on the near
north side in a horse-drawn carriage. The men waited under the steps of her brownstone, armed with revolvers.
When she pulled to the curb and her driver helped her up
the stairs, Karl and Lars sprang from their hiding place,
expecting to easily overpower their prey. The driver shot
them both in the face at point-blank range with a custom-
made six-shot Derringer.

The three surviving members of the Bergland-DeVries
combine fled to St. Paul, Minnesota, with eighteen thousand dollars in cash and jewelry. Hasse Berglund wanted
to kill Piet DeVries. One night, drunk, he tried. Willem
Berglund interceded, beating Hasse senseless with a lead-
filled cane. Hasse was irreparably brain damaged, and
Willem was distraught with guilt. To assuage Willem's
guilt, Piet placed the now childlike Hasse in an asylum,
paying the director of the institution two thousand dollars
to keep him there in perpetuity.

Where were two immigrants, one Norwegian, one
Dutch, with sixteen thousand dollars, without wives or
children, and above all else, without land, to go? Their
dream was dairy farming, but now that was impossible.
Sixteen thousand dollars would not purchase two dairy
farms, and co-ownership was out of the question—the two
men were bound by spilled blood, but hatred lay in abey-
ance beneath that bondage. So they traveled, living frugally, drifting through Minnesota and Wisconsin until
they ended up, in 1910, thirty miles east of Lake Geneva in
a little town in the middle of a giant cabbage field.

They married the first girls from their home countries
who were nice to them: Willem Berglund wed Anna Ny-
borg, seventeen, Oslo-born, tall and blond, with a frail

body and a face of cameolike loveliness. Piet DeVries wed
Mai Hendenfelder, the daughter of a ruined Rotterdam
shipping magnate, because she loved Brahms and Beethoven, had a beautiful thick body, and could cook.

Tunnel City in 1910 had cabbage, but it also had aspira-
tions to the ultimate Wisconsin trade: cheese. Piet De-
Vries, thirty-seven-year-old Dutch dairy farmhand, and
Willem Berglund, thirty-nine-year-old Norwegian bank
teller and part-time milkman, wanted to settle for nothing
less than a dairy dukedom, but with their depleted funds
they found themselves reluctantly looking for other options.

The land had the last laugh—huge lots of it were bought
by wealthy cheese farmers, acreage stretching all the way
to Lake Geneva, acreage whose soil temperature and con-
sistency soon proved to be almost totally unsuitable for
grazing large numbers of milk cows. But it was *wonderful*
soil for growing cabbage.

So Piet DeVries and Willem Berglund reluctantly joined
the crowd, plopped down their sixteen thousand dollars
and bought cabbage acreage, two adjoining parcels of land
separated by nothing but a dusty country road.

Cabbage brought them moderate prosperity, and family
life—at first—brought them moderate happiness. Willem
and Anna soon had twin sons, Will and George; while Piet
and Mai produced Marcella and John, two years apart.

Willem played solitaire chess and went for long exhaust-
ing runs down country roads. Piet taught himself to play
the violin, and listened to scratchy Beethoven on his newly
purchased Victrola. The two men formed a truce, at once
bitter and steeped in mutual respect. Though not of the
same blood, their ties went deep. Despite the close proxim-
ity of their property, they seldom socialized; when they
did, they treated each other with the exaggerated deference of the mutually fearful.

Both men were considered anomalies by their fellow
townspeople. They held a separate designation, based, people said, not on their aloofness but on something in their
eyes, some fascinating secret knowledge.

It was a knowledge passed on to the second generation.
The people of Tunnel City discerned that, too, as soon as
little Will and Marcella were old enough to walk and talk

and react to the environment that they knew wasn't good enough for them.

Marcella DeVries and the twins Will and George Berglund were born three months apart, in 1912. Marcella was born first. Piet was ecstatic. He had wanted a girl and he got one—chubby and pink and redheaded like him. Willem Berglund wanted a male heir, and got what he wanted—twice over. But George was a sickly infant, born at half the weight of his healthy twin brother, and was quickly diagnosed as hopelessly backward. At the age of three, when Will was well on his way to speaking in the precisely modulated tones of an educated adult, George was unable to stand, drooled like an idiot, and flapped his arms like a chicken.

Willem hated the child. He considered him a hideous punishment, perpetrated by a hateful God for whom he no longer had any use. He hated his wife, he hated God, he hated cabbage, and he hated Tunnel City, Wisconsin. But most of all he now truly hated Piet DeVries.

Piet seemed to be flourishing. He loved his wife, he loved his violin, he loved his Victrola, and he loved his children: precocious Marcella of the red hair and translucent green eyes, whose dark freckles seemed to float in clusters all about her pretty face, who, although willful and spoiled to the point of becoming tyrannical when she didn't get her way, was nonetheless the fiercely loving daughter he had always dreamed of; and little Johnny—thirteen pounds at birth—laughing, happy, bungling in his hugeness, adoring of his family. Always, always laughing. "My little dinosaur," Piet would call him, then pull a nonexistent tail on the boy's rump until father and son collapsed in tears of joyous laughter.

George Berglund, who never walked or spoke a human sound, died of scarlet fever in 1919. He was seven years old. Willem buried him in a burlap bag in a shallow grave next to the toolshed adjoining his house.

Piet crossed the road to offer condolences to the man to whom he hadn't spoken in over a year. Willem slapped him before he could say a word.

Hasse Berglund died the following year. Sodomized repeatedly by his fellow inmates at the asylum, he could stand the abuse no longer and threw himself off a high

ledge into a granite quarry that the inmates were forced to
work in.

The director of the asylum wrote Willem a letter
demanding two hundred dollars for a "decent Christian
burial" for the "boy." He never got his money. Willem simply forgot to send it; he had other things on his mind. He
had to destroy Piet DeVries. He talked about it to Anna,
late at night. Young Will listened at the bedroom door:
Piet had been responsible for the deaths of Lars and
Hasse—and even little idiot Georgie. That was the past,
and it was enough. But now Piet and his little redheaded
vixen daughter were trying to destroy Willem's golden
Will, his only remaining true blood, with poetry and music
and God knew what else. God! Willem would then exclaim
hysterically to the sobbing Anna that there was no God beyond his land and his family, and that, by God, he would
teach Piet that.

Marcella and Will knew each other by instinct, by mind,
and by rote. With the discernment of highly attuned animals they found each other across the dusty country road
that separated the two farms, across the legacy of ambition
and violence that bound their fathers. The inevitability of
the two was so correct that Willem Berglund and Piet De-
Vries just sat back and let it happen.

It happened. When the children were four they would
toddle into the cabbage field together and construct man-
sions out of the brown soil that ran through the irrigation
furrows. Often after a day of play in the fields they would
return to the DeVries farmhouse and pick out tunes on
Mai's piano.

When they were seven, the year of George's death, they
discovered the town, and would walk hand in hand down
Main Street to the public library and read together for
hours, lugging huge armfuls of books out to the pergola
that stood behind the white brick building. In the wintertime they would hide in the wooden feed bin at the edge of
the Berglund property, make a fire out of twigs, and tell
stories until they fell asleep.

No one—not Willem, nor Piet, nor their wives, nor the
neighbors—took exception to this arrangement. Somehow,

it was implicitly understood that these two children were the uneasy truce between the families, and if they remained free to be together there would be no more tragedy.

But the twenties came, and Willem took to drink, and his nighttime rantings against Piet took on a renewed vehemence. Will, now ten, had long ceased to believe that his father would ever carry out his threats, but things were changing. He and Marcella were changing. Their conversations were more and more frequently being interrupted by roughhouse horseplay that inevitably led to touching and kissing and probing. Soon they were lovers in the flesh, and soon it seemed that everyone knew and loathed and feared it.

Marcella at twelve was taller than Will, already full breasted with smooth freckled skin stretched taut over wide hipbones. Men from the town looked at her and felt immediately guilty for their thoughts. The same men looked at Will and hated him for what they knew he had.

The poetry-reading, nature-loving golden children who strolled down Main Street, lost in each other, drew much attention in the staid little farming community. Small-town talk—compounded by the strangeness of Piet and Willem—made resentment and curiosity fester, and the two lovers began to take their love clandestinely to wherever they could find a knoll or a mantle of grass or a field overgrown with foliage where they could lie together.

In 1926 Willem made his first overt move against Piet, dumping large piles of compost into his irrigation sluices. Piet knew about it and did nothing to retaliate. A week later Piet's collie dog was found bludgeoned to death. Still Piet did nothing.

Late at night Will would hear his father cackle drunkenly to the wife who had come to hate him. Piet was a coward, he said, gone soft from his sissy music. A man who won't avenge his land is less than a dead dog, Willem shrieked, and by God, a coward had no right to own land.

Will was watching and listening through a spy hole in the ceiling that Piet had long ago told him to construct. Will knew that it was different this time, that his father's timidity, so long held in check by his fear of Piet, was wan-

ing. Willem was awestruck at Piet's reluctance to retaliate, and young Will knew that his father would take his revenge as far as he could.

Will loved Piet, and told him what he knew. Piet shook
his head and told Will two things: "Don't tell Marcella,
and tell your mother to go and stay with her family in
Green Bay."

Anna Berglund left for upstate Wisconsin the following
day, and Marcella already knew, informed by the almost
telepathic rapport between herself and Will.

And *she* retaliated. Marcella knew that Willem spent
his Thursday mornings in town, withdrawing money from
the bank to pay his farmhands and buying provisions. She
waited for him there, in the lobby of the Badger Hotel,
armed with hatred for her lover's father and fierce love
and contempt for her own.

Townspeople sensed that something was about to happen: Marcella DeVries, straight-A student, was not in
school, was instead sitting in an overstuffed chair fuming
silently, her normally pale skin as florid as her bright red
hair, twisting her hands into knots and staring straight
through the plate glass window, watching the National
Bank. A crowd formed outside the hotel.

Willem showed up at nine o'clock, when the bank
opened. Marcella waited until he finished his transactions,
then walked across the street to wait for him. He came out
the door a few minutes later, carrying a brown paper bag
full of money. When he saw Marcella there was a fearful
silence, then she rushed at him and flung the paper bag to
the ground, spilling its contents. Greenbacks drifted down
Main Street in the April wind, and the crowd watched in
horrified awe as fourteen-year-old Marcella DeVries
wreaked her revenge. She punched, scratched, kicked, and
bit Willem Berglund, pummeling him to the ground, pulling the whiskey bottle out of his waistband and spilling
the contents over his head, cursing him in English, Dutch,
and German until her throat and rage gave out.

She reserved the worst of her wrath for her father, her
mother, and her lover. They were cowards too, and it was
worse because she loved them.

Marcella cleaned house that Wisconsin Walpurgis-
nacht; informing her gentle mother that this farmhouse

was no place for a weak woman, that she was to get out until such a time as her father was strong enough to shelter a woman of her kind. Piet made no move to stop his daughter. As much as he loved his wife, he was in awe of the red-headed girl who bore his features.

Mai Hendenfelder DeVries left that night for the shelter of friends in Lake Geneva. Marcella had directions for Papa, too: he was not to tinker with his violin or play his Victrola or read until he exhausted himself in the fields each day like the cheap German immigrant labor he hired. Shamed and humiliated beyond words, Piet mutely agreed. Marcella raged on: he was to renounce God and Jesus Christ and the Dutch Reformed Church. Piet balked. Marcella raged. Piet continued to balk until Marcella said simply, with brutal finality—"If you don't, you will never see Johnny or me again."

Sobbing, abject, and utterly degraded, he agreed.

Will had not helped Marcella humiliate his father. Marcella considered this the ultimate betrayal.

They were through, of course, the golden elite were now just tarnished fragments; but that wasn't enough for Marcella. She wanted further revenge—something that would solidify her contempt for the Berglund family and all of Tunnel City, Wisconsin.

Will and Marcella had exchanged love letters for years, explicit ones, full of references to lovemaking and dripping with contempt for the picayune small-town ways of Tunnel City. In those letters the genitalia of prominent townspeople were derided, Tunnel City High School teachers were excoriated as buffoons and Willem Berglund was satirized and dissected in vicious detail.

Marcella savored the letters her weakling lover had sent her. She considered her options and decided to wait before using them.

Small-town talk continued as Willem endeavored to drink himself to death; Piet worked side by side with his laborers, and Marcella and Will went to high school and never spoke to each other.

Marcella had a new cause: her brother, Johnny. Johnny, at fourteen, was six foot six, and blond like his mother. He was a wild but quiet boy who preferred the company of ani-

mals, often raiding the outdoor pantries of neighboring
farmhouses to steal sides of beef and pork to feed to the le-
gions of homeless dogs and cats who roamed the outskirts
of town.

Marcella, now bereft of a lover, became the aimless giant's benefactor, counselor, tutor, and anodyne. She held
her brother fiercely close in the wake of her loss, and
taught the bright but lazy boy subjects as diverse as geom-
etry and poetry, medieval history and calculus. She awakened in him more than he knew he possessed, and by doing
so reached deep for her best.

The new DeVries combine had a dream; a dream that ex-
pressed both Marcella's elitist contempt and Johnny's love
for animals: medicine. Marcella the microbe hunter, the
doctor who would go into "pure research," and Johnny, the
veterinarian who would surround himself with the love of
strays and foundlings seeking to be healed. It was a powerful dream, one that would take them far from the hated
confines of Tunnel City, Wisconsin. But first Marcella had
to have her revenge on the town.

In June of 1928, at sixteen, she graduated from Tunnel
City High School, the youngest member of her class. Piet
was very proud. Mai, still estranged from her family, returned from Lake Geneva at Piet's urgings to see the
daughter she hated smile contemptuously in gown and
mortarboard on the stage of the school auditorium as she
was lauded in small-town hyperbole for her academic ac-
complishments. After the ceremony, Mai returned to Lake
Geneva, never to see her family again.

Diploma in hand, Marcella went about her business.
There were eighty-three letters from Will. On the Monday
morning after her graduation, Marcella spent hours deciding where each letter should go to achieve the maximum
insult and harm. This accomplished, she went on her mission. Main Street was first, where Marcella dropped little
packets of vitriol with the mayor, town alderman, librar-
ian, sheriff, barber, and every businessman on the four
commercial blocks of Tunnel City.

"Read this," she said to each recipient. "See if you recognize any of your friends."

The churches were next: Dutch Reformed, Catholic,

Presbyterian, and Baptist all received messages of hate tailored to offend at the level of both faith and viscera.

Marcella then traversed the residential streets of Tunnel City in a concise, well-mapped-out pattern until her brown paper bag was empty. Then she walked home and told her brother to pack his bag, that they would be leaving soon to pursue their dream.

Their departure was delayed. Marcella figured she would wait two days, to collect her thoughts and savor the first ripples of shocked reaction from the town before stealing her father's cache of gems and heading for New York City with Johnny.

She holed up in her bedroom reading Baudelaire and thumbing through East Coast college catalogues. On Tuesday night she heard her father weeping in his bedroom. That meant that he knew.

Marcella decided to go for a last walk in the cabbage fields. She skipped down the dusty road that separated the DeVries and Berglund farms. Willem Berglund was waiting. He was stone cold sober and carrying a straight razor. He grabbed Marcella and threw her to the ground and raped her, the razor at her throat. After he finished he lay on top of her as she stared off into the sky, teeth clenched, refusing to make a sound. When he regained his breath, Willem stood up and urinated on Marcella's prostrate form. Then he walked back into the darkness of his cabbage fields.

Marcella lay there for an hour, then hobbled home. She forced herself to cry. Her father was still awake, tinkering with his violin. Marcella told him what had happened, then turned and went to bed. Piet didn't. He stayed up all night, playing the Beethoven symphonies in chronological order on his Victrola and executing the most difficult passages of the Kreutzer Sonata on his violin.

In the morning, while Marcella and Johnny were still asleep, Piet walked to the home of one of his farmhands and asked to borrow a 10-gauge double-barreled shotgun. Varmints, Piet said. The man gave his employer the gun and shells with his good wishes. Piet then walked to the Berglund farmhouse, the loaded shotgun cradled in the crook of his arm. He knocked on his neighbor's door. Willem answered immediately, as if expecting someone.

Piet stuck the shotgun into Willem's chest and fired, ripping him apart at the level of the lower torso. The top half of Willem's body flew back into his living room, while the lower half crumpled at Piet's feet. Piet reloaded and stepped into the living room, gathering the two pieces of what had once been his friend into a pile next to the fireplace. He dipped his hand into Willem's blood and smeared "God's mercy on us" on the wall, then stuck the shotgun into his mouth and squeezed both triggers.

If it was more than she had bargained for she never told anyone, not even Will years later when they were reconciled and corresponded voluminously.

Marcella gathered up her brother and her father's jewelry shortly after dark on the night he died and headed south, on foot, toward Chicago. As they passed the far border of what were once the Berglund and DeVries cabbage farms, Marcella took an ax and smashed the connecting points of the irrigation sluices that fed water to the farmland. She didn't know if this would flood the cabbage fields or render them dry as a bone, and she didn't care; she only wanted the land on both sides of the dusty country road to suffer as she had.

They traveled southeast, by train and by bus. Marcella decided on a circuitous route, to give Johnny time to accept his father's death. Although they were only sixteen and fourteen, no one bothered them; Marcella had the competent look of a woman in her twenties and Johnny was too big to be considered anything but an adult.

They arrived in New York City two weeks later. Marcella had half-expected a sheriff's posse of Tunnel Cityites to follow them, but no one pursued. New York City sweltered in a summer heat wave, and Marcella sold the jewels and set about trying to register in premed at Columbia and New York universities. She was not accepted at either school, or at Brooklyn College, New York City College, or at the half-dozen other schools she applied to.

There was a simple reason for this: Tunnel City High School would not forward her transcript, and she could not return to pick it up, lest she be held and placed in a home for wayward girls. Marcella thought about this. She had seven thousand three hundred dollars in a bank account, she had Johnny, and she had her will to succeed. She had a two-room flat near Prospect Park in Brooklyn, and she had her brains.

Marcella decided that fate was on her side. She was right. On Independence Day, 1928, she went walking and passed the Fletcher School of Nursing on Jamaica Avenue in Queens. Next door to it was the Fletcher School of Pharmacology. Both schools were "fully accredited"—it said so right there above the door. Marcella had a feeling that this was her destiny, at least for the time being. She was right again.

Willard Fletcher took one look at the hard-eyed young redhead seated across the desk from him and knew that she could give him things his wife never could. He told Marcella this on their first night in bed together.

The admissions office was quiet that day as Marcella explained that her small-town high school had recently burned down and their records were destroyed in the fire. She was a straight-A student, as was her brother John, and she wanted to take the Fletcher School of Nursing's three-year course before transferring to a prestigious university medical school. John eventually wanted to study veterinary medicine, but that was out of the question now. The Fletcher School of Pharmacology would serve as good preveterinary training, didn't Mr. Fletcher agree?

Mr. Fletcher did indeed. He took Marcella's registration fees, and she and Johnny were enrolled for the fall semester. It was that simple. Except, he explained, for the matter of her records. The schools had a reputation to uphold, and before the semester started he wanted to be sure that Marcella was bright and competent enough to tackle the curriculum. Perhaps if they got together socially he could gently quiz her on her academic background, get to know her better, and satisfy himself that she was up to Fletcher School of Nursing standards. Would that be possible? Marcella smiled in anticipation of playing the game.

"Of course," she said.

Marcella played the game well. Her scholastic performance was so superior and her hold over Willard Fletcher so absolute that after three semesters of study she had convinced her benefactor-lover to forge complete academic records going back to the first grade at various secondary schools in the Bronx.

Her fake transcript in hand, she applied to the nursing school of New York University, where she was immediately accepted.

She continued to be the nominal mistress of Willard Fletcher until she was well established at N.Y.U. Then she dropped him like a hot rock, causing an awful scene in the banquet room of a large Atlantic City hotel where they were attending a convention of medical supply wholesalers.

Marcella took her nurse's cap in June of 1931. Johnny was graduated from pharmacy school a year later, with scholastic honors and a codeine habit.

It was the height of the Depression, and their frugally spent money had run out. Marcella considered her options again: med school was out, for now. Money was too tight. She took a job at Bellevue Hospital, patching up derelicts brought to the emergency room. Johnny went to work in the hospital pharmacy, compounding the sedative mixtures used to knock the mental patients into harmless oblivion. He himself remained in a state of oblivion in his off-hours, only he wasn't so harmless—the once-gentle giant, now almost seven feet tall, had become a fearsome barroom brawler. Marcella was continually bailing him out of jail and taking him home to their Brooklyn Heights apartment, where she would stroke his battered head as he whimpered for his dead father.

When Pearl Harbor was bombed on December 7, 1941, Will Berglund was a twenty-nine-year-old English teacher at the University of Wisconsin at Madison, Marcella DeVries was the head nurse at a Catholic hospital on Staten Island, and Johnny DeVries was New York City's leading supplier of illegal codeine.

War brought forth in these disparate individuals the same rush of patriotism that seized millions of other Americans. Will joined the army, received a commission, and was sent to the Pacific. His career as a soldier ended quickly: he caught mortar fire in both lower legs and was repatriated to the naval hospital at San Diego, California, where he underwent several operations and extensive therapy to restore his shattered nerve tissue.

It was there, in the hospital, that he was reunited with Marcella, now a thirty-year-old Wave lieutenant. The events of the previous fifteen years were shunted aside. Will loved Marcella as fiercely now, in her white uniform, as he had when she wore the gingham dresses of her childhood. Time and place and the necessity of healing obliterated the familial bloodletting of Tunnel City, and Marcella and Will again became lovers; the changing of bandages and emptying of bedpans metamorphosed into a late night love ritual that cleansed and healed them both. For the first time in their lives, their mutual small-town ghost was consigned to oblivion.

Johnny DeVries rounded out the San Diego triumvirate. A pharmacist's mate second-class assigned to the hospital pharmacy, he dispatched palliative compounds to the ships moored at the San Diego Naval Yard and moonlighted by running marijuana over the border from Tijuana. Johnny had modified his drug use, switching from codeine to reefers, and his violent behavior modified along with it. The seven-foot brawler was now content to spend his evenings in the Coronado Bay apartment he shared with Marcella and Will.

Marcella and Will would talk, and Will would gamely trundle across the living room to strengthen his now brace-clad legs, and Johnny would smoke hop in his bedroom and listen to Glenn Miller records.

The happy trio stayed together until the spring of 1943, when Marcella met the man who was to shatter her illusions and her life.

"When he walked and spoke, you knew that he *knew;* that he understood all of life's dark secrets—on the level of animal instinct—some highly attuned animal superior to man," Marcella wrote to Will years later. "He is the handsomest man I have ever seen; and he knows it and knows that *you* know it—and he respects you for your supreme good taste and treats you as an equal for wanting to know what it is he knows."

Marcella's infatuation and curiosity took flight, and three days after meeting Doc Harris, she announced to Will: "I cannot be with you. I have met a man I want to the

exclusion of all else." It was brutally final. Will, who had
known that Marcella would ultimately have to move on,
accepted it. He moved out of the apartment and back to the
hospital. He received his medical discharge a week later
and returned to Wisconsin.

Doc Harris was a genius, Marcella decided. He could
think two steps ahead of her, and of course she bordered on
genius herself. He spoke five languages to her three, he
knew more about medicine than she did, he could drink
her under the table and never show it, he could dance like
Gene Kelly, and at forty-five could do a hundred one-
handed push-ups. He was a god. He had won twenty-nine
fights as a professional light heavyweight during the Jack
Dempsey era, he could lampoon small-town mores better
than she and Will at their best, and he could cook Chinese
food.

And he was enigmatic, willfully so: "I'm a walking euphemism," he told Marcella. "When I tell you I run a
chauffeur service, it may or may not be the literal truth.
When I tell you I use my medical background to benefit
man, look for the riddle. When you wonder at my connec-
tions to the big brass here in Dago, wonder at what I can do
for them that they can't do for themselves."

Marcella's mind ran with many possibilities regarding
her new lover: he was a gangster, a high-ranking navy de-
serter, a remittance man devoted to a life of anonymous
good. No explanation satisfied her, and she constantly
thought about the literal truths she knew regarding this
man who had taken over her life. She knew that he had
been born near Chicago in 1898, that he had attended public schools there; that he had been a hero in World War I.
She knew that he had never married because he had never
found a woman to match the force of his personality. She
that knew he had plenty of money but never worked. She
knew that he had worked at odd jobs, gaining life experience after leaving med school at the beginning of the Depression. She knew that his small beachfront apartment
was filled with the books she herself had read and loved.
And she knew that she loved him.

One night in the summer of 1943 the lovers went walking on the beach near San Diego. Doc told Marcella that he

was resettling in the Los Angeles area; that he had the "opportunity of a lifetime" there. His only regret, he said, was that they would have to part. Temporarily, of course —he would come down to Dago to visit. He wanted to be with her every spare moment; she was the only woman who had come close to touching the core of his heart.

Marcella, moved to the core of *her* heart, set about pulling strings to be with the man she loved. She was a consummate string-puller, and within two weeks she brought Doc the happy news: she was to be transferred to the naval hospital at Long Beach, a half hour's drive from Los Angeles. Her brother Johnny, now a master pharmacist's mate, was to be a hospital liaison there, procuring drugs and other hospital supplies from wholesalers in the Los Angeles area.

She beamed at Doc, who marveled aloud for several minutes at Marcella's gifts of manipulation. Finally he took her hand. "Will you marry me?" he asked. Marcella said yes.

They honeymooned in San Francisco, and moved to a spacious apartment in the Los Feliz district of Los Angeles. Marcella, newly promoted to lieutenant commander, took over her duties at the naval hospital, as did Petty Officer John DeVries, who had rented an apartment near the newlyweds.

It went well for a while: the Allies had turned the tide, and it was now only a matter of time before Germany and Japan capitulated, Marcella was satisfied with her supervisory duties, and Johnny and Doc had become great friends.

Doc had become the father that Johnny had lost. The two would spin off together in Doc's LaSalle convertible for long, aimless jaunts all over the L.A. basin. That was the trouble, Marcella decided. Doc was never around, and when he was he was deliberately mysterious and darkly elliptical.

It soon became obvious to her that her husband's "opportunity of a lifetime" was the receiving of stolen goods from an L.A.-based robbery gang. Johnny, high on hop one night, had told her that Doc had garages filled with stolen merchandise all over the city. He fenced the contraband

goods—furs, jewelry, and antiques—to army and navy high
brass, hangers-on in the movie industry, and the gamblers
and other assorted con artists who frequented Hollywood
Park and Santa Anita racetracks.

Doc was a loving, solicitous husband when he was
around, but Marcella started to worry. She began drinking
to excess and corresponding voluminously with Will to assuage the fears that were building in her about the man
she loved. He seemed to be laughing at her, thinking always two or even three steps ahead of her, and always, always smiling darkly with what she imagined to be an evil,
absolutely cold light in his eyes.

Marcella decided she needed a vacation by herself. She
needed to cut down her intake of alcohol and collect her
thoughts. She told Doc this, and he readily agreed. She had
a month's accumulated leave time coming, and her superiors were more than willing to let their fiercely competent
nurse take some time off to relax.

She drove to San Juan Capistrano and swam in the sea
and wrote long letters to Will, who had—amazingly—reset-
tled in Tunnel City. Astounded by this, Marcella telephoned him there. Will told her that he had found it necessary to confront his tragic past. He had become a seeker of
the spiritual path. It worked, he told her; he was at peace
here, running the town movie theater, going on book-
buying missions to Chicago for the Tunnel City Public Library, and meditatively walking the cabbage fields he had
once hated so terribly.

Marcella returned to Los Angeles to find she was pregnant and that Johnny was once again addicted to codeine.
He had taken up with a young woman that Doc had considered unworthy and had decreed that he not see again.
Cowed by his father-surrogate, Johnny had agreed, and
the woman had left Los Angeles.

Marcella was angry at her husband's hold over her
brother, and hurt. She had exercised authority over
Johnny much more benignly. Doc would coldly order
Johnny about, tell him to drive him places, instruct him on
what to wear and eat; and always, always with that cold
smile on his face.

Marcella was troubled. But when she told Doc the news
of her pregnancy, she was overjoyed to see the laughing,

witty, and tender Doc of their courtship reemerge. He was solicitous, he was considerate, he anticipated her moods perfectly. She was never happier, she wrote to Will, not ever.

Michael was born in August of 1945, and Marcella's letters to Will became less frequent. She never mentioned her new child and ignored Will's written queries about him.

"Trouble, trouble," she wrote Will in October of that year. "John and I are being questioned about a drug robbery on an aircraft carrier. We have been singled out because of Johnny's addiction. It is a terrible, terrible thing."

"Trouble, awful trouble from all quarters," she wrote in November of '45, three months after the end of the war. It was their last contact for almost six years.

Will and Johnny had run into each other in Chicago late in '49. Johnny had looked terrible: emaciated, his skin a ghastly gray. Will had sought to comfort him, had told him about the "Order of the Clandestine Heart" to which he belonged. Johnny seemed interested, but became nervous when Will pushed the point.

John DeVries was murdered in Milwaukee in 1950. His killer was never found. When Will read of Johnny's murder in the Milwaukee newspapers, he tried to contact Marcella. It was no use—he sent telegrams to her last known address only to have them returned stamped "Gone, No Forwarding Address." He called every William Harris in the Los Angeles directories, to no avail. Finally, he drove to Milwaukee and talked to the two detectives assigned to investigate the killing.

Johnny had been found at dawn on the grass at a park a few blocks off Milwaukee's skid row. He had been stabbed repeatedly with a butcher knife. He was a known morphine addict and sometime dealer. His death was obviously tied in to the drug underworld. The detectives, Kraus and Lutz, were considerate and kind to Will, but closed-minded about broadening their investigation. Although they told Will they would keep him informed, he drove back to Tunnel City troubled and feeling powerless.

He was to see Marcella one last time. She knocked on his door in the summer of 1951. It was the most startling event of his life. Marcella had lost weight and was close to hysteria. They talked of John's death and she sobbed in Will's arms. Will told Marcella of the Clandestine Heart monastery, and she seemed to listen and gain brief solace.

Marcella drank herself to sleep that night, passing out on Will's living room sofa. When Will awoke early the next morning she was gone. She had left a note: "Thank you. I will consider what you have said. I will seek what I have to seek. I envy your peace. I will try to gain what peace I can."

Will Berglund anticipated my one question: "I'll call those policemen in Milwaukee. I'll tell them you're coming."

I nodded at the farmer-lover-spiritual seeker. He seemed to take my brief turn of the head as absolution, and a slow trickle of tears ran from his eyes.

It was 5:00 A.M. I walked back to the Badger Hotel. My room had been gone through—magazines had been turned over and the bed had been tousled. I checked the contents of my suitcase. Everything was there, but my gun had been unloaded. I packed and walked downstairs and through the lobby, getting curious and hostile looks from some early-rising townspeople. I walked down Main Street feeling awed and humbled—and also powerful; I had been handed the wonder on a platter, and now it was up to me to put it in order.

20

It took me two hours to get to Milwaukee. The Wisconsin
Dell Highway was deserted as I drove past small towns
and through deep green grazing land. I had been awake for
more than twenty-four hours, had traversed fifty years of
history and was now nowhere near tired. All I could think
of was the history lying in wait for me in Milwaukee, and
how to synthesize all the knowledge that only I could tie
together.

I thought of pharmacist's mates John DeVries and Eddie Engels. Had they known each other at the Long Beach
Naval Hospital? Was Eddie connected to Marcella there?
Was that the genesis of the train of deadly events that
erupted in 1950 and continued through this summer?

Coming into Milwaukee on Blue Mound Road—an incon-
gruously named, smog-choked four-lane highway—I said
to myself: don't think.

Milwaukee was red brick, gray brick, white brick, factory smoke, and rows and rows of small white houses with
small Wisconsin green front lawns, all modulated by the
breeze wafting from Lake Michigan. I parked in the base-
ment of the Greyhound Bus Depot on Wells Street, then
shaved and changed clothes in the huge lavatory.

I checked my image in the mirror above the basin. I decided I was an anthropologist, well suited to dig into the
ruins of blasted lives. This conclusion reached, I threaded
my way down a corridor laced with sleeping winos to a pay
phone, where I dialed the Operator and said, "Police Department, please."

* * *

Detectives Kraus and Lutz were still partners and were working the Eighth Precinct, located on Farwell Avenue, a few blocks from the sludgy, waste-carrying Milwaukee River. The old three-story police station was red brick, sandwiched between a sausage factory and a parochial school. I parked in front and walked inside, feeling nostalgia grip me in a bear hug: this had been my life once.

I showed my phony insurance business card to the desk sergeant, who didn't seem impressed, and asked for the detective division. Nonplussed, he said, "Third floor" and pointed me in the direction of the Lysol-smelling muster room.

I took the stairs two at a time in almost total darkness, and came out into a corridor painted a bright school-bus yellow. There was a long arrow painted along the wall underlining "Detective Division: The Finest of Milwaukee's Finest." I followed the arrow to a squad room crammed with desks and mismatched chairs. Nostalgia gripped me even harder: this was what I had once aspired to.

Two men occupied the room, conferring over a desk underneath a large ceiling fan. The men were blond, portly, and wearing identical gaudy hand-tooled shoulder holsters encasing .45 automatics with mother-of-pearl grips. They looked up when they heard my footsteps and smiled identically.

I knew I was going to be the audience for a cop comedy act, so I raised my arms in mock surrender and said, "Whoa, pardner, I'm a friend."

"Never thought that you weren't," the more red-faced of the two men said. "But how'd you get past the desk? You one of Milwaukee's finest?"

I laughed. "No, but I represent one of the finest insurance companies in Los Angeles." I fished two business cards out of my coat pocket and handed one to each cop. They responded with identical half nods and shakes of the head.

"Floyd Lutz," the red-faced man said, and stuck out his hand. I shook it.

"Walt Kraus," his partner said, extending his hand. I shook it.

"Fred Underhill," I returned.

We looked at one another. By way of amenities I

said, "I take it Will Berglund called you about me?"

By way of amenities, Floyd Lutz said, "Yeah, he did. Who choked Johnny DeVries's sister, Underhill?"

"I don't know. Neither do the L.A cops. Who sliced Johnny DeVries?"

Walt Kraus pointed to a chair. "We don't know," he said. "We'd like to. Floyd and I were on the case from the beginning. Johnny was a beast, a nice-guy beast, don't get me wrong, but seven feet tall? Three hundred pounds? That's a beast. The guy who cut him had to be a worse beast. Johnny's stomach was torn open from rib cage to belly button. Jesus!"

"Suspects?" I asked.

Floyd Lutz answered me: "DeVries pushed morphine. More correctly, he gave it away. He was a soft touch. He could never stay in business for long. He'd always wind up on skid row, sleeping in the park, passing out handbills and selling his blood like the other derelicts. He was a nice, passive guy most of the time, used to hand out free morph to the poor bastards on skid who had got hooked during the war. Floyd and me and most of the other cops did our best not to roust him, but sometimes we had to: when he got mad he was the meanest animal I've ever seen. He'd wreck bars and overturn cars, bust heads and fill skid row with dread. He was a terror. Walt and I figure his killer was either some bimbo on the row he beat up or some dope pusher who didn't like a soft touch on his turf. We checked out every major and minor known heroin and morph pusher from Milwaukee to Chi. Nada. We went back over Johnny's rap sheet and checked out the victims in every assault beef he ever had—over thirty guys. Most of them were transients. We ran makes on them all over the Midwest. Eight of them were in jail—Kentucky to Michigan. We talked to all of them—nothing. We talked to every skid row deadbeat who wasn't too fucked up on Sweet Lucy to talk. We sobered up the ones who *were* too fucked up. Nothing. Nothing all the way down the line."

"Physical evidence?" I asked. "ME's report?"

Lutz sighed. "Nothing. Cause of death a severed spinal cord or shock or massive loss of blood, take your pick. The coroner said that Big John wasn't fucked-up on morph when he was sliced—*that* was surprising. *That* was why

Walt and I figured the guy who sliced him had to be a beast or a friend of Johnny's—someone who knew him. Anyone who could slice a guy like that when he was sober had to be a monster."

"Did Johnny have any friends?" I asked.

"Only one," Lutz said. "A chemistry teacher at Marquette. Was. He's a wino now. He and Johnny used to get drunk together on the row. The guy was nutso. Used to teach a semester, then take off a semester and go on a bender. The priests at Marquette finally got sick of it and gave him the heave-ho. He's probably still on skid; the last time I saw him he was sniffing gasoline in front of the Jesus Saves Mission." Lutz shook his head.

"What was the guy's name?" I asked.

Lutz looked to Kraus and shrugged. Kraus screwed his face into a memory search. "Melveny? Yeah, that's it—George 'The Professor' Melveny, George 'The Gluebird' Melveny. He's got a dozen skid row monickers."

"Last known address?" I queried.

Kraus and Lutz laughed in unison.

"Park bench," Kraus said.

"Slit trench," Lutz rhymed.

"No dough."

"Skid row." This sent the two detectives into gales of laughter.

"I get the picture," I said. "Let me ask you something: where did a skid row bum like Johnny DeVries get morphine?"

"Well," Floyd Lutz said, "he was a pharmacist by trade, before the dope got him. I always figured he was using George 'The Gluebird's' lab to make the shit. We checked it out once; no go. Beats me where he got the stuff; Johnny was kind of formidable in a lot of ways; you got the impression that maybe he was hot stuff once." Lutz shook his head again, and looked at Kraus, who shook his, too.

I sighed. "I need a favor," I said.

"Name it," Kraus said. "Any pal of Will Berglund's is a friend of mine."

"Thanks, Walt. Look, Will told me that maybe Johnny DeVries and his sister were involved in a drug robbery at the naval hospital in Long Beach, California, during the war. They were both stationed there. Could you call the provost marshal's office there at the hospital? A request from an official police agency might carry some weight. I'm just an insurance investigator—they won't give me the time of day. I—"

Lutz interrupted me. "Are you fishing in the same stream as us, Underhill?"

"All the way. A big load of morph was stolen, I know that, and that would explain where Johnny got the stuff he was pushing."

Kraus and Lutz looked at each other. "Use the phone in the skipper's office," Lutz said.

Kraus jumped up from his desk and walked to a cubicle partitioned off and festooned with Milwaukee Braves' pennants.

"All the particulars, Walt," Lutz called after him.

"Gotcha!" Kraus returned.

I looked at Lutz and popped my next request: "Could I see DeVries's rap sheet?"

He nodded and went to a bank of filing cabinets at the far end of the squad room. He fumbled around in them for five minutes, finally extracting a file and returning to me.

I was getting nervous. Kraus had been on the telephone a long time, and it was only 6:00 A.M. in L.A. His protracted conversation at that hour struck me as ominous.

The manila folder had "DeVries, John Piet; 6-11-14" typed on the front. I opened it. When I saw the series of mug shots clipped to the first page my hands started to shake and my mind recoiled and leaped forward at the same time. I was looking at the face of Michael Harris. Every curve, plane and angle was identical. It was more than a basic familial resemblance; it was purely parental. Johnny was Michael's father, but who was his mother? It *couldn't* have been Marcella. With shaking hands I turned the first page and went into double shock: John DeVries had listed Margaret Cadwallader of Waukesha, Wisconsin, as next of kin when he was arrested for assault and battery in 1946.

I put down the folder and suddenly realized I was gasping for air. Floyd Lutz had rushed to the water cooler and was now shoving a paper cup of water at me.

"Underhill," he was saying. "Underhill? What the hell is the matter with you? Underhill?"

I came out of it. I felt like a madman restored to sanity by a divine visitation; someone viewing reality for the first time.

I made my voice sound calm: "I'm all right. This guy DeVries reminded me of someone I knew as a kid. That's all."

"You holding out on me? Man, you look like you just got back from Mars."

"Ha-ha!" My laughter sounded phony even to my own ears, so to forestall any more questions, I read through John DeVries's rap sheet; scores and scores of arrests for drunkenness, assault and battery, petty theft, and trespassing; a dozen thirty- and forty-five-day incarcerations in the Milwaukee County Jail; but nothing else related to blood. No further mention of Maggie Cadwallader, no mention of Marcella, no mention of children.

When I finished I looked up to find Walt Kraus staring down at me. "I pulled some tails and got what you wanted," he said. "The robbery was big-time, off an aircraft carrier bound for the Pacific. Forty-five pounds of morph—enough to supply every hospital ship in the fleet and then some. Three Marine liaisons were guarding it. Someone slipped them something, and they passed out. The snatch was made at three o'clock in the morning. The infirmary was picked clean. It never made the news because the navy high brass kiboshed it. DeVries and his sister and two others were strong suspects—they were all assigned to pharmaceutical supply, but they all had tight alibis. They were all questioned repeatedly, jailed as material witnesses, and finally released. The dope was never recovered. They—"

"What were the names of the other two suspects?" I blurted out.

Kraus consulted some papers in his hand. "Pharmacist's mates Lawrence Brubaker and Edward Engels. Underhill, what the hell is the matter with you?"

I stood up, and the squad room, Kraus and Lutz reeled in front of me.

"Underhill?" Lutz called as I started to walk away. "Underhill!"

"Call Will Berglund," I think I shouted back.

Somehow I made it out of the police station and out into

the hot Milwaukee sunlight. Every car and passerby on the street, every fragment of the passing scene, every inundation of the red brick midwestern skyline looked as awesome and incredible as a baby's first glimpse of life out of the womb and into the breach.

There was only one Cadwallader in the Milwaukee-Wau-
kesha area phone directory: Mrs. Marshall Cadwallader,
311 Cutler Park Avenue, Waukesha. Rather than call
first, I drove directly there, straight back over Blue Mound
Road.

Cutler Park Avenue was a block of formerly ritzy town-
houses converted into apartment houses and four-flats.
Cutler Park itself—"Wisconsin's Greatest Showplace of
Genuine Indian Artifacts"—stood across the street.

I parked my loaner and went looking for 311, checking
out house numbers that ran inexplicably out of sequence.
Number 311 was at the end of the block, a two-story apartment house guarded by a plaster jockey with one arm outstretched. The front door was open, and the directory in
the small entrance foyer told me that Mrs. Marshall Cadwallader lived in apartment 103. My suspicion was that
Mrs. Cadwallader was a widow, which suited my purposes:
a single woman would be easier to question.

I felt my pulse race as I recalled the photographs Maggie
had shown me of her adventurous-looking father. I walked
down a hallway lined with cheap prints of southern planta-
tions until I found number 103. I knocked, and the very image of what Maggie Cadwallader would have looked like at
sixty-five answered the door.

Startled by this permutation of time and place, my now
familiar insurance cover story went out the window and I
stammered: "Mrs. Cadwallader, I'm a friend of your late
daughter's. I investigated her . . ." The woman blanched
as I hesitated. She looked frightened, and seemed about to
slam the door in my face when I caught myself and contin-

ued: ". . . her death for the Los Angeles Police Department back in 1951. I'm an insurance investigator now." I handed her one of my cards, thinking that I almost believed I *was* in the insurance racket.

The woman took the card and nodded. "And you . . ." she said.

"And I believe there are other deaths tied in to Margaret's."

Mrs. Cadwallader showed me into her modest living room. I seated myself on a couch covered with a Navajo blanket. She sat across from me in a wicker chair. "You were a friend of Maggie's?" she asked.

"No, I'm sorry, I mean . . . I didn't mean that. I was one of four detectives assigned to the case. We—"

"You arrested the wrong man and he killed himself," Mrs. Cadwallader said matter-of-factly. "I remember your picture in the paper. You lost your job. They called you a Communist. I remember thinking at the time how sad it was, that you made a mistake and they had to get rid of you so they called you that."

I felt the queerest sense of absolution creep over me.

"Why are you here?" Mrs. Cadwallader asked.

"Did you know a woman named Marcella DeVries Harris?" I countered.

"No. Was she Johnny DeVries's sister?"

"Yes. She was murdered in Los Angeles last month. I think her death was connected to Margaret's."

"Oh, God."

"Mrs. Cadwallader, did Margaret have a child out of wedlock?"

"Yes." She said it sternly, without shame.

"In 1945 or thereabouts?"

"On August 29, 1945."

"A boy?"

"Yes."

"And the child . . ."

"They gave up the child!" Mrs. Cadwallader suddenly shrieked. "Johnny was a drug addict, but Maggie had good stuff in her! Good Cadwallader-Johnson stock! She could have found herself a good man to love her, even with another man's baby. Maggie was a good girl! She didn't have to take up with drug addicts! She was a *good* girl!"

I moved to the grandmother of Michael Harris and tentatively placed an arm around her quaking shoulders. "Mrs. Cadwallader, what happened to Maggie's child? Where was he born? Who did Maggie and Johnny give him up to?"

She shrugged herself free of my grasp. "My grandson was born in Milwaukee. Some unlicensed doctor delivered him. I took care of Maggie after the birth. I lost my husband the year before, and I lost Maggie and I never even saw my grandson."

I held the old woman tightly. "Ssshh," I whispered, "Ssshh. What happened to the baby?"

Between body-wrenching dry sobs, Mrs. Cadwallader got it out: "Johnny took him to some orphanage near Fond du Lac—some religious sect he believed in—and I never saw him."

"Maybe someday you will," I said quietly.

"No! Only half of him is my Maggie! The dead half! The other half is that big, dirty, Dutch drug addict, and that's the part that's still alive."

I couldn't argue with her logic, it was beyond my province. I found a pen on the coffee table and wrote my real phone number in L.A. on the back of my bogus business card. I stuck it in Mrs. Cadwallader's hand.

"You call me at home in a month or so," I said. "I'll introduce you to your grandson."

Mrs. Marshall Cadwallader stared unbelievingly at the card. I smiled at her and she didn't respond.

"Believe me," I said. I could tell she didn't. I left her staring mutely at her living room carpet, trying to dig a way out of her past.

"My baby. My love."

"Where is he?"

"His father took him."

"Are you divorced?"

"He wasn't my husband, he was my lover. He died of his love for me."

"How, Maggie?"

"I can't tell you."

"What happened to the baby?"

"He's in an orphanage back east."

"Why, Maggie? Orphanages are terrible places."
"Don't say that! I can't! I can't keep him!"

I ran through Cutler Park searching for a pay phone. I found one and checked my watch: ten-fifteen, making it eight-fifteen in Los Angeles. A fifty-fifty chance: Either Doc or Michael would answer the phone.

I dialed the operator, and she told me to deposit ninety cents. I fed the machine the coins and got a ringing on the other end of the line.

"Hello?" It was unmistakably Michael's voice. My whole soul crashed in relief.

"Mike, this is Fred."

"Hi, Fred!"

"Mike, are you okay?"

"Sure."

"Where's your father?"

"He's asleep in the bedroom."

"Then talk quietly."

"Fred, what's wrong?"

"Ssshh. Mike, where were you born?"

"Wha-what? In L.A. Why?"

"What hospital?"

"I don't know."

"What's your birthday?"

"August 29."

"1945?"

"Yes. Fred—"

"Mike, what happened in the house on Scenic Avenue?"

"The house—"

"You know, Mike; the friends you stayed with while your mother went on her trip four years ago—"

"Fred, I . . ."

"Tell me, Mike!"

"Da-dad hurt the guys. Dad said that they were never going to hurt any other little boys."

"But they didn't hurt you, did they?"

"No! They were nice to me! I told Dad that—" Michael's voice had risen into a shrill wail. I was afraid he would wake Doc.

"Mike, I have to go now. Will you promise not to tell your father I called?"

"Yes, I promise."

"I love you, Mike," I said, not believing my own ears and hanging up before Michael could respond.

This time it took me a scant twenty-five minutes to make the run back to Milwaukee. Blue Mound Road had become an old friend in the course of three harried hours.

Back within the city limits where Blue Mound Road turned into Wisconsin Avenue, I stopped at a filling station and inquired with the attendant about the whereabouts of Marquette University and Milwaukee's skid row.

"The two are within shouting distance," the youth said. "Take Wisconsin Avenue to Twenty-seventh Street, turn left until you hit State Street. Don't hold your breath, but hold your nose."

Marquette University extended a solid ten blocks on the periphery of a skid row that rivaled L.A.'s Fifth Street for squalor and sheer despair—bars, package liquor stores, blood banks, and religious save-your-soul missions representing every faith and sect imaginable. I parked my car at Twenty-seventh and State and went walking, dodging and sidestepping knots of winos and ragpickers who were passing around short-dogs and gesticulating wildly at one another, babbling in a booze language compounded of loneliness and resentment.

I took my eyes off the street for five seconds and went crashing to the pavement; I had tripped over an old man, naked from the waist up, his lower body wrapped in a gasoline-soaked tweed overcoat. I got to my feet and brushed myself off, then attempted to help the old man up. I reached for his arms, then saw the sores on them and hesitated. The old man noticed this and began to cackle. I reached instead for a hunk of his overcoat, but he rolled himself away from me like a dervish until he was lying in the gutter in a sea of sewer water and cigarette butts. He cursed me and feebly flipped me the finger.

I left him and continued walking. After three blocks, I realized I had no real destination, and moreover that the denizens of the row had taken me for a cop: my size and crisp summer suit got me looks of fear and hatred, and if I played it right I could use this to my advantage without hurting anyone.

I recalled what Kraus and Lutz had told me: George "The Professor" Melveny, George "The Gluebird" Melveny, former Marquette chemistry teacher, last seen sucking on a rag in front of the Jesus Saves Mission. It was almost noon, and the temperature was soaring. I felt like shedding my suitcoat, but that wouldn't work: the skid row inhabitants would then know I wasn't packing a gun and was therefore not the heat. I stopped in my tracks and surveyed the row in all directions: no sign of the Jesus Saves Mission. On impulse I ducked into a liquor store and purchased twenty short-dogs of Golden Lake muscatel. My liver shuddered as I paid, and the proprietor gave me the strangest look I have ever encountered as he loaded the poison into a large paper bag. I asked him for directions to the Jesus Saves Mission, and he snickered and pointed east, where the skid row dead-ended at the Milwaukee River.

There was a line of hungry-looking indigents extending halfway around the block as I approached the mission, obviously waiting for their noon meal. Some of them noticed my arrival and jabbed at one another, signaling the onslaught of bad news. They were wrong; it was Christmas in July.

"Santa Claus is here!" I shouted. "He's made a list and he's checked it twice, and he's decided that all of you folks deserve a drink!"

When all I got was puzzled looks, I dug into my paper bag and pulled out a short-dog. "Free wine for all!" I yelled. "Free cash to anyone who can tell me where to find George 'The Gluebird' Melveny!"

There was a virtual stampede to my side. The Jesus Saves Mission and its lackluster luncheon were forgotten. I was the man with the real goodies, and scores of winos and winettes started reaching fawningly toward me, poking tremulous hands in the direction of the brown paper bag I rested out of their reach on my shoulder. Information was screeched at me, tidbits and non sequiturs and epithets:

"Fuck, man."

"Glueman, Gluebird!"

"Sister Ramona!"

"Wetbrain!"

"Gimme, gimme, gimme!"

"See the sister!"

"Handbill!"

"Glueman!"

"Oh, God. Oh, God."

"Warruuggh!"

The crowd was threatening to drive me into the gutter, so I placed my brown bag on the sidewalk and backed off as they descended on it like starving vultures. Pushing and shoving ensued, and two men wrestled into the street and began feebly clawing and gouging at each other's faces.

Within minutes all twenty bottles were broken or snatched up, and the sad boozehounds had dispersed to consume their medicine, except for one particularly frail, sad-looking old man in ragged pants and a Milwaukee Braves T-shirt and Chicago Cubs baseball cap. He just stared at me and waited at the head of the bean line, along with the few other indigents who hadn't seemed interested in my offering.

I walked over to him. He was blond, and his skin had been burned to a bright cancerous red after years of outdoor living. "Aren't you a drinking man?" I asked.

"I can take it or leave it," he said, "unlike some others."

I laughed. "Well put."

"What do you want the Gluebird for? He don't hurt nobody."

"I just want to talk to him."

"He just wants to suck his rag in peace. He don't need no cops bothering him."

"I'm not a cop." I opened up my suit coat to show I was bereft of hardware.

"That don't prove nothin'," he said.

I sighed and lied: "I work for an insurance company. Marquette owes Melveny some money on an old employee claim. That's why I'm looking for him."

I could tell the wary man believed me. I took a five-spot out of my billfold and waved it in front of him. He snatched it up.

"You go down to Sister Ramona's; that's four blocks west of here. It's got a sign out front that says 'Handbill

Passers Wanted.' The Gluebird's been working for the sister lately."

I believed him. His pride and dignity carried authority. I took off in the direction he was pointing.

Sister Ramona was a psychic who preyed on Milwaukee's superstitious lower middle classes. This was explained to me by one "Waldo," an ancient bum lounging in front of the storefront where she recruited the winos and blood bank rejects who carried her message via handbill into Milwaukee's poorer enclaves. She paid off in half gallons of wine that she bought dirt cheap by the truckload from an immigrant Italian wine maker from Chicago. He jacked up the alcohol content with pure grain spirits, which weighed in his vino at a hefty one hundred proof.

Sister Ramona wanted to keep her boys happy. She provided them with free outdoor sleeping quarters in the parking lot of the movie theater she owned; she fed them three grilled cheese sandwiches a day, three hundred and sixty-five days a year; and she bailed them out of jail if they promised to repay the money by donating their blood for free at the blood bank owned by her gynecologist brother, who recently lost his license from poking too many patients in the wrong hole.

This came out in a torrent of words, unsolicited. Waldo went on to explain that the only trouble with Sister Ramona's scam was that her boys kept kicking off of cirrhosis of the liver and freezing to death in the winter when her parking lot became covered over with snowdrifts that she never bothered to clear out. Ol' sister had a high turnover, yes, sir, Waldo said, but there were always plenty of recruits to be found: sister was a wine cono-sewer supreme and she made a mean grilled cheese sandwich. And she wasn't prejudiced, Waldo said, no sir, she hired white men and Negroes alike and fed them the same and provided them with the same flop-out space in her parking lot.

When I pulled a five-dollar bill out of my pocket and said the words "George 'The Gluebird' Melveny," Waldo's eyes popped out and he said, "The Genius," in a voice others reserved for Shakespeare and Beethoven.

"Why is he a genius, Waldo?" I asked as the old man deftly snatched the five-spot out of my hands.

He started jabbering, "Because he's smart, that's why!
Marquette University professor! Sister made him a crew
chief until he couldn't drive no more. He don't sleep in her
parking lot, he sleeps in a sleeping bag in the summertime
on the beach by the lake, and in the wintertime he sleeps
in the nice warm boiler room at Marquette. He so smart
that sister don't pay him with no booze—he don't drink no
more; sister pays him off with model airplanes 'cause he
like to build them and sniff the glue! The Gluebird is a genius!"

I shook my head.

"Whassa matter, man?" Waldo asked.

"You think that's five dollars' worth of information?"

"I sure do!"

"So do I. You want to make another fin?"

"Yeah, man!"

"Then take me to the Gluebird, now."

"Yeah, man!"

We went cruising, in the front seat of my sweltering
Ford sedan, zigzagging the streets of Milwaukee's lower-
class neighborhoods in a random pattern until we spotted
pairs of ragged men tossing handbills onto lawns and front
porches. Some venturesome winos even jammed them into
mailboxes.

Waldo said, "This is what sister call 'saturation bomb-
ing.' Bomb 'em right into her parlor, she says."

"How much does she charge?"

"Three dollars!" Waldo bellowed.

I shook my head. "Life's a kick in the brains, isn't it,
Waldo?"

"Life's more like a kick in the ass," he said.

We drove on for another half hour. The Gluebird was not
to be found among his colleagues. Exhaustion was catching up with me, but I knew I couldn't sleep.

Finally Waldo exclaimed, "The hobby shop!" and
started jabbering directions. All I could pick out was
"Lake Michigan," so I turned around and pointed the car
toward a bright expanse of dark blue that was visible
from our hilltop vantage point. Soon we were cruising
down Lake Drive, and Waldo was craning his head out the
window looking for the Gluebird.

"There!" he said, pointing to a row of shops in a modern shopping center. "That's it."

I pulled in, and finally spied a joint called Happy Harry's Hobby Haven. At last my exhausted, dumbfounded brain got the picture: Happy Harry was George Melveny's glue supplier.

"Stay here, Waldo," I said. I parked and walked into the little store.

Happy Harry didn't look too happy. He was a fat, middle-aged man who looked like he hated kids. He was suspiciously eyeing a group of them, who were holding balsa wood airplanes over their heads and dive-bombing them at one another, exclaiming "Zoom, karreww, buzz!" Suddenly, I felt *very* tired, and not up to sparring with the fat man, who looked like he would give a good part of his soul to converse with an adult.

I walked up to him and said, "George 'The Gluebird' Melveny."

He said in return, "Oh, shit."

"Why 'Oh, shit'?" I asked.

"No reason. I just figured you was a cop or something, and the Bird set himself on fire again."

"Does he do that often?"

"Naw, just once or twice. He forgets and lights a cigarette when his beard is full of glue. He ain't got much of a face left because of that, but that's okay, he ain't got much of a brain left either, so what's the diff? Right, Officer?"

"I'm not a cop, I'm an insurance investigator. Mr. Melveny has just been awarded a large settlement. If you point me in his direction, I'm sure he will repay the favor by purchasing glue by the caseload here at your establishment."

Happy Harry took it all in with a straight face: "The Bird bought three models this morning. I think he crosses the drive and goes down to the beach to play with them."

Before the man could say anything more, I walked out to the lot and told my tour guide we were going beachcombing.

We found him sitting in the middle of the sand, alternately staring at the white, churning tide of Lake Michigan and the pile of plastic model parts in his lap. I handed

Waldo five dollars and told him to get lost. He did, thank-
ing me effusively.

I stared at the Gluebird for several long moments. He
was tall, and gaunt beyond gaunt, his angular face webbed
with layers of white scar tissue burned to a bright red at
the edges. His sandy hair was long and matted sideways
over his head; his reddish-blond beard was sparkling with
gooey crystalline matter that he picked at absently. It was
a breezeless ninety degrees and he was still wearing wool
slacks and a turtlenecked fisherman's sweater.

I walked up to him and checked out the contents of his
lap as he stared slack-jawed at a group of children building
sand castles. His bony, glue-encrusted hands held the plastic chassis of a 1940 Ford glued to the fuselage of a B-52
bomber. Tiny Indian braves with tomahawks and bows
and arrows battled each other upside down along the
plane's underbelly.

The Gluebird noticed me, and must have seen some sad-
ness in my gaze, because he said in a soft voice: "Don't be
sad, sonny, the sister has a cozy drift for you and I was in
the war, too. Don't be sad."

"Which war, Mr. Melveny?"

"The one after the Korean War. I was with the Manhat-
tan Project then. They gave me the job because I used to
mix Manhattans for the fathers. By the pitcherful, with
little maraschino cherries. The fathers were cherry themselves, but they could have told the sisters to kick loose,
but they were cherry, too. Like Jesus. They could have got
fired, like me, and left the sisters to work for the sister."
Melveny held his mound of plastic up for me to see. I took
it, and held it for a moment, then handed it back to him.
"Do you like my boat?" he asked.

"It's very beautiful," I said. "Why did you get fired,
George?"

"I used to be George, and it was George with me, but
now I'm a bird. Caw! Caw! Caw! I used to be George, by
George, and it was George by me, but the padres didn't
know! They didn't care!"

"Care about what, George?"

"I don't know! I used to know, when I was George, but I
don't know anymore!"

I knelt beside the old man and placed an arm around his

shoulders. "Do you remember Johnny DeVries, George?"

The old Gluebird began to tremble, and his face went red—even the white scar tissue. "Big John, Big John, squarehead kraut-eater. Big John, he could recite the table of elements backwards! He had a prick the size of a bratwurst! Eight foot four in his stocking feet, Big John. Big John!"

"Was he your friend?"

"Dead friend! Dead man! Guy Fawkes. Welcome back, Amelia Earhart! Redevivus Big John! Big John Redux! Didn't know a bunsen burner from a bratwurst, but I taught him, by George, I taught him!"

"Where did he get his morphine, George?"

"The nigger had the dope—Johnny just got the cat's bones. The nigger got the pie and Johnny got the crust!"

I shook the Gluebird's bony shoulders. "Who killed Johnny, George?"

"The nigger had the pie, Johnny had the crumbs! Johnny Crum-bum! Johnny said the slicer paid the piper, the slicer's gonna get me, but I got my memoirs at the monastery! Buddha's gonna get the slicer! And make my book a best-seller!"

I shook the Gluebird even harder, until his glue-streaked beard was in my face. "Who's the slicer, goddamnit?"

"Ain't no god, Johnny-boy. The Buddhist's got the Book and they don't believe in Jesus. Turnabout's fair play, Jesus don't believe in Buddha! George don't believe in George, by George, and that's George!"

I let go of the Gluebird. He caw-cawed at the sea gulls flying above the lakefront, and flapped his emaciated arms in longing to join them. On the extreme off chance that God existed I said a silent prayer for him. I walked back to my car knowing I had gleaned enough from his ravaged mind to take me at least as far as Fond Du Lac.

22

I got a room in a motor court on Blue Mound Road and slept for sixteen hours straight, dreaming of Michael and Lorna floating on life rafts in a sea of airplane glue. It was just before dawn when I awoke and called Will Berglund in Tunnel City. Did the Clandestine Heart have a monastery near Fond Du Lac? Yes, he said, his voice blurred by sleep, it did. Did it have an orphanage? No, it didn't. Before I hung up I got explicit directions on the shortest route to the order. Will Berglund came awake as he sensed the anxiety in my voice, and he said he would call the prelate at the monastery and tell him I was coming.

I stopped for gas and a quick breakfast, then swung north in the direction of the lake country, certain that what awaited me at the Clandestine Heart Monastery would not be dull.

Two hours later I was skirting a crystal blue lake dotted with small pleasure craft. Sunbathers were jammed together on the narrow sandy lakefront, and the pine forests that surrounded Fond Du Lac were alive with camera-toting tourist families.

I checked the directions Will Berglund had given me: edge of lake through mountains to farmland, past three farmhouses, one mile to the road with the sign depicting major faiths.

I found the mountain road, then the flat grazing land and the three farmhouses. It was sweltering, close to one hundred degrees, but I was sweating more from nervous anticipation as I turned onto the road. It cut through a half mile of sandy-soil pine forest before ending at a clearing where a plain whitewashed cement building stood, three stories high without ornamentation or architectural style or signs of welcome. A parking area had been created next to the building. The cars that were parked there were spare, too: World War II vintage jeeps and a prewar Willys sedan. They looked well kept up.

I stared at the large wooden door as if expecting an austere miracle. Gradually I realized I was scared and didn't want to enter the monastery. This surprised me; and by reflex I got out of my car and ran to the door and banged on it as hard as I could.

The man who answered had a fresh, well-scrubbed look. He was small and refined looking, yet I got a distinct impression that he had known protracted bad times and had surmounted them. He nodded demurely and bade me enter into a long corridor of the same whitewashed cement as the exterior of the building.

At the end of the hallway I could see a meeting or worship hall of some kind.

The man, who could have been anywhere between thirty and forty-five, told me that the prelate was with his wife and would see me in a few minutes.

"You guys can get married?" I asked.

He didn't answer me, just shoved open a small wooden door in the corridor wall and pointed me inside. "Please wait here," he said, shutting the door behind me. The room was a monk's cell, with few furnishings and no adornment. I checked the door. It was unlocked. In fact, it held no locking mechanism—I was free to leave if I chose. There was one unbarred window, at about the eye level of a tall man. I peeked out and saw a garden behind the monastery. A man in dirty farmer's overalls was hoeing a row of radishes. I put my fingers in my mouth and whistled at him. He turned his head in my direction, smiled broadly, waved, and went back to his work.

For five minutes I stared in eerie silence at the naked light bulb that illuminated the cell. Then my escort returned, telling me that the prelate had been contacted by Will Berglund and was anxious to give me all the help he could. He went on to add that although members of the Clandestine Heart Order eschewed the trappings of the world, they recognized their duty to participate in the world's urgent matters. In fact, it was in many ways the basic tenet of their faith. The whole spiel was as ambiguous as the rest of the religious rebop I had heard in my life, but I didn't tell the man that, I just nodded mutely and hoped I looked properly reverent. He led me past a main worship room and into a small room about double the size of the monk's cell, this one furnished with two metal folding chairs stenciled "Milwaukee General Hospital" on the back. He told me the prelate would join me momentarily, then padded out the door, which he left ajar.

The prelate showed up a minute later. He was a robust, stocky man with jet black hair and a very dark, rough-looking razor stubble. He was probably somewhere in his forties, but again, his age was hard to discern. I stood as he entered the room. We shook hands, and as he motioned me back to the chair he gave me a look that said he was all business. He sat down and let loose with a startling belch. It was a superb icebreaker.

"Jesus," I said spontaneously.

The man laughed. "No, I'm Andrew. He wasn't even one of the apostles. Are you versed in the scriptures, Mr. Underhill?"

"I used to be. I was forced into it. But I'm not what you'd call a believer."

"And your family?"

"I don't have a family. My wife is Jewish."

"I see. How did Will Berglund impress you?"

"As a guilt-ridden man. A decent, gentle man. Possibly an enlightened man."

Andrew smiled at me. "What did Will tell you about our order?" he asked.

"Nothing," I said. "Although I admit it must have some appeal to the intellect or an intelligent man like Berglund wouldn't have been so hopped up on it. What interests me, though, is why John DeVries—"

"We'll talk about John later," Andrew said, interrupting me. "What *I* am interested in is what you will do with any information I give you."

The ascetic surroundings and Andrew's patient voice started to irritate me and I felt the periphery of my vision begin to blacken. "Look, goddamn you," I said harshly, "John DeVries was murdered. So was his sister. These are lives we're talking about, not biblical homilies. I . . ." I stopped.

Andrew had gone pale beneath his dark stubble, and his huge brown eyes were clouding over with grief. "Oh, God, Marcella," he whispered.

"You *knew* her?"

"Then it was true . . ."

"Then what was true, goddamnit?!"

Andrew faltered while I tried to control my excitement. He stared at his hands. I gave him a few moments to calm himself, then said gently: "Then what was true, Andrew?"

"Marcella told my wife and me last month that she was in danger, that her husband wanted custody of their son, that he was going to kidnap him."

"Last month? You saw Marcella Harris last month? *Where?*"

"In Los Angeles. Some awful town east of L.A. El Monte. Marcella phoned my wife. She said she needed to see us, that she needed spiritual counsel. She wired us plane fare and we flew to Los Angeles. We met Marcella at a bar in El Monte, my—"

"On a Saturday night? June 21? Does your wife have a blond ponytail?"

"Yes, but how do you know that?"

"I read it in the papers. The L.A. cops were looking for you as suspects in Marcella's murder. She was killed late that very night, after she left you at the bar. You should have listened, Andrew."

I let that sink in, watching Andrew sink into his grief. The calmness of that grief was unnerving: I got the feeling he was already bartering with God for a way off the hook. "When did you first meet Marcella?" I asked gently. "Tell me how she came to call on you for help last month."

Andrew hunched over in his chair in an almost supplicant's position. His voice was very soft: "Marcella came to the order four years ago. Will Berglund had told her about us. She was distraught, she told me that something terrible was going to happen and she was powerless to stop it. I told her that the Clandestine Heart Order is a spiritual discipline based on anonymous good deeds. We have a few wealthy patrons who own a print shop that prints up our little tracts, but basically we operate our farm here and support ourselves and give our food away to hungry people. We have three hours of silent meditation every day and a day of fasting every week. But mostly we journey to the cities. We put our little tracts in missions on skid rows, in jailhouse chapels, wherever there are lonely, despairing people. We walk city streets, picking lonely, drunken people out of gutters, feeding them, and giving them comfort. We don't actively seek recruits—ours is a severe discipline, and not for the capricious. And we are anonymous: we take no credit for the good we do. I told Marcella all this when we talked back in '51. She told me she understood, and she did. She was a tireless worker. She picked rag women up off the street and bathed and fed them, spending her own money to buy them clothes. She tendered love as no one I have ever seen. She waited outside the gates of the Milwaukee County Jail and drove the released prisoners into the city and talked to them and bought them dinners. She stood guard for twenty-four-hour stretches outside the emergency room at Waukesha General Hospital, offering her nursing skills for free and praying for accident victims. She gave and she gave and she gave, and in so doing transformed herself."

"Into what, Andrew?"

"Into someone who accepted life, and herself, on God's terms."

"And then?"

"And then she left, as abruptly as she came."

"How long was she with the order?"

"For about six weeks."

"She left in August of '51?"

"Yes . . . Yes, that's correct."

Something crashed within me. "I'm sorry I was abusive," I said.

"Don't be sorry, you want justice."

"I don't know what I want. Johnny DeVries came here independently of his sister, is that right?"

"Yes. Will Berglund sent him also. I think it was around Christmas of '49. He was no Marcella. He was a volatile drug addict with a lot of self-hatred. He tried to buy his way in here. Dirty money he'd earned from selling drugs. He made half-hearted attempts to listen to our message, but—"

"Have you ever operated an orphanage here?" I interjected.

"No, that requires a license. We serve anonymously, Mr. Underhill."

"Did John DeVries ever mention a woman named Margaret Cadwallader? Or a child he fathered with her out of wedlock?"

"No, mostly John talked about chemical formulas and the women he had sexual relations with, and—"

I stabbed in a darkness that was becoming increasingly brighter. "And he left his memoirs here, right, Andrew?"

Andrew hesitated. "He left a carton of personal effects, yes."

"I want to go through it."

"No, no. I'm sorry, you can't. That's absolute. John entrusted them to the order. I went through the carton and saw that there were no drugs, so I did John the decency of assuring him that his things would always be safe here. No, I can't let you see them."

"He's dead, Andrew. Other lives may be at stake in this thing."

"No. I won't belie his trust. That's final."

I reached inside my coat and into my waistband and pulled out my .38. I leaned over and placed the barrel in the middle of Andrew's forehead. "You show me that carton, or I'll kill you," I said.

It took him a moment to believe me. "I have work to do that requires me to acquiesce to you," he said.

"Then you know why I have to do what I'm doing," I said.

The carton was musty and mildewed and covered with spiderwebs. And it was heavy; reams and reams of paper weighted down with dampness. I hauled it out to my car under Andrew's watchful eye. He gave me some sort of two-handed benediction as I locked it in my trunk.

"Shall I return it to you?" I asked.

Andrew shook his head. "No, I think you've let me off the hook as far as God is concerned."

"What was that sign you made?"

"I was asking for God's mercy on readers of dark secrets."

"Have you read any of it?"

"No."

"Then how do you know what it is?"

"You wouldn't have come here if those pages contained joy."

"Thank you," I said. Andrew didn't answer; he just watched me drive away.

I rented a room at a motel in Fond Du Lac and settled in to read John DeVries's memoirs.

I emptied the musty carton onto my bed and arranged the paper into three neat piles, each one about a foot high. I gave each stack a cursory look to see if the writing was legible. It was. The black ink was smeared by dampness and age, but DeVries had a neat, concise handwriting and a narrative style that belied his drug addiction and rage; there was both chronological and thematic unity in his writing. The pages were not compiled by date, but each sheet was dated at the top. I went through all three piles and collated them according to month and year.

John DeVries's journals covered the war years, and more than anything else they detailed his fascination with and subservience to Doc Harris, who had taken over the life of Johnny's domineering sister; who had become his father and teacher and more; who had taken his aimless rage and given it form. "Johnny the enforcer" had only to stand by his avatar's side and look intimidating, and by so doing gained more respect than he had ever known.

Johnny had been given the job of bringing back into line the recalcitrant burglars and buyers that Doc dealt with as middlemen:

November 5, 1943

This morning Doc and I drove out to Eagle Rock, ostensibly to move a supply of radios out of our garage there and up to our buyer at San Berdoo. Doc lectured on moral terror as I drove. He talked of the smallness of 99.9% of all lives, and how this smallness generates and regenerates until it creates an effect that is a "snowballing apocalypse of picayunity." He then said that the natural elite (i.e.—us, and others like us) must send messages to the potential elite by "throw-

ing a perpetual monkey wrench into the cogs of the
picayunist's machinery." He explained that our buyer
in San Berdoo was continually trying to bring us down
in price by the intimidation tactic of threatening to
look elsewhere for radios. Doc said that it could be tolerated no longer and that I should visit the man with a
spiritual message that would teach him humility. Doc
said no more until we had loaded our radios into the
truck and were almost to San Berdoo, then he told me:
"This picayune has a cat he dotes on. Picayunes love
dumb animals because by comparison they are even
more powerless than they themselves are. I want you
to strangle that cat in front of its picayune owner. If
you grab the cat lengthwise by its head, and wrap
your little finger and thumb around its neck and
squeeze abruptly with your first two fingers stationed
firmly above its eyebrows, it will cause the cat's eyes
to pop out of its head as you strangle it. Do this for me,
Johnny, and I will teach you other ways to consolidate
your power: the real mental power that I know you
have." I did it. The buyer pleaded with us, pledging all
his business to us exclusively and offering Doc three
hundred dollars as a bonus. Doc declined the money
and said, "My bonus is the lesson you have learned
and the good that will come from it for you and many
others."

I read on through 1943, as Doc Harris consolidated his
hold over John DeVries, moving him into a widening
arena of violence interspersed with counseling on the philosophy and psychology of terror. Johnny beat up and
robbed homosexuals at Doc's command; he broke the arms
and legs of bet welchers; he pistol-whipped burglars who
Doc thought were holding out on their take. And he never,
ever questioned his mentor. The philosophy with which
Doc dominated him was Hitlerian-Utopian, tailored to fit
Johnny's history of overdependence on supportive figures:

"You, Marcella and I are the natural elite. You
must respect Marcella for saving you from Tunnel
City, Wisconsin, and respect her as your blood; but
know that she has her faults. She is weaker than we

on the level of action; you and I have reached for the
beast within ourselves and have externalized it. We
will always do what we have to do, regardless of the
consequences to others, rendering ourselves above all
of man's laws and moral strictures designed to keep
that beast at bay. Marcella will never reach that
point, yet she is a valuable comrade for us at the level
of wife and sister. Respect her and love her, but keep
your emotional distance. Know that ultimately she is
not of our morality.

"The Navy has you now, John, but soon we will
have the Navy. Keep your uniform neatly pressed and
shine your shoes. Play your part well, and you will be
a rich man for life. Your sister is pregnant with the
child who will be your nephew and my son and *our*
moral heir. Watch your intake of hop and you will
have the power of hop over millions. Listen and trust
me, John. You must acquiesce more, and when you do
that I will tell you of the literal power of life and death
I have exercised over many people."

I saw where that paragraph was taking me, so I flipped
ahead in time to August, 1945. What I already knew was
strongly confirmed: John DeVries, Eddie Engels, and Lawrence Brubaker had robbed the infirmary of the aircraft
carrier *Appomattox* of forty-five pounds of undiluted morphine. Doc Harris was the mastermind. DeVries, Brubaker, and Engels were questioned, then released. Doc's
intimidation of Johnny was so absolute that Johnny never
cracked under questioning. The diary indicated that
Engels and Brubaker were equally cowed, equally in the
grip of the incredible Doc Harris's stranglehold. What I
had strongly suspected was also confirmed; Marcella Harris did not participate in the crime—she was in the naval
hospital in Long Beach miscarrying her expected child.

It was then, for the first time, that Johnny saw Doc Harris shaken. Due to complications, Marcella would now be
barren for life. It was then that Johnny came to his mentor's aid to offer to him what Doc would never himself
achieve with Marcella—Johnny told Doc that the girlfriend of whom Doc had disapproved was now pregnant in
Wisconsin, and due to give birth in two weeks.

Doc and Johnny flew there. Doc delivered the child in a
house trailer parked in a wheat field south of Waukesha.
Maggie had wanted to keep the baby, but Doc, aided in the
birth by Larry Brubaker, had terrorized her into releasing
the child to him, for safe delivery to a "special" orphanage
for "special" children. Doc returned to Los Angeles and his
wife with the child she so desperately wanted and his own
"moral heir."

Again I skipped ahead in time, only to find that time abruptly stopped, shortly after Johnny described the events
of August, 1945. But there were at least a hundred sheets
of paper remaining, undated but crowded with words.
Johnny had inexplicably switched to red ink, and in a few
moments I realized why: Johnny had sought Doc's absolute knowledge, and Doc had given it to him in gratitude
for his moral heir. Here was the story of "the literal power
of life and death" that Doc had exercised over many people. Here it was, appropriately in red, for it was the story
of the insane Doc Harris's murderous ten-year career as a
traveling abortionist on the underside of skid rows
throughout the Midwest, armed with scalpel for cutting,
cheap whiskey for anesthesia, and his own insane elitist
hatred as motivation.

Johnny continued to quote his teacher verbatim:

"Of course, I knew since medical school that it was
my mission and my learning process; that the power of
life and death was the ultimate learning ground. I
knew that if I could effectively carry out this dreadful
but necessary process of birth and elimination and
withstand any emotional damage it might cause, I
would possess the inviolate mind and soul of a god."

I read on as Doc described his process of selection to an
awed and finally sickened Johnny:

"If the girls were referred to me by a lover or a pimp
then, of course, they had to be allowed to live. If they
were bright and charming then I performed the job
with all my considerable skill and acumen. If the girls
were ugly or whining or slatternly or proud of their

promiscuity, then the world was of course better off without them and their offspring. Such creatures I would smother with chloroform and abort after their death—perfecting my craft to save the lives of the unfortunate young women who *deserved* to live. I would then drive out into the country with dead mother and unborn child and bury them, late at night, in some kind of fertile ground. I would feel very close to these young women and secure in my knowledge that they had died so that others could live."

Doc Harris went on to describe his abortion techniques, but I couldn't go on. I began to weep uncontrollably and cry for Lorna. Someone rapped at my door, and I grabbed the pillow off the bed, smothered my cries and fell onto the floor thrashing and kicking convulsively. I must have fallen asleep that way, because when I awoke it was dark. The only light in the room came from a desk lamp. It took me a few seconds to recall where I was and what had happened. A scream rose up in my throat and I stifled it by holding my breath until I almost passed out.

I knew I would have to read the rest of the journal. Gradually I got to my feet and steeled myself for the task. Fearful and angry tears covered the remaining pages as I read the horrifying accounts of life and death and blood and pus and excrement, and life and death and death and death and death.

Johnny DeVries had finally become as sickened as I was, and had run to Milwaukee's skid row with a private supply of morphine. His prose style by this time had degenerated into incoherent rambling interspersed with chemical formulas and symbols I was incapable of understanding. Fear of Doc—"The slicer! The slicer! No one is safe from the slicer!"—covered the last pages.

Shaken, I locked my room and went for a walk. I needed to be with people who bore a semblance of health. I found a noisy cocktail bar and entered. The room was bathed in an amber light that softened the patrons' faces—to the good, I thought.

I ordered a double bourbon, then another—and another; a very heavy load for a nondrinker. I ordered yet another double and discovered I was weeping, and that the people at the bar were looking at me in embarrassed silence. I finished my drink and decided I didn't care. I signaled the bartender for a refill and he shook his head and looked the other way. I threaded my way through a maze of dancing couples toward a pay phone at the back of the room. I gave the operator Lorna's number in Los Angeles, then started feeding the machine dimes and quarters until the operator cut in and told me I had deposited three times the necessary amount.

When Lorna came on the line I just stammered drunkenly until she said, "Freddy, goddamnit, is that you?"

"Lor-Lorna. Lorna!"

"Are you crying, Freddy? Are you drunk? Where the hell are you?"

I brought myself under control enough to talk: "I'm in Wisconsin, Lor. I know a lot of things I have to tell you about. There's this great big little boy that might get hurt like Maggie Cadwallader . . . Lorna, please, Lor, I need to see you . . ."

"I didn't know you got drunk, Freddy. It's not like you. And I've never heard you cry." Lorna's voice was very soft, and amazed.

"I don't, goddamnit. You don't understand, Lor."

"Yes, I do. I always have. Are you coming back to L.A.?"

"Yes."

"Then call me then. Don't tell me anything about great big little boys or the past. Just go to sleep. All right?"

"All right."

"Good night, Freddy."

"Good night." I hung up before Lorna could hear me start to weep again.

Somehow I slept that night. In the morning I put Johnny's history of terror into the trunk of my car and drove to Chicago.

I stopped at a hardware store in the Loop and bought a reinforced cardboard packing crate, then spent an hour in the parking lot sifting through and annotating the memoirs. From a pay phone I called L.A. Information, and learned that Lawrence Brubaker's residence address and the address of Larry's Little Log Cabin were the same. This gave me pause, especially when I recalled that there was a post office directly across the street from the bar when Dudley Smith and I had braced him in '51.

Before transferring the mass of paper from the musty carton to the new one I checked my work: all references to Brubaker and the drug robbery were underlined. I dug some fresh sheets of stationery out of the glove compartment and wrote a cover letter:

> Dear Larry—
> It is time to pay your dues. You belong to me now, not Doc Harris. I will be in touch.
> > Officer Frederick U. Underhill
> > 1647

Next I drove to a post office, where I borrowed masking tape and sealed up the carton tight as a drum. I addressed it to:

> > Lawrence Brubaker
> > Larry's Little Log Cabin Bar
> > 58 Windward Avenue
> > Venice, California

For a return address I wrote:

> > Edward Engels
> > U.S.S. Appomattox
> > 1 Fire Street, Hades

A nice touch. A just touch, one that would appeal to Lorna and other lovers of justice.

I explained several times what I wanted to the patient postal clerk: insured delivery, to the post office across the street, where the recipient would be required to produce identification and sign a receipt before getting his hands on the package. And I wanted the carton to arrive in three days' time; no sooner. The clerk understood; he was used to eccentrics.

I left the post office feeling light as air and solid as granite. I drove to O'Hare Field and left off the rented car, then caught an afternoon flight home to Los Angeles and my destiny.

VI

THE GAME FOR SHELTER

23

Three days later at seven in the morning I was stationed on Windward Avenue in front of a liquor store that afforded me a view of both the Venice Post Office and Larry's Little Log Cabin.

I waited nervously for the post office to open its doors at seven-thirty, fully aware that my plan would work to psychological perfection only if the postal messenger roused Brubaker early enough so that he was alone at his bar. His joint was no longer open the maximum hours—the current hours posted on the door were a more demure 10:00 A.M. to midnight. It could work only to my benefit—I would come down on Brubaker under any conditions, but I wanted him and his Little Log Cabin to myself if possible. So I lounged in front of the liquor store, knowing I might be in for a long day.

I thought mostly of Lorna. I hadn't phoned her when I returned to Los Angeles. I wanted to recapture a parity I thought I had lost on the night I called her, sobbing. The two days I had spent at my apartment trying not to think about her had been days of complete defeat; I thought of little else, and pictured every possible resolution between us in the light of what I knew had to happen before we could be together again. I had to will myself, there on seedy "Wineward" Avenue, wearing a seedy windbreaker to cover my gun, not to think about what I wanted most, and not to think about dead women, dead unborn children and my own past that wouldn't die.

My trying not to think was interrupted at eight-twenty, when a postal clerk in uniform trotted across the street toward Larry's Little Log Cabin. I watched as the man con-

sulted a slip of paper in his hand and knocked loudly on the
front door. A moment later the door opened and a pale-
skinned Negro in a silk robe was standing there, blinking
against the brightness of the day. Brubaker and the post-
man talked, and from half a block away I could tell that old
Larry's curiosity was whetted.

Brubaker came back out the door five minutes later,
dressed in slacks and a sport shirt. He jaywalked directly
across the street to the post office while my body started to
go alternately hot and cold all over.

I figured on another five minutes. I was wrong: three
minutes later Brubaker was running back across the
street, my carton in his arms, his face the picture of absolute panic. He didn't run for his front door—he bypassed it
and ran for the parking lot adjacent to his building. I was
right behind him, and as he plopped the carton down on
the trunk of a Pontiac roadster and groped in his pocket for
the keys, I came up behind him and jammed my gun into
his spine.

"No, Larry," I said as he cut loose with a sound that was
half wail and half shriek, "not now. You understand?" I
cocked the hammer and dug the barrel into the fleshy part
of his back. Brubaker nodded his head very slightly.

"Good," I said. "Eddie is in hell, but I'm not, and if you
play your cards right you won't be either. Do you dig me,
Larry?" Brubaker nodded again. "Good. Do you know who
I am?"

Brubaker twisted slightly to see my face. When recognition flashed into his pale blue eyes he whimpered, then
covered his mouth with his hands and bit at his knuckles.

I motioned him toward the back door of his cocktail
lounge. "Pick up the box, Larry. We have some reading
and talking to do."

Brubaker complied, and in a few moments we were
seated in his modest living quarters at the rear of the bar.
Brubaker was quivering, but holding on to his dignity,
much as he had on the day Smith and I had questioned
him. I pointed with my gun barrel to the carton that lay between us.

"Open it up and read the first ten pages or so," I said.

Brubaker hesitated, then tore into it, obviously anxious
to get it over with. I watched as he hurriedly read through

the sheets I had annotated, setting each one aside with trembling hands as he continued reading. After ten minutes or so he had gotten the picture and started to laugh hysterically, but with what seemed like an underlying sense of irony.

"Baby, baby, baby, baby," he said. "Baby, baby, baby."

"You ever kill anyone, Larry?" I asked.

"No," Brubaker said.

"Do you have any idea how many people Doc Harris has killed?"

"Lots and lots," Brubaker said.

"You're a sarcastic bastard. You feel like surviving this thing, or going down with Doc?"

"I went down on Doc in 1944, baby. So did Eddie, so did Johnny DeVries. Just to seal our pact, you understand. I didn't mind: Doc was a gorgeous hunk. Eddie didn't mind, he was a switch-hitter. But it ate Johnny up, no pun intended. He liked it, and he hated himself for it till the day he died."

"Who killed him?"

"Doc. Doc loved him, too. But Johnny was talking too much. He never turned his share of the stuff over. He was giving it away to all the hopheads on Milwaukee skid. Then he started talking about kicking. We were friends. He called me and told me he wanted me to hold his stuff until he got out of the hospital. He wanted to kick, but he didn't want to lose the money he could get by pushing the stuff, you dig?"

"I dig. So you were afraid that if he got clean he'd blab and implicate you, and you told Doc."

"That's right, I told Big Daddy, and Big Daddy took care of it."

Brubaker managed to keep his pride, though he was clearly accepting of his subservience and self-hatred. I honestly didn't know if he wanted to go on living or die with his past. All I could do was go on asking my questions and hope that his detachment held.

"What happened to the rest of the dope, Larry?"

"Doc and I are turning it over, a little at a time. Have been, for years."

"He's blackmailing you?"

"He's got pictures of me and a city councilman in what

you might call a compromising position," Brubaker
laughed. "I fixed the councilman up with Eddie. Eddie was
a status fiend, the guy was in love with status and horses,
and that councilman had both. Doc took some pictures of
them, too, but the councilman never knew it. Eddie did,
though—that's how Doc got him to take the fall for
Maggie."

I started to tremble. "Doc killed Maggie?"

"Yes, baby, he did. You got the wrong man when you
popped Eddie. But you paid, baby. It's funny, baby, you
don't look like a Commie." Brubaker laughed, this time directly at me.

"Why?" I asked. "Why did he do it?"

"Why? Well, Maggie was living here in L.A., unknown
to all us sailor-boys. Her mother wrote to her about Johnny
being sliced in Milwaukee. She ran into Eddie, acciden-
tally someplace, and started shooting off her mouth. Eddie
told Doc, and Doc told him to sweet-talk her and fuck her
and keep an eye on her. Then Doc started getting nervous.
He borrowed Eddie's car one night and went to Maggie's
apartment and choked her. It was a setup—Doc knew he
could always trust me, but he wasn't sure about Eddie. He
knew Eddie was insane about anyone knowing he was gay;
that he'd rather die than have his family find out, so he
showed Eddie the pictures of him and the councilman and
that sealed it. Either the cops would never find out who
choked Maggie, which would be hunky-dory, or Eddie
would buy the ticket. Which he did, baby, and you were the
ticket taker." I was jolted back to that night in '51 when I
had first tailed Engels—he had had a violent confrontation
with an older man in a homosexual bar in West Hollywood. My faulty memory sprung back to life—that man
had been Doc Harris. Feeling self-revulsion start to creep
in like a cancer, I changed the subject. "Did Marcella Harris know Maggie? Know that Doc was going to kill her?"

"I think she knew. I think she guessed. She had always
liked Maggie—and she knew that Maggie was really Michael's mother. Doc told Marcella to stay away from Maggie. Doc and Marcella were divorced, but still friendly.
Marcella took off on a trip somewhere; she left Michael
with some boyfriends of hers. See, baby, she always knew
Doc was a little cold. When she found out Maggie was

dead, she knew how cold, but it wasn't until later that year that she found out Doc was the night train to Cold City."

"What are you talking about? Didn't she know Doc killed Johnny?"

Brubaker shook his head and gave me an ironic hipster's smile. "Negative, baby. If she'd known, she would have killed him or herself. That woman loved that crazy brother of hers, and did she have a will! I was Doc's alibi, baby. He was with me on a three-day poker-drunk when he was really in Milwaukee slicing Big John."

I shuddered because I already had an idea about the answer to my next question. "Then what did Marcella find out later that year?"

"Well, baby, to give old iceberg Doc his due, he does love his 'moral heir,' as he calls him. When Marcella went gallivanting all over hell in '51 and left Michael with her partying pals, Doc was frantic, not knowing where his boy was. When he and Michael got together, and Michael told him he was with some nice fellas in Hollywood, Doc got real upset. He went up there with a butcher knife and did some cutting. He got three of them. It was in all the papers, but you probably didn't read about it—you was recently on the headlines yourself and probably hiding out. What's the matter, baby? You're a little bit pale."

Brubaker went to the sink and drew me a glass of water. He handed it to me and I sipped, then realized what I was doing and hurled it at the wall.

"Easy, baby," Brubaker said. "You're learning things you don't want to?"

I almost choked on the words, but I got them out, in part: "Why did Doc . . ."

"Kill Marcella? For the boy, baby. He knew Marcella knew of all the shit that had hit the fan; maybe she even suspected he killed Johnny. But if she ever went to the cops she knew she'd never see her little boy. That ate at her. She started hitting the juice and popping pills harder than ever. She started sleeping around harder than ever. Doc had this sleazy private detective checking her out. He told Doc that Marcella had more rubber burned in her than the Pomona Freeway. That private eye disappeared shortly thereafter, baby. So did Marcella."

Brubaker drew a silent finger across his throat, indicat-

ing the end of Marcella's potentially splendid life. I was
outraged beyond outrage, but not at Brubaker.

"But Michael was with Doc when Marcella was strangled," I said calmly.

"That's correct," Brubaker said, equally calmly. "He
was. Doc drove out to El Monte. He knew that Marcella
usually stumbled home from Hank's Hot Spot down Peck
Road by the high school. He knew she never took her car.
He was parked by the school. He picked her up and talked
to her for a couple of hours, then strangled her. Michael
was asleep in the back seat. Doc had fed him three Sec-
onals. When he woke up at home the next day he never
knew where he spent the night. Ain't parental love a kick,
baby?"

I jumped up, and with a trembling hand held my gun
inches from Brubaker's smiling face, the hammer cocked,
my finger on the trigger.

"Shoot me, man," Brubaker said. "I don't care, it ain't
gonna hurt for long. Shoot me."

I held my ground.

"Shoot me, goddamnit! Ain't you got the guts? You
afraid of a nigger queer? Shoot me!"

I raised the gun barrel into the air and brought it down
full force onto Brubaker's head. He screamed, and blood
burst from a vein over his nose. I raised my gun again,
then screamed myself and threw it against the wall. I
stared at Brubaker, who wiped his bloody face with his
sleeve and returned my stare.

"Are you with me or with Doc?" I said finally.

"I'm with you, baby," Brubaker said. "You've got all the
aces in this hand. In fact, you're the only game in town."

24

It *was* the only game in town, I knew that, but I didn't feel I'd been dealt aces. I felt like I was holding a dead man's hand, and that even after it was over Doc Harris would be laughing at me from wherever he went, secure in the knowledge that I could never again lead a normal life, if indeed I ever had.

Larry Brubaker and I drove north, toward the farm country east of Ventura. I was armed with a 10-gauge shotgun, a .38, and a hypodermic syringe; Brubaker with a masochistic delight at the predicament he was in. He knew I was armed for bear—he had supplied me with the syringe and he knew what I had to do. Brubaker was driving, but he knew only the barest outline of my plan; he knew only the territory where the game was to be played.

I stared at him out of the corner of my eye. He was a skillful driver, deftly weaving through traffic like a rider jockeying for post position, and even with his head bandaged from the result of my outrage he maintained an icy calm.

He had supplied the details, and he had agreed to sign a confession to all his knowledge of Doc Harris's malfeasance and his own part in the drug robbery. He was an accessory to murder and much more. That confession was now, four days later, lying in my Bank of America safe-deposit box. After signing his name with a flourish to the twenty-three-page indictment I had drawn up in his cluttered back room, Brubaker had said: "There's only one way to play this game and win. Doc owns a plot of land east of Ventura. Just a nasty little good-for-nothing pile of dirt.

331

It's his tax sting; he's got no visible means of support, being a respectable middle-class dope pusher like he is. So he writes off his rockpile and pays a C-note a year in income tax. That's where he hides his stuff. He gives it to me and I turn it over for him. We meet there once a month, on the fifteenth, to make the trade: I give Doc the month's take, he gives me the stuff. That's the place to take him. You dig, baby?"

I dug, and I wanted to make sure Brubaker reciprocated. "Yeah, I dig. You dig that if this thing doesn't come off, I'm going to kill you right there?"

"Of course, baby. It's the only game in town."

I saw a clock as we passed Oxnard—8:42 A.M., and I noted the time and place—Saturday, July 15, 1955, and I thought of what I wanted from Doc Harris on the biggest day of my life and the last day of his: I wanted a dialogue before the strychnine-laced morphine entered his veins. Remorse was beyond his capability, but I wanted a crumbling, or at least an expression of grief, as my personal revenge. And more importantly, I wanted information on the state of mind of his "moral heir." How far had he gone in perverting Michael's mind? How conscious and subtle were his methods of brainwashing? And I wanted him to die knowing that Michael would live free and sane because of his death.

We passed the Ventura County line and headed east. I felt like I was going to vomit, and reflexively looked at the cold mien of Larry Brubaker for signs of stress. I was rewarded: he had tightened his hands on the steering wheel until his pale brown knuckles had turned a throbbing white.

"You want to hear a joke, Larry?" I said.

"Sure, baby."

"It's my definition of a sadist. Are you ready? Someone who's kind to a masochist."

Brubaker laughed, first uproariously, then obscenely. "That's the story of my life, baby! Only I was playing both parts. It's too bad you ain't gonna get the chance to know Doc. He would have dug your act."

"Tell me about the setup. How do you and Doc work it?"

"He drives up alone; I do likewise. He's got the stuff buried in a watertight chest in this little grove of trees next to this little shed. We make the trade and we have a drink or two and talk politics or sports or old times, and that's it."

"Would Doc's car fit in this shed?"

"Probably. How do you expect to get Doc to sit still while you hot-shot him? That's what you're planning to do, ain't it, baby?"

"Don't you worry about it. And your meeting time is always ten, and Doc is never early?"

"Right, baby. Now *you* don't worry. You can see Doc coming from half a mile away. I *always* come early, to observe nature. You dig?"

"I dig."

Ten minutes later we were there.

We turned off the shoulder and drove for a quarter mile over a dusty road. When we came up to the site it was just as Brubaker described it: soft brown dirt strewn with rocks, dust, and a white clapboard shack on the edge of an expanse of dead-looking eucalyptus trees.

We parked next to the shack. Brubaker set the brake and smiled at me. I didn't know what the smile meant, and suddenly I was terrified.

Brubaker looked at his watch. "It's nine-fifteen," he said. "We've got forty-five minutes, but you better get out of sight to be safe. I'll stand outside my car like I usually do. Hot, ain't it? But pretty. God, do I love the country!"

I got my shotgun out of the back seat, wishing it were an automatic, and walked into the grove of trees. I placed it at the back of the tree closest to Brubaker's car, where it could be grabbed quickly when Doc Harris arrived. I got out my .38 and checked the safety, then stuck it back in my waistband and walked toward a dark patch of shade at the middle of the little forest.

"I'll whistle once when he shows," Brubaker called to me. For the first time I noticed tension in his voice.

"Right," I called back, noting my own voice was stretched thin.

I leaned up against a tree trunk that afforded me a view of Brubaker and his car as well as the road. I was so light-headed from nervous tension that it was easy not to think. My mind was totally blank, and I caught myself slipping into a state of complete nervous exhaustion. I cleared my throat repeatedly and started to scratch and pick at myself, almost as if to prove that I was still there.

I heard a rustle of dried leaves in back of me, and whirled around, my hand on the butt of my gun. It was nothing—probably just a scurrying rodent. I heard the rustle again and didn't turn around, and then suddenly I heard the *ka-raack!* of a shot and the tree trunk splintered above my head. I pitched to the ground and rolled in the direction of a large mound of fallen branches. I pulled my .38 from my waistband and flipped off the safety and held my breath. I dug in behind the branches, burrowing through dried leaves for a place to aim. Finding a small spot of daylight that provided aiming room and protection, I dug deeper and scanned the direction from which the shot had come.

There was nothing: no movement of any kind, no noise but the frantic slamming of my own heart and the sharp wheeze of my breath. I risked sticking my head above the mound of branches and quickly scanned the grove of trees. Still nothing. Was the sniper Brubaker?

"Brubaker," I called. There was no response.

I glanced over to my left. The shotgun was still resting against the tree trunk. I crawled over to where I could see Brubaker's car and the little shack. No Brubaker and no movement. I was starting to calm down a little, and starting to get angry. As I crawled back toward my hiding place I caught a glimpse of trouser legs off to my left near the far edge of my vision. Three shots rang out, and the dirt in front of me blew up in my face. I started rolling toward the shotgun when I saw a man charging me. Dimly I knew it was Doc Harris. I was within inches of my shotgun and still rolling when he fired two shots at me from within ten yards. The first shot narrowly missed; the second grazed the side of my head. I flailed my .38 in front of me, wasting precious seconds. Doc Harris saw what I was doing and aimed dead at me. He pulled the trigger, and got an empty click. Livid, he was on top of me, and he kicked me in the face just as I got my gun free, causing me to fire three quick shots in the wrong direction.

He flung himself on my gun arm and grabbed my wrist with both hands. As a precaution I fired the remaining three rounds into the dirt. This infuriated him and he brought his knee into my groin. I screamed, and vomited onto his shirt front. He reached up reflexively to fend it off, thereby easing some of the pressure on my chest. I squirmed partially free and twisted myself in the direction of the shotgun. Just as I got my hands on the butt, Harris renewed his attack. I feebly swiped at him with the gun butt, grazing him in the chin. He grabbed for the trigger, hoping to force a shot in my direction, but my right hand was securely clamped around the trigger guard. We rolled into a tree trunk, and I tried to squash Harris into it, banging him at chest level with the gun barrel that was between us like a wedge. It was no use; he was too strong. I wrapped my middle finger around the trigger and squeezed. The shotgun exploded and the barrel buckled, hitting Harris in the face. He panicked for just an instant, withdrawing his hand slightly and looking startled.

We both drew ourselves to our feet. Harris had retightened his grip on the gun, then realized it was useless and let go, causing me to fall to the ground. He smiled down at me through clenched teeth and pulled a switchblade knife from his back pocket. He pressed a button on the handle and a gleaming, razor-sharp blade popped out. He advanced toward me. I was trying to get to my feet when I saw Larry Brubaker inching up in back of him, wielding a tire iron. Harris was within three feet of me when Brubaker brought it down with a roundhouse swing onto his shoulders. Harris collapsed to the ground at my feet and was silent.

Brubaker helped me up. I checked Harris's pulse, which was normal, then rounded up the two handguns from their resting place. Harris had a .32 Colt revolver. I put it in my back pocket, and reloaded my own .38 and placed it in my waistband. Brubaker was kneeling over Harris, gently stroking his thick gray hair and staring at him with a look that was equal parts longing and amazement.

I walked up to him. "Get the syringe from the glove compartment, Larry. There's a paper bag on the front seat with a bottle of water, a spoon, some matches and a little vial. Bring it to me."

Brubaker nodded and went to the car.

I dragged Doc Harris over to a large tree and propped his back up against it. I could barely manage the pulling: my arms were numb from tension and exertion, and my head slammed from the shot that had grazed me. Brubaker returned with the paper bag.

"You know where the stuff is buried," I said.

Brubaker said, "Yes, baby," very softly.

"Go get a handful of it. A **big** handful. Then come back here. I want you to cook Doc up a little cocktail."

Harris came awake a moment after Brubaker departed. When his eyelids started to flutter, I reached for my .38 and trained it on him. "Hello, Doc," I said.

Harris smiled. "Hello, Underhill. Where's Larry?"

"He went to fetch you a little surprise."

"Poor Larry. What will he do now? Who will he follow? He's never had anyone else."

"He'll survive. So will Michael."

"Michael likes you, Underhill."

"I like Michael."

"Like attracts like. You and I are Renaissance men. Michael is attracted to Renaissance men."

"What have you done to him?"

"I've told him stories. I taught him to read at three. He's got an amazing I.Q. and an astounding sense of narrative, so I've been giving hm parables since he was old enough to listen. I was going to write my memoirs for him, when he was a few years older and capable of understanding them. Of course, now that will never be. But he has had enough of me to form his character, I think."

"You lost, Harris. Your life, your moral heir, your 'philosophy,' all of it. How does that feel?"

"Sad. But I've been to mountaintops that you and the rest of the world don't know exist. There's a certain solace in that."

"How did you know I'd be here?"

"I didn't. But I knew you knew about me. I've had a feeling since I read about you and poor Eddie in the papers back in '51 that you'd be coming for me someday. When you showed up at my door I wasn't surprised. I figured you might use Larry as a wedge, so I showed up here early without my car as a precaution."

Brubaker returned with both hands overflowing with

white powder. I tasted the most minute amount I could put on a finger. It was very, very pure.

"I was going to shoot you up, Doc," I said. "But I haven't got the heart for it."

Still holding my gun, I scooped a handful of morphine from Brubaker's outstretched palms and dug the water bottle out of the paper bag. I uncapped it, and walked up to Harris.

"Eat it," I said, shoving the morphine at his mouth.

Harris opened his mouth and stoically took death's communion. I tilted the water bottle to his lips as one last act of mercy. Doc shuddered and smiled. "I don't want to die like this, Underhill."

"Tough shit. You've got five minutes or so until your heart bursts and you suffocate. Any last words? Any last requests?"

"Just one." Harris pointed to the ground in back of me. "Will you hand me my knife?" he asked.

I nodded and Brubaker got the knife and handed it to him.

Harris smiled at us. "Goodbye, Larry. Be gracious in victory, Underhill. It's not your style, but do it anyway. Be as gracious in victory as I am in defeat."

Harris unbuttoned his shirt and slowly removed it, then took the knife in both hands and slammed it into his abdomen and yanked it upward to his rib cage. He shuddered as blood spurted from his stomach and burst forth from his mouth and nostrils. Then he pitched forward onto the ground, his hands still gripping the knife handle.

We buried him in the spot where he had stored his morphine, jamming him into the deep narrow space he had originally created to hold a huge steamer trunk full of death. We covered him over with rock-strewn dirt and covered the dirt with a spray of dried leaves.

I hauled the trunk over to Brubaker's car, siphoned gas from his tank, and drove the car off to a safe distance. Then I lit a match and set the trunk on fire. Brubaker, who had remained silent since the moment of Doc's death, stared at the flames musingly.

"Have you got a valedictory, Larry?" I asked.

"Yeah," he said, and quoted Cole Porter: " 'Goodbye

now and amen, here's hoping we meet now and then, it was great fun, but it was just one of those things!' You like that, baby?"

"No, you're too hep for me, Larry," I said, throwing dirt on the charred remains of the trunk. "Let's get out of here. I'll drive."

I took Pacific Coast Highway back. Brubaker was silent, and it troubled me.

"You saved my life," I said. "Thanks."

"He was going to kill me, baby. I knew it. He swooped down on me and took me aside and told me you were dead meat, and then things would be copacetic. But I knew he was going to kill me." Brubaker turned in his seat to face me. "I would have let you die otherwise," he said.

"I know. You were in love with him, weren't you?"

"From the moment I met him, baby. From that very moment." Brubaker started to sob quietly, sticking his head out the window to avoid my watching him. Finally he turned to face me. "But I cared, too, baby. When you and that big Irish cop rousted me years ago I knew you were an okay guy. You just didn't have too good an idea about what was going on. You dig?"

"I guess so. If it's any consolation, I used to have a friend, a drunk who was sort of way ahead of his time, who used to say there was a city of the dead, existing right here where we are, but invisible to us. He said that when people go there they carry on exactly the way they did on earth. That's not much consolation to me, but I think it may be true."

Brubaker didn't answer. He just sobbed out the window, his head wedged tightly against the doorjamb. He was still sobbing when I left him at his bar in Venice.

25

I staked out the apartment building on Beverly Boulevard for three days. Huddled low in the seat of my car, I watched Michael read comic books on his front lawn, noting that he wore thick glasses to read. I watched him throw a tennis ball against the wall of the building and usually blow the catch when it returned to him. I watched him pick at his acne, and I watched him thrash at the tennis ball with an old rusted putter. I watched him lie on the dead grass and dream. I noted that the other kids in the neighborhood avoided him like the plague. I noted that by the time he was twelve he would be far taller than I am.

At the end of those three days I knew that I loved him.

He just stared at me when he flung the door open in answer to my knock. I stared back for a moment, then broke the silence.

"Hi, Mike. May I come in?"

"Sure."

I moved my way through the modest little apartment, looking for something to give me something to say. "Where's your puppy?" I asked finally.

"She ran away," Michael said.

It was obviously my cue. "Your father is dead, Mike."

Michael said, "I figured he was," then looked out the window to the stream of cars moving along Beverly Boulevard. "I knew he had to die—because of the stories. He thought I was a smart kid, but he didn't know how smart. He used to think he was fooling me. He used to think I didn't know that the stories were real."

"What stories, Mike?"

Michael turned his gaze from the street to me. "I won't tell you. Not ever. Okay?"

"Okay. Do you miss your dog?"

"Yes, she was my friend."

"I've got a dog. A hell of a good dog."

"What kind?"

"A big black Labrador. He loves people, but he hates cats."

"I don't like cats either. They're slimy. What's going to happen, Fred?"

"You're going to come and live with me. Do you want to?"

"Are you married?"

"I don't know. I think so."

"What's your wife like?"

"She's very smart and strong and very beautiful."

"Will the Lab be my dog, too?"

"Yes."

"Then okay."

"Pack your stuff. Leave your father's things, I'll get rid of them later."

Ten minutes later the back seat of my car was packed with a meager collection of clothes and assorted other stuff—and a huge collection of books. I drove to a pay phone and called Big Sid at home and told him I had a guest for him to look after for a few days. The monster mogul was bewildered, but ecstatic when I told him it was a bright young boy who loved horror movies.

Sid was there on the front lawn of the huge house on Canon Drive waiting for us when we pulled up. I introduced Michael to him, and Sid double-taked on the huge youngster and offered him a cigar. Michael fell on the lawn in his laughter, then got up and hugged me before running off in the direction of the house.

From a pay phone I called Lorna's office. Her secretary told me she was down in San Diego for a convention. She was staying at the El Cortez Hotel and would be returning in two or three days. I couldn't wait. I got a tank of gas and highballed it south on the San Diego Freeway.

It was turning dusk when I got to Dago. A drunken sailor gave me directions to the El Cortez, a pink Spanish-style building with an outside elevator enclosed in glass.

I ditched my car in the parking lot and tore through the lobby to the front desk. The clerk told me that the guests who were here for the American Bar Association convention were at the banquet in the Galleon Room. He pointed to a large banquet hall off to his left. I ran in, catching glimpses of a stern-looking man at the podium, who was speaking ambiguously about something called justice.

I walked quietly along four walls, scanning every rapt and bored face at every table. There was no Lorna. There was an exit at the rear of the room, and I went for it, hoping it would provide access to an elevator to the hotel proper.

I opened the door into a hallway just as Lorna limped out of the ladies' room, talking to another woman. "I only come for the food, Helen," she was saying. Helen noticed me first, and must have known something was up, because she nudged Lorna, who turned around and saw me and dropped her purse and cane and said, "Freddy, what—"

Helen said, "Excuse me, Lorna," and darted out of sight.

I smiled and said, "I never liked phones, Lor."

"You lunatic. What's happened to you? You look different."

"I think I am different."

I bent down and handed Lorna her cane and purse. Impulsively I threw my arms around her and said, "It's over, Lor. It's over." I grabbed her waist and lifted her off the floor and held her way over my head until she shrieked, "Freddy, goddamnit, put me down!"

I held her higher still, tossing her up to where her head almost banged the ceiling.

"Freddy, goddamnit, please!"

I lowered my wife to the lushly carpeted floor. She retained her hold around my neck and looked into my eyes sternly and said, "So it's over. And now?"

"There's us, Lor. There's a great big little boy who needs us. He's with your father now."

"What great big—"

"He's Maggie Cadwallader's son. That's all I'll tell you. I want you back, but it's no good without him."

"Oh, Jesus, Freddy."

"You can teach him justice, and I can teach him whatever I know."

"He's an orphan?"

"Yes."

"There are legalities, Freddy."

"Fuck the legalities; he needs us."

"I don't know."

"I do. I want you back."

"Why? You think it will be different this time?"

"I know it will be."

"Oh, God, Freddy!"

"We'll never know unless we try."

"That's true, but I just don't know! Besides, I've got two more days down here at the convention."

"We'll never know unless we try."

"It's a standoff, Freddy."

"It always has been, Lor."

Lorna dug into her purse and pulled out her keys. She detached the ones for the house in Laurel Canyon and handed them to me. She smiled, and brushed tears out of her eyes. "We'll never know unless we try," she said.

We held each other tightly for several minutes, until we heard applause coming from the banquet room.

"I have to go now," Lorna said. "I'm on in a few minutes."

"I'll see you at home."

"Yes."

We kissed, and Lorna composed herself, opened the door and moved into the banquet room to the sound of dying applause for the last speaker.

As she limped to the dais, I thought of Wacky Walker and wonder and the constituency of the dead and mad Dudley Smith and poor Larry Brubaker and orphanhood and the strictures of my once inviolate heart. Then I thought of redemption, and got my car and caught the freeway back to L.A.